DOUBLE IMAGE

ALSO BY DAVID MORRELL

FICTION

First Blood (1972)
Testament (1975)
Last Reveille (1977)
The Totem (1979)
Blood Oath (1982)
The Hundred-Year Christmas (1983)*
The Brotherhood of the Rose (1984)
The Fraternity of the Stone (1985)
The League of Night and Fog (1987)
The Fifth Profession (1990)
The Covenant of the Flame (1991)
Assumed Identity (1993)
Desperate Measures (1994)
The Totem (Complete and Unaltered) (1994)*
Extreme Denial (1996)

NONFICTION

John Barth: An Introduction (1976)
Fireflies (1988)

*Limited edition with illustrations. Donald M. Grant,
Publisher, Hampton Falls, New Hampshire.

DAVID MORRELL

DOUBLE IMAGE

WARNER BOOKS

A Time Warner Company

Warner Books, Inc., 1271 Avenue of the Americas, New York, NY 10020
Visit our Web site at http://warnerbooks.com

 A Time Warner Company

Printed in the United States of America
First Printing: May 1998
10 9 8 7 6 5 4 3 2 1

Library of Congress Cataloging-in-Publication Data

Morrell, David.
    Double image / David Morrell.
        p.   cm.
    ISBN 0-446-51963-4
    I. Title.
PR9199.3.M65D68   1998
813'.54—dc21   97-32283
                                                                                                              CIP

Book design by Giorgetta Bell McRee

To Stirling Silliphant (1918–1996)
For *Route 66, Naked City,* and all the
other wonderful things you wrote that made
me want to become a writer. Dear friend,
you accomplished what all true writers aim
toward—you changed someone's life.

The terms *shoot* and *take* are not
accidental; they represent an attitude of
conquest and appropriation. Only when
the photographer grows into perception
and creative impulse does the term *make*
define a condition of empathy between the
external and the internal events. Stieglitz
told me, "When I make a photograph, I make
love!"

—Ansel Adams

DOUBLE
IMAGE

ONE

1

THE PIT SMELLED OF LOAM, mold, and urine. It was three feet wide, seven feet long, and three feet deep, the size of a shallow grave. Coltrane had been lying in it for thirty-six hours, a rubberized sheet under him, an earth-colored nylon sheet suspended over him, anchored by dead branches and further camouflaged by fallen pine needles. Two hundred yards below the wooded slope on which he was concealed, vehicles were arriving. Six big open-backed trucks jounced along a narrow road into a clearing in the deserted valley. With an echoing rumble, a bulldozer and a backhoe struggled to keep up. A few flakes of snow drifted to the frost-hardened ground as the convoy stopped next to a rectangular area, roughly fifty by a hundred feet, where the ground had been disturbed.

Having waited so long, Coltrane frowned toward the increasingly dark clouds drifting into the valley and prayed that the weather wouldn't turn against him. He raised one of the four cameras arranged before him, focused its zoom lens, and started taking photographs. Men in tattered winter clothes, clutching automatic rifles, jumped from the trucks and scanned the slopes around them. Despite the care with which Coltrane had hidden himself, he tensed when they concentrated in his direction. Afraid he'd been spotted, he ducked his head and pressed himself harder against the floor of the pit. When the men changed their attention to another area of the valley, Coltrane let out his breath, taking more pictures. A bandy-legged, heavy-chested, beefy-faced man with dense dark hair and a thick mustache waved directions to the bulldozer and the backhoe.

Got you, you bastard. Coltrane pressed the shutter button, unable to get over his good fortune. Back in Tuzla, his contact on the UN inspection team had spread out a map and indicated a dozen areas that they intended to investigate. Of course, they wouldn't get around to those areas until they finished with the dozen areas they were *already* investigating. The schedule depended on the weather, which was due to worsen now that November was almost half over. By the time the investigators reached all the suspected areas, the men they wanted to prosecute would have eliminated the evidence against them.

Coltrane had chosen the most isolated spot, his compass and terrain map preventing him from getting lost as he made his way, burdened by two knapsacks, across streams and ridges toward this slope. Concealed among bushes, waiting two hours, he had studied the rugged landscape for any sign that he had been noticed. Only after dark had he constructed his primitive shelter and crawled into it, exhausted, craving sleep but knowing that food had to come first, the cheese sandwiches and dry sausage he had brought along. But even before eating, there was one thing he knew he absolutely had to do: check his cameras.

Throughout the next day and night, Coltrane had remained in his cold hiding place, permitting himself movement only when he ate more sausage, drank from a straw inserted in his canteen, or turned onto his side, urinating into a plastic bottle. All the while, he had second-guessed himself, telling himself that he was wasting his time, that he had chosen the wrong location, or that nothing was going to happen in *any* location and he might as well hike out of here. The dingy bar where his fellow photojournalists hung out in Tuzla was beginning to seem more and more appealing. But he hated to surrender to impatience. Giving up wasn't in his nature. And now he was overjoyed that he hadn't. Not only was he getting prime photos of what the UN inspection team had suspected was happening at various sites but he was also documenting the participation of the man they most wanted to nail.

Dragan Ilkovic. A perfect name for a monster.

The son of a bitch leaned his rifle against the front of a truck and braced his hands on his powerful-looking hips, watching with satisfaction as the bulldozer went to work, plowing earth. The backhoe moved into position behind it. Heart pounding against the rubber sheet, Coltrane kept rapidly taking pictures, glad that he had brought four cameras, each with a different lens and film speed, some with black-and-white film, some with color, so that he wouldn't have to waste time changing film.

Below him, a man with a rifle shouted, pointing fiercely at what the bulldozer had exposed. The beefy-faced man hurried over, yelling commands at the backhoe's driver. For a frustrating moment, the commotion hid what agitated them, but the group quickly parted, some of them rushing to help unload a large piece of equipment from a truck, and Coltrane reacted with horror, the small image in his viewfinder intensified by the magnification of his zoom lens.

He was staring at corpses, a soul-searing countless jumble of them. The bodies had been thrown into the mass grave with such careless haste, so tangled among one another, that it was impossible to know which leg belonged to which torso, which arm to which shoulder to which neck to which skull. The confusion became more manifest as the weight of the bulldozer crushed spines and rib cages. Clothes had disintegrated, flesh had rotted, creating a common putrescent black mush from which gray bones protruded and lipless mouths gaped in silent, eternal anguish.

During the war, this region in eastern Bosnia was supposed to have been a UN-controlled safe haven for Muslims. From hundreds of miles around, as many as fifteen thousand Muslims had hurried here, seeking protection. The target had been too tempting for the Serbs, who surrounded the area and bombarded it, forcing the UN troops to surrender. Surprisingly, the Serbs had let the Muslim children go. But they raped the women—to breed the Muslims out of existence by forcing Muslim women to bear Serbian children. And as for the men . . . Coltrane's mouth filled with bile as he worked the cameras, taking more and more photographs of what remained after the Serbs had loaded the Muslim men into trucks and driven them to isolated valleys like this one, where they dug pits with bulldozers and backhoes, lined the Muslim men up on the edge of the pits, and shot them.

Some of the pits, like the one Coltrane photographed, held as many as four hundred corpses, he had been told. It took a lot of hate and determination to get the job done, but the Serbs had been up to the challenge. When they had finally shot the last Muslim in the back of the head, they had used the bulldozers to spread earth over the bodies, and that was that—problem solved, everything neat and tidy. Except, when the war ended and Bosnia had been carved into Serb, Croat, and Muslim regions, the UN had started talking about outrages against humanity. A war-crimes tribunal was convened in the Netherlands, and suddenly a lot of Serb commanders, like Dragan Ilkovic down there, had become wanted men. They had to be tidier.

The roar of a large machine attracted Coltrane's notice toward the cumbersome piece of equipment that the men had unloaded from one of the trucks. It had a huge funnel on one side and a spout on the other. It resembled the device that city cleanup crews used to pulverize fallen tree limbs. In this case, the machine was a *rock* pulverizer that Dragan Ilkovic had brought from one of the many nearby mines. The backhoe was dropping bones into the funnel. The spout on the other side was spewing horrifying pebbles into the back of a truck. The pebbles would be eliminated in a shaft in one of the mines, Coltrane's informant had suspected. The trouble was, no one could prove that this sanitizing was actually taking place.

Until now, Coltrane thought with fury. Abruptly he noted how quickly the clouds were darkening and thickening. The few flakes of snow had become flurries. He had to work fast. He got a close-up of Dragan Ilkovic, switched to a wide-angle view, and felt his heart stop as the camouflage sheet suspended over him was torn away.

2

HANDS GRABBED HIS ARMS AND SHOULDERS. Guttural voices barked. Coltrane barely had time to snag the straps on his cameras before he was jerked from the pit. The hands spun him, bringing him face-to-face with two muscular men wearing outdoor clothes, their features flushed with anger. The repeated clicks of his cameras must have alerted them as they searched for intruders. Conversely, the clicks—amplified in the confinement of his narrow shelter—had prevented him from hearing their footsteps creep toward him.

"Okay, guys, calm down." Coltrane had no hope that they understood him. But if his tone communicated his intent, the men had absolutely no interest in calming down. Instead, they shoved him backward.

Coltrane made a futile placating gesture. "Look, I was only camping. No hard feelings. Why don't I grab my stuff and leave?"

The men unslung assault rifles from their shoulders.

Several times, in Nicaragua at the start of Coltrane's career, later in Lebanon and Iran, armed men had confronted him about photographs he had taken. Their attention had always been on his cameras. But *these* men barely glanced at his cameras. As they raised their weapons, all they seemed to care about was his chest.

Jesus. Coltrane reacted without thinking. Pretending to stumble back, he twisted as if to try to regain his balance, and *kept* twisting, spinning to face his attackers again, swinging his heaviest camera by the end of its strap. The bulky zoom lens collided with the chin on the man to Coltrane's right, bone crunching. With a groan, the man lurched to Coltrane's left, jolted against the second man, and threw off his aim, the second man's assault weapon blasting chunks from a tree.

Coltrane rushed the men as they toppled into the pit. Swinging the camera again, he cracked it across the second man's forehead. Blood flying, the man collapsed.

Startled voices echoed from the valley. Coltrane jerked his gaze in that direction. The small figures below had heard the gunshots. They were glaring toward this slope, some of them pointing, others shouting. The heavy-chested man grabbed his rifle and scrambled toward the slope.

Coltrane raced toward the ridge top, entering the dense fir trees on the opposite side. Shadows enveloped him. His cameras banged against him. The one he had used as a weapon was smeared with blood. The lens had shattered. If only the camera isn't cracked, he hoped. If only the film hasn't been exposed to light. Despite the frenzy of his descent, he pressed the rewind button and heard a whir, relieved that the motor hadn't been damaged. Immediately, he lost his balance, a mat of fir needles slipping out from under him. His back struck the ground so hard that his teeth snapped together. He fought to dig in his heels to prevent himself from sliding faster down the slope, but the needles kept giving way. He tumbled, walloped to a stop against a tree, and grimaced from a sharp pain on his right side, finding where the camera had rammed against him.

Have to get the film, protect the film. Hands trembling, he freed a catch at the side of the camera, flipped open the back, and pulled out the rewound film. His elation lasted barely a second as shouts crested the ridge behind him. Fear rocketed through him. Struggling to catch his breath, he shoved the film into a pocket, dropped the damaged camera, and charged down the remainder of the incline.

Even on a sunny day, the massive fir trees in this region were dense enough to filter light, but this had not been a sunny day, the dark clouds massing, turning the afternoon into dusk. The air became colder. Snow started falling again, at first sporadically, then steadily, a gentle blanketing that made a whisper as it settled through the fir boughs.

Behind him, the shouts became more angry. A staccato burst of gunshots shredded tree limbs.

Coltrane reached an ice-rimmed stream, almost tried to leap across but realized it was too wide, and veered to the left. For certain, he couldn't just jump in and wade to the opposite bank. The water was so cold that it would give him frostbite or hypothermia.

He had to try to find a fallen log that bridged it. But the stream widened as he ran along it, and there weren't any logs. The color of his clothing—brown woolen pants, a green ski jacket, a matching knit cap that he had pulled down around his ears—had been chosen to help him blend with the evergreen forest. He tried to assure himself that at least he had that advantage. The thought didn't give him much confidence when another stuttering burst of gunshots riddled the trees. Despite the unfamiliar language, the tone of the shouts behind him left no doubt that the men were cursing.

Slowed by the slippery accumulation of snow, Coltrane saw a fir tree close to the stream and noticed that one of its boughs—dead, about nine feet off the ground—extended over the water. He leapt. His leather-gloved hands fought for a grip on the bough. The snow made the bark slick. Straining, he tightened his fingers, dangled, felt the awkward weight of his remaining three cameras hanging from his right shoulder, and struggled hand over hand across the bough.

Behind him, closer, branches cracked. Footsteps thundered. He dropped to the ground on the opposite side of the stream, straightened, and raced deeper into the forest. Determined to get the film from his cameras, he pressed their rewind buttons. Without warning, something yanked him backward. The jolt had such force that he thought he'd been shot. But instead of falling, he hung on an angle, his boots on the ground, his body suspended over the gathering snow. A moment of disorientation cleared and he realized in dismay that a stout branch had snagged one of his camera straps. The branch had torn the right shoulder on his ski jacket. It had gouged his skin. He slipped painfully free of the strap, heard the camera's rewind motor stop whirring, opened its back, stuffed the roll of film in a pocket, abandoned the tangled camera, and charged onward.

If I can just keep going. The snow's falling harder. It'll fill my tracks, he thought. Behind him, heavy splashes told him that some of his pursuers had jumped into the stream, too impatient to wait in line to go hand over hand on the branch. Wails followed, the icy water shocking their bodies. At least *some* of them will be slowed, Coltrane tried to assure himself.

But *he* was also slowing. The forest sloped upward. Gasping for breath, he struggled higher, the pain in his ribs getting sharper. Although he had jettisoned two cameras, he still had two others and continued to fear that something would happen to the film in them. Grabbing one as he ran, he pawed open its back and yanked out its rewound film, only to moan in despair when he dropped the cylinder into a drift. Rushing, he stooped to fumble through the snow and retrieve it, shoving it into the jacket pocket where he had put the others.

The camera he had just unloaded blew apart, the explosive force throwing him onto the snow. He felt intense heat, then bitter cold along his left side. Nausea swept through him as he realized that a bullet meant for his back had struck the camera, deflected off it, and sliced through his left side. He rolled toward the cover of a fir tree as the far-off crack of a rifle echoed through the forest. He had to find where the shooter was to avoid his line of fire. Struggling to his feet, he risked a glance through an opening in the trees, toward the direction from which he had come. Snow settled on his eyes, making him blink repeatedly. The wind stopped. The snow eased just for a moment, and he shivered at the sight of a bandy-legged, bulky-shouldered man on a ridge across from him, Dragan Ilkovic's thick features braced against the sights on his rifle.

Ilkovic fired again, the bullet whizzing past Coltrane, tearing up snow and earth. Enraged, Ilkovic switched his rifle from single shot to full automatic, releasing a burst that went wild as the snow swirled back in greater force. Ilkovic vanished in the storm, and Coltrane felt a bone-deep chill. Clutching his bleeding side, stumbling higher up the slope, he fled the louder noises of his pursuers.

3

THE WIND HAD WORSENED TO A GALE by the time Coltrane reached the top. If not for his injuries, he might have hurried over the crest, in which case he would have died, for the other side of the slope was a cliff, its bottom invisible in the gusting snow. Which way? Right or left? As far as his limited vision allowed him to determine, the cliff continued in both directions. But whichever way he chose, following the ridgeline was predictable. All his pursuers would have to do would be to separate and outflank him.

I can't go back the way I came, he thought. He saw an outcrop ten feet below him, squirmed over the edge, ignored the pain of his injuries, and hung to the agonizing limit of his arms. When he released his grip and hit the ledge, he fell to his knees, then his chest, hugging the rock. He feared he was going to pass out.

But he couldn't allow himself to give in to weakness. He had to get far enough down the cliff that his pursuers wouldn't be able to see him in the snowstorm. Pulse racing, he peered over and saw another ledge, but it was farther down than the first one had been. Even hanging by his arms, he would still have to drop several yards, and the force of the landing would almost certainly throw off his balance, plunging him over the edge. As the angry voices rushed closer to the top, he imagined what would happen when his hunters got there. Staring down, their sullen faces would break into smiles when they saw him crouching helplessly ten feet below them. Their grins would broaden when they opened fire. He had to—

The snow gusted at an object that weighed on Coltrane's injured shoulder: his remaining camera. He frowned at its nylon strap. If he didn't get off this ledge in the next thirty seconds, he wouldn't be going anywhere again. Frenzied, he extended the strap to its maximum length, about four feet, hoping it would hold him. His lungs heaved so much that he feared he might faint when he looped the strap over an outcrop and squirmed down, pretending he was clutching a rope. It wouldn't get him to the next ledge, but at least it would get him closer. The snow buffeted him. Trembling, he eased lower, the ledge not yet close enough to drop to, almost a body length away. Spasms shuddered through him—because he hadn't moved his hands to get lower. The *strap* had done it for him. It had stretched. It groaned. Every impulse urged him to hurry, but he didn't dare.

Any strong motion might cause the strap to stretch to its breaking point. Closer.

The strap broke. Scrabbling against the cliff face, he felt the wind shove him into space. He fell, clawed at the rock, and landed, half on, half off the ledge. The wind struck him harder. His gloves lost their grip. Slipping over, he tensed in panic, his stomach soaring toward his throat as he anticipated his impact on the rocks far below. With startling abruptness, he jolted to a stop much sooner than he expected, his legs buckling, his body collapsing. It took him a moment to realize that he had landed on another ledge. He might have passed out. He couldn't tell. One thing he did know was that, as he lay on his back, blinking upward through the thickening snow, he couldn't see the top of the cliff, which meant that *he* couldn't be seen, either.

But he didn't dare rest. The snow might lessen at any moment and reveal him. He had to keep moving. Another wave of nausea swept through him as he forced himself to sit up. When he peered over the side, his vision cleared enough for him to see that the next ledge was only four feet down. Wincing, he lowered himself onto it. The next time he peered down, he discovered he was on a slope that led to the bottom.

The snow rose above his ankles. Shuffling through it, his legs kept threatening to give way, but he refused to let them surrender. I have to get the film out of here, he urged himself. The air dimmed, the snow becoming gray, his vision narrowing, his thoughts blurring. When he stumbled into a fir tree, its icy needles stinging his face, he realized that he must have been walking half-asleep. He could barely see his hand in front of his face. If he didn't find shelter, he was going to freeze to death. Sinking to his hands and knees, he crawled weakly beneath the drooping boughs of the snow-laden fir tree. In the space under them, he reached ground that was bare except for fallen needles, and he had just enough room to slump with his back against the trunk. The bark smelled sharply of resin. Except for that, in the gathering darkness, hearing the wind outside, he had the sensation of being in a tent.

He passed out.

4

A SMOTHERING BLACKNESS SURROUNDED HIM, so absolute that he feared he'd gone blind or was in hell. Immediately his pain jerked him fully awake. Muffled, the shrieking wind seemed far away. It was night. The dense blanket of snow on the needled branches made the air around him feel heavy, compressed. He licked his dry, cracked lips. Completely disoriented, racked with pain, he feared he was going to die in here.

He took off his right glove and mustered the strength to reach under the left side of his jacket. There, his sweater and his thermal underwear were soaked with a warm sticky liquid. His gentle touch made him shudder. The wound seemed as long as his hand, as wide as a finger. The deflected bullet had gouged a furrow along his side. And kept going? he wondered. Or was it still inside him? Had it hit only fat, or ruptured the abdominal wall?

He had never felt so powerless and alone. His feeling of isolation increased when he reached for the comfort of a camera and recalled that he had started out with four of them and not one of them remained. But I had the fourth camera with me on the cliff. Didn't I take it off the strap and cram it into a pocket? In dismay, he pawed at the jacket but didn't feel the camera. What he did feel were three cylinders of film. The fourth camera and, more important, the film inside it were lost to him.

He fought to rouse his spirit. Hey, I saved the other three rolls. That's still a lot. If I can get them out of here . . .

The sentence didn't want to be completed.

Yes? he asked himself. If I can get them out of here?

Are those photographs worth dying for?

This time, he didn't hesitate. Are you kidding me? The UN inspection team is desperate to get its hands on evidence like this. The film will prove that the atrocities committed here were much worse than anyone imagined. That bastard Ilkovic will finally have to pay for what he did.

Maybe.

Coltrane felt uneasy. I don't understand.

Oh, the photos you took are shocking enough to get Ilkovic convicted, all right. But what if the politicians become involved and declare an amnesty for the sake of peace in the region? What if nothing changes? Are your pictures worth getting killed for?

Coltrane didn't have an answer. Again, he groped for the reassuring touch of a camera. A homicide detective friend of his had once joked that Coltrane felt about cameras the way police officers did about backup guns—naked without one. "Come to think of it," the detective had continued joking, "cameras and guns both shoot people, don't they?" But it wasn't the same at all, Coltrane insisted. His kind of shooting didn't kill people. It was supposed to make them immortal. That was the reason he had become a photographer. When he had been twelve, he had found a trove of photographs of his dead mother and had fantasized that they kept her alive.

Those pictures of his mother had been beautiful.

As shivers seized him and his consciousness faded into a place that was despairingly even darker, he managed one last lucid thought.

Then why have I been taking ugly pictures for such a long time?

5

HEARING A RUMBLE, he woke in alarm. His first panicked thought warned him he was about to be smothered by an avalanche. But the moment he raised his head, trying to move, the pain that radiated from his left side almost made him pass out. The rumble increased. As his consciousness fought to clear itself, he understood that he had to be wrong, that the ridges here weren't steep enough for avalanches. Besides, the rumble seemed to come from *below* him rather than from above. It didn't make sense. What was causing the noise?

Find out. Spots swirled in front of his eyes as he placed his hands on the ground, barely aware of the fir needles under his knees. He crawled from beneath the snow-covered boughs, the glare of sunlight off drifts nearly blinding him. The air was shockingly cold, pinching his nostrils.

When he squinted below him, he feared he was hallucinating, unable to make himself believe that he was on a hill above a road, that the rumble came from a convoy of tanks that had NATO markings. He wobbled like a tightrope walker, struggling for balance as he waved his arms and waded as fast as he could down through snowdrifts, which wasn't fast at all, but it didn't matter, because the lead tank's driver had seen him and was stopping, soldiers jumping out as he fell and tumbled to the bottom, the soldiers blurting German as they rushed to help him.

Three days later, against a UN doctor's orders, he was on a plane home. From hell to the City of Angels.

TWO

I

As Coltrane twitched from a nightmare that was indistinguishable from the trauma of his wide-awake memories, he seemed to have been running forever. He fell from the impact of the bullet that shattered his camera, rolled desperately to avoid Ilkovic's line of fire, and flinched as hands grabbed his shoulders, pushing him.

A moan escaped him. His eyes jerked open in a panic, the hands continuing to press him down, a gentle voice whispering, "Ssshh, it's only me. It's Jennifer."

"Uh." Sweat slicked him. His chest heaved.

"You're home. You're safe."

". . . Uh."

"You were having a nightmare. I had to grab you before you rolled out of bed."

Coltrane's heart hammered so fast that he feared it would burst against his ribs. His tongue felt dry and thick. ". . . Jennifer?" In the shadows of what he now recognized was his bedroom, he peered up at her. Still disoriented, he seemed to see her through an imaginary viewfinder, framing her lovely oval face, her light blue eyes, and the dark worry behind them. His gaze lingered on her appealing curved lips, her smooth tan cheeks, and her short blond hair that resembled corn silk.

His heartbeat no longer made his chest feel swollen. At last, he seemed to be getting enough air. He eased back onto his pillow.

"Here." Jennifer reached for a glass of water on the bedside table. Adjusting a straw, she placed it against his parched mouth. He took several deep swallows, luxuriating in the wonderful coolness, ignoring the drops that rolled down his chin.

"Guess I'm the last person you expected to see, huh?" Jennifer asked.

Coltrane didn't know what to say. The last time he had seen her was six months ago when they had broken up.

"Daniel sent for me," she said.

Coltrane nodded, the motion aggravating a headache. Daniel was a friend who lived in the town house next door.

"When you showed up at his place this morning, you really spooked him. He took care of you during the day, but he's working nights at the hospital, and he needed somebody to watch you." Jennifer smiled awkwardly. "He phoned me at the magazine." She hesitated, then made a mock salute. "Nurse Nightingale reporting. Unless you can find somebody better, I guess you're stuck with me."

"I can't think of *anybody* better."

Jennifer's smile was now filled with pleasure. "Can I get you anything? Daniel said I should give you Tylenol for your fever. And this antibiotic. Your wound's a little infected."

"Whatever the doctor ordered." Coltrane swallowed the pills, then took several more sips of water. His body seemed to absorb the fluid instantly.

"How do you feel?" Jennifer asked.

Coltrane tilted his right hand from side to side, as if to say, Not so good.

"Daniel told me what you told *him*. There are a couple of blank parts. You can fill them in later. When you get your strength back. That's all I want you to concentrate on—getting better."

"Need . . ."

"Tell me."

"The bathroom."

"Put your arm around my shoulder. I'll help you stand."

When Jennifer pulled off the covers, Coltrane realized that he was wearing only boxer shorts and a T-shirt. His shirt hiked up, making him conscious of the bulk of the new bandage that Daniel had taped over the stitches on his side. There was dried blood below the bandage, scrapes on his stomach, and bruises on his legs.

Coltrane leaned on her.

"Can you manage by yourself?" Jennifer asked as they entered the bathroom. "Should I stay here with you?"

"I'm fine." But Coltrane lost his footing, and Jennifer had to grab him.

He sank to the seat. "Not my best profile, I'm afraid."

"Just do what you have to."

"I'm okay. You can wait outside."

"You're sure?" Jennifer asked.

"Thanks."

"As long as you're certain you won't fall on the floor."

Coltrane nodded, watching her start to leave the bathroom. He whispered her name.

She looked back.

"I mean it," he said. "Thanks."

2

I'VE BROUGHT TWO PRESENTS FOR YOU," Jennifer said the next evening, "but the first one doesn't count."

Curious, Coltrane watched her bring her left hand from behind her back. She set down a copy of *Southern California Magazine,* a photograph of the windmill electrical generators outside Palm Springs on the cover. "The latest issue. I've made a lot of improvements. I don't know if you've been keeping up with it since . . ."

"I haven't missed an issue."

Her light blue eyes glittered.

"Even when I've been out of the country, I had it forwarded. It kept my memories warm on a lot of cold nights. If this is the gift that doesn't matter, I can't imagine what you've got behind your back in your other hand."

Jennifer showed him a flat, stiff object, about eight by ten inches, gift-wrapped. She watched intently as he shook it.

"Doesn't rattle. Feels like glass. I wonder what . . ."

She watched him pull open the wrapping. But the discomfort on Coltrane's face at what he saw caused her anticipation to change to confusion. "Your third *Newsweek* cover," she said. "It came out yesterday. I thought you'd like it framed."

Coltrane somberly studied the stark black-and-white image of the backhoe dropping bones into the pulverizing machine while Dragan Ilkovic watched with satisfaction. ". . . Thanks."

"You don't sound as if you mean it."

"It was very thoughtful of you."

"Then why aren't I convinced?"

The room filled with silence.

"What you told Daniel about how you got wounded," Jennifer said. "I already knew some of it—from the CNN interview you did while you were in the hospital over there."

"That's why I snuck out of the hospital and caught the first plane back to here. After CNN tracked me down, I knew it wouldn't be long before a lot of other journalists would be swarming around me. I had no idea the UN would release the photographs so quickly. I couldn't bear talking about them."

"You unplugged your phone."

"It kept ringing. I couldn't sleep. A half a dozen TV talk shows asked me to be a guest."

"People think you're a hero."

"Please." With distaste, Coltrane set the framed *Newsweek* cover aside. "I was lucky to survive."

"You'll get another Pulitzer Prize."

"I hope not. Not for *those* photos. It didn't take a genius to get those pictures, only a damned fool who was willing to lie in a hole in the ground for a day and a half."

Jennifer looked baffled. "I've never heard you talk this way before."

"Did the pictures make a difference? Was Ilkovic charged with war crimes and arrested?"

"He disappeared. Nobody knows where to find him."

"Great." The word sounded like a curse.

"They'll get him."

"Sure."

"I don't understand what's happened to you," Jennifer said. "You were always proud of scraping through tough spots."

"I had a lot of chance to think while I was trying to get through the night without freezing to death. I got to wondering if I'd ever taken any photographs that made people feel glad to be alive because they'd seen my work. Maybe it's time I became a real photographer."

"But there isn't anybody better."

"I'm not a photographer. Stieglitz, Steichen, Strand, Weston, Adams, Berenice Abbott, Randolph Packard—*they* were photographers. *They* knew what a camera was for."

A somber moment lengthened.

Jennifer interrupted it. "I brought some Chinese food. Do you think you could eat it if I go downstairs and bring you a plate?"

Instead of answering, Coltrane caught her by surprise. "How have you been, Jennifer?"

"Fine. Working hard. The magazine's doing well."

"But what about *you*? Are *you* doing well?"

"It's been lonely."

"Yes."

She seemed to hold her breath.

"The same with me. I've missed you, Jennifer."

Her eyes misted. She walked slowly toward him and knelt, her face level with his, stroking his beard-stubbled cheek. "I'm sorry. I needed too much from you. I think I smothered you. I'll never act that way again."

"It was my fault as much as yours."

"No. I've changed. I promise."

"We both have." Ignoring the tightness in his side, Coltrane leaned forward and kissed her.

3

COMING EVENTS

Legendary photographer Randolph Packard will have a rare showing of his prints at the Sunset Gallery in Laguna Beach, from 5:00 to 7:00 P.M. on Friday, November 21. Packard, whose work documents the changes in Southern California, is generally considered to be one of the great innovators in modern photography. He was born in . . .

4

COLTRANE COULDN'T GET OVER IT. If he hadn't opened the copy of *Southern California* Jennifer had given him, happening to scan its calendar section, he wouldn't have known about Packard's opening until it was too late. Even then, he barely had enough time, suddenly realizing that today was the twenty-first and that it was almost three. Fortunately, he had already mustered the strength to get out of bed and clean himself up. His sneakers, jeans, and denim shirt weren't exactly what he would have chosen for what sounded like a formal reception, but he didn't have time to change, only to grab a sport coat, a camera, and a copy of one of Packard's collections, then get to his car.

The effort exhausted him, but he didn't think twice about its worth. Leaving Los Angeles, driving south as fast as possible amid the smog-shrouded traffic on the San Diego Freeway, he felt as if he'd been told that someone had risen from the dead. Good God, how old would Packard be? In his nineties? The bulk of his work had been done in the twenties and the thirties. From then on, his output had dwindled, until, by the fifties, he had disappeared from public view. As the *Southern California* article had noted, paraphrasing a quotation from F. Scott Fitzgerald, "For Randolph Packard, there wasn't a second act." But his *first* act had certainly been remarkable. The rumors about drugs and orgies, about his frequent unexplained trips to Mexico, had rippled through California's artistic community and generated publicity for his work.

Not that Coltrane had needed the article to tell him any of this. When he had first been learning about photography, Randolph Packard had been one of his idols. He owned every Packard collection that had been published. His work had been deeply influenced by Packard's theory that every effective photograph ought to tell the viewer something that merely looking at the subject of the photograph in its natural setting could not.

Packard's famous portraits of silent-screen movie stars, for example: Rudolph Valentino, Clara Bow, Ramon Novarro, a lot of others, many of whom nobody would remember if Packard hadn't immortalized them. Each portrait presented its subject in a splendor of light. But the actors didn't radiate the light. Instead, they absorbed it. The brilliance was so intense, Packard seemed to think of them as *literally* being stars, but of a special sort, sucking up energy until, because of their egos and their frantic lifestyles, they would either burst or collapse upon themselves and be consumed.

Heading into the wall-to-wall cities that made up Orange County, Coltrane felt his anticipation swell. He was reminded of when the county had literally been covered with oranges, grove after grove of them, and how Packard's classic sun-bright photograph of the area had depicted more oranges on the ground than in the trees, an abundance of ripeness on the verge of decay.

Packard had also photographed Laguna Beach, not the town (which had been only a few cottages back in the twenties and thirties) but the curve of sand along the ocean. That area of the Pacific Coast Highway was still as winding as it had been in Packard's day, but now it had been overbuilt, the same as everywhere else in Southern California—gas stations, gift shops, and restaurants jammed next to one another. The crowded four-lane road felt like the narrow two-lane it had replaced. At dusk, in late November, the beach itself was almost deserted, cold waves crashing onto the sand. When Packard had photographed the area, he had made it seem an unoccupied paradise. But if the viewer looked closely at Packard's most reproduced depiction of the beach, *Horizon, 1929*, the telltale imperfection, the poignant regret for time passing that was typical of Packard's work, became evident: distant smoke belching from a passing freighter.

Coltrane managed to find a parking space on Forest Avenue across from the beach. He slung his Nikon single-lens reflex around his neck and took a deep breath, surveying the lights of art galleries along the tree-canopied street. When he reached back into his car to get his copy of Packard's *Reflections of the City of Angels*, he suddenly felt light-headed and almost collapsed across the seat. His side in pain, he grabbed the steering wheel, took another deep breath, and straightened. Sweat chilled his face.

Maybe this isn't such a good idea, he told himself. It's a wonder I didn't faint driving down here. I belong in bed, not getting crushed by strangers at a cocktail party.

No, he thought, feeling much older than his thirty-five years. I need to start over.

5

THE RECEPTION IN THE RUSTIC-LOOKING SUNSET GALLERY had spilled out onto the street. Coltrane stepped past trendily dressed couples wearing expensive jewelry, their makeup and hair perfect, and ignored the looks they gave his sneakers. The gallery was crammed with people who spoke with pseudo-British accents. Many of them had lips so tight, they seemed to have lockjaw. They sipped from flutes of champagne, but Coltrane had no interest in finding the bar. He heard music playing from hidden speakers, a CD of a string quartet, it sounded like, but he couldn't be sure—the conversations were too loud. All he cared about were Packard's photographs, and even before he worked his way through the crowd, it was obvious that the sheer number of them was astonishing.

Protecting his side, he struggled to the nearest wall of photographs and felt excitement build in him when he realized that he had never seen any of them before. Again and again, a card next to a photograph indicated that each was from Packard's own collection. Their dates ranged from the fifties to the nineties, making clear that Packard *hadn't* given up photography in his later years. He had simply chosen not to let the public see his work. Coltrane's excitement changed to dismay when the force of the images hit him. This second act of Packard's career emphasized the decay that he had only hinted at in his earlier work. Each photograph was devoted to blight—a dead seagull trapped in an oil spill, an emaciated child eating garbage, a brush fire destroying a spindly multimillion-dollar house perched ridiculously on a Los Angeles hilltop.

Repelled, Coltrane forced his way to another wall, oblivious to the annoyed looks people gave him as he shoved past. The next pictures were even more disturbing—policemen standing around a woman's corpse in an alley, a caged pit bull snarling at children who taunted it with sticks, a man attacking another man during a riot. The black-and-white images had been printed to emphasize their shadows, the bleakness chilling. The only thing missing was a photograph of jumbled skeletons being clawed from the earth by a backhoe. Stumbling away, wanting nothing more than to leave, Coltrane felt the back of his legs bump against an upright metal circle with spindles and nearly toppled backward over it, catching his balance just in time, sensing with embarrassment that what he had struck was a wheelchair.

He quickly turned. "I'm very sorry. I didn't . . ." His apology froze in his throat when he recognized the chair's occupant.

Randolph Packard was wizened, but he still bore an uncanny resemblance to photographs that had been taken of him in his prime. Even in a wheelchair, he was tall, his thinness emphasizing his height. His trademark shock of hair over his forehead had receded, becoming wispy and white, but it was nonetheless recognizable. The hypnotic eyes were darker, the face narrower, the nose more blade-like. But despite being withered, with liver spots, his slack skin barely concealing his skull, he was unmistakably Packard.

"This chair's taken, thank you." Packard coughed, as if he had sand caught in his throat.

"I apologize. I should have looked where I was going," Coltrane said. "Are you hurt?"

"The truth *never* hurts. Tell me what you think of my photographs."

Coltrane was taken by surprise. "They're, uh . . ."

"Indescribable, evidently."

". . . impressive."

"You don't make it sound like a compliment."

Coltrane was determined to be tactful. "They're technically perfect."

"Technically?" Packard coughed more forcefully, still unable to get the sand from his throat. "That camera around your neck—is that a fashion statement? Don't tell me you're a photographer."

"Yes." Coltrane stiffened. "Yes, I'm a photographer."

"Oh, well, then. Since you're a photographer. What don't you like about these photographs?"

Coltrane felt bile in his stomach. "They're too bleak for my taste."

"Is that a fact."

"Actually, if you want to talk about facts, they're ugly."

"Ugly?"

"Coming here was important to me. I needed hope, not despair."

Packard didn't say anything for a moment, only steadied his wrinkle-rimmed eyes on Coltrane, then nodded. "Well, good for you."

"I beg your pardon?"

"I asked for the truth. You're the only person in this room who gave it to me. What are you holding there?"

"One of your collections."

"You brought it for an autograph?"

"That was my intention."

"But now you're not sure."

"That's right."

"And you're really a photographer?"

Coltrane nodded.

"Then tell me something else that's true. Why did you become a photographer?"

Coltrane turned to leave. "I won't bother you any longer."

"I asked you a question. Quick now. Don't think about it. Answer me. Why did you—"

"To stop time."

"Indeed?" Packard's sunken eyes assessed him. "What's your name?"

"Mitchell Coltrane."

"Mitchell . . ." Packard's gaze went inward, then focused on him more tightly. "Yes, I know your work."

Coltrane couldn't tell if that meant the same as stepping in dog shit.

"Tell me why you want to stop time," Packard demanded.

"Things fall apart."

"And the center cannot hold? I didn't know anybody read Yeats anymore."

"And people die."

"How very true." Packard coughed again, painfully.

At once, an effusive, colorfully dressed man burst from the crowd. "There you are, Randolph. I've been looking everywhere." He was in his forties, overweight, with a flushed face, a salt-and-pepper mustache, and several thousand dollars' worth of designer labels. "Some people came in you absolutely have to meet." The man gripped the back of Packard's wheelchair. "Excuse us. Coming through, everyone."

"Just a moment." Packard's frail whisper carried amazing force. He motioned for Coltrane to step close. "This is my card. I'd like you to come for lunch tomorrow. One o'clock sharp. Bring the book. I'll sign it then."

And Packard was gone.

6

Well, what did I expect? Coltrane asked himself, struggling through the crowd to get out of the reception. There were many mysteries about Randolph Packard, but everything Coltrane had read about him was clear about one thing: his personality. Even to his most sympathetic biographer, Packard was haughty. His overbearing attitude was variously explained as the consequence of having been spoiled by wealthy parents whose fortune he had inherited at the age of sixteen after the parents died in a boating accident, or as the imperious manner of a genius whose sensibility was constantly being assaulted by those around him.

Whatever its cause, Coltrane had definitely had a taste of it. Angry, he escaped from the art gallery, so distracted by his emotions that he didn't notice the change in the weather until he got to where he'd parked his Chevy Blazer near the intersection of Forest and the South Coast Highway. At almost six o'clock in late November, darkness was natural. But not *this* much darkness. A remnant of the sunset ought to have been visible on the ocean's horizon; despite the glow from streetlights, stars should have started to glitter. But now the sky was absolutely black, and the horizon was indistinguishable from the ink that had become the ocean. A wind stung his cheeks, flinging sand from the beach. The first drops of rain pelted his windshield as he hurried to unlock his car and get in.

For about twenty minutes, as he headed north along the slippery, glistening 405 back to Los Angeles, the storm matched his mood. Then it seemed to cleanse him. Although the rain-slowed traffic would normally have made him impatient, he felt oddly content just to gaze past his flapping windshield wipers. He put on one of his favorite tapes and listened to Bobby Darin sing heartbreakingly "The Gal That Got Away." As he admired Darin's perfect phrasing, it occurred to him that almost no one had ever spoken favorably about Bobby Darin as a human being. Because of a heart condition,

Darin had known that the odds were he wouldn't live past his thirties. Feeling the pressure of limited time, he had so devoted himself to his career that no one else had mattered. *Self-centered* didn't begin to describe him. Nor did *cruel.* Talent, it seemed, wasn't any guarantee of noble character. Mulling over these issues, Coltrane made the obvious application to Randolph Packard: Maybe it's not a good idea to meet one of your idols.

7

THROUGH THE STORM, Coltrane's headlights revealed Jennifer's red BMW parked at the curb in front of his town house. It troubled him. He had left a message at Jennifer's office, telling her he wouldn't be home. Why had she come over, regardless? Worried that their problems might be starting again, he pressed his remote-control garage opener, steered into the single stall, and shut off the engine. After hours of listening to the cacophony of rain drumming on his roof, he sat motionless, wearily enjoying the comparative silence. Then he pressed the remote control again and got out of the car. Despite the rumble of the descending garage door, he heard another door, the one at the top of the stairs. Kitchen light spilled down.

"Mitch?"

As Jennifer appeared above him, he saw her through an imaginary camera, its lens intensifying her. Nimbuslike, her blond hair seemed to radiate the light behind her. She wore gray slacks and a crewneck navy sweater. Her lips had a touch of pale orange lipstick.

"Are you all right?" She took several steps down toward him.

"Didn't your assistant give you my message?"

"Message?" Jennifer looked confused. "No. I was away from the office all afternoon. By the time I had a chance to call in, my assistant was gone."

Coltrane's shoulders relaxed. It had just been a simple misunderstanding. It wasn't going to be like before. He gripped the railing and climbed to her.

"I got worried when you weren't here," Jennifer said. "Then I finally noticed the open magazine on your kitchen table. When I saw the article in the calendar section, the time and date for the Packard exhibit, I figured out where you'd gone."

"If you ever decide to get out of the magazine business, you'd make an awfully good detective." Coltrane shut the kitchen door. "You wanted to know if I'm all right. No." He stroked her hair and kissed her; her lipstick tasted of apricots. "I was a fool. I should have stayed home. With you."

The compliment made Jennifer's blue eyes seem as clear as the Caribbean when the sun emerges from behind a cloud. Then something else he had said registered on her, making her frown. "Why did you call yourself a fool?"

"Let's just say meeting Randolph Packard wasn't what I'd hoped it would be."

"You have awfully high standards."

Her remark puzzled him. "I've admired his work since I was old enough to tell a good photograph from a bad one."

"Then I don't know what more you could want. From everything I hear, things couldn't have gone better."

"Everything you hear?" Coltrane creased his brow.

"Packard phoned fifteen minutes ago."

"*What?* You're kidding me."

"He got your number from the magazine photographers directory. He thought you'd be back by now. When I told him you weren't, he talked about you. You made quite an impression on him."

Coltrane felt a dizzying sense of unreality.

"He said he hasn't met anybody as honest as you in a long time. What on earth did you say to him?"

Coltrane sank onto a kitchen chair. "Actually, I insulted him."

Jennifer's mouth hung open.

"I told him I thought his photographs at the exhibition were ugly."

"You certainly know how to win friends and influence people."

"Believe me, I wasn't exaggerating about his photographs. They're as ugly as the ones *I've* been taking."

"And the ones you removed from your wall?"

Coltrane turned toward his living room. During the day, he had taken down all his framed photographs. His *Time* cover of an American soldier spooning food into a skeletal child's mouth in Somalia, his two *Newsweek* covers (one of which showed a widow keening, holding her dead daughter in one arm and her dead husband in the other after a rocket attack in northern Israel), and his much-reprinted Associated Press photo of the first wave of American helicopters to invade Panama. These and other sensational highlights of his career were now stacked on a closet shelf. "It takes one shitty photographer to recognize another."

"Maybe that's why he wants to do a project with you," Jennifer said.

Coltrane wasn't sure he'd heard her correctly. "Do a project with . . ."

"He says he knows your work and thinks it's impressive."

"You're making this up."

"Not at all. But he says *you'll* be putting in most of the effort. *He'll* supply the advice and the original photographs for a photo essay in *Southern California.*"

"What are we talking about?"

"His famous series of L.A. houses in the twenties and thirties."

Coltrane straightened. That series of twenty photographs was a masterpiece. Packard's depiction of various styles of houses in widely separated areas of the not-yet-overgrown city not only had been hauntingly beautiful but had seemed to mourn the impending loss of the innocence it celebrated.

"Packard thinks they ought to be done again," Jennifer said. "Go back to the same neighborhoods. Find the same spots where he set up his camera. Choose the same angles. Shoot what's there now. He says he's been thinking about a continuation of the series for a long time, but now he isn't well enough to do it."

"All he's asking me to be is his assistant?"

"More. Even if he *could* take the photographs, he says he *wouldn't.*

He agrees with your opinion of his recent work—he can't see beauty anymore. He's hoping, if *you* take the photographs, the same places all these years later, maybe you'll find the beauty he can't find."

"I'll be damned."

8

SOMETIME IN THE NIGHT, Coltrane woke to find himself reaching for her. His lips touched hers, but as he continued to roll onto his injured side, he winced from pain. "Lie still," she whispered. "Let me do the work." He felt her warmth when she leaned over him, kissing his neck. She trembled from the brush of his hands against her breasts. Floating. Flowing. Pain stopped. So did time.

9

WE SHOULD NEVER HAVE SPLIT UP," he said.

The bedside lamp was on. They had just returned from the bathroom. Naked, Jennifer sat next to him on the bed, her legs curled under her.

"I didn't give you a choice," she said.

His emerald eyes studied her. "I didn't pay enough attention to you."

She shook her head. "We both know the truth. I crowded you until you had to back off." She looked at her hands. "There's something I never told you."

Coltrane frowned, wondering what she was getting at.

"This is hard for me to . . . I was married once."

He turned his head in surprise.

"Ten years ago. I found out later he'd screwed my best friend the night before the wedding. That was after I found out he'd been screwing every woman he could all the time he was married to me, which wasn't long, just under a year."

"Why on earth didn't you tell me?"

"It's not something I'm comfortable talking about. All the story proves is that I'm a fool."

"But why did he marry you if he didn't intend to be faithful?"

"He said he loved me." Jennifer's tone was filled with self-mocking. "Lord knows, I loved *him*. I think being married to me gave him the chance to play the field and have an excuse why he couldn't marry those other women. I was compliant enough to give him a home and make his meals and not pester him when he said he had to work late and wouldn't be home."

"I can't tell you how sorry I am."

"Not as much as *I* was. The point is, I had a hard time trusting men after that. I kept suspecting that anybody who showed an interest in me was really trying to take advantage of me." Jennifer bit her lip. "I guess that's another way of saying I didn't believe I could be special enough to any man that he'd never look at another woman. So . . ." She shrugged fatalistically. "I overcompensate. I wanted you to love me on an impossible level. But I swear that won't happen again. Word of honor. I won't make demands."

"You should have told me about this before. It helps me understand a lot of things."

"That's why I'm telling you now. I lost you once, Mitch. I don't want to lose you again."

10

PACKARD'S ADDRESS WAS IN NEWPORT BEACH. Coltrane's *Thomas Guide* led him to a Spanish-style mansion partially concealed by a high stucco wall. Both the wall and the house were pale pink, severely sun-faded, although the clouds from Friday night's storm lingered, cloaking everything in gray. Driving through an open iron gate, Coltrane saw pools of water around cracks in the driveway's blacktop. Shrubs needed trimming. Avocados rotted on the ground.

The overweight, colorfully dressed man who had wheeled Packard away at the reception answered the doorbell. He looked as if he'd had a hard night. His red sport coat matched the flush of his heavy cheeks. His gray-and-white mustache seemed to push down his mouth. He was holding a half-finished glass of what Coltrane assumed was a Bloody Mary. "I'm not convinced this is a good idea," the man murmured.

Coltrane couldn't tell if he meant drinking his lunch or inviting Coltrane in.

"The reception was very hard on him," the man said.

"I wouldn't have guessed. He seemed to be in fine form."

"Because he was spirited? That's when you know he feels most vulnerable." The man shifted his Bloody Mary to his left hand and offered his right. The hand was cold from the ice in the glass he'd been holding. "Duncan Reynolds."

"Mitch Coltrane."

"I know. A word to the wise. Watch him carefully. I haven't the faintest notion what he's up to this time."

When Coltrane frowned, Duncan frowned in return. "Something the matter?"

"I guess I'm not used to someone's friend warning me about the other friend. At least not the first time we have a conversation."

"Friend?" Duncan tucked in his chin, creating wrinkles in his puffy neck. "You think Randolph and I are friends? Good God, no. I'm his assistant. Chief cook and bottle washer. His private nurse."

From somewhere in the house, a bell rang.

"I wouldn't keep him waiting," Duncan said.

Throughout this exchange, the front door had remained open. Now, when Duncan shut it and Coltrane followed him along a muffled corridor, he realized how dark the interior was. Dense draperies covered the windows in several indistinct rooms he passed. By com-

31

parison, the last room had muted recessed lights that seemed almost bright. The furniture was surprisingly sparse—a few padded chairs, a coffee table, and a sofa, all showing signs of wear. There was nothing on the walls. The draperies had been parted, but not the lace curtains behind them. Past a wall of windows, filtered gray daylight showed a strip of lawn littered with leaves. Beyond was a yacht moored at a dock, both looking in need of maintenance. Even the water seemed dingy.

Coltrane heard a subtle hissing sound. At first, he thought it came from a pump on a fish tank, but when he finished taking in the room and focused on Packard, who sat in his wheelchair next to a fireplace, Coltrane saw plastic prongs in the old man's nostrils, connected to a tube that led to a small oxygen tank at the back of the wheelchair. Packard seemed to be drowning in a pair of green silk pajamas and a matching robe. His narrow face looked more shrunken than the previous evening, his eyes filmy, his white hair sparse, his skin mottled with brown. When he coughed, the sand that had seemed wedged in his throat at the reception no longer bothered him. His present problem was a lot of phlegm.

Coltrane looked discreetly away while the old man used a handkerchief. "Perhaps if I came back another time . . ."

"Nonsense," Packard whispered hoarsely. "I asked you to lunch."

Barely able to hear him, Coltrane stepped closer.

"I rarely invite anyone to the house."

Now Coltrane was close enough that, if he wanted to, he could touch him. There was something oddly intimate about Packard's forced whisper.

"And I certainly don't go back on offers I make." The old man cleared his throat with difficulty. "But I'm afraid my appetite isn't what it should be." The oxygen continued its subtle hiss. "No doubt something I ate at the reception last night. I hope you don't mind if I don't share the meal with you."

"Since you're not feeling well, why don't we do this another time?"

"I won't hear of it. Duncan, bring our young man something to eat. Is there anything you particularly enjoy?"

"A sandwich is fine. Whatever."

"I was thinking of something a little more elaborate than a sandwich." Packard cocked his wizened head. "If the Dom Pérignon is properly chilled, Duncan, would you bring it out now?"

Duncan saluted with his Bloody Mary and left.

11

THE ROOM BECAME SILENT, except for the hiss of oxygen. The contrast between this conversation and the one the previous evening was more striking. Coltrane decided that Packard not only had worn makeup at the reception but had been energized by some kind of drug. The drug must have put him on edge. That would explain why his present tone was so agreeably the opposite of the one he had used at the reception.

"I see you brought the collection for me to sign. Which one is it?"

"*Reflections of the City of Angels.*"

Packard sounded oddly sad. "That has always been my favorite. How on earth did you find a copy? It's very rare. And very expensive."

"I spent a lot of time haunting rare-book stores."

"You certainly must have." Packard took the oversized book and the fountain pen Coltrane offered him. When he opened the cover, he drew his spindly hand affectionately along a page. "*I* got older. This paper, the finest I could find, remains the same as when the book was printed in 1931. A lifetime ago." With a nostalgic shake of his head, he uncapped the pen and managed the strength for a solid flourish of a signature.

"There." He looked mischievous as he returned the pen and the book. "Now it's even more rare and more expensive. While you're holding that pen, I wonder if you'd return the favor and sign something for me."

Coltrane didn't understand. Baffled, he watched Packard reach into a pouch on the side of the chair and bring out a copy of *Through a Lens Darkly,* Coltrane's only collection of photographs, images from war zones.

"You *do* know my work," he said in amazement.

"A Pulitzer Prize–winning photographer has a way of attracting my attention," Packard said. "You're very good."

"Thank you." Coltrane's voice thickened. "Coming from you, that means a great deal." He managed to control his hand when he signed the book. "But I wish I'd devoted my career to something besides war and pain. I've been having a lot of second thoughts."

"The day you're satisfied with your work is the day you'll stop being an excellent photographer," Packard said.

The old man suddenly coughed.

The cough increased alarmingly.

"Is there anything I can . . ."

"No." Packard strained to speak through the handkerchief pressed to his mouth.

Coltrane felt helpless, wanting to pat him on the back but afraid the old man was so frail that he might injure him.

At last, Packard straightened. "It's this weather. The chill in the air. I shouldn't have gone out last night."

"Then why did you?" The abrupt voice was Duncan's. He entered with an ice bucket, a champagne glass, a white towel, and the Dom Pérignon.

"To remind myself of how blind people are," Packard said. "The only person who recognized the inferiority of my recent photographs is our young man here."

"Or maybe everyone else was being polite." Duncan popped the champagne open and poured the glass for Coltrane.

"That still makes Mr. Coltrane the only credible person at the reception."

"Except me. I always tell you what *I* think." Duncan set the bottle into the ice bucket, placing the towel next to it.

"And what are you thinking now?"

"That I'll prepare lunch." His lips barely revealing a smile, Duncan left.

Coltrane felt the champagne bubbles touch the tip of his nose when he sipped.

"I see you also brought . . ." Packard gestured toward the Nikon that hung from a strap on Coltrane's shoulder. " 'To stop time,' you said."

The change of subject threw Coltrane off.

"I asked you why you became a photographer. That was your answer. Then you added, 'Things fall apart. . . . And people die.' "

"Yes."

"Who?"

"Excuse me?"

"Who died?"

12

COLTRANE LOOKED AT THE FLOOR.

"My question makes you uncomfortable?"

". . . Yes."

"At my age, I find that it saves time"—Packard paused to catch his breath—"if I ask new acquaintances to tell me the most important thing I need to know about them."

"A lot of people don't like to be reminded of the most important thing about them," Coltrane said.

The oxygen hissed.

"Was it a sister?"

The champagne suddenly had an acidic edge.

"A brother?"

Coltrane set down the glass. "My mother."

"I see."

"And my father."

"When you were young? My own parents died when I was young. Not far from here. In a boating accident off Santa Catalina."

"Yes, when you were sixteen."

Packard didn't seem surprised that Coltrane knew any detail of his life.

"My parents died when I was eleven," Coltrane said, "although really both of them were dead a long time before—it just took several years to work it all out."

Packard frowned.

"My father beat my mother."

Packard didn't move, didn't speak. If he had reacted in any way, Coltrane would have ended the subject right there. But Packard seemed to sense Coltrane's ambivalence. The old man's presence was hypnotic. As the silence lengthened, except for the hiss of the oxygen, Coltrane found himself wanting to continue.

"My father didn't beat my mother because he was a drunkard or because he was worried about his job or any of the other excuses you sometimes hear. I never saw him take a drink. He had his own successful business, a chain of dry-cleaning shops that kept expanding every year. Maybe it was work pressures I didn't know anything about. Or maybe *his* father liked to beat *his* mother. Maybe that's why he did it. Maybe he thought it was normal. For a while, *I* thought it was normal. I thought *every* kid's father beat up . . ."

Coltrane felt taken back in time. He blinked, coming out of a trance, and picked up the champagne. Regardless of how much the acid of his memories tainted it, he took a long swallow. He felt an odd need to keep explaining, as if Packard, more than anyone else in the world, would understand.

"One night, after my father had given my mother an especially thorough work-over, he did something he'd never done before—he started on *me*. He knocked out one of my teeth. The next morning, he said he was really sorry and it wouldn't happen again and I should tell my teacher I'd fallen off my bike and that was how my face got messed up and honest to God he would make it up to me for hurting me. Then he drove off to work. The minute his car disappeared around a corner, my mother rushed me upstairs and helped me throw clothes into two suitcases. Then she filled two suitcases of her own, and I remember all the while she was glancing frantically out the bedroom window, afraid that my father might drive back."

Coltrane studied the bubbles in his champagne glass. They seemed to get larger. Again he was tugged back into the past. "She must have been planning it for a long time. She kept the garage door closed while she put the suitcases in her car—so the neighbors wouldn't see. Then she and I drove to the bank. After that, she drove to a bus station and made me wait there with the bags while she left the car somewhere else—at a train station, she later told me, so my father would think that was how we'd gotten out of town. An hour later, she came back to the bus station, and for the next three years we were on the run, stopping in towns across the country, where my mother worked at any job she could find until she had enough money saved to keep running. I later reconstructed the route. From New Haven, Connecticut, to Trenton, New Jersey, to Harrisburg, Pennsylvania, to Youngstown, Ohio, to Sedalia, Missouri, to Boulder, Colorado, to Flagstaff, Arizona, and finally to Los Angeles."

Very thirsty, he finished the glass of champagne and poured another. He might as well have been drinking water. "We kept changing our names. My mother told me she looked for cash-only jobs, like housekeeping, that didn't force her to pay taxes and get her Social Security number recorded in a government computer. She told me if we didn't leave a paper trail, if we didn't try to get in touch with friends and relatives back home, my father wouldn't be able to find us. I still don't know how . . ." Emotion tightened Coltrane's throat. "One afternoon after my mother picked me up from a library where she always told me to wait after school till she was done with work, we went to get an ice cream cone, just one—we couldn't afford two. Then we took a bus to the trailer where we were living, and when we went in, we found my father sitting on a stool at the kitchen counter, playing solitaire.

"As calm as I'd ever seen him, he got up, sighed, pulled out a gun, said, 'Togetherness is next to godliness,' and shot my mother in the face. Just like that. When my father made up his mind to do something, he was unstoppable. I felt as if somebody had slammed hands against my ears. The inside of my head was ringing, but somehow, I

37

thought I heard my mother moan as she fell. Maybe *I* was the one moaning. I felt wet, sticky stuff all over my face. The next thing, my father pointed the gun at *me.* He gave me a funny little frown, looked at my mother's body, looked at *me* again, shook his head, and blew his brains out."

When Coltrane lifted his glass to his lips, he realized that it was empty once more. "They told me I didn't speak for a year."

13

COLTRANE BRACED HIMSELF TO CONTINUE. Packard's intensely sympathetic gaze was eerily compelling, urging him on.

"After my grandparents flew to Los Angeles to get me, after they packed up the clothes and things that my mother and I had in the trailer, after they took care of the bills and arranged for the bodies to be transported back to Connecticut, after all the legal technicalities were out of the way and I went to live with them in New Haven, I couldn't remember what my mother looked like. I used to spend hours at a stretch, hiding in the basement, trying to remember her face, but all that came to me was the image of her blood splattering when my father's bullet hit her. I desperately wanted to remember her voice, but all I heard in my mind was the sound of the shot. That was my reality, not what was going on around me in my grandparents' house. I must have eaten and slept, bathed and dressed and watched television and gone to school, but the images and sounds I actually experienced were in my memory.

"I had no idea of time passing. Eventually I found out it was a year later when I heard someone crying in a room above me while I hid in the cellar. A fog seemed to clear as I crawled from behind the furnace and made my way upstairs, following the sobs through the kitchen to the living room, discovering that they belonged to my grandmother. She was hunched forward on a chair, her face in her hands, sobbing so hard that tears dripped through her fingers and landed on the clear plastic sheets that protected photographs in an album lying open on the coffee table.

"I came around her chair and peered down at the photographs. One of them had been taken in blazing sunlight that made everything overbright and harsh. I recognized a swing, a slide, and a teeter-totter that someone had put up at the trailer park where my mother and I had lived. I recognized a trailer in the background. I studied a boy in the swing and a woman pushing him. I leaned closer, squinting at the woman's long, windblown sand-colored hair, at her high, slender neck and delicate face, at her beaming smile. The woman wore a brown-and-white-checkered shirt with its sleeves rolled up and its bottom hanging over her jeans. The shirt and the jeans looked too big for her, emphasizing how delicately thin she was. Pushing that laughing child, she looked to be having the time of her life.

"Slowly, I became aware that the sobbing had stopped. When I turned, I saw that my grandmother had lowered her hands and was staring at me, her face raw from tears.

" 'That's my mother,' I said, the first time I'd spoken in a year. 'That's what she looks like. I remember now.' "

14

So YOU BECAME A PHOTOGRAPHER to try to preserve the past?" Packard asked.

"The *present*. That album, and others my grandparents had, showed my mother growing up and getting married. Then she was big with me. Then she was holding me and bathing me and raising me. Time was suspended. She existed on the page. Mercifully, I didn't find any photos of my father. My grandmother told me that she had

39

burned every image of him, cursing him all the while. *He* was dead. But not my mother. She was still alive in the photographs.

"But she was more perfect in some than in others. As I studied them endlessly, I became frustrated. Some of the photos were slightly blurred. Others had too much or too little light. Some were too close, others too far. Some didn't emphasize what I absolutely needed to see, a glint in my mother's eyes or what she was doing with her hands. I kept imagining better images. I kept praying that they could have been *made* better."

"And the next step was to start learning about photography?"

"You've heard the stories about photographers who go to primitive regions, where the natives won't let the photographers take pictures of them because the natives are afraid the cameras will steal their souls. I have no idea if those stories are true, but if they are, the natives are wrong. The camera doesn't steal anything. It *gives*: immortality. That's what I thought when I was a young man. I wanted to take photographs of everybody I met, to memorialize them with pity and love—because one day they were going to die. But not in my photographs. As long as my photographs existed, I thought, so did those people."

"Wanted? Thought? You keep using the past tense."

"Somewhere along the line, I went wrong. I started taking pictures that didn't celebrate living but fixated on dying. I started documenting despair instead of hope." Coltrane shook his head sharply. "No more. I want to glorify life."

"Then by all means"—Packard coughed painfully—"I want you to photograph *me.*"

15

WHEN DUNCAN BROUGHT IN A TRAY of six different kinds of caviar, translucent eggs of gold, black, gray, brown, gray-green, and greenish black, Coltrane's already-tentative appetite deserted him. Emotion on top of the champagne had soured his stomach. Increasingly, Packard (his eyes drooping, his whisper more filled with phlegm) didn't have the strength to continue the conversation. So, after finalizing the details of their project, Coltrane said good-bye.

The afternoon light remained dismal. Driving back to Los Angeles, Coltrane struggled against an overwhelming exhaustion. He reached his apartment at 4:30 but still wasn't hungry. In fact, he feared he was going to be sick. He lay on his leather sofa, tried to analyze what had just happened to him, and sank into an agitated sleep. At one point, the phone rang, but he was in too dark a place to answer or hear if anyone left a message.

16

DID YOU PHONE ME LAST NIGHT?" Coltrane asked.

It was eleven Sunday morning. He sat with Jennifer on the narrow balcony of her condominium overlooking the harbor in Marina del Rey. The clouds continued to be gray. The breeze was cool; even wearing a sweater, Coltrane felt slightly shivery. But he couldn't shake the sensation of being hungover and told himself that all he needed was fresh air to perk him up.

Jennifer shook her head. "We agreed you were going to find out how you managed on your own."

"So you didn't?"

Jennifer looked amused. "There was a time when I called you a little too often, remember?"

"I was just wondering. Last night while I was asleep, somebody phoned but didn't leave a message. When I checked the machine this morning, its light was flashing. I had plenty of messages from earlier in the day—more reporters and TV talk shows wanting an interview about those Bosnia photographs. But then at the end, all I got was fifteen seconds of some kind of classical music and then click."

"Wasn't me," Jennifer said.

Coltrane rubbed his forehead and fortified himself with a sip of steaming French-roast coffee. "A reporter wouldn't have been shy about leaving a message."

"You wonder if it was Packard?"

"The thought occurred to me." Despite Coltrane's sunglasses, the light seemed awfully intense. He squinted toward a sailboat, its motor chugging, as it made its way along the crowded harbor toward the exit from the marina.

"Maybe it's my Virgo personality," Jennifer said.

"What do you mean?"

"This is definitely a done deal, right? You and Packard are going to collaborate for the magazine?"

"Packard promised he'd FedEx you the prints and the signed permission forms tomorrow," Coltrane said.

"But if it *was* Packard who phoned you last night, do you suppose he was planning to tell you he'd changed his mind? Maybe you should phone him today and confirm the arrangement."

"And make him worry I'm going to be a nuisance?"

Jennifer chewed her lower lip. "Yeah, sometimes I don't know when to leave well enough alone."

17

CLIMBING THE STAIRS FROM HIS GARAGE, entering his kitchen, Coltrane heard a voice call his name. About to continue up to his darkroom on the second floor, he tensed, immediately changed direction, and stared into the living room.

The front door was open, light streaming in from the patio. A red-haired man was setting a large cardboard box next to another one. Like Coltrane, he was in his mid-thirties. His thinning hair emphasized the fullness of his face. His pale skin contrasted with his freckles.

"Just in time," the man said. "I signed for these boxes and brought them in for you."

"Daniel." Coltrane grinned. "I've been wanting to call you, but I know you're working nights in the emergency ward. I didn't want to wake you during the day."

"I appreciate the thought. This week's been rough."

"I guess I didn't make it any better when I hammered on your door Wednesday morning."

"It's a good thing you did. Your stitches needed a little maintenance. How are they?"

"Fine."

"Seeing's believing. Up with the sweater and the shirt."

Coltrane sighed and did what he was told.

"Not bad." Daniel bent, peering closely. "The antibiotic I prescribed must be working. You had the start of an infection, but the redness around the edges has almost disappeared now. How's your fever?"

"Gone."

"You've got a hell of a constitution, my friend. I doubt I'd have lived through what *you* did."

Coltrane shrugged.

"Make sure you finish the antibiotics. Keep drinking plenty of fluids. In a couple of days, I'll take out the stitches."

"Daniel"—Coltrane put a wealth of meaning into the next word—"thanks."

"It's nothing."

"No, it's very definitely something. You're always there when it counts."

"What did you expect me to do—tell you to go away, that I'd just gotten home from the hospital and I needed to sleep?"

"You're a friend."

"I hope you didn't mind my bringing in Jennifer. I couldn't think of anybody else I could count on to help."

"Mind? Not at all. Things are working out great."

"Admit it—you missed having her around. The three of us had a lot of good times. If Jennifer tried too hard, it's because she cared."

"Or *I* didn't try hard enough." Coltrane changed the subject. "Tell me about these boxes."

"A man from a limousine service was camped outside your door. I noticed him when I was going out for some much-needed exercise." Daniel patted the slight protrusion at the belly of his blue jogging suit. "The boxes must have gold in them or something—they certainly weigh enough. The delivery guy was reluctant to let me sign for them. He only agreed when he saw I had a key to your town house."

"A delivery on *Sunday?*"

"The driver said the man who sent them was very insistent."

"There isn't a label. Did the driver say who—"

"Randolph Packard."

"*Packard?*"

"Why should that name mean something to me?"

Coltrane quickly explained as he opened one of the large boxes. Inside, an envelope lay on top of a generous amount of bubble wrap. He broke the seal, finding a handwritten card.

I trust you know what to do with this.

Baffled, Coltrane pulled away the bubble wrap, his bewilderment changing to amazement when he discovered a tripod and a foot-square black box whose front and back were connected by bellows.

"What *is* it?" Daniel asked.

"A camera."

"I've never seen any camera that looks like a miniature accordion."

"It's called a view camera." Realizing the significance of what he was holding, Coltrane felt awestruck. "These days, only studio photographers use them, but in the old days, in Packard's prime, it was the standard for every serious photographer. Packard would have taken one with him everywhere."

"How come it looks so weird?"

"I guess you don't know anything about f-stops and shutter speeds," Coltrane said.

"Thank God. Just give me my 'point and shoot' Kodak and I'm a happy camper."

"Right." Coltrane chuckled. "You can't imagine what it was like to take pictures when a camera didn't come equipped with a built-in light meter and automatic focus and all the rest of the bells and whistles."

"Progress."

"Maybe, but don't you sometimes get frustrated with the pictures those automatic cameras take? They often look overexposed. There's no texture to the image. The colors are harsh."

"They're good enough for snapshots."

"But if you want a first-rate photograph, you have to go a different route. You need to use a meter to judge the light as accurately as you can. Then you need to adjust the lens opening and the shutter speed so the correct amount of light strikes the negative. This view camera has precise controls that allow you to do that. Its focusing is just as precise. You expand or contract these bellows, like an accordion, pulling the lens closer or farther away from the view plate at the back, until the image is perfectly crisp. A camera this large takes an eight-by-ten negative. You can print the image as an eight-by-ten transfer, with none of the graininess you get when you enlarge an image from a dinky thirty-five-millimeter negative. You get an image so sharp and clear, you won't be able to tolerate snapshots from an automatic camera."

"Looks awkward."

"Worse than you think. Hold this while I pull the tripod from the box." Coltrane expanded the tripod's legs and locked them, then secured the camera to the tripod. He draped a black cloth over the back. "Now stoop under there and look at the viewing screen."

Daniel did so, then quickly reappeared from the cloth, rubbing his eyes in discomfort. "Everything's upside down."

"And reversed," Coltrane said. "The photographer has to imagine the way the image would look normally. Not only that—the camera's heavy. It uses negatives protected by a lightproof holder, two negatives to a holder, so if you want to take a hundred exposures, you need fifty holders, and *they're* heavy. And then, of course, you need various filters and lenses, which you have to carry with you, and which, I assume, are in the other box. Taking a view camera on a photo assignment can be like going on a safari."

"You're sure it's worth it?"

"Right now, I wouldn't have it any other way." Coltrane stared reverentially at the camera. "Look at the scratches on it. Old." He studied the manufacturer's name imprinted on the metal rim at the back. "Korona. I'm not sure that company's still in business."

Numbed, Coltrane sank onto the sofa, struck by the implications. This must be the same camera that Packard used to photograph his famous series of L.A. houses, he thought. In a way he had never imagined, this assignment to re-create that series was going to be an education. He had known that he would be literally following Packard's footsteps: doing his best to find where Packard had placed his camera, trying to reproduce the same camera angles. But Coltrane had assumed that he would use contemporary cameras. Now he understood that modern equipment would skew the experiment, drawing more attention to how *photography* had changed than to how the *city* had changed since the twenties. The further implication was that by wanting Coltrane to use the same camera *he* had, Packard was telling him to do everything possible to try to identify with Packard, to pretend to *be* Packard. Only then would Coltrane understand the decisions Packard had made when photographing those houses.

The phone rang.

Maybe it's the old man, Coltrane thought. "Hello?"

"You'll never guess what a messenger just delivered," Jennifer said excitedly. "The prints and the signed permission forms. This is very definitely a done deal."

"And *you'll* never guess what a messenger just delivered to me. The view camera Packard used."

"What?"

"Get over here. You've got to see this camera."

18

Hello." Duncan's voice sounded thick, as if he'd been drinking.

"It's Mitch Coltrane."

No response. Coltrane pressed the phone harder to his ear, wondering if there was something wrong with the connection. "Duncan?"

"This is about the camera?"

"I can't get over how generous he's being. Is this a good time to talk to him? I'd like to thank him and swear he'll get everything back in perfect condition."

"No, I'm afraid this isn't a good time."

"Then I'll call back. When do you think he might be feeling—"

"Randolph died two hours ago."

A chill started at Coltrane's feet and went all the way to his scalp. "No. How . . . Yesterday . . ."

"He put up a good front. His breathing got worse around three this morning. Even with the oxygen at its highest setting, he still had to fight for air."

"Jesus."

"I phoned for his doctor, but Randolph left strict instructions that he didn't want to go to a hospital. All we could do was make him comfortable. By early afternoon, he was finally at peace."

"The camera." Coltrane had difficulty getting his voice to work. "When did . . ."

"We discussed it last evening. That's also when he signed the photo-permission forms, which I assume your editor has by now, along with the prints. The project can go forward as planned. For some reason, Randolph thought it important that someone retrace his steps."

"I won't let him down."

"He didn't think you would. You'd be surprised how close he was beginning to feel toward you. 'A fellow orphan' is how he described you. I want to be sure you understand. Randolph found it almost impossible to speak near the end, but he managed an amazing effort to make me promise to tell you."

"Tell me?"

"The camera is yours."

". . . What?"

"It's not a loan. It's a gift. I guess you could call it an inheritance."

19

So, WEIGHED DOWN WITH GRIEF, Coltrane brought Packard back to life. He couldn't help thinking that way as he worked in the darkroom, a faint amber safelight over his head. Jennifer stood next to him, watching somberly as he used tongs to slide a sheet of photographic paper into a tray of developing solution. He stirred the solution. Briefly, the sheet remained blank. Then the magic took place, an image coming to life on the paper, a black-and-white picture of the old man gazing up.

Jennifer wasn't able to speak for a moment. "It's fabulous."

Sorrow negated any tone of satisfaction that Coltrane might have felt. The odor of chemicals was bitter. "I took a dozen exposures, but this is the one I knew I wanted."

The image showed Packard looking shrunken in his pajamas and his housecoat, sitting in his wheelchair, the fireplace in the background. The aperture setting Coltrane had used had allowed him to keep that background in focus, specifically part of a burnt-out log in the hearth, the kind of symbolic detail that Packard had liked to use in his early work.

"His eyes," Jennifer said.

Coltrane nodded. "The expression in them constantly changed—from arrogance to impatience to irony to amusement to calculation. But this particular expression was the one I wanted. Earlier, when he'd looked at the collection of his photos I brought for him to autograph, his eyes became sad. There wasn't a hint of pride in his reaction to what he'd created. Instead, the only thing the photographs seemed to do was remind him of the passage of time."

"Did you have any trouble getting him to hold the book in his lap?"

"Not at all. He told me, 'I surrender myself.' "

"So now we have a photograph of a fragile old man who happens to be a genius, inspecting the contents of one of his books. A photograph about a photographer and his photographs."

Coltrane's voice was filled with melancholy. "His photos stayed the same, but he got older."

"But now he stays the same in this photo."

"I wonder what it'll feel like, going where Packard did, doing what he did, trying to be him."

THREE

I

A<small>PPROACHING THE</small> B<small>EVERLY</small> H<small>ILLS</small> H<small>OTEL,</small> Coltrane steered left off Sunset Boulevard and headed up Benedict Canyon Drive. It was a little after eight Wednesday morning, the day after Packard's funeral. Determined to start the project, he and Jennifer had set out early. They drove through the shade of towering palm trees, past expensive homes concealed behind meticulously trimmed hedges and tall house-hugging shrubs. The sky was clear and bright for a change, the clouds having moved on.

"Don't keep me in suspense. Which house is first on the list?" Jennifer asked.

"Falcon Lair." Coltrane wore his typical work clothes: leather hiking boots, jeans, and a navy sweatshirt.

In contrast, Jennifer had an orange sweatshirt with a *Southern California Magazine* logo. Her short blond hair was tucked beneath a baseball cap, making her face look attractively boyish, reminding Coltrane of the movie actor she now mentioned. "Rudolph Valentino?"

"The sheik himself."

"I never understood why he called the place Falcon Lair."

"In the mid-twenties, Valentino's second wife was trying to get the studio to let her supervise the production of one of his movies. The picture was called *The Hooded Falcon.* But she ran up costs so much that the studio canceled it. To make her feel better, Valentino named the mansion they were building in honor of the aborted project. They got divorced shortly afterward."

"And what happened to Valentino?"

"When his wife left him, he threatened to blow his brains out. In-

50

stead, he bought tons of antique furniture—suits of armor and Moorish screens, crap like that. It was more than Falcon Lair would hold, but he managed to cram it all in there. In the end, he almost spent himself into bankruptcy. He worried about his career until he died at the age of thirty-one from a bleeding ulcer."

2

PACKARD'S MUCH-PRAISED PHOTOGRAPH OF FALCON LAIR had been taken from a neighboring hilltop. It showed the thirteen-room mansion tiny in the distance, surrounded by a high white wall, perched on a flattened ridge, looking so isolated that it bore an intriguing resemblance to a Spanish monastery. None of the many hills beyond it had any houses on it, but tentaclelike roads predicted the invasion about to take place. On the bottom left of the photograph, amid exposed earth on one of the slopes, a developer's sign announced BEVERLY TERRACE. The implication was clear. Soon the area would be filled with comparable estates. The remoteness that made the location attractive would be destroyed. As if commenting on the impending invasion, Packard had managed to capture a bird of prey hovering in the foreground.

3

NEAR THE TOP OF BENEDICT CANYON DRIVE, Coltrane chose a secluded street to the left and headed higher into the wooded hills. The neighborhood became increasingly deserted the more the houses looked expensive.

"How do you know this is the way?" Jennifer asked.

"I don't. Monday, I bought a contour map and tried to orient it with Packard's photo and a Beverly Hills street guide. Falcon Lair is on one of those bluffs to the right, so we have to go in the opposite direction to find the spot where Packard took the photograph."

Jennifer shook her head. "These streets weren't here back then. There's no way to tell which route Packard used."

"And all these trees cut off the view, so we don't know where we are in relation to Falcon Lair."

Six hours later, dogged determination was all that kept them going. "This assignment needs an explorer, not a photographer," Coltrane said as he steered onto yet another side street.

Jennifer squirmed. "My rear end hurts. I feel as if I've driven to Vegas and back." Empty coffee cups, along with scrunched-up junk-food wrappers, littered the floor of the passenger seat—from several bathroom trips to West Hollywood. "I bet I put on ten pounds."

"Maybe getting me to do this project was Packard's idea of a practical joke." Coltrane reached the crest of what seemed the hundredth side street and pointed toward a walled estate on the left. "Do you think *this* is where he took the photograph?"

Jennifer glanced from the estate toward the barely glimpsed view to the right. "Let's give it a try. Anything to get out and see if my legs still work."

A breeze smelled sweet. Despite the recent rain, Coltrane heard a lawn sprinkler.

"Could be." He studied the estate. It was higher than the street. In fact, it was on the highest spot around. "From inside, we might be able to see over the trees toward the opposite side of the canyon."

Jennifer checked her watch. "Ten after two. The light will soon be perfect."

"Yeah, maybe the day won't be a total waste. Maybe I can still get some shots."

The rhododendron-lined driveway had a closed metal gate. A smaller closed gate had a sidewalk leading onto the property. An intercom was mounted on an ivy-covered wall.

Coltrane pushed the button.

"Hello?" A female voice, sounding tinny, came from the intercom.

"Ma'am, I'm sorry to bother you, but I'm a photographer for—"

"You're early."

Coltrane exchanged a puzzled look with Jennifer.

"Excuse me, ma'am?" he said to the intercom.

"You're not supposed to be here until Saturday."

"Saturday?"

"For our daughter's wedding."

"I'm afraid there's been a misunderstanding."

"My God, don't tell me you can't be here for the wedding!" the woman said.

"I don't know anything about that. I work for *Southern California Magazine* and—"

"Magazine? But I *don't want* any magazines."

Jennifer started to giggle.

"Ma'am, I'm not selling magazines. What I want to do is take some photographs of a house across—"

"*Photographs of our house?* My husband will go insane. He hates anybody knowing anything about our private life. The last movie he produced was about Arab terrorists. He says, if they find out where we live, they'll blow us up in our sleep."

Jennifer bent over, trying to stifle her laughter.

"Ma'am, I have no intention of photographing your house. I want to photograph *Rudolph Valentino's* house."

"Rudolph Valentino? You're not making sense! For all I know, *you're* a terrorist. Young man, I can see you from the house. If you don't leave right now, I'm calling the police!"

"Please, let me explain!"

The intercom had been making a slight buzzing sound. Now it went dead.

When Coltrane turned to Jennifer for moral support, he found her slumped on the curb, holding herself, laughing. "Only nineteen more houses to go," she managed to say between guffaws. "At this rate, you'll be done by next summer."

"Maybe not," a voice said.

4

JENNIFER STOPPED LAUGHING. They spun toward the gate, where an attractive, delicate-looking woman in her late twenties studied them. She was tall and slim, wearing tan slacks and a brown cardigan. Her arms were crossed. A kerchief covered her hair.

"Are you really from *Southern California Magazine*?"

Jennifer stood and showed her best winning smile, gesturing toward the logo on her sweatshirt. "Cross my heart."

"Just a second." The woman reached through the bars on the gate and pressed the intercom.

The tinny voice responded immediately. "Young man, I told you—"

"Mother, don't call the police. These people seem all right. I'm going to let them in."

"But—"

The woman took her finger off the intercom's button, then pressed numbers on a keypad on the other side of the gate, freeing an electronic lock. "You're serious about photographing a house across the canyon, Mr. . . ."

"Mitch Coltrane. This is my editor, Jennifer Lane."

"Diane Laramy."

They shook hands and stepped through the gate.

"What's this about Rudolph Valentino?"

Coltrane explained the assignment as they climbed a smooth slanted lawn, stopping with their backs to a lemon tree at the hill's highest point.

"And there it is." Jennifer sounded amazed. She showed Packard's photograph to Diane, then pointed down toward a curving street of houses on an opposite but lower hill. One sprawling red-roofed structure stood slightly apart, perched on an eroded slope, solitary on a dead-end road. Its walls were still white. It still looked like a Spanish monastery. But there the similarity ended. The invasion that

Packard's photograph had predicted made Falcon Lair look besieged.

"I was beginning to think this project couldn't be done," Coltrane said.

"Eerie," Diane said. "Looking at that photograph and then at the house, I feel as if I'm in the past and the present simultaneously."

"That's the idea," Coltrane said.

He and Jennifer crisscrossed the hill, leaning this way and that, all the while comparing their view of Falcon Lair to the perspective in Packard's photograph, trying to find the exact spot where Packard had set up his camera.

Scraping his back against the lemon tree, Coltrane smiled. "Well, I'll be . . . Yes. Right here."

"Let me see." Jennifer hurried to Coltrane's left.

Bemused, Diane joined Coltrane on his right. He raised the photo so that it obscured the view, then lowered it, the Falcon Lair from the 1920s replaced by the Falcon Lair of the present.

"It's like a weird kind of double exposure," Diane said. "This lemon tree wouldn't have been here then."

"Or the lawn," Jennifer added. "And obviously not your house."

"And none of these other houses." Coltrane continued to raise and lower the photograph, the effect hypnotic.

"So many years ago. Someone stood exactly where I'm standing now and took that picture."

"He died on Sunday," Coltrane said.

Diane suddenly shivered.

"Is something wrong?" Coltrane asked.

"No. There's just a chill in the air."

But Coltrane couldn't help wondering if Diane had shivered for another reason. Her delicate features began to trouble him. Her skin was so translucent that he could see the hint of blue veins in her cheeks. Her eyes seemed sunken, possibly because she had lost a lot of weight. Her slacks and cardigan hung on her. Her kerchief covered her head so completely that he didn't see any of her hair.

"Well . . ." Coltrane felt awkward. "We're taking up your time."

"No problem," Diane said. "I'm enjoying this."

"Even so . . ." Coltrane studied the sky. "The light's about as good as I can hope for. I'd better get started."

5

WHEN HE AND JENNIFER WENT BACK TO THE CAR TO GET THE camera, the tripod, and the bags of equipment, Diane insisted on helping, out of breath even though she carried only a small camera bag to the crest of the hill. Coltrane didn't have time to think about the implications. He had only about two hours of effective light remaining and needed to hurry.

It took almost fifteen minutes to get the heavy camera secured on the tripod. After that, he used a light meter, calculated the necessary shutter speed and aperture setting, chose a lens, poked his head beneath the black cloth at the rear of the camera, used the bellows to adjust the focus, and compared what he saw to Packard's photograph. Getting everything lined up was more difficult than he had anticipated. After forty-five minutes of concentrating on an upside-down reversed image, he felt light-headed, as if *he* were upside down.

He made twelve exposures, but he wasn't satisfied. Framing the image to make its perspective identical to that in Packard's photograph wasn't going to produce a brilliant photograph, he realized. The result would merely be a visual trick. He had to build on what Packard had done, to find a metaphor equivalent to the bird of prey hovering over Falcon Lair.

"Mitch?"

Coltrane rubbed the back of his neck.

"Mitch?"

"Huh?" He turned toward Jennifer.

"You haven't moved in the last ten minutes. Are you all right?"

"Just thinking."

"You've got only forty-five minutes of light," Jennifer said.

"*Forty-five?*" Startled, Coltrane checked his watch. He had lost more time then he realized.

Yet again, he poked his head beneath the black cloth at the rear of the camera. Earlier, when he and Jennifer had driven toward the estate, Coltrane had wondered, not seriously, if Packard had been playing a practical joke on him by suggesting this project. Now that idea struck him as being *very* serious. With one foot in the grave, had Packard been determined to show Coltrane—typical of all would-be Packards—that Coltrane didn't have a hope of competing with him? Was this project the old man's way of proving one last time how superior he was?

"Mitch?"

Coltrane noticed slight movement on the focusing screen. He heard a far-off echoing *whump-whump-whump* and peered up from the camera to search the sky, seeing that the movement was a distant whirling speck: a helicopter. He inserted an eight-by-ten-inch negative and grabbed the shutter release. "Come on," he whispered tensely. He held his breath as the chopper's glinting blades crossed the horizon.

"*Now.*" He squeezed the shutter release.

The camera clicked.

He breathed out. Packard's bird of prey had symbolized Valentino's bad ending and the impending invasion of the land. Now a helicopter and all *it* symbolized about the mechanization of the twentieth century had taken the falcon's place.

"If that picture turns out the way I hope . . ." Coltrane watched the helicopter recede into the distance. "That was a one-time only chance. Even if another helicopter flies past, the odds are it'll never be in the same spot as Packard's falcon."

Jennifer studied the sky. "You're losing the light faster than we expected."

"There might be enough for a couple more."

A soft voice asked, "Do you suppose . . ."

Puzzled, Coltrane looked at Diane.

"When you're finished taking pictures of the house . . ." Diane hesitated.

"Yes?"

"Could you take one of me?"

"Of course. It would be my pleasure."

"You're sure I'm not imposing?"

"Not at all. You made us feel welcome. I'd enjoy repaying the favor. If you turn this way . . . yes . . . with the sunset on your face . . ." Coltrane smiled. "It'll be lovely."

6

She's dying," Coltrane said, driving from the mansion.

"Something's definitely wrong," Jennifer said.

In his rearview mirror, Coltrane saw Diane standing in her driveway, her arms crossed on her oversized sweater, forlornly watching them head back toward Benedict Canyon Drive. Then he rounded a corner, and she disappeared.

"Studying her through the camera made it even more obvious," Coltrane said. "The hollows around her eyes. I don't think she has any hair under that kerchief. I think she's bald from chemotherapy. I think getting married on Saturday is her attempt to grab at life."

Jennifer didn't say anything for a moment. "Yes. To grab at life."

It was after dark, around six, when they pulled into the garage beneath Coltrane's town house in Westwood. Jennifer's BMW was at the curb.

"Do you want to get something to eat?" she asked.

"What I'd really like to do is go into the darkroom and develop these negatives."

The photographs of Falcon Lair turned out to be excellent. Most were a close match to the angle Packard had used, but close wouldn't do it. For the exercise to work, the match had to be perfect. The one with the helicopter in place of the falcon did the trick. All Coltrane had to do was crop it a little and print a slight enlargement of the cropped area so that Falcon Lair was precisely the same size in both photos. Eerily, the helicopter was almost exactly where the falcon had been. By modifying the development period, Coltrane was able to get the same crisp black-and-white definition that Packard had. When he glanced from Packard's photo to his own, he had the odd sensation that he was looking at time-lapse photography, that both pictures had been taken by the same person, who had made himself wait motionless in one spot for two-thirds of a century. Staring at that relic from the past, he couldn't help recalling that after Valentino's death, Buster Keaton had moved into the area and put up an Italian villa. John Gilbert had built a Mediterranean palace. Other movie stars—their names no longer familiar—had built their own mansions. All lost and gone. Only Falcon Lair remained. And *would* remain as long as Packard's photo and his own survived.

"It's a keeper." Jennifer put an arm around him.

But the photograph of Falcon Lair wasn't the treasure of the day. That honor went to the image of Diane.

He had done it in color. The glow of sunset chased the wanness from Diane's cheeks. Her face was raised yearningly, her recessed eyes sad, her gaunt features determined, her frail shoulders braced as she smiled wistfully toward the sunset of her life.

"*That* I want my name on," Coltrane said. "Her bravery's an inspiration."

"Packard would have been pleased to take that picture," Jennifer said.

While they worked in the darkroom, they heard the phone ring on three different occasions. Each time, it stopped after four rings, the limit Coltrane had set for the answering machine to engage. "It's probably more reporters wanting an interview about those war-atrocity photos. I hope my fifteen minutes of notoriety soon stop," he said.

But after he finished making the prints and went to the living room to press the play button on his answering machine, he frowned when all he heard was mournful classical music.

Jennifer stopped next to him. "The same as on Saturday night?"

Coltrane nodded, troubled. "And this time, we know it wasn't Packard."

7

REPRESSING HIS MISGIVINGS ABOUT THE PHONE CALLS, Coltrane left his apartment the next morning shortly after seven. He brimmed with energy, never having been this enthusiastic about any project. First, a few blocks away, he stopped at a mailbox to drop in an envelope addressed to Diane. Along with three copies of her photograph, the package contained a copy of Packard's Falcon Lair photograph and Coltrane's parallel version of it. His note read, "Here are some mementos of our photographic adventure. Enjoy your honeymoon. I wish you every happiness." He watched the lid close on the mailbox. To grab at life, he thought.

With that, he went to work.

There was a time, he knew, when pepper trees had grown on Hollywood Boulevard, when Beverly Hills had bridle paths, when streetcar tracks occupied the route that freeways now did, when Sherman Oaks, North Hollywood, Burbank, Tarzana, Encino, Van Nuys, and all the other communities in the San Fernando Valley (how Coltrane loved the litany of their names) were distinct villages separated by farmland. Each had a different architecture, English-style cottages in one contrasting with mission-style bungalows in another, Victorians in this area, colonials in that. The distinctness of each area was destroyed as the farmland shrank and the communities merged, although sometimes, driving from community to community, if Coltrane ignored where the borders met and concentrated only on the historical core of each area, he could still see the contrast between one community and another.

Randolph Packard had managed to capture those differences. He recorded a sense of welcoming space, of sun-bathed separateness. As always in his photographs, a detail here and there predicted the impending doom—the tiny figures of surveyors on a field in the background, for example, or a half-completed skeleton of a building on a distant hill. Coltrane brooded about those changes as he took the 405 into the smog-filled valley. He imagined what it must have been like in Packard's youth to have a clear view of the now-haze-shrouded San Gabriel Mountains. As he followed Packard's route, trying to see with Packard's eyes, he had the sensation of going back in time.

8

THE TRAILER COURT WAS IN GLENDALE—drab rows of dilapidated mobile homes, overflowing Dumpster bins at the end of each row, gravel in front of each trailer, no grass anywhere, no trees, just a few flower boxes here and there, spindly marigolds and geraniums drooping over their rims. Coltrane drove down to the third row and turned left, passing an elderly man wearing suspenders over a T-shirt and carrying a basket of laundry toward a clothesline at the side of his trailer.

Halfway along, Coltrane reached a small playground, stopped the car, got out, and approached the playground's rusted waist-high chain-link fence. The swings and the teeter-totter were tarnished and unpainted. The ground was like concrete. A thin black woman pushed a young boy in a swing. The woman's dark hair hung in half a dozen braids. She wore sandals, wrinkled shorts, and a red pullover, which, although faded, was the only bright spot in the trailer court. As the boy stretched his legs to give more force to his upward momentum, the soles of his running shoes were visible— and their holes.

The woman narrowed her eyes toward Coltrane, then returned her attention to the boy.

"Hi," Coltrane said.

She didn't answer.

"I used to live here," he said.

The woman stayed silent.

"Every once in a while, when I'm in the neighborhood, I come back."

The woman shrugged.

"My mother used to push me in those swings," Coltrane said.

"You want something?"

"I'd like to take your picture."

"Why?" The woman tensed.

"Somebody once took a picture of me and my mother exactly where you're standing. I'd like to feel what the photographer felt. I'd like to try to take the same picture."

The woman looked baffled.

"Go back to what you were doing. I won't bother you. I'll just take one picture and leave."

The woman's gaze faltered as she struggled with her suspicion. At last, after another shrug, she returned her attention to the boy and started pushing him again.

Coltrane selected a fast shutter speed to avoid blur, then peered through his viewfinder. Knowing that Packard's camera was too awkward for this situation, he was using his Nikon. Through the viewfinder, in miniature but somehow intensified, the woman pushed. The boy went up in the air, then swung back down. The woman gave another push, her body leaning into the motion. The boy looked up, as if his goal were the sky. As he veered back down, Coltrane adjusted the focus. He readied his finger on the shutter button. There wasn't any question about the position he wanted them to be in. He had studied that position thousands of times in the photograph that had made him want to be a photographer.

In *Sightings*, a book that Packard had written about photography, the master had devoted a chapter to his theory of anticipation.

Once you see the elements of the image you want, it's too late to release the camera's shutter. By the time you do, those elements will have changed. In that

62

instant, clouds will have shifted, smiles will have weakened, branches will have been nudged by a breeze. It is the nature of life for things to be in motion, even if they do not appear to be, and the only way to capture the precise positioning of your subject as you desire it is to study your subject until you understand its dynamic—and then to anticipate what your subject will do. The photographer's task is to project into the future in order to make the present timeless.

Do it now, Coltrane thought. He pressed the shutter button, and in the ensuing millisecond, as the camera clicked, the woman and the boy achieved perfect balance. Through the viewfinder, time seemed suspended. Coltrane sighed and lowered the camera. The boy reached the limit of his upward glide, hovered, and began to descend. Time began again.

"Thanks," Coltrane said. "What's your name and address? I'll send you a couple of prints."

"Do I look that stupid? You think I'm gonna tell you my name and address?"

Coltrane's spirit sank.

He turned from the playground and studied the trailer behind him. The three concrete steps to its entrance were cracked. The screen had been torn from the bent aluminum door. One of the windows had cardboard in it.

He crossed the gravel lane. The bent door creaked when he opened it. The metal door behind it shuddered when he knocked. He waited, not hearing any sound. He knocked a second time but still didn't get a response. When he knocked a third time, he started to worry, only to see the door open and a stooped, wrinkled black woman with short silver hair frown out at him.

"You." The woman clutched a tattered housecoat to her chest. "Where you been? Ain't seen you in a couple of months."

"I was away on several business trips—out of the country."

"Got to thinkin' somethin' had happened to you."

"Well, as a matter of fact, it did. Is this a convenient time?"

"The same as before?"

"Yes."

"Get it over with."

Entering, Coltrane smelled ancient cooking odors. He faced an oblong living room filled with tattered furniture. To the left, a fold-down card table had a jigsaw puzzle on it. Farther to the left, a counter separated the living room from the murky kitchen.

It seemed barely yesterday that he and his mother had stood where he now stood, the door open behind him, sunlight gleaming in, when his father had turned from playing solitaire at the kitchen counter and raised the gun toward his mother's face.

Coltrane heard the shot slam his ears. He gaped at his mother falling, at the blood around her on the floor. He stared down for the longest time.

Finally, he raised his head and turned to the elderly woman. "Thank you."

"What do you get out of this?"

"I'm not sure." Coltrane gave the woman three hundred dollars.

"Real generous this time."

"Well, I'm going through some changes. I might not be back."

9

SCHOLARS ANALYZING PACKARD'S CONTRIBUTION TO photography had documented the location of each house in his series, but Coltrane never knew what he was going to find when he reached each address. Some of the houses no longer existed, variously replaced by an apartment building, a four-lane street, and a supermarket. Others had been renovated, their facades altered to the point where they weren't recognizable. A few had been maintained. Most had decayed. But if finding them wasn't difficult, locating the spot from which Packard had photographed them turned out to be almost as arduous as figuring out the vantage point from which he had photographed Falcon Lair.

In the following two weeks, each of Coltrane's setups—in locations as various as Arcadia, Whitley Heights, Silver Lake, and Venice—turned out to have a story behind it, some as poignant as his meeting with Diane, others comic or repulsive or ennobling, and in two cases violent. In Culver City, he lugged the view camera, its tripod, and its bags of equipment to the top of a warehouse that had not existed when Packard took his photos. In Gardena, he paid for permission to shoot from an upstairs bedroom window of an eighty-year-old widow's house. Other places, he photographed from an alley, a school yard, the side of a freeway, and the back of a pickup truck. He escaped a pack of vicious dogs. He saved the life of a drug addict who had overdosed in a drainage ditch. He talked his way out of a confrontation with a street gang. He met a blind novelist, a one-armed songwriter, and an aging actor who had once played a policeman on an ensemble TV show and was now an insurance salesman. He took pictures of everything.

Some nights, he got home too late to call Jennifer. Other nights, he had so much work to do in the darkroom that he kept the conversation short. "I'll tell you all about it when I'm finished. I'm afraid I'll jinx this if I talk about it or interrupt it. I haven't felt this involved in an awfully long time. The project'll be done soon. Then we'll go away for a couple of days. Up to Carmel. Anyplace you like."

Each night, when he checked his answering machine, there was always at least one hang-up call and that strange mournful music.

FOUR

I

IN A CITY OF IMITATION, the house was unique. Designed by Lloyd Wright, the son of Frank Lloyd Wright, it had been constructed in 1931 for a movie producer whose films were unoriginal but who knew enough to let an original-minded architect do his job. In an area prone to earthquakes, it was made from reinforced concrete. Its staggered three stories created a castle effect. Glinting windows dominated the upper rooms, which were flanked by shrub and flower-filled terraces. Pounded copper sheets displaying pre-Columbian designs that resembled arrowheads led up each corner and along the parapets.

In Packard's photograph of it. But Coltrane had no idea if the house still existed. Using his *Thomas Guide* and information from one of Packard's biographies, he approached the area via a densely built, narrow, tree-lined street that curved up one of the numerous hills near the Hollywood Reservoir. Doubt made him uneasy, but as he crested the hill, peering over and down toward the middle of the congested area across from him, he felt his heart beat faster when he recognized what he was looking for.

His breath was taken away. This was one case where Packard's photograph didn't do justice to its subject. For one thing, the house had a presence, a solidity, an immediacy that the photograph, even using tricks of perspective and shadows, only hinted at. For another, Packard's photograph had been in black and white, leaving Coltrane unprepared for the greenish blue of the hammered copper trim along the corners, or for the coral tint of its stucco and the red and yellow of the flowers on the terraces.

After so much effort trying to find the sites from which Packard had photographed the other houses, he had chanced upon the exact spot he needed for this house on his first try. He couldn't get over it. Excitement swelling in him, he got out of his Blazer, opened the back hatch, and arranged his equipment. Waiting for a truck to pass, he set up the view camera in the street (he was amazed by how efficiently he was now able to handle it), made the necessary adjustments to match the image with the perspective in Packard's photo, inserted an eight-by-ten-inch negative, and took the picture.

His chest relaxed with satisfaction. To make sure there hadn't been a mechanical failure, he decided to take a dozen more exposures, but basically he had gotten the job done—and there wasn't any need to find details that commented on the difference between the past and the present, because in this case there *wasn't* any difference. Although the neighborhood had become overgrown, the house had been maintained exactly as it had once looked in Packard's photograph. It was as beautiful as ever.

A horn sounded behind him. He waved for a station wagon to squeeze around him, then redirected his attention to the house below him. After retrieving the exposed negative, he decided to check that the camera hadn't shifted slightly, and he stooped to peer beneath the black cloth, concentrating on the upside-down image on the focusing plate.

Movement caught his attention—someone coming out of the house's front door, a portly man carrying a large cardboard box to a Mercedes sedan, then returning to the house. The man wore a green sport coat and had a distinctive rolling gait.

No. Coltrane frowned. It can't be.

2

HE WAS WAITING AT THE MERCEDES when Duncan Reynolds again came out of the front door, carrying another cardboard box.

As heavy as the last time Coltrane had seen him, his face as ruddy, Duncan set down the box beside an azalea, closed the door behind him, picked up the box again, and only then noticed Coltrane at the curb.

Duncan hesitated, concealing his surprise, then walked down a sloping concrete path to the street. "I don't suppose I need to ask what you're doing in the neighborhood."

"Want some help?"

"Why not? Since you're here." Duncan, his eyes a little bloodshot, surrendered the box and unlocked the Mercedes's trunk.

When Coltrane set the box inside next to three others, he got a look past an open flap, seeing binders of sleeve-protected photographs and negatives.

Coltrane stepped back from the car. "So we know why *I'm* in the neighborhood. . . ."

"I'm just taking care of the final details," Duncan said.

Coltrane shook his head, not understanding.

"The movers were here earlier, carting away the furniture. But I didn't trust them to handle the photographic materials."

Coltrane continued to look perplexed.

"Of course." Duncan gestured with realization. "You didn't know."

"Know?"

"This house belonged to Randolph."

"Belonged to . . . This was *his*?"

"After Randolph photographed it, he couldn't get it out of his mind. He was so haunted by the unusual design that he bought it."

Coltrane continued to feel amazed. "None of his biographers ever mentioned that."

"Well, as you must have gathered by now, Randolph liked to keep many details about his life confidential. He bought the house through an intermediary and put the title in the name of one of the corporations he inherited from his parents. Sometimes, he came here to reminisce about his youth. Mostly, though, he used it as an office, an archive, and a darkroom. Would you like to see the inside?"

3

A BROAD CHECKERED SKYLIGHT BATHED THE ENTRYWAY IN brilliance. Stairs led down and up, the areas beyond as bright as the entryway. Coltrane had never been in a house that collected so much light. Following Duncan, he climbed the steps and faced a white room with a wall of windows that looked down on a garden. The room's lack of furnishings made its clean lines even more elegant.

"Bedroom and bathroom to the right." Duncan pointed through a corridor into another sunlit area. "Dining room to the left. Note that its walls are draped with chromium beads. Original Art Deco design. The kitchen's beyond it."

As the stairs continued upward, Coltrane's movements made a hushed echo. The next level was equally sunlit.

"A bathroom, a bedroom, and a study. Another balcony."

One final set of stairs, and Coltrane reached a single room with four walls of windows and a skylight. A glass door in the middle of each wall led onto a flower-filled terrace.

"The master bedroom."

Coltrane pivoted, spellbound.

"But I haven't shown you the most important section," Duncan said.

Curious, Coltrane followed him back down to the entryway, from where they descended toward the lowest level. In back, past a darkroom, windows looked out onto a narrow pool, its water reflecting the house's coral stucco. Beyond was a flower garden.

But Duncan paid no attention to the view and instead guided Coltrane to the left, toward a white door within a white wall. When Duncan pulled at a recessed latch, he revealed not another room but another door, and this one was metal. He unlocked it. "This area used to be another bedroom. Randolph converted it into . . ." Beyond the door was an area more murky than the darkroom. ". . . a vault."

Cool air spilled out, making Coltrane step back.

When Duncan flicked a light switch, a harsh glare exposed a windowless area that was filled with librarylike metal shelves, all but one of which were empty. "This is where Randolph stored all his important negatives and master prints."

For no reason Coltrane could understand, he didn't want to enter.

"A separate air conditioner keeps the area cooled to a constant fifty-five degrees." Duncan's footsteps scraped as he walked along the concrete floor.

Reluctant, Coltrane followed, the cool air making him shiver.

"The area is reinforced by steel to withstand earthquakes," Duncan said. "It's insulated against fire and sealed against flood. As a further precaution, a halon-gas fire-extinguisher system is recessed into the ceiling."

What's the matter with me? Coltrane thought. There's plenty of space in here. Why do I feel smothered?

Hearing a metallic click, he turned, to discover that the door had swung shut. "Does the lock work from the inside as well as the out?"

"Of course. There's no danger of being trapped in here. Randolph thought of everything." Duncan reached the only shelf that wasn't empty. "I have only a few more boxes. If you'll give me a hand."

"Gladly."

In truth, Coltrane couldn't wait to get out. He breathed normally only after he and Duncan carried the boxes into the soul-warming light and Duncan locked the darkness behind them. The change was immediate. Again, Coltrane felt at one with the house.

4

OUTSIDE, AT THE CURB, he helped Duncan put the boxes into the Mercedes. Turning, he peered toward the property and recalled the almost-mystical quality of brightness in it.

Except for the vault, he reminded himself.

But the vault doesn't count, he thought. It was never intended to be part of the house.

"So what happens now?" he asked Duncan. "Where are you taking those boxes?"

"UCLA. Randolph established a special collection there. For the past few days, I've been making trips back and forth. It's time-consuming. Maybe I could have trusted someone else to do the job. But somehow it gave me a sense of peace."

"And the house?"

"Will go on the market." Duncan hesitated. "You know, it's odd. Randolph didn't particularly care for where he lived in Newport Beach. You saw how badly maintained it was. But here, where he came only occasionally, he kept this house in perfect shape."

"It's being put up for sale?"

"That's what the trustees of his estate have decided to do. Randolph willed the Newport Beach house to me, but he made no provisions for this one."

"Duncan, would you do me a favor?"

"That depends."

"Ask the trustees to delay putting the house on the market."

5

"YOU WANT TO BUY A HOUSE?" Jennifer asked in disbelief.

Daniel looked astonished. It was Saturday, 2:30 in the afternoon. They were in Coltrane's Chevy Blazer, heading past Christmas decorations on Hollywood Boulevard.

"*That's* what all the mystery's about?" Daniel asked. "You're taking us to look at a *house?*"

"You ought to feel complimented. I wouldn't think of taking a drastic step like this without some input from the two of you."

71

"But you're out of town a lot—sometimes for months," Jennifer said.

"Maybe not anymore."

"I'll believe that when I see it. When would you find time to look after a house?"

"I could hire people to maintain it." Coltrane steered left onto Beachwood Drive, heading up into the tangle of streets in the Hollywood Hills.

"But right now, if you need to leave in a hurry, all you have to do is lock your place and drive away," Daniel said. "No muss, no fuss. Not to mention, you've got *me* next door to come over and check on things. And you've got Jennifer. Why on earth do you want to complicate your life?"

"I was hoping to simplify it." Coltrane steered to the right, heading up a eucalyptus-lined zigzag road. "I want to put down roots."

"Then plant a tree," Daniel said. "I'm telling you—this could be a mistake."

Coltrane crested a hill. Excitement made him smile as the house appeared below him. He had been afraid that upon returning to it, he wouldn't feel the same magic. But if anything, it gripped him more strongly.

"There." He stopped in front.

The car became silent.

"So what do you think?"

Neither Jennifer nor Daniel said a word.

"Well?" Coltrane asked.

"Shit," Daniel said.

"What's the matter?"

"It's fantastic."

"What about *you,* Jennifer?"

She still didn't say anything.

"Jennifer?"

". . . It's one of the houses Packard photographed."

"Right."

"Why didn't you tell me?"

"I didn't want you to have preconceptions."

Jennifer raised a hand to shield her eyes from the sun. "I wouldn't have believed it. As impressive as it is in Packard's photograph, he didn't do it justice."

"Then you understand why I'm tempted to buy it," Coltrane said.

"The question that comes to mind is how. Have you got an oil well or something I don't know about?"

"Exactly what I was thinking," Daniel said. "This is a major piece of real estate. The asking price must be over a million."

"And a half," Coltrane said.

"How the . . . What makes you think you can afford . . ."

"My father's going to buy it for me."

They looked at him as if he'd lost his mind.

"*Your father?*" Jennifer asked.

"The son of a bitch had twenty dry-cleaning shops," Coltrane said. "After he shot my mother and himself, the shops were sold. The proceeds were put in a trust account that my grandparents managed while they were raising me. Except for feeding and clothing me, paying my medical bills and my college expenses, the money was never used. Until I was twenty-one, I didn't even know the account existed. I thought my grandparents were paying the bills. If I'd known where the money was coming from . . . Several times, I almost gave it away. What stopped me were my grandparents. *They* didn't want the money, either, but I kept worrying that if something terrible happened to them, if they had catastrophic medical bills or . . . I wanted to be in a position to pay them back for all the years and the love they put into raising me. So I let the money stay—in case. The last thing I expected was to use it for myself." Coltrane tasted something bitter. "But finally the asshole who called himself my father is going to do something for me."

An emotional silence was broken by the stutter of a hard-to-start lawn mower down the street.

"Okay," Jennifer said. "I can see you've got your mind made up."

"Why are the two of you being so negative?"

They looked at each other.

Daniel glanced down in embarrassment. "I guess we do sound

73

negative. The truth is, I enjoy having you as a neighbor. The last thing I want is for you to move."

"But it's not like I'd be moving to another city. We'd still see each other."

"It wouldn't be the same, though."

"No." Coltrane felt a twinge of melancholy. "No, it wouldn't."

"All we want is what's best for you," Jennifer said. "Don't you think you should at least check to make sure the house doesn't have structural damage from the last quake? Maybe it's about to fall over. Or maybe its plumbing is all messed up, or the house is sitting on a swamp."

Coltrane chuckled. "I sort of planned on getting it inspected." He pulled out a key that Duncan had lent him. "Would you like to see for yourself about the swamp?"

6

THE VAULT," Daniel said when they came out.

"I know," Coltrane said. "But there's an easy way to fix the problem."

"I don't see how."

"Rip the damned thing out. Restore the house to its original condition."

"You sound as if . . ."

"I've made up my mind. I'm going to buy it."

"Let me ask you something, and then I'll shut up," Jennifer said.

"Okay."

"If you just happened to be driving along that street and the house had no association with Packard and you noticed it was for sale, would you have suddenly wanted to buy it?"

Coltrane thought a moment. "Probably not."

"So you're buying the place because Packard photographed the house and made it famous?"

Coltrane hesitated. "I don't think so."

"It's because Packard *owned* the house? You want to identify with him that much?"

Coltrane didn't answer.

7

I'VE GOT SOMETHING ELSE I WANT TO SHOW YOU," Coltrane said.

They looked puzzled as they got out of his car in his garage.

"But I confess I'm a little nervous about it. Lord, I hope you're more enthusiastic."

"About what?" Jennifer asked.

"You have to wait here until I get everything ready."

They looked even more puzzled when he disappeared upstairs.

Two minutes later, Coltrane called down to the garage, "Okay, you can come up now."

He had put on a CD of Miles Davis's *Kind of Blue.* He had glasses of chilled chardonnay ready when they reached the top of the stairs.

"What's this all about?" Daniel asked.

"Well, I figured if I was going to have a showing, I might as well set the mood."

"Showing?" As Jennifer sipped the wine, she peered into the living room and was momentarily frozen.

Coltrane didn't need to explain. What he wanted to show them was obvious, everywhere, on the walls, the bookshelves, the furniture, any place he could hang them or set them: eight-by-ten-inch mounted photographs.

"My God, Mitch."

"That's why I didn't want to go out to dinner last night," Coltrane said. "I was working like crazy to finish the prints."

"They're . . ." Words failed her.

Coltrane's updates of Packard's photos were eerily suggestive of the originals. "Time warps," he had called them as he worked on them. He had done his best to replicate the texture of Packard's photographs, down to the slightest shadows and subtlest streaks of light. Juxtaposed, his images and Packard's evoked powerful emotions within the viewer, creating the illusion of being in two time frames simultaneously.

Jennifer and Daniel seemed spellbound, moving from photograph to photograph, studying them while Coltrane didn't say a word but merely sat on a stool at the entrance to the living room, sipping wine, studying *them*.

But the project was devoted to more than just Packard's houses. Interspersed among the time warps were other mounted photographs, which—beginning with the heartbreaking depiction of Diane—recorded the emotional encounters Coltrane had experienced while retracing Packard's steps.

Jennifer shook her head in wonder.

Daniel looked at Coltrane, as if seeing him with new eyes.

"This is the best stuff you've ever done," Jennifer said. "I have a hunch you won't mind talking about *these* pictures."

"No," Coltrane said, relief ebbing through him. "I won't mind talking about them at all."

"Well, I was wrong about one thing," Jennifer said. "I thought this would be suitable for a feature in the magazine."

"You've changed your mind?"

"Definitely. There's too much here, and I don't want to leave anything out. For the first time, there's going to be a special issue."

". . . I don't know what to say."

"I do," Daniel said. "Where'd you put the wine?"

Coltrane laughed.

Jennifer kissed him. "I'm so proud of you."

As she and Daniel returned to the photographs, Coltrane noticed the red light blinking on his answering machine. He pressed the play button.

His stomach tightened when a chorus sang mournful classical music.

"Again?" Jennifer looked up from a photograph he had taken of the elderly black woman at the trailer court. "This is annoying."

"I can think of less polite ways to put it," Coltrane said. "I wish I had one of those machines that shows the number of whoever's calling. Then I could phone the jerk back and play music to *him*— except I'd have trouble finding music as weird as this."

"Verdi isn't what I'd call weird." Daniel didn't glance away from the photo of the young black woman pushing a boy in a swing. Coltrane had juxtaposed it with the faded photo of his mother pushing *him* in the same swing twenty-four years earlier.

"Verdi?"

"You ought to get more culture. If you listened to something other than jazz, if you went to those classical concerts I invited you to . . . The music on your answering machine is by Verdi."

"Italian. That's why I can't understand what they're singing."

"Well, in this case, what they're singing isn't Italian—it's Latin. Let me hear the music again."

Coltrane pressed the repeat button.

"No doubt about it," Daniel said. "That's from the Requiem."

"The music for a funeral mass?" Jennifer asked.

"Hear what they're singing? '*Dies irae.*' 'Day of wrath.' That's definitely from the Requiem."

Coltrane gestured in frustration. "But why would anybody phone me every day and play music for a funeral?"

"A prankster with a sick sense of humor."

" '*Dies irae.*' What's that mean?"

"Something about a day," Daniel said. "If you're really curious, I can go next door and get my copy of the Requiem. The liner notes have a translation."

It was a vinyl LP, Coltrane saw when Daniel returned. Daniel was fond of lecturing that vinyl had a richer, more lifelike sound than the CD format. "Bernstein conducting. Domingo soloing. This is one of the best—"

"Just tell us what the Latin means, Daniel."

"Right." Daniel looked mischievous, as if he knew he was making them impatient. "It should be . . ." He unfolded the double-platter album and ran his index finger down the translation on the inside. "Here. *Dies irae.*'

> *'The day of wrath, the day of anger,*
> *will dissolve the world in ashes. . . .*
> *How horrid a trembling there will be*
> *when the judge appears*
> *and all things are scattered.*' "

Daniel lowered the album. "Well, I guess a little fear of the Lord is a good thing at a funeral. Keeps our priorities straight."

"But there's no hidden message that I can figure out," Coltrane said. "What about you, Jennifer?"

"The only message I get out of it is that I'd better say my prayers more often. We were right the first time. It's just a prankster with a weird sense of—"

The phone rang.

"Hello."

Verdi's Requiem blared at him again.

8

YOU'RE NEVER HOME," a thickly accented, gravelly voice said.

Coltrane's skin tingled. "What? Who *is* this?"

"The judge."

"Mitch?" Jennifer was alarmed by the look on Coltrane's face. "What's the matter?"

"Now listen to me, you sick bastard," Coltrane said into the phone. "Quit calling me and—"

"There'll come a time when you'll wish with all your heart that the only thing I had done was phone you." The voice sounded like pebbles being rattled in a cardboard cup. "Jennifer is correct about saying her prayers more often."

Coltrane's scalp prickled. "How did you know she said—"

"The day of wrath will dissolve the world in ashes when *I* appear and all things are scattered."

Coltrane's entire body felt as if an electrical current had surged through him. He spun to stare at the living room, his alarmed expression making Jennifer and Daniel more startled. *"You've got a microphone in here?"*

The voice chuckled, its crustiness reminding Coltrane of a boot stomping dried mud. "Oh, I've got much more than that in your apartment. Go up to your bedroom. I've left you some souvenirs."

The connection was broken.

9

COLTRANE FELT SUSPENDED BETWEEN HEARTBEATS. Abruptly he dropped the phone and raced toward the stairs in the kitchen.

"Mitch, what's the matter? Who *was* that?" Jennifer's urgent questions overlapped with Daniel's, their footsteps pounding on the stairs behind him.

He reached the upper corridor and ran past the door to his darkroom, then the door to the bathroom, at once slowing, afraid of what he would find in his bedroom. When he looked cautiously in, what greeted him made him feel as if a hand was pressed against his chest and was shoving him backward.

The bedroom was arranged in a parody of the display he had set up for Jennifer and Daniel downstairs in the living room. Photographs were everywhere, on the floor, the bureau, the bedside tables, the bed itself. Eight-by-tens, the same dimension as the photographs from Packard's view camera. But even at a distance,

Coltrane could tell that *these* photographs were too grainy to have been taken with a view camera. They were blowups from a 35-mm negative. What they depicted, though, made up for their lack of detail.

Jennifer and Daniel crowded behind him.

"What's going on?" Daniel asked. "Who was that on the phone?"

Coltrane didn't answer. Muscles compacting, he entered, stepping between photographs, staring down, then all around.

"This is insane," Jennifer said.

Image after image showed Coltrane setting up the view camera, taking photographs of the houses in Packard's series or of the people and places he had encountered as he followed Packard's route. There was even a photograph of him and Jennifer saying good-bye to Diane in the rhododendron-lined driveway of her parents' estate. Another showed Coltrane at the trailer court in Glendale as he photographed the young black woman pushing the boy in the swing. Wherever he had gone in the last two weeks, someone had been following him, taking *his* picture.

"When we said good-bye to Diane, I didn't notice anybody on the street taking pictures of us," Jennifer said.

"With a telephoto lens, the camera could have been a block away."

He turned toward the bed, toward images of a backhoe dropping jumbled bones into a rock pulverizer while a bandy-legged, barrel-chested, beefy-faced man watched, his huge hands braced on his hips, his drooping mustache raised in a smile of satisfaction.

"These are the photos I saw in *Newsweek*," Daniel said.

"No," Coltrane said. "You never saw *these* photos. This set was never published." Fearing he might throw up, he took a tentative step toward a dismaying object braced against the bed's headboard—all the photographs seemed to be arranged to draw attention to that spot. "They *couldn't* have been published. The negatives were in a camera I lost on a cliff while I was trying to escape from . . . *This* camera. Someone found it and developed the negatives."

He stared again at the photographs of the barrel-chested man watching with delight as the rock pulverizer spewed out chunks of bones. The freshly healed wound in his side throbbed.

"Dragan Ilkovic," Coltrane said.

"What did you say?" Daniel asked.

Fire seemed to shoot through Coltrane's nervous system. "We have to hurry. Jennifer, grab all these photos. Daniel, get the ones downstairs. Now! It isn't safe in here! We have to get out!"

10

THE CRIMSON RAYS OF SUNSET haloed six sweat-slicked men playing basketball. They dodged, ducked, and pivoted with amazingly deft precision, throwing, leaping, dunking, matching one another's points. Four of the men were black. All were approximately Coltrane's age—mid-thirties. They played with such concentration and enthusiasm that the past and the future didn't matter, only now and only the game.

Coltrane watched from concrete bleachers on the street side of one of the many basketball courts at Muscle Beach in Venice. Behind him, bicyclists and roller skaters floated by. Ahead, the sunset-tinted ocean silhouetted the players. It was like watching expressionistic dancers on a stage. A moment later, the sun slipped a degree too low, shadows deepened, and the players faced one another, bending forward, hands on their knees, chests heaving as the ball rebounded off the backboard, missed the hoop, and bounced among them.

"Can't hit a hoop I can't see."

"Never mind the hoop. I can't see the *ball*."

"Hey, you can't quit now. We're only two points from beating you."

"Next time, bro. It's your turn to buy the beers."

"It's *always* my turn."

As the group headed past a palm tree toward the walkway, one of the black men said, "Go on without me. There's a guy over here I have to talk to."

"See you next week."

Joking with one another, comparing shots, the group avoided two skateboarders and headed toward a café along the walkway.

Coltrane stood from the empty bleachers and approached.

The black man reached into a gym bag, pulled out a towel, and dried the sweat on his face.

"Greg."

"Mitch."

They shook hands.

Coltrane was six feet tall. The man he had come to see was two inches taller. They were both about the same weight—two hundred pounds. Coltrane's hair was curly and sand-colored, long enough in back that it hung to his collar. In contrast, the man he spoke to had wiry dark hair cut close to his scalp. Both had strong, attractive features, but the black man's were broader and gave the impression of having been carved from ebony, whereas Coltrane's seemed chipped from granite.

"Just happened to be passing by?" Greg looped the towel around his neck and tugged his sweatshirt from his chest.

A cool December breeze gusted off the ocean and made Coltrane shiver. "Don't I wish. I phoned your house. Your wife told me where you'd be."

"I get the feeling you didn't drop by to catch up on old times."

"Afraid not." Coltrane held up a box. "Got something I want you to look at."

Greg frowned at the box, redirected his attention toward Coltrane, and sighed. "Come on up to the house. Lois will be glad to see you again. You can stay for supper."

"I don't think that's a good idea."

"Oh?"

"The kind of trouble I've got, you don't know what I might bring with me to your house."

11

GREG'S LAST NAME WAS BASS. He was a lieutenant in the Los Angeles Police Department. Coltrane had met him two years earlier
when the *L.A. Times Sunday Magazine* had asked him to do a photo
essay on the police department's Threat Management Unit, the only
law-enforcement squad in the United States devoted exclusively to
stalkers. What had attracted the *L.A. Times* was that, because of the
clandestine nature of their harassment, stalkers were sometimes described as "invisible criminals." The idea was that a photographer as
inventive and accomplished as Coltrane could perhaps make some
stalkers *very* visible.

Coltrane's liaison at the Threat Management Unit had turned out
to be Greg, and over the course of the assignment, they had developed a friendship, Coltrane earning Greg's respect by being of considerable help to one of the many terrified women the Threat
Management Unit was trying to protect. By lying in the bushes outside the woman's home several nights in a row, Coltrane had managed to capture a picture of the woman's heretofore-unknown
harasser—a man she had dated twice five years earlier—as he
dumped gasoline on the woman's lawn at three in the morning. The
stalker had gone to prison for eighteen months. Since then, Coltrane
had helped Greg on three other cases.

They sat facing each other in the back booth of a tavern. Both of
them sipped Budweiser, neither of them speaking, while Greg finished assessing the last photograph, thought about them, stacked
them, and put them back into the box.

"So basically you're telling me that this guy thinks it's cool to tie
people's hands behind their back with baling wire, line them up facing a pit, and shoot them in the back of the head so they topple forward into the pit and nobody has to move the bodies to bury them.
Sounds like he and Hitler would have been pals."

"Except that Hitler was a Nazi. Ilkovic came out of the *Commu-*

nist system when Bosnia was part of Yugoslavia, so Stalin would probably be closer to his ideal."

"Politics as an excuse for mass murder." Greg shook his head.

"Ilkovic worked his way up through the Communist system, learned English, and was trained to be a diplomat. For a time, he was stationed at the Yugoslavian consulate in London. As thugs go, he's very sophisticated. Not to mention calculating. As soon as the Soviet system collapsed, he went back to what is now Bosnia and took advantage of the civil war. He gained his power base by urging the Serbs not to just win the war but to exterminate the enemy. I suppose he figured that after the Serbs killed all the Muslims, he could get them to eradicate the other ethnic group in the region, the Croats. Then the Serbs would control all of Bosnia, and since *he* controlled the Serbs . . . Meanwhile, Bosnia became his private killing field."

"I bet he loved every minute of it. Dragan Ilkovic. Quite a mouthful. And you've got this bastard after you because you took pictures that linked him to war crimes and ruined his chances of controlling Bosnia's government."

"It's kind of hard to rule a country when you're in prison because of crimes against humanity," Coltrane said.

"Except he isn't in prison," Greg said. "He's here in Los Angeles, looking to pay you back."

12

AMBULANCE ATTENDANTS HURRIED TO PUSH A YOUNG MAN ON a gurney into the emergency ward. The young man had an oxygen mask over his face. His chest, which wasn't moving, was covered with blood.

Coltrane got out of their way, then followed through electronically controlled glass doors that hissed shut behind him. Two nurses and a physician rushed to the young man on the gurney, guiding him into a cubicle, tugging a curtain shut, casting urgent shadows as other nurses and physicians worked on other patients in other cubicles and more patients huddled on benches along the walls.

"Can I help you, sir?"

Coltrane turned toward a weary-looking bespectacled woman who wore a green hospital top and held a clipboard.

"Are you hurt? Do you need . . ." Her voice dropped as she studied him and couldn't see anything obviously wrong.

"I'm looking for Dr. Gibson."

At that moment, Daniel—his red hair emphasized by the greens he wore—came out of a cubicle and walked quickly toward a counter in the middle of the area.

"There. I have to see him for a moment."

"Sir, you'll have to wait your turn. There are patients ahead of you who—"

"*Daniel.*"

Hearing his name, Daniel turned. "Mitch?" Frowning, he came over. "What are *you* doing here?"

"I need to talk to you."

Daniel's frown deepened with puzzlement. "I just finished with a patient." He cocked his head toward the approaching wail of an ambulance outside. "Typically busy Saturday night. This'll have to be quick."

Daniel guided him through a door and into a stairwell. The door banged shut, echoing.

"I won't be home for the next couple of days. Maybe weeks," Coltrane said. "I wanted you to know so you wouldn't worry."

"A photo shoot?" Daniel sounded hopeful.

"No, the guy who broke into my apartment while we were out this afternoon."

"I was afraid you'd say that."

"I just got finished talking to a friend who's with the LAPD antistalking unit. He says if this guy could plant a bug in my living room, what's to stop him from planting a bomb? I'm not supposed to go home—not until this creep is caught."

"But who knows how long . . . Where will you go?"

"I'm not sure. If I need to reach you, I'll leave a message for you here at the hospital. The reason I didn't leave a message *this* time, Daniel, is that my friend also had some advice for *you*. I wanted to give it to you in person."

Daniel looked uneasy.

"I don't think you should go back to your apartment," Coltrane said. "This guy can as easily break into your place as mine. He might decide to pay *you* a visit and find out where I've gone."

"But you haven't told me where you're going."

"*He* doesn't know that. Tell the hospital you need some time off. Take a lot of streets at random and watch for any headlights following you. When you're sure you're safe, get out of town. Maybe in a couple of days my friend will have caught him, and you can come back. But Daniel, listen to me. No matter how much you're tempted, don't stay with a friend."

Daniel paled as he understood the implications.

"I didn't do anything wrong," Coltrane said. "But I can't tell you how sorry I am that I put you at risk."

The stairwell door banged open. "Doctor, we need—"

"Yes." Daniel hurried back to the din of the emergency ward. "Jennifer." He looked back. "What about—"

"I'm on my way to warn her."

13

WHEN THE HEADLIGHTS OF A CAR VEERED OFF BEVERLY GLEN Boulevard onto Knob Hill Drive, Coltrane watched from where his Blazer was parked among other cars in the darkness at the side of the road. In this secluded residential area of Sherman Oaks, there was almost no traffic at 10:00 P.M., even on a Saturday. This was only the third set of lights in the past fifteen minutes. Identifying Jennifer's BMW as it slowed on a curve and passed him, Coltrane redirected his attention toward the entrance to this street. One minute became two, then three. After five minutes, Coltrane decided that if Ilkovic had been following her, other headlights would certainly have appeared by now. Picking up his car phone, he pressed the numbers for Jennifer's car phone, let it ring three times, and broke the connection, the signal to Jennifer that it was safe for her to keep descending into the valley and wait for him at the Sherman Oaks Recreation Center. He didn't speak on the car phone because Greg had emphasized how easy it was for someone to use an audioscanner to overhear conversations on that type of phone.

The recreation center's arc-lit parking lot was almost deserted as Coltrane pulled up next to Jennifer's BMW. Her blond hair was suddenly visible, catching the glare of the security lights as she scrambled into his Blazer.

She hugged him tightly. "You've got me scared to death. What's going on? Why the pay phone? Why did you ask me to meet you here?"

Coltrane had called her at home in Marina del Rey and told her to go to a specific phone booth near the docks, where he had gone earlier and noted the number. When she'd had enough time to get there, he had called from another pay phone in the area, telling her the route he wanted her to drive.

"You think my phone's tapped?"

"I assume *mine* is," Coltrane said. "Hell, my apartment's bugged, so why not my phone? Why not Daniel's? Why not yours?" Coltrane summarized his conversation with Greg. "We're away from our homes so much, getting in and bugging our phones wouldn't be hard to do. It's a logical thing for Ilkovic to try, to keep pressure on me by knowing everything I'm up to."

Hating what he had to say next, Coltrane hesitated. "Greg says that Ilkovic might be tempted to use you to get at me."

Jennifer looked at him sharply.

"He thinks you're at risk. He says you ought to stay away from your condo for a while."

"What?"

87

"He says we ought to keep away from each other. When Ilkovic can't figure out where I've gone—"

"Where you've gone?"

"I'm going to disappear, Jennifer. When Ilkovic can't figure out where, he'll probably follow you, hoping that you'll lead him to me. Or he might decide to do worse, to force you to tell him what you know, even if it isn't anything. There isn't a choice. *You've* got to disappear, too."

Jennifer pressed her hands against her stomach. "I thought I was scared driving over here, but that's nothing compared with what I'm feeling *now*. My God, there's got to be a . . . Where do you plan to hide?"

Coltrane didn't answer.

"I'm going with you," Jennifer said.

"But you just heard me explain—"

"It makes more sense for both of us to disappear together. That way, we don't have to worry if he'll be following me. He won't be able to use me to get at you. We'll *both* be safe while your friend tries to catch him."

"I'm not sure that . . ."

"Mitch, this isn't about crowding you. It's about survival."

14

JENNIFER RUSHED INTO THE AIRPORT. While she bought tickets for America West's 11:45 shuttle to Las Vegas, Coltrane left his car in the parking garage. Out of breath, they met at the gate as the straggle of late-night passengers was boarding. Placing himself at the end of the line, Coltrane checked to make sure that no one followed them into the aircraft. Only after the jet pulled away from the terminal did he breathe easier.

"I need a drink," Jennifer said.

"Me, too. But I'm afraid I'll have to settle for coffee. We need to be awake for quite awhile."

The jet arrived in Vegas at 12:44. They hurried to the America West counter and bought tickets on the next flight back to Los Angeles. By the time they reached the gate, the 1:45 shuttle was already boarding.

"Lord, I hope this fools him," Jennifer said.

"I don't see why it won't work," Coltrane said. "If Ilkovic did manage to follow us to the airport, we know he didn't get on the plane with us. He has no way of figuring out we caught the next flight back to L.A. As far as he's concerned, we're in Vegas, and that's where he has to search for us."

"But what about when we get to L.A.?" Jennifer's usually bright eyes dimmed with exhaustion. "Where will we hide? A hotel?"

"That's the logical choice."

But Coltrane had another idea, although he didn't tell her. Their plane reached LAX at 2:41. A van took them to the Avis lot, where a weary clerk gave Coltrane documents to sign.

"A midsize car. Nothing flashy," Coltrane said.

"A Saturn all right?"

"Perfect." With so many Saturns on the road, nobody would notice another one.

The dashboard clock showed 3:31 as they drove out of the lot. The streetlights hurt Coltrane's eyes. Using La Cienega Boulevard, he headed into the heart of the temporarily quiet city.

Jennifer yawned. "What hotel are we going to use?"

"Greg doesn't want us to go anyplace that's fancy, where we'll attract attention when we check in without luggage. I know a couple of quiet places in West Hollywood."

Jennifer yawned again. "As long as it's got a decent bed."

"We'll be a little while getting there. Why don't you close your eyes and go to sleep?"

Without traffic, Coltrane made good time, reaching his destination at 3:54. He got out of the car, unlocked the front door, and pressed buttons on an entryway monitor that disarmed the security system. To the left, he stepped into the single-stall garage and pressed a button that activated the door opener. As the overhead motor rumbled and the door rose, he returned to the car, pausing when he saw that Jennifer had wakened.

Groggy, she rubbed her eyes. "Are we there? Is this the hotel?"

"Yes, but it's not exactly a hotel."

Jennifer concentrated to focus her vision, gaping through the windshield when she realized what she was seeing. The glare of the headlights revealed a house that resembled a castle, its coral-colored stucco lovely even when harshly lit, the edges of its parapets trimmed with green copper strips that glinted in the shape of pre-Columbian arrowheads.

"*Here?*" she asked in disbelief.

"Yes," Coltrane said. "Packard's house."

FIVE

I

"BUT THIS IS CRAZY." Jennifer's voice echoed in the empty house. "We don't have a right to be here. The neighbors will think we broke in. They'll call the police."

"This late, I doubt anybody noticed, but just in case, we won't turn on the lights," Coltrane said. "Tomorrow morning, I'll go around to the neighbors and explain that I'm buying the place, that the estate let me move in a little early."

He paused on the entryway's landing, peering toward the darkness of the bottom floor. The vault was down there, and he had no intention of going in that direction. Upstairs, a night-light guided the way to the living room. Despite shadows, the white walls and hardwood floor looked clean and pure, myriad windows along the back wall enhancing a glow from streetlights and stars.

"But suppose the neighbors don't believe you," Jennifer said. "Suppose the estate gave them a number to call if anything seemed wrong."

"The estate won't have a problem."

"How can you be sure?"

"Before I phoned you tonight, I called Packard's assistant. While the Realtor's getting the paperwork ready, it's okay for us to stay here. That's how I got the code for the security system. And we don't have to worry about Ilkovic. He doesn't know about this place."

"But he followed you to all the houses you photographed."

"Not this one," Coltrane said. "When I saw the photographs he took of me, something seemed missing. Later, I realized what it was. There wasn't any photograph of me at this house. He didn't follow me that day."

"You can't be sure. His camera might not have been working."

"That still doesn't make a difference. Even if he did follow me, as far as he knows, this is just one more house in Packard's series. He has no way to tell I'm planning to buy it. Granted, I went back there yesterday with you and Daniel, but we definitely know Ilkovic didn't follow us then—because while we were gone, he was in my bedroom, setting up his surprise. He *can't* know I'm interested. He doesn't have the slightest reason to suspect I'd hide here tonight."

Clouds must have obscured the stars, because the room became darker.

"You feel that certain," Jennifer said.

"Otherwise, I wouldn't have come."

"You just can't keep away from this house."

"Hey, it's better than staying in a hotel."

"Is it? What kind of hold does Packard have on you?"

2

EVEN WITH SUNLIGHT STREAMING THROUGH THE WINDOWS, they managed to sleep until almost eleven.

Jennifer stood awkwardly and rubbed her back. "Ouch."

Coltrane knew what she meant—from sleeping on the hardwood floor, his neck felt as if he'd been karate-chopped.

"You really know how to show a girl a good time," Jennifer said. Rummaging through a bag of toiletries that Coltrane had bought at a convenience store on the way from the airport, she pulled out toothpaste, a toothbrush, and a bottle of shampoo. "Salvation."

"Don't forget the doughnuts I bought."

"If I weren't so hungry, I would. Really, this would be paradise if only we had clean underwear."

Her sarcasm made him chuckle.

"Some towels wouldn't hurt," she added.

"Let's make a supply run down to Hollywood Boulevard. First things first, though. I'd better speak to the neighbors."

"In that case, you're going to need this." Jennifer handed him shaving cream and a razor.

By early afternoon, they returned with a fresh change of clothes, a coffeemaker, a few dishes and pans, and enough food to last them a couple of days. They scanned the street but didn't see anyone who aroused their suspicion. They felt encouraged when they found that the alarm system was still engaged. But they didn't relax until they had searched the house—except for the vault, which Coltrane had locked after showing it to Jennifer and Daniel the previous day, and which, Coltrane assured himself, remained that way.

Only then did they carry in their purchases. Coltrane had never been much for Christmas decorations, but saying that he might as well make the house a home, he had bought a two-foot-tall artificial Christmas tree that had ornaments attached to it. He placed it in the middle of the living room and spread out two sleeping bags.

"All the comforts," he said.

They showered and put on jeans and pullovers they had bought. Then they made coffee and munched on bagels topped with smoked salmon, sliced tomato, cream cheese, and capers.

"I'm beginning to feel like a human being." Jennifer stretched.

"Don't move."

"What's wrong?"

"That pose is too good to . . ." Coltrane had kept his Nikon and his photographs when he abandoned his Blazer at the airport. He snapped her picture. "Beautiful."

"I hate to say this."

"Then you'd better not."

"No, you'll want to hear it. This house is beginning to appeal to me. The space and—"

"The light."

Jennifer nodded. "I imagine it with Art Deco furnishings."

"That would have been the style when this place was built."

"I wonder what it looked like when . . . Were you serious about wanting to rip out the vault and restore the house to its original design?"

"Top of my list."

"Then maybe . . ."

"What are you thinking?"

"I'll be right back," Jennifer said.

"Where are you going?"

"The garage. When we carried the groceries in, I noticed something."

Coltrane raised his eyebrows with interest when she came back with a long cardboard tube.

"This was on a shelf," Jennifer said. "Whoever moved everything out of here was meticulous—no junk left behind, nothing. Except for this."

"You're thinking it might *not* be junk?"

"When my parents bought an old Victorian five years ago over on Carroll Avenue"—Jennifer referred to an area near Echo Park that was famous for its Victorians—"they found a tube like this in the garage."

Coltrane didn't understand what she was getting at.

"The tube contained the house's original blueprints," Jennifer explained.

"You're not suggesting . . ."

"It's a logical place to leave them for a new owner." She opened the tube and upended it, gently pulling out its contents.

Coltrane stared at a set of tightly rolled sheets of thick blue-tinted paper. They were faded and smelled musty with age. Helping her spread them out on a clean section of the counter, he marveled that the detail of the diagrams and notations was still visible.

"By God." He ran his finger down the top sheet, stopping at a matted-off section on the lower right side that indicated the name of the architect and the year the house had been built. "Lloyd Wright—1931."

3

As much as I can tell"—Jennifer studied the entrance to the vault, then shifted her gaze to the blueprints—"there was a bedroom here."

"That's what Packard's assistant said."

"Its dimensions were the same as the garage above it."

"No, that doesn't sound right," Coltrane said.

"How come?"

"The garage has room for only one car—typical of the thirties. But the vault seems bigger, almost the size of a *double* garage."

"So the renovation was more like an addition," Jennifer said.

"I could be wrong. I felt a little queasy in there."

"Well, I felt the same, and I've never been claustrophobic. The vault can't be *that* much bigger than the garage if we both felt hemmed in." Jennifer checked a detail on the blueprints. "The garage is fifteen feet square. Since we don't have the blueprint for the renovation, I guess there's only one way to tell how much room was added. Pace it off. Have you got the key?" Jennifer unlocked the door and pushed it open.

As cool air cascaded out, the darkness made Coltrane shiver. "Ah, if you don't mind, I'll wait out here."

"Since when have you been claustrophobic?"

"Only when I'm in that vault."

Reaching to the left, Jennifer flicked the light switch on the inside wall. An oppressive overhead glare made Coltrane squint, seeming to reflect off the concrete floor, revealing the stark gray metal library shelves.

"One, two . . ." Jennifer entered, pacing the vault.

"Definitely bigger," she said when she came back. "The garage is fifteen feet wide, but this is twenty-five."

"Closer to thirty," Coltrane said.

"What do you mean?"

He gestured toward a corridor next to the vault. "I paced it from the outside."

"Thirty? Are you sure? We must have paced it differently."

"Probably we did. But since my feet are longer than yours, *I'm* the one who should have the lower number. You should have needed *more* paces and have had the higher number."

"We're doing something wrong. Let's try it again. This time, *you* go in."

"Are you kidding me?"

"I've never seen you so timid."

She's right, Coltrane thought. What's the matter with me? I have to get over this. Ignoring pressure in his chest, he braced himself. The glare became harsher, the temperature cooler, the air thicker as he forced himself to enter the vault. "One, two . . ."

He restrained himself from walking fast. It's only a windowless room, he told himself. He breathed easier when he returned to Jennifer in the welcoming light. "I got more or less what you did: twenty-five feet."

"Then we're still doing something wrong." Jennifer frowned. "I paced off the corridor and got what *you* did: thirty feet. How can a room be—" She spun in alarm. *"Somebody's in the house."*

4

As THE FRONT DOOR CLICKED SHUT, Coltrane rushed toward the stairs. Above him, the landing creaked. A figure appeared, hands raised.

"I didn't mean to startle you," the man said.

Coltrane faltered, his heart no longer hammering as he took in the red jacket that Duncan Reynolds wore.

"It's just that we weren't expecting visitors," Coltrane said.

Duncan put a key in his jacket. "I was in the neighborhood, so I thought I'd drop by and see how you were settling in. I'd have phoned, but . . ."

"There *isn't* a phone."

"Exactly. I don't want to intrude. If this is a wrong time."

"Not at all," Coltrane said. "I want you to meet my friend Jennifer Lane. Jennifer, this is Randolph Packard's assistant, Duncan Reynolds."

They shook hands.

Still calming herself, Jennifer smiled. "It must have been fascinating working for a genius."

"*Fascinating*'s one word. So is *hair-raising*. I finally decided to call it an adventure."

"Can I get you some coffee?" Coltrane led him up to the living room.

Duncan surveyed the sleeping bags next to the small artificial Christmas tree. "*This* looks like an adventure. About the coffee—no thanks. But something stronger would do nicely."

"I'm afraid we didn't buy . . ."

Duncan's face drooped.

"But we did pick up some wine," Jennifer said.

Duncan brightened. "Forgive the pun, but any port in a storm."

"White or red?"

"Whatever you have more of."

Jennifer headed to the left, toward the kitchen.

"We found a set of blueprints in the garage," Coltrane said.

"Yes, I put them there," Duncan said. "I discovered them when I was going through Randolph's things at the Newport Beach house. I decided to bring them here before they got mislaid."

"You didn't happen to come across the blueprints for the renovation, did you?"

Duncan shook his head no. "I've still got a lot of things to sort through. Why?"

"Just curious. There's a discrepancy that puzzles us."

"Come into the kitchen," Jennifer called.

"Excellent," Duncan said. "We can talk while you pour."

They crossed through the dining room, its chromium bead–

draped walls reflecting light, and entered the sun-bathed kitchen. It had a butcher-block island in the middle, where Jennifer uncorked the wine. "Paper cups will have to do."

"It's the only way to go when you're roughing it."

"And I hope you like cabernet sauvignon."

"I have what might be called an indiscriminate palate. It all tastes good to me." Duncan sipped and nodded. "Perfect. You mentioned a discrepancy?"

"We were trying to figure out how much space had been added when the vault was installed," Coltrane said. "We kept getting conflicting numbers. Do you have any idea when the vault was put in?"

Duncan took another sip. "All I know is, it was here when I came to work for Randolph in 1973."

"Was he living here then?"

"No. If he ever lived in this house, I never heard him say so. But he certainly adored it. With the exception of the vault, he went to elaborate lengths to keep the property, including the landscaping, exactly the same as it had appeared when he took his photograph of it in 1933. Too bad the furniture was gone by the time you saw the interior."

"Why?" Jennifer asked.

"It was the same furniture that was in the house when he photographed it."

"You can't be serious." Coltrane leaned forward. "You mean imitations, right? The original furniture would have fallen apart by now."

"Not *this* furniture." Duncan wiped a purple drop from the edge of his mustache. "The furniture was designed by Warren McArthur, a noted modernist of the thirties. His work is characterized by shiny metal and glass. The supports were tubular. Everything glinted. Of course, the cushions eventually had to be replaced, but Randolph was careful to replicate the textured red fabric. Here and there, he also had some Mies van der Rohe chrome tables. You can understand why the furniture was removed. Those tables and sofas have considerable value. Christie's is going to auction them."

"I want you to bring them back," Coltrane said.

98

Duncan almost spilled his wine. "Bring them back?"

"I want to buy them."

"But you're talking about an enormous price."

"I want the house to be exactly as it was."

Jennifer looked astounded.

"And I think it would be great if you could get me more information about the house's history," Coltrane said. "You told me Packard used this for an office, a darkroom, and an archive. But who lived here before he owned it? His biographers say it was designed for a film producer named Winston Case. Is that who Packard bought it from, or did somebody else own it in the meantime? What about *after* he bought it? Did someone else live here then?"

"But it was all so long ago. Why should it matter?"

Coltrane didn't have an answer.

5

THE LAST RAYS OF SUNSET AGAIN OUTLINED SIX BASKETBALL players on a court at Muscle Beach in Venice: the same court where Coltrane had met Greg the previous day. Almost exactly twenty-four hours ago, Coltrane thought. Seated with Jennifer on the same level of the same concrete bleacher at the sideline, an eerie sense of doubling overtook him.

"Greg ought to be here anytime now," Coltrane said.

An ocean breeze made Jennifer shiver. "I'm surprised he didn't ask you to meet him at the police station."

"He lives only a few blocks away. I guess he figured it would be more convenient to meet down here."

The sun dipped into the ocean, its crimson now so faint that the players stopped. Coltrane overheard their conversation: gibes at one another, plans to get a beer, promises to meet next week. Déjà vu made him squirm.

The players headed along the walkway. The sun eased below the horizon. Skateboarders became fewer as the temperature cooled. Streetlights struggled to dispel the darkness.

"He's fifteen minutes late," Coltrane said.

"Maybe he got held up by a phone call."

"Greg has a thing about being on time. I've never known him to keep me waiting."

Another fifteen minutes passed.

"It must be an awfully long phone call," Jennifer said. "So what do you think we should do?"

"I guess we don't have any choice except to stay here until—"

"Is that him?"

Coltrane looked toward where Jennifer pointed. A heavyset man wearing sneakers, jeans, and a leather windbreaker stepped from behind a shadowy wall next to the court and approached them.

"No." Uneasy, Coltrane stood.

"Does he look like Ilkovic?"

"I can't tell in the dark at this distance. He doesn't have a mustache. But Ilkovic might have shaved his."

They stepped from the bleachers.

"He keeps coming in this direction," Jennifer said.

"Then why don't we walk in *that* direction."

They started past palm trees, heading up the beach.

The man followed.

"Shit," Coltrane said.

They started to run.

"Wait!" the man called.

They ran faster.

"Mr. Coltrane, stop! Lieutenant Bass sent me!"

They faltered.

As the man hurried to catch up, Coltrane turned, straining to see in the shadows, wondering if he was making a mistake. His misgivings lessened when a streetlight revealed the badge the man pulled out.

"I work with Lieutenant Bass in the Threat Management Unit," the man said. Tall, he had a solid-looking body, his chest, shoulders, and upper arms developed like a weight lifter's. His brown hair was trimmed to almost military shortness. His matching brown eyes had a no-nonsense steadiness. "Sergeant Nolan."

Coltrane shook hands with him—not surprisingly, Nolan's grip had force—then introduced Jennifer.

"Greg couldn't get here?" Coltrane asked.

"It's complicated. He didn't think it would be safe."

Jennifer visibly tensed.

"I've been watching you to see if *anybody else* is watching you," Nolan said.

"And?" Apprehensive, Coltrane glanced around. It was hard to tell in the darkness, but the beach seemed deserted.

For the first time, Nolan's gaze lost its steadiness. "Why don't we get out of the open? We need a place to talk."

6

THE RESTAURANT HAD A CHEERY CHRISTMAS ATMOSPHERE—a tinsel-covered tree in a corner, strings of winking lights on the walls, tiny wreaths around candles on the tables, all of which were lost on Coltrane as he and Jennifer sat across from Nolan. Again, Coltrane endured an intense overlapping of time, as though he still sat across from Greg the previous evening.

"Okay, the good news first," Nolan said. "Lieutenant Bass contacted the FBI, who in turn got in touch with the UN war-crimes tribunal. Interpol got involved. They're trying to find how Ilkovic left Europe. The FBI's doing the same on *this* end—to learn how he entered the country. They're checking the passenger manifests on all flights that came into this country from Europe during a one-week time frame: from when you left Bosnia to when you started getting the messages on your answering machine. The UN tribunal has asked various European nations to compare the names on those airline manifests to lists of sanctioned passport holders. The FBI's doing the same with passports issued by the United States. If we can determine the alias Ilkovic is using, that'll take us a long way toward tracking him down."

"Assuming he keeps the name he traveled under," Coltrane said.

"Assuming." Nolan looked uncomfortable. "Meanwhile, an LAPD bomb squad went through your town house. Behind your furnace, they found enough plastic explosive to level half the block."

"That's the *good* news?" Jennifer murmured.

"After the bomb was disabled, a team of LAPD electronic-surveillance specialists went through your home. Ilkovic had microphones in every room. I hope you didn't discuss any secrets there."

Coltrane felt as if a chunk of glass was wedged in his throat.

"They also found microphones in your friend's place next door," Nolan said, "and at *your* place, Ms. Lane."

"Jesus," she said.

"I don't know what you mean by good news," Coltrane said. "I haven't heard any so far."

"It's *very* good. Where did Ilkovic get the plastic explosive? The microphones—where did *they* come from? Every alphabet-soup agency you can think of is following those leads. A lot of muscle is being flexed to give you help."

"Then if everything's so positive, why do you look like you need root canal?"

Nolan glanced down at his hands, then fixed his gaze on Coltrane, reluctantly continuing. "The reason Lieutenant Bass didn't meet you as planned is that you were followed when you went to talk to him yesterday."

"What?"

"After you and he concluded your conversation and separated, the person who followed you—we have to assume it was Ilkovic—shifted his attention to Lieutenant Bass."

"Are you telling me something happened to Greg?"

"No. Lieutenant Bass—"

"Stop calling him that. Please. He's my friend. Call him—"

"Greg hasn't been harmed. Nor has his family."

Coltrane breathed out.

"But last night, his home was broken into."

"*What?*"

"That doesn't mean it was Ilkovic." Jennifer tried to sound hopeful. "It might have been a crackhead breaking in, looking for something to steal to sell for drugs."

"Unfortunately, we know for certain it *was* Ilkovic," Nolan said. "The message left absolutely no doubt."

"Message?" Coltrane felt pressure behind his ears.

Nolan hesitated. "Before I explain, I want you to know how sorry I am about all this. So is Lieutenant Bass. Greg. He wants me to tell you he'd have been here to talk to you himself, but that would have compromised your safety. Now that you've disappeared, there's too great a risk that Ilkovic might be following Greg in the hopes that Greg will lead him to you."

"Sergeant Nolan, why don't you tell me what you're doing your damnedest not to."

Coltrane had seldom seen anyone appear more uneasy. The sergeant glanced down again, seemed to muster his resolve, looked up, sighed, and pulled out a Walkman from his windbreaker pocket. "Ilkovic left an audiotape on the coffee table in Greg's living room."

Coltrane reached.

"But I'm not sure you want to listen to the copy we made," Nolan said.

"I don't understand. Why wouldn't I want to?"

"Sometime after midnight last night, Ilkovic went to the hospital where your friend worked."

"Oh my God," Jennifer whispered.

"The nurses and physicians your friend worked with in the emergency ward say he went to the cafeteria to get something to eat around one A.M. He never came back."

Coltrane felt so great a tightness in his chest that he feared he might be having a heart attack.

"The break-in at Greg's house occurred around *four* A.M.," Nolan said. "We know that because when he left, he threw a lamp through

103

a window so Greg would be startled awake. A little after four—
that's when Greg found the tape."

"From one until four." Jennifer's voice was taut.

Nolan seemed to be waiting for them to make conclusions.

"That's how much time"—Jennifer shook her head—"Ilkovic
had with . . ."

"It's Daniel on the tape?" Coltrane's stomach cramped.

"I deeply regret having to tell you. The bomb squad found his
body in his living room when they went in to search his town house
this morning."

Coltrane's mind swirled. I'm going to pass out, he thought.

Jennifer's hand found his and squeezed. He held her, feeling her
tears mixing with his own.

After what seemed forever, he eased away, hardly aware that customers in the restaurant were staring at him—because the only thing
that occupied his attention was the Walkman.

He reached for it.

"I don't recommend that," Nolan said. "Greg felt you had a right
to hear it if you were determined to. But I really don't—"

"I have to know."

The Walkman had a set of small earphones. Hands shaking,
Coltrane put them on. He felt disturbingly remote from his body, as
if he was seeing everything through the reverse end of a telescope.
With a finger that didn't seem to belong to him, he pressed the
Walkman's play button.

A scream made him flinch. It was the most pain-ridden sound he
had ever heard. Daniel.

It stopped.

"Say a few words to your friend," a guttural voice with a Slavic accent ordered, sounding amused.

Daniel's scream reached a new pitch of agony. It dwindled and became strident breathing.

"Speak to him!"

"Mitch . . ." Daniel sounded pathetically weak. "I didn't tell him
a thing."

"You didn't betray him because you *don't know* anything!" the guttural voice said. "But you would have!"

Daniel shrieked again, on and on, communicating agony beyond endurance.

Silence again. Coltrane had no doubt that he had just heard Daniel dying.

"Photographer," the guttural voice said. "I've got pictures of the party. I'll mail them to your home. Why don't you stop by and pick them up?"

A click was followed by the hiss of blank tape.

Tears streaming down his face, Coltrane removed the earphones. Jennifer took them and put them on, her normally tan face ashen as she rewound the tape and pressed the play button.

Coltrane's throat felt paralyzed. "There's an echo. It sounds like"—he strained to make his voice work—"like they're in a cellar or something."

"Which your friend's town house doesn't have, although it does have a garage underneath," Nolan said. "But the garage showed no evidence that your friend was killed there."

"You're talking about blood."

Nolan spread his hands, seeming to apologize. "There would have been a lot of it. Ilkovic used a knife."

Jennifer yanked off the earphones and jabbed the Walkman's stop button. Her eyes were dilated, the black of their pupils so huge that the blue of her irises had almost disappeared. "I've never heard . . . What kind of monster . . ."

"I'm not sure there's an answer to that question," Nolan said. "I've never dealt with anything like this. You need to move to a safe site where we can protect you."

"Move?"

"A hotel we're familiar with. A place where we can control the environment and watch you around the clock."

"You mean put us in a trap and make us targets," Coltrane said.

"It wouldn't be like that at all. Security would be so tight, Ilkovic wouldn't have a chance of finding where you were."

"Yeah, right."

"I'm serious."

"So am I," Coltrane said. "Jennifer and I aren't going to let ourselves be prisoners in a hotel."

"Then we can guard you where you're staying now. If you think it's more comfortable—"

"It's safer," Coltrane said. "The reason it's safer is that nobody knows where it is, including the police. Suppose I told you where we're staying. What if Ilkovic grabbed you? What if he did to you what he did to Daniel? From what I heard on the tape, I think Ilkovic was right: The only reason Daniel didn't tell him where I was is that Daniel didn't know."

7

AFTER GREAT PAIN, A FORMAL FEELING COMES. Coltrane remembered having read that in an English class when he was in college at USC. A poem by Emily Dickinson. It had impressed itself upon him because it had so perfectly described the emotion with which he most identified: grief. *This is the hour of lead*—He felt like that now. Having struggled to maintain his survival instincts, to get back to the sanctuary of Packard's house, he had only enough energy left to make sure that the doors were locked and that he and Jennifer were alone.

In shadows, he sank onto one of the sleeping bags in the living room. After a time, he heard Jennifer settle wearily next to him. The house was so perfectly quiet that he heard her weeping. Hollowness overtook him. He stared up at the murky ceiling, absolutely emotionally exhausted, but he knew that a further torture awaited him, that no matter how much he craved the release, he wouldn't be able to sleep. He shivered. *As freezing persons recollect the Snow—/First Chill—then Stupor, then the letting go—* But he couldn't manage to let go. "Daniel," he whispered. "Daniel."

8

HE AWOKE AS EXHAUSTED AS WHEN SLEEP HAD FINALLY overtaken him. The faint light of dawn glowed through the windows. Turning onto his side, toward Jennifer, he groggily noted that she wasn't there. He assumed that she must have gone to the bathroom. He closed his eyes. But when he opened them again and the light was brighter and she still wasn't next to him, he sat up, worried.

Various explanations occurred to him. Perhaps she had decided to lie down in another room. Then why hadn't she taken her sleeping bag with her? Perhaps she was showering. Then why didn't he hear the muted hiss of water?

When he stood, his body ached, grief racking it. The hope that this had all been a nightmare and that Daniel was still alive dwindled the more his troubled consciousness took control. He glanced at his watch. A little after seven. Perhaps she's getting something to eat in the kitchen, he thought. But when he checked, she wasn't there. Perhaps she was using the tub instead of the shower. In that case, the water would already have been run; sleeping, he wouldn't have heard it. But the bathroom on this floor wasn't occupied.

There was a bathroom on each of the two upper levels, however. He wondered if she had gone up to one of them—to avoid making noise and waking him. Hopeful, he climbed the steps to the next level, failed to find her, continued to the last level, but he didn't find her there, either. He peered onto the flower-filled terrace. It, too, was deserted.

"Jennifer?" Taking two steps at a time, he hurried down to the entryway and stared anxiously toward the bottom level. Until now, the silence in the house had seemed so profound that he had felt reluctant to call her name, concerned that she might in fact be dozing somewhere and he would wake her. "Jennifer?" he called again, and again received no answer.

About to descend toward the vault, he decided to look into the garage and see if the rented car was still there. But when he raised a hand to press the numbers on the security system's keypad to deactivate the alarm so that he could open the garage door, his hand froze—because an illuminated message on the keypad's display screen indicated READY TO ARM. The security system had already been deactivated.

Why? Where had Jennifer gone? Breathing rapidly, Coltrane yanked open the garage door. In the reverberating echo, he saw that the Saturn was where he had left it. Wild, he stared down the steps toward the vault, then charged lower, fearful that Jennifer had somehow become trapped in there. But as he reached the bottom, about to open the hidden white door that concealed the metal entrance to the vault, another door caught his attention—across the large open area at the bottom of the stairs—one of the French doors that led out to the lap pool.

That door was open. He hurried outside, his nostrils tingling from the early morning's chill. Mist floated over the long, narrow rose-tinted pool. He rushed along it, afraid that he might find her facedown in the water. Oblivious to the glint of dew on flowers and shrubs, he studied the ivy-covered slope at the back and the privacy wall that capped it.

"Jennifer?"

"What?" She appeared around the far left corner.

His knees became weak with relief.

"Is something else wrong?"

Coltrane shook his head. "I couldn't find you. I got worried."

"Sorry." Jennifer looked as fatigued as he'd ever seen her. Her blond hair was lusterless. "I couldn't sleep. I thought maybe if I went outside . . ."

"You look cold." Coltrane put an arm around her.

She leaned against him.

"Don't let Ilkovic do this to you, Jennifer. Don't let him win."

She shrugged. "Not that it matters—I solved our little mystery."

Coltrane didn't know what she meant.

"The different numbers." She shrugged again.

"Numbers?"

"Twenty-five versus thirty."

At last, he realized what she was talking about. "When we paced the inside and the outside of the vault?"

"There's a door around the side. To a utility area."

Hoping to distract her, Coltrane said, "Show me."

9

FLANKED BY WELL-TENDED BUSHES, a door was situated in the middle of the narrow side of the house. To the left of the door, a window provided an inside view of the corridor next to the vault. Coltrane understood. Inside, when he had paced down to this window, he had thought that the vault occupied the entire length of the corridor, when in fact a small area with an outside entrance took up part of the space. He opened the door, seeing the shadowy outlines of a water heater and a furnace/air-conditioning unit. "You're right. Mystery solved." His voice was flat. "Come on back inside. It's cold out here."

10

AT 10:00 A.M., using a pay phone outside a convenience store in Studio City, Coltrane called the Threat Management Unit. Jennifer stood next to him in the phone booth, her head against his so she could overhear the other end of the conversation. Now that she had showered and forced herself to eat a little, her blue eyes had regained some of their brightness. But not much, Coltrane thought. Not enough.

"Lieutenant Bass or Sergeant Nolan, please," Coltrane said.

He heard office noises in the background—phones ringing, people talking—then a click and silence as the call was transferred. Outside the phone booth, the rumble of traffic made him press the phone harder against his ear.

"This is Lieutenant Bass," a sonorous no-nonsense voice said.

Recognizing it, Coltrane almost smiled, pleased to be in touch with someone he trusted. "Greg, it's Mitch."

Greg's voice quickened, its bureaucratic flatness gone. "Thank God. I was hoping this would be you. Are you all right?"

"Shaky."

"No shit. Listen, I can't tell you how sorry I am about your friend."

Coltrane paused, a renewed shock of grief jolting through him. "Ilkovic is going to be even sorrier."

"That's the way I want to hear you talk."

"What about your family? Are they okay?"

"They weren't hurt, but are they okay? Hell no. They're scared to death. I've moved them out of the house. I sent them to—"

"Stop," Coltrane said.

"What?"

"Not over the phone."

"What are you talking about?"

"I don't trust it. This guy's too good with microphones."

"You're not seriously suggesting Ilkovic could figure out a way to get into the Threat Management office and—"

"There aren't many people in your office on Sunday. He might have pretended to be a janitor. Are you willing to bet your family's life that he didn't?"

Greg didn't answer.

"When he was in your home Saturday night, he had time to bug *that* phone, too," Coltrane said. "Did you use it to make arrangements about where to send your wife and kids?"

For a moment, all Coltrane heard were the background noises in the office.

"Jesus," Greg said. "Don't hang up."

Click. On hold, Coltrane listened to dead silence that stretched on and on and—

Abruptly Greg was back on the line. "I've got a team going out there to search for microphones."

"Your family. If Ilkovic *did* bug that phone, you have to warn them," Coltrane said.

"But not on *this* phone. The son of a . . . How can I get back to you? If he can hear us, you can't tell me the number to call."

"Greg, do you remember when we first met? I helped a woman identify a stalker."

"Yes, you hid outside her house and photographed him pouring gasoline on her lawn in the middle of the night."

"Do you remember where she lived?"

"I can look it up."

"There's a Pizza Hut two blocks east of her house," Coltrane said. "Go to its pay phone."

"Give me an hour."

Coltrane hung up and left the phone booth.

Jennifer frowned at him.

"Something the matter?"

"Where did you learn about hidden microphones?" she asked.

"A couple of times, when I was on assignment, the CIA and I crossed paths." Coltrane started with her down the exhaust-hazed street.

"The CIA?" The reference made Jennifer's eyes widen.

"In Beirut, there was one operative in particular. He showed an awful lot of interest in the photographs I was taking. So I worked out a deal with him. I promised I'd make him a better photographer than the Agency had trained him to be, and in return, he had to teach me some of what *he* knew."

"Hold it. This isn't the way back to the car. Where are we going?"

"Into this sporting-goods store."

"But what do you need in—"

"A twelve-gauge pump shotgun."

111

11

COLTRANE CARRIED THE SHOTGUN, concealed by a leather sleeve, back to where they had parked the Saturn around the corner from the convenience store. In five days, after the federally mandated waiting period, he planned to come back and pick up a Beretta 9-mm semiautomatic pistol that he had also purchased. For now, the shotgun would have to do. He locked it and a box of buckshot in the trunk, then headed toward the next block.

"*Now* where are we going?" Jennifer asked.

"Down the street. That Pizza Hut."

"Are you telling me that's the same . . ."

"Yep. Greg's going to show up there in about thirty-five minutes. I need to get the number of its pay phone."

The phone turned out to be on the wall to the left, just inside the front door. A large window provided a view of the restaurant's parking area, a crowded intersection, and a Burger King diagonally across the intersection.

"Perfect."

Five minutes later, when they entered the Burger King, its air thick with the smell of charcoal-cooked meat, Coltrane discovered that the arrangement was even more perfect than he had imagined. Standing at the pay phone, which was near a window next to the front door, he could see across the intersection to the pay phone in the Pizza Hut.

"The next best thing to meeting in person," Coltrane said. "Now comes the hard part—the waiting."

"All those times you went away on assignment, you lived like this?"

"Not always. It depends on where I was sent."

"I'm beginning to think I don't know you."

"When the time comes, watch the street. If Ilkovic follows Greg, there's a chance we can spot him."

"And?"

"Then maybe *we* can follow *him.*" Coltrane glanced toward the menu on the wall behind the counter. "We're going to need food in front of us so we don't appear to be loitering."

They each ordered a burger, fries, and coffee. Carrying their tray of food, Coltrane avoided a booth by the window and instead chose a table one row in—less chance that they'd be seen from the street. He positioned Jennifer so that her back was to the window. That way, facing her, he could appear to be talking to her but would actually be looking past her, concentrating on the Pizza Hut. Eating slowly, which wasn't difficult, given the state of their appetites, they tried to distract themselves with small talk. It didn't work.

Twenty minutes dwindled to fifteen, then to ten. With five minutes to go, Coltrane inwardly flinched when a kid with a ring in his nose dumped a tray of crushed wrappers and an empty paper cup into a trash receptacle, then picked up the phone. No!

Five minutes became zero.

Coltrane placed himself next to the kid.

"Hey, do you mind. I'm having an important conversation," the kid said.

"Here's five bucks to have it somewhere else."

"Later," the kid said into the phone. He hung up, grabbed the money, shook his head as if he thought Coltrane was a fool, and walked out.

Immediately, Coltrane picked up the phone, shoved coins into it, and pressed the numbers that he had written on a notepad.

On the other end, the phone barely had a chance to ring. "Mitch?"

Partially concealed, Coltrane peered across the street toward Greg at the pay phone in the Pizza Hut. "While you're there, why don't you order a medium pepperoni and mushroom for me?"

"Yeah, it's definitely you. That bastard *did* bug my home. And you were right: My office phone and my desk were bugged, too. If I get my hands on him—"

"You mean *when,* don't you?"

Greg didn't respond for a moment. "Interpol thinks he used a forged passport under the name of Haris Hasanovic to fly out of Bosnia. His route was from Tuzla to Hamburg to London. After that, MI-Six got into the act. They think he changed his name to Radko Hodzic, but there's no record of anyone with that name applying for a Bosnian passport. The rest of the Slovak countries came up blank, as well. So did Germany. The FBI established that Radko Hodzic arrived in Los Angeles two days after you did. He would have needed IDs for Radko Hodzic to rent a car or a hotel room. The FBI's checking that."

"Or else he switched back to being Haris Haranovic."

"We thought of that, too. We're checking it."

"Or he had a third set of documents, and he's somebody else now."

"Mitch, we're trying our best."

"But where's he getting the electronic-surveillance equipment? Damn it, what kind of explosive did he put behind my furnace? Where would he have gotten—"

"*I told you we're working as fast as we can.*"

A jarring crash made Coltrane whirl. When he saw that it had been caused by a tray of food that a nervous-looking woman with two pouting children had dropped, he still had trouble controlling his breathing. "Greg, tell me how to have a nice day."

"We'll keep trying to find out where he got the microphones and the explosives. We're also trying to find out where he got those photographs of you developed. That many eight-by-ten enlargements aren't common. We're hoping somebody will remember the order."

"I'm getting that cold, sinking feeling again," Coltrane said.

"We're also pursuing another angle. A profiler from the FBI says somebody as twisted as Ilkovic often feels compelled to go back to where he terrorized his victims. It's a compulsion to reexperience the thrill of what he did to them. That would explain why he went back to the mass grave in Bosnia, where you took his picture."

Coltrane stared harder at Greg across the smog-hazed, traffic-cluttered street. "So what does that mean? He's going to go back to where he tortured Daniel? We don't know where that happened."

"But we know where Daniel's going to be buried."

The statement made Coltrane feel as if a fist had been driven into his stomach. He tasted coffee, french fries, and chunks of hamburger, and he fought the urge to throw up. Daniel's funeral. He had been so fixated on what had been done to his friend that he hadn't considered what would happen next.

"Daniel's ex-wife went out of her mind when she found out he'd been murdered," Greg said. "For being divorced, she sure seems close to him."

"They were talking about getting back together."

Greg didn't say anything for a moment. "Well, she's making all the funeral arrangements. The visiting hours are tomorrow evening. A closed casket."

Coltrane wanted to weep.

"Then Wednesday afternoon at one, there'll be the funeral, and the burial around two-thirty. The FBI profiler thinks Ilkovic won't be able to resist coming around to relive his triumph. All those grieving people. It'll give Ilkovic a thrill to see how much power his actions have."

"There's another reason Ilkovic won't be able to resist going to Daniel's funeral," Coltrane said.

"I was wondering if you'd figure it out."

"A sociopath like him will automatically assume I can't control my emotions enough to stay away. He'll want to be somewhere at the funeral because he'll count on me to be there. It's his best chance to follow me." Coltrane mustered the strength to make a decision he absolutely did not want to make. "So let's give him what he wants."

"Are you saying what I *think* you're saying?"

"Nobody I'm close to is safe. Who will he go after next? My grandparents?" Coltrane suddenly realized that he had to warn them. "I'm sick of letting him control me. It's time I controlled *him*. Where's the funeral?"

"It's too risky for you to—"

"Fine. Don't tell me. I'll look it up in the newspaper."

"St. John's Church in Burbank. Daniel's ex-wife lives over there. The burial's at Everlasting Gardens."

"God, I hate the names of cemeteries. . . . Two days from now,"

Coltrane said. "Does that give you and the FBI enough time to button down those areas without making it obvious to Ilkovic?"

"It's a lot of space to cover. Especially going from the church to the cemetery."

"Then let's forget about the church. I'll show up only at the cemetery. It'll be more believable to Ilkovic. By avoiding the church, I'll look as if I'm trying to be cautious."

"And *then* what? We can't cover every building that surrounds the cemetery. Suppose he decides to blow your head off at three hundred yards with a sniper's rifle?"

"No," Coltrane said. "That's one thing I'm sure he *won't* do. He loves to do his work up close and personal."

"You still haven't answered my question. *Then* what?"

"I let him follow me."

12

COLTRANE HUNG UP, returned to Jennifer at the table, and helped her study the intersection.

"Nobody attracts my attention," she said.

"I don't see anybody, either."

In the distance, Greg remained at the Pizza Hut window, the phone pressed to his ear.

"He's making another call," Jennifer said.

"Pretending to. I finally told Greg I was where I could see him. He did a good job of hiding his surprise and not staring in this direction. He suggested he pretend to stay on the line a little longer, to give us a longer chance of spotting Ilkovic if he's around here."

"Good idea."

"But it doesn't seem to be helping. If Ilkovic *is* in the area, he's blending well," Coltrane said.

"For all we know, he shaved his mustache, got his hair cut, dyed it light brown, bought a decent suit, and looks like a businessman."

"Or he went in the opposite direction, made himself scruffy, and looks like he's homeless," Coltrane said. "In that case, for a lot of people, he *would* be invisible."

"Greg's hanging up."

Ten seconds later, Greg came out of the Pizza Hut and headed around to the parking lot at the side of the restaurant.

"I still don't see anybody who looks suspicious," Jennifer said.

"Let's see if anybody follows Greg when he drives away."

"In this traffic? *Everybody* will seem to be following him," Jennifer said. "Even if we do see a car go after him, we won't be able to get to *our* car in time to do anything about it."

"We can try to get the plate number."

Coltrane watched Greg take out his key and unlock his car.

Which disintegrated.

13

THE FIREBALL SPEWED ACROSS THE PARKING LOT AT THE SAME time the shock wave shattered windows in every direction. The force of it threw Coltrane and Jennifer backward out of their chairs, slamming them onto the floor, glass spewing over them. For a dazed instant, his ears ringing but not enough to shut out the wail of children, Coltrane felt jolted back to when he had been photographing a violence-torn village in Northern Ireland and an IRA bomb had blown a school bus apart. Straining to clear his mind, he sensed Jennifer squirming next to him and reached for her.

"Are you all right? Are you hurt?"

"Don't know." Chunks of glass had cut Jennifer's hands and forehead.

"Greg," Coltrane moaned. He struggled to his feet, then helped

Jennifer up. "Greg," he said with greater force, turning toward the glassless windows. The intersection was in chaos. Cars had slammed into one another. Horns blared. Drivers peered around in a daze. Pedestrians lay motionless on the sidewalk. Beyond, in the restaurant's parking lot, the explosion that had devastated Greg's car had blown apart other cars, igniting their fuel tanks, sending numerous fireballs roaring into the sky. Black greasy smoke topped the area like a curse.

"Greg," Coltrane said a third time, the word coming out as a sob. He struggled around a table, lurching, trying to go through a gaping window. Have to get to the parking lot. Have to help Greg.

Someone grabbed Coltrane's shoulders, dragging him backward. *"What are you doing?"* Jennifer blurted. "You can't show yourself!"

"My friend needs . . ."

Wavering, Coltrane saw the astounded expression in Jennifer's eyes and realized that he must sound insane. Save Greg? How in God's name was he going to do that when his friend was in a million pieces? "Oh Jesus."

"Somebody *help* me!" a woman screamed.

Coltrane spun toward the far-left corner of the Burger King, seeing the panic of a gray-haired woman who knelt beside a young girl with a six-inch shard of glass embedded in her right arm. Blood spurted.

"Help me!"

He couldn't count how many times, in how many languages, he had heard that wail. In northern Israel after a Shiite Muslim rocket barrage. In Chechnya, after a Russian artillery assault on a rebel village. How many times had he taken photographs of victims as doctors and nurses raced across blood-covered streets?

"HELP ME!"

And how many times had he hurried toward the victims, hoping that one of the doctors would understand his desperate English and tell him what to do?

If he couldn't help Greg, he was going to help *somebody*, by God.

In a rush, he untied a kerchief from the woman's neck and twisted it around the girl's arm, above the embedded glass. The girl, who had been trying to stand, sank back onto the glass-covered floor.

"Hold the kerchief tightly, Jennifer."

He knelt beside the girl, gripped the shard, and pulled it free. The girl turned instantly pale. Blood continued to gush.

"Twist the kerchief tighter."

Approaching sirens wailed.

"She needs a pressure bandage."

The girl had a sweater tied around her waist. Coltrane tugged it free, wrapped the sleeve around the wound, and used his belt to secure it tightly. The sweater, which was blue, turned pink. But it didn't turn crimson. The belt's pressure on it was partially sealing the wound.

"That'll buy some time. You have to get her to a hospital," Coltrane told the woman.

Outside, the sirens wailed to a stop.

"Take her to one of those ambulances. Hurry." Even as Coltrane said that, it became obvious that the woman was in no condition to carry the girl outside. But no matter how determined he was to make sure the girl was safe, he didn't dare risk carrying her out there himself. Ilkovic might spot him.

Alarmed by how pale the girl was, watching her tremble, he realized that the child was going into shock. "No, don't move her. We have to lay her flat. Prop her feet on that overturned chair. Keep them above her head. Somebody cover her with something."

A man in a windbreaker stared.

"You," Coltrane said. "Take off your jacket. Cover her."

In a daze, the man complied.

As other sirens wailed, Coltrane spun toward a young woman in a jogging suit. "Get to one of those ambulances. Bring help."

The direction broke the woman's paralysis. She scrambled toward the littered sidewalk.

The moment Coltrane saw the woman speak urgently to an ambulance attendant, he stepped away. "We have to get out of here," he told Jennifer. "Through the back."

Jennifer stared at him as if she had never seen him before.

14

W HERE DID YOU GET PARAMEDIC TRAINING?"

Coltrane sped around a corner, saw a gas station, and steered toward a pay phone next to the rest rooms at the side.

Jennifer persisted. "This isn't the first time you've had to—"

Before she could finish her sentence, Coltrane skidded the car to a stop and jumped out. After hurrying to the phone booth, he shoved in coins and pressed numbers.

"Threat Management Unit," an authoritative voice said.

"Give me Sergeant Nolan. This is an emergency."

"I'm afraid he isn't—Wait a minute. He just walked in."

Coltrane gripped the phone tighter.

"Sergeant Nolan here."

"Greg's dead."

"What?"

"I'm telling you—"

"Who *is* this? Coltrane? Slow down. What are you—"

"I made an appointment to talk to him on a pay phone at a Pizza Hut in Century City."

"He told me."

"Ilkovic must have followed him. While Greg was in the restaurant, the bastard slipped a bomb under his car. It took out half a block. *He's dead.*"

"Jesus, Mary, and Joseph."

"Go to Greg's house." Coltrane couldn't stop feeling breathless.

The sudden change of topic startled Nolan. "What for? What are you talking about?"

"Greg sent a surveillance team over there to look for microphones. I need to talk to you. We can trust that phone."

The instant Coltrane broke the connection, he pulled out a credit card and placed a long-distance call to New Haven, Connecticut—to his grandparents.

Although the sky threatened rain and the temperature was in the fifties, he sweated as he listened to the phone ring.

It rang again.

Pick it up, Coltrane thought.

It rang a third time.

A fourth.

Come on, come on, he thought urgently.

"Hello," an elderly male voice said.

"Grandpa, it's Mitch. I—"

"You have reached the number for Ida and Fred," the frail voice said. "We're away from the phone at the moment. Please leave a brief message, and we'll call you back."

Beep.

"Grandpa, it's Mitch," he said quickly. "As soon as you hear this, take Grandma and leave the house. Go to the police. Ask them to contact Sergeant Nolan at the Threat Management Unit of the Los Angeles Police Department. He'll explain what's happening. I don't want to scare you, Grandpa, but there's a very dangerous man after me, and you're going to need protection. Don't trust anybody you don't know except the police. Make sure they help you."

Beep.

The machine had reached the end of the time limit for the message. Coltrane hung up and stood tensely motionless in the phone booth, debating whether to call back and leave a further message. But he didn't know what he would accomplish other than to frighten his grandparents even more than he already had.

Maybe that's a good thing, he thought. Being afraid of Ilkovic is a survival skill.

"Mitch?"

Jennifer's voice surprised him. He turned.

"You've been staring at the phone for two minutes now. Are you waiting for someone to call back? Are you okay?"

"First Daniel. Now Greg. How many others are going to die because they're close to me?"

15

As THE GARAGE DOOR RUMBLED SHUT, Coltrane got out of the Saturn, unlocked the trunk, and took out the pump-action shotgun, along with the box of buckshot.

Jennifer stepped back from the weapon.

"You're going to have to feel comfortable with this," Coltrane said. "You're going to have to learn how to use it."

Jennifer continued to look uneasy.

It was midafternoon. Coltrane had driven around the valley, taking an erratic route that would have required Ilkovic to stay close and make his presence obvious. Amid the chaos of the explosion's aftermath, with rescue workers arriving, victims being taken away, and onlookers milling, he didn't think it likely that Ilkovic would have managed to see Jennifer and him leave the back of the Burger King and follow them to the car, but Coltrane couldn't take anything for granted.

The first two times he had phoned Greg's house, someone from the electronic-surveillance team had answered. On the third try, he had gotten Nolan, and as alternating surges of grief and anger swept through him, he had bitterly told Nolan the plan that he and Greg had worked out.

"Nothing's changed. I'm still going through with it."

"I can't sanction this. It's too dangerous. We've already lost Greg. Don't add yourself to the body count."

"Well, sanctioned or not, I'm going to show up at that cemetery Wednesday afternoon, so are you going to make sure I have backup or aren't you?"

". . . Yes."

"That's all I ask. Give me the cooperation Greg would have given."

"I want to give you something else. Police protection until Wednesday."

"Hey, if I had accepted police protection, if I'd been with Greg, *both* of us would have gotten blown up. Staying on my own is working out fine."

"Phone me tomorrow at ten. Be careful."

"After what happened to Greg"—it had hurt Coltrane to say Greg's name—"*you* be careful."

Taking care was exactly what Coltrane was doing now. After prying the lid off the box of buckshot, he pushed three shells into the slot on the side of the pump-action shotgun. Telling Jennifer to stay behind him, he checked every section of the house, including the vault, even though the intrusion detector gave no indication that anyone had entered. Finally, he returned with Jennifer to the living room and unloaded the shotgun so that he could show her how the weapon worked without any danger that it might go off.

He held up one of the thumb-sized red plastic shells. "This contains gunpowder and hundreds of lead pellets. Depending on what you want to shoot—"

"But I don't want to shoot *anything*."

"—the pellets come in different sizes. The ones in this shell are called buckshot. They're large, about the size of BBs. When the shell goes off, the pellets spew out the barrel and spread into a thirty-inch pattern."

"Mitch, you might as well save your breath. I'm not—"

"So as long as you're aiming in Ilkovic's general direction, you have a damned good chance of hitting him with one of these. At close range, the pellets would really chew him up. Now, to hold the shotgun—"

Jennifer shook her head forcefully. "I really don't—"

"See that grip underneath the barrel. Put your left hand there. Then put your right hand here at the thin part of the stock, just behind the trigger guard. Raise the butt of the stock to your shoulder."

"Mitch, you're not listening to me."

"Cradle the stock against the meaty part of your shoulder. Raise the gun and aim along—"

"*Will you stop?*"

Coltrane looked at her in surprise.

"How many times do I have to tell you? I'm not going near that thing."

"You're telling me that if Ilkovic broke in here, you wouldn't defend yourself?"

"I don't want to think about it."

"But what if—"

"Guns scare me to death."

"I'm not exactly crazy about them, either," Coltrane said.

"Then how come you know so god-awful much about them?"

Coltrane tried to calm himself. "When the Soviets invaded Afghanistan, I met an arms dealer in West Pakistan who smuggled weapons to the Afghans. I crossed the border with him. But not before he insisted I learn about some of his weapons so I could help protect the convoy if there was trouble."

Jennifer stared.

"Three days later, he was killed in a Soviet gunship attack. The rest of us buried him under rocks and moved on. The photograph of that rock pile and his sons staring at it was reprinted in the *New York Times*. It was the start of my career."

"And did you ever have to use any of those weapons?"

Coltrane looked away.

"Did you?"

"What difference does it make?"

"It does."

"Yes," Coltrane said, "I had to use some of those weapons."

Jennifer shuddered. "I feel like I'm in a blizzard. I don't want to hear any more."

"Then you shouldn't have asked."

Now it was Jennifer's turn to look away.

"Remember, you had a choice to be on your own, but you insisted on hiding with me."

"Great," Jennifer said. "This is something else we can curse Ilkovic for. He's got us arguing. About guns."

16

ALTHOUGH THEIR SLEEPING BAGS LAY NEXT TO EACH OTHER, Coltrane felt a disquieting sense that he and Jennifer slept apart. Not that he was able to get much sleep. Preoccupied, he lay awake in the darkness, staring toward the ceiling. He kept thinking of the last thing Jennifer had said to him before emotional exhaustion forced them to lie down. "Hiding with you in this house, I could almost pretend that we're in a secret, magical place where Ilkovic can't get to us. But seeing that gun on the floor next to you reminds me that there *isn't* any magical place."

Thinking of all the pain and despair he had photographed, Coltrane quietly agreed. It was yet another reason to curse Ilkovic. After having worked so hard to turn his back on the direction in which his career had been taking him, Coltrane again found himself enmired in bleakness. Street smarts and survival skills that he had hoped never again to use were depressingly familiar. Ilkovic had dragged him back. And for that, and for Daniel and Greg and the tension between Jennifer and himself and his fears about his grandparents, Ilkovic was going to pay.

The silence smothered him. His cheeks felt warm. He had never associated grief with a fever, but now that he thought about it, grief was one of the worst illnesses anybody could suffer. Before he realized what he was doing, he stood, approached the murky stairway, and descended toward the bottom level.

Not bothering to look toward the entrance to the vault, he passed the corridor that separated the vault from the darkroom and reached the French doors that led outside to the pool. The illumination of stars and the moon made glints on the still water. He saw the vague outlines of the nearest shrubs and flowers.

His cheeks feeling warmer, he reached to open one of the doors, to let the night air cool him, and at once stopped himself, remembering that he had to disarm the security system before he went outside. Besides, what if Ilkovic had somehow tracked him here? It would be foolish to expose himself by leaving the house.

And what about Jennifer? What if she woke up and couldn't find him? All too vividly, he remembered what *that* dismaying emotion had been like—this morning, when Jennifer had gotten up earlier than he did and he had frantically searched the house, at last discovering that she was outside in the back garden.

"I solved our little mystery. The different numbers. Twenty-five versus thirty," she had said distractedly.

It had taken him a moment before he understood what she was talking about. "When we paced the inside and the outside of the vault?"

"There's a door around the side. To a utility area."

Yes, mystery solved. The missing five feet were easily accounted for, taken up by an area devoted to a water heater and a furnace/air conditioner. It's amazing how we ignore the obvious, Coltrane thought, glancing behind him toward the corridor that paralleled the vault. It was also amazing how an emotion-ravaged mind sought distractions.

There was something about that utility area. . . . A thought struggled to surface, then sank back into the roiling depths of his subconscious.

He shook his head, unable to clear it. Glancing at the luminous dial on his watch, he saw that the time was ten after two. You need to try to sleep. You've got only a day to figure out the details of what to do if Ilkovic follows you from the cemetery on Wednesday.

His hand cramping on the shotgun, Coltrane stepped back from the wall of windows and the glass-paneled door. About to turn to go upstairs to Jennifer, he paused as the thought that had struggled to surface made another attempt.

Something about the utility area.

Yes, it was deep enough to account for the five-foot difference between the inside and the outside of the vault. But what about . . .

How wide was . . .

The thought broke free. The utility area doesn't stretch all the way along that section of the house, he realized. When I looked inside, it was only about eight feet from left to right.

But the vault's fifteen feet wide. If the utility area takes up eight feet of that, what's in the remaining seven feet of the strip along that side?

Coltrane's cheeks became cold, blood draining from them. There wasn't another door on the outside wall. That meant if there was a seven-by-five-foot area farther along, the only way to get into it would have to be . . .

Jesus.

It was the first time Coltrane had ever wanted to enter the vault.

17

PULLING THE KEY FROM HIS JEANS, Coltrane approached the vault's entrance. As he opened the outside door, exposing the blackness of the metal door, he set the shotgun against the wall and inserted the key into the metal door's lock. For something so heavy, the door swung open smoothly, requiring almost no effort for him to push it.

He reached in to the left, brushed his hand against the wall, found the light switch, and flicked it, squinting from the harshness of the overhead lights. Again, the chill of the place overwhelmed him. The rows of gray metal library shelves had never seemed bleaker. The concrete walls and floor seemed to shrink. Overcoming the sensation of being squeezed, he picked up the shotgun and entered the vault.

His gaze never wavered from the left section of the opposite wall. But he couldn't get there directly. He had to walk straight ahead until he reached the last row of shelves, then turn left and proceed to the area that held his attention. The wall was lined with shelves. Facing them, positioning himself in the middle, he glanced to the right. Behind those shelves and that section of the wall was the utility area. But what was behind the shelves and the section of the wall on the *left?*

Again he set down the shotgun. He leaned close to the shelves on the left section of the wall. The metal frame that supported them was bolted to the concrete behind them. He tugged at the shelves but had no effect; they remained firmly in place.

He ran his hands along the back edges of the shelves. Crouching, then stretching, he checked above and below them, also along the sides, wherever they met the concrete. It won't be something difficult, he told himself. Packard was in a wheelchair. The old man didn't have the strength for anything complicated or awkward. It would have to be . . .

At wheelchair height, Coltrane touched a slight projection of metal at the back of the right side of the shelves.

Something easy, he thought.

He pulled down on the wedge of metal, but it didn't budge.

Something simple and . . .

He pulled *up* on the wedge of metal. It immediately responded.

Clever.

He heard the click of metal, of a latch being released.

Yes.

This time when he pulled at the shelves, they *did* budge. Not a lot. Not enough to move forward. But enough to indicate that they were no longer secured to the wall. What else do I have to . . .

He shifted to the left side of the shelves, crouched at wheelchair height, reached to the back where the side met the concrete, and touched a corresponding wedge of metal. When he pulled it upward, another latch snicked free, and now the shelves moved smoothly forward, seeming to float.

No matter how rapidly Coltrane breathed, he couldn't seem to get enough air. He stepped to the right, out of the way, and continued to pull on the shelves, their outward movement so smooth that even an aged man in a wheelchair could have controlled them. Viewing that section of the wall from the side, he saw that what had appeared to be solid concrete was actually a concretelike stucco attached to a partition of oak. On the left, large foldout hinges at the top, bottom, and middle made the false wall capable of being moved in and out.

He stepped inside.

18

THE RADIANT WOMAN FACING HIM MADE HIS HEART STOP. Despite her alluring features, he almost recoiled in surprise at finding her, except that he couldn't—his legs were powerless. Her hypnotic gaze paralyzed him. For a startling instant, he thought that she had been hiding behind the wall. But the face was too composed, showing no reaction at having been discovered.

Nerves quivering, he stepped into the chamber, so drawn that he overcame his fear of being enclosed. What he was looking at was an amazingly life-sized photograph of a woman's face. It hung on the chamber's back wall, exactly where the woman's face would have been if she had actually been standing there. Indirect light from the vault dispelled many but not all of the shadows in the chamber, so that the area where the woman's body would have been was partially obscured, creating the illusion that her body was in fact there. Although the photograph was in black and white, the absence of color seemed lifelike because of the woman's extremely dark hair and dusky features.

Either she spent a lot of time in the sun, Coltrane thought, or there was an ethnic influence, possibly Hispanic. Certainly the white lace shawl she wore reminded Coltrane of similar garments he had seen in Mexico. Her dark eyes were riveted on where the camera would have been, on where Coltrane's eyes now studied her, with the effect that he felt she was peering into him. Her lush hair hung thickly around her shoulders, with such a sheen that it gave off light regardless of how black it was. Her lips were full, their arousing curves parted in a smile, the glint from which seemed to shoot from the photograph. The combination of her features was typical of classic beauty—large eyes, high cheekbones, a smooth, broad forehead, an angular jawline, a narrow chin. She sparkled and smoldered.

But as captivated as he was by her image, he was equally captivated by the medium in which she was presented. He had seldom seen a black-and-white portrait that demonstrated such perfect control of its essential elements, of the juxtaposition of darkness and light. The technique required more than just a careful positioning of the subject and a precise calculation of light. Afterward, the real work was in the developing process, dodging and burning, underexposing some portions of the print while overexposing others, *making* the image rather than simply *taking* a picture. Coltrane knew of only one photographer who had absolute mastery of this technique. Even if he hadn't found this photograph in this particular location, Coltrane would have known at once who had created it: Randolph Packard.

19

A NOISE MADE HIM SPIN. Startled, he grabbed the shotgun, about to raise it, then immediately checked himself when he saw Jennifer at the entrance to the vault.

"That's one of the reasons I don't like guns," she said.

"You weren't in danger. I would have looked before I aimed."

"Glad to hear it." Jennifer's eyes were still puffy from sleep. "When I woke up and didn't find you, I got worried. This is the last place I expected you to be."

"Believe me, *I'm* surprised. But not as surprised as I am by *this.*" Coltrane pointed. "Our little mystery wasn't as solved as we thought."

As Jennifer approached, she ran a hand through her short, sleep-tousled hair.

"And maybe it's not such a little mystery after all," Coltrane said, then explained how he had found the chamber.

Fascinated, he watched her peer inside.

"My God," she whispered. From the side, Coltrane could see that her eyelids came fully open. "She's the most beautiful . . ."

"Yes."

"Who? Why?"

"And a hundred other questions. The only thing I know for sure is, Packard took that photograph. The style is unmistakable."

Jennifer appeared not to have heard. She raised a hand toward the photograph, held it an inch away from the woman's face, then lowered it. "This is fabulous. I don't understand why he hid it."

"Not just *it*," Coltrane said. "Look over here." To the right, metal shelves rose to the ceiling. "Look at all the boxes."

Each was about two inches deep. Grabbing one, Coltrane carried it from the shadows toward the lights in the vault. In a rush, he set the box on a shelf and opened the lid, inhaling audibly when he found the woman's sultry face peering up at him in another pose.

"How many?" Coltrane flipped through the rest of the eight-by-ten-inch photographs in the box. "There must be at least a hundred. Every one of them shows her."

Jennifer brought out another box. "This one holds sixteen-by-twenties." She set it on a shelf next to him, tugged the lid open, and lifted a hand to her chest, overwhelmed. "Mitch, get over here. You've got to see this."

Coltrane quickly joined her. The top image, twice as large as the ones he had flipped through in the first box, gave him his first full-body view of the woman. She was on a deserted beach, stepping out of the ocean, so that the water came just below her knees, one leg ahead of the other, her movement languid even though it was fixed in time. Her bathing suit was dazzlingly white against her tan skin, a one-piece costume that was modest by contemporary standards, its bottom line level with the top of her thighs, its upper line almost to her collarbone, inch-wide straps hitched over her shoulders. But for all its modesty, the suit had an arousing effect, clinging to her supple body, the smooth, wet material emphasizing the curves of her hips, waist, and breasts. Those curves seemed an extension of the undulation of the waves from which she emerged. Water glistened on her silken face, arms, and legs. She didn't wear a bathing cap. Her midnight-colored hair, drenched by the ocean, was pulled back close to her scalp, the contrast with the lush appearance of her hair in the other photographs reinforcing the classical beauty of her high cheeks. But what most attracted Coltrane's attention, what mesmerized him in this photograph, as in the others, was the woman's soul-invading gaze.

Jennifer sorted through the other photographs in the box, showing Coltrane additional images of the woman on the beach. The scene changed; the woman was on the rim of a cliff with the ocean below her. Sunlight was full on her face, but the other details of the photograph suggested an oncoming storm. The waves in the background were tempestuous. Wind gusted at her hair, sweeping it back. It also gusted at the white cotton dress she wore, blowing it against her body, molding the soft, pliant fabric to her legs, stomach, and breasts. The scene changed yet again; the woman was in a luxuriant garden, oblivious to the flowers around her, gazing pensively toward something on the right while a fountain bubbled behind her.

In wonder, Coltrane glanced back into the chamber, toward the numerous boxes. "There must be—" his calculations filled him with an emotion that was almost like fear—"*thousands* of photographs."

"And every one so far is a masterpiece," Jennifer said. "Prints of this quality don't just get churned out. They take meticulous care. Sometimes a day for each one."

Coltrane knew that she wasn't exaggerating. Packard had been legendary for insisting that photographers who didn't develop their own prints were contemptible. He had been known to spend a day on one print alone, and if the result had even the slightest blemish, some faint imperfection that only he would have realized was there, he tore the print to shreds and started over.

"Everybody thought his output dwindled," Coltrane said. "But if anything, it increased unimaginably."

"All of the same amazingly beautiful woman."

"Packard certainly didn't lack ego," Coltrane said. "He went out of his way to let everybody know how great he was. When he had a photograph that satisfied even *his* standards, he bragged about it. These are among the best images he ever produced. Instead of showering them upon the world, why the hell did he build a secret room and hide them?"

"Did Packard ever use this model in any of the photographs he made public?" Jennifer asked.

"No. I have no idea who on earth she is."

"Was," Jennifer corrected. "Take another look at that bathing suit. That style hasn't been in fashion since . . . My guess is the forties. More probably the thirties. How old does she seem to you?"

"About twenty-five."

"Let's split the difference between decades and say the photograph was taken in 1940. Do the math. She'd be in her eighties now. Assuming she's still alive, which the odds are against. Even if she *is* still alive, she won't be the woman in that photograph. *That* woman exists only in these prints."

"Immortality," Coltrane said. The irony wasn't lost on him. "I'm not sure I'll be alive beyond Wednesday, and here I am wondering about a woman in photographs taken a lifetime ago." He steadied his gaze on the woman's. "Whoever you are, thank you. For a little while, I forgot about Ilkovic."

SIX

I

I HAVE TO PUT MYSELF IN ILKOVIC'S PLACE, Coltrane thought. If I'm going to get through this alive, I have to imagine what I'd do in his situation.

In the dark, lying next to Jennifer, he couldn't get his mind to shut off. He strained to fix his imagination on the woman's haunting face, but it melted into a fleshless skull, which swiftly became Ilkovic's big-boned features. Terror overcame him. He kept worrying about his grandparents. He kept wondering how he was going to survive on Wednesday.

Maybe Nolan's right. Maybe it's foolish to offer myself as bait.

At once a part of him said, But the cemetery's one of the few places where Ilkovic is likely to show up. He won't be able to resist the pleasure of watching Daniel's mourners. He'll be hoping to see *one* mourner in particular: me. The police and the FBI will have a chance to catch him.

But what if they fail?

I have to think like Ilkovic. Is he just going to show up on Wednesday and wander around?

Of course not. He'll assume the police are there. He'll change his appearance or hide or watch from a distance.

And what's the safest way for him to figure out where to hide?

The answer felt like an electrical jolt. In a rush, Coltrane sat up. My God, he'll want to get to the cemetery a day ahead of time so he can scope it out and make sure he protects himself.

A day ahead of time meant . . .

Today.

2

THREAT MANAGEMENT UNIT," a crisp voice said.

"Give me Sergeant Nolan. It's urgent."

"Who's calling?"

Coltrane quickly gave his name. He and Jennifer were at a pay phone on Hollywood Boulevard.

"Well, well. Just the man I want to talk to."

"I beg your pardon?"

"This is FBI Special Agent James McCoy." The voice became crisper. "I want you and your friend to report here at once."

"Why? What's the—"

"We're taking you into protective custody."

"But I already told Sergeant Nolan I think we're safer on our own."

"When *he* offered protection, he was making a suggestion. In *my* case, I'm giving you an order."

"You remind me of my father. *He* liked to give me orders."

The special agent seemed not to have heard. "We're going to guard you around the clock."

"Sure, right. And how long is that going to last?"

"Until we catch Ilkovic."

"Three months? Six months? A year?"

"I certainly hope we'll have caught him in a matter of days."

"Is that a fact? And how many leads do you have?"

The special agent didn't answer.

"You've got *one* lead—you're hoping he'll show up at the cemetery on Wednesday."

The special agent still didn't respond.

"And if I'm not there," Coltrane said, "he'll never tip his hand. He'll go to ground and wait until the bureau runs out of money and patience guarding us and puts us back on the street."

"I'm afraid I don't agree with your assessment."

"Well, since it's not your life at risk, I don't much care *what* you agree with."

"In that case, you leave me no choice. There's been a new development you need to know about."

"What's happened?"

"It's better if I inform you about it in person rather than on the phone."

"Tell me now."

"It would be more humane if we discussed this in person."

"*Humane?*"

"It's about your grandparents."

3

THE THREAT MANAGEMENT OFFICE HADN'T CHANGED MUCH since Coltrane had last been there two years earlier—an additional desk, a couple of new computers—but it could have been painted scarlet instead of white and have had a pool table instead of filing cabinets for all he noticed when he stormed into the room. Two detectives, their jackets draped over the back of their chairs, peered up from monitors they were studying. A third man, his blue suit coat neatly buttoned, crossed the room.

"Mr. Coltrane?"

"I want to see Sergeant Nolan."

The rigidly postured man was slender, with thin lips and narrow eyes. He held out his hand. "I'm Special Agent McCoy." He glanced toward Jennifer, who was standing behind Coltrane.

Coltrane didn't shake hands. "I said I want to see Sergeant Nolan."

McCoy reached for his shoulder. "Why don't we go over to the Federal Building and—"

"Stay away from me."

"Mr. Coltrane, I realize you're under a lot of stress, but—"

"Get your hand off me, or I'll break it."

The room became still. The two detectives braced themselves to stand. McCoy's mouth hung open in surprise. As Coltrane's face reddened, Jennifer stepped between them.

Footsteps sounded in the corridor. Nolan appeared at the entrance to the office, his tan blazer slightly oversize to compensate for his weight lifter's shoulders. "Getting acquainted?"

McCoy stood straighter. "More like threatening a federal officer."

"You implied something terrible had happened to my grandparents. You refused to tell me over the phone. You forced me to risk my life by coming here."

"I hardly think coming to the police qualifies as risking your life," McCoy said.

"If it was just a ploy to get me here, if there's nothing wrong with my grandparents—"

"Time out, gentlemen."

"*Did* something happen to my grandparents?"

"Yes." Nolan glanced toward the floor. "I keep giving you bad news. I'm sorry."

Coltrane felt as if a cold knife had pierced his heart.

"Did you phone the New Haven Police Department yesterday evening?" McCoy asked.

Coltrane directed his answer toward Nolan. "I called my grandparents several times, but I kept getting their answering machine. So I got worried and asked the New Haven police to send a patrol car over to their house to make sure everything was okay."

"Your call was logged just after eight P.M. eastern time," McCoy continued.

"Not you. *Him*." Coltrane pointed toward Nolan. "If I'm going to hear something terrible about my grandparents, I want it to be from somebody I know."

"There was a major freeway accident in New Haven shortly after your call," Nolan said. "Most patrol cars were called in to sort out the confusion. By the time a car was free to go to your grandparents' house, it was after eleven at night."

"Quit stalling and tell me."

"They found newspapers for Friday, Saturday, Sunday, and Monday on the front porch. The mail hadn't been picked up, either." Nolan paused, uncomfortable. "They broke in and searched the house. . . . Your grandparents were in the basement."

Coltrane could barely ask the next question. "Dead?"

"Yes."

"How?"

Nolan clearly didn't want to say it. "Ilkovic hanged them."

Coltrane wanted to scream.

"The reason we're sure it was Ilkovic," Nolan said, "is that Federal Express tried to deliver a package to your town house yesterday. When there was nobody to receive it, the driver delivered it to a secondary address that the sender had specified."

"Secondary?"

"Here. It arrived at the station in midafternoon, but because it was addressed to you, it went from office to office, after an all clear from the bomb squad, until someone in the Threat Management Unit recognized your name."

Coltrane sounded hoarse. "What's in the package?"

"A videotape."

4

THE ROOM BECAME SMALLER. Coltrane glanced from Nolan to McCoy to Jennifer to Nolan. He felt as if he was spinning. "Videotape?"

"Like the audiotape of . . ." Jennifer's voice trailed off.

"I want to see it," Coltrane said.

"No," Jennifer said. "Take their word for what happened."

"I *have* to see it."

"What will that accomplish?" Jennifer asked. "You know how

devastated you felt when you heard Daniel on the audiotape. That's exactly what Ilkovic wants. Don't give him the satisfaction."

"She's right," McCoy said.

"Why don't you sit down?" Nolan said. "Can I get you a cup of coffee or—"

"Let me understand this," Coltrane said. "Are you telling me you *refuse* to show me the tape?"

"No, but—"

"Then where *is* it?"

The group exchanged glances.

McCoy shrugged fatalistically. "A man ought to know what he wants."

Nolan shook his head in frustration. He opened a desk drawer and removed a videocassette. "There's a room down the hall that has a TV and a video player."

Coltrane waited for him to lead the way.

"But I want to emphasize—" Nolan said.

"That you don't think this is a good idea," Coltrane said. "Fine. Now let's go."

Jennifer held back.

"You're not coming?"

"No."

"I understand," Coltrane said. As she sank into a chair, he placed a hand on her shoulder and squeezed reassuringly. "Take it easy. I won't be long."

He considered her another moment, his emotions in chaos, then followed Nolan and McCoy out of the office.

In the corridor, Nolan said, "You might be wrong about how soon you're going to be back."

"I don't understand."

"Ilkovic set this tape for a six-hour recording speed."

"So?"

"All six hours are full."

5

THE SHADOWY ROOM WAS NARROW. It had no windows. The TV was a battered nineteen-inch with a video player on a shelf underneath it. As Nolan put the tape into the player, Coltrane shifted a metal chair in front of the screen.

Solemn, McCoy shut the door.

Although the image, recorded on slow speed, was grainy, it struck Coltrane with horrifying vividness. The yellow glare of an overhead bulb in his grandparents' basement—how well Coltrane remembered the time he had spent down there in his youth—showed his grandmother and grandfather standing on tiptoes on a bench. Their hands were secured behind their backs. Their mouths were covered with duct tape. Their aged eyes bulged from panic and from the rope that was tied around each neck, secured to a rafter in the ceiling. Coltrane's grandfather was wearing pajamas, his grandmother a housecoat. Both had slippers, their bare heels angled upward as they braced themselves on their toes.

"My grandmother has asthma." Coltrane could hardly speak. "That duct tape on her mouth must be agony. Look at her chest heave."

A guttural voice with a Slavic accent spoke from behind the camera. "Are we comfortable? Are the ropes too tight? I hope I haven't cut off your circulation."

Coltrane's grandfather strained to speak through the duct tape.

"Please," the guttural voice said. "My instructions were clear. Don't make any unnecessary motions."

Coltrane's grandfather stopped trying to speak. He closed his eyes and seemed to concentrate on controlling his breathing.

"Good," the voice said. "Now I'm going to have to be rude and leave you alone for a moment. I haven't had breakfast. I'm sure you won't mind if I go upstairs and make a plate of those waffles you

140

didn't have a chance to eat. Blueberries are my favorite. I'd bring you some, but you're occupied."

Wood creaked, the sound diminishing, as if someone was climbing stairs.

Coltrane's grandfather and grandmother exchanged looks of desperation. And other emotions: determination to survive, sorrow for what the other was suffering, most of all love.

The image blurred. Tasting salt, Coltrane realized that he was crying. He wiped his shirt sleeve across his eyes, one of the most effortful things he had ever done. But not as hard as the effort his grandparents were making to stand on their toes. Their posture wasn't exaggerated. They weren't in the extreme stance of ballet dancers on their toes. The space between their heels and the bench they stood on was only about an inch and a half. Nonetheless, Coltrane inwardly cringed at the thought of the effort they would have to make to stand in that position for any length of time, especially because each had arthritis.

Wood creaked, but this time the sound grew louder, someone returning down the stairs. Coltrane's grandfather and grandmother tensed.

"There," the guttural voice said. "I hope you didn't get into mischief while I was gone."

Coltrane identified the sounds of a plate being set onto something, then a knife and fork scraping on it, food being cut.

"I can't recall when I ate waffles this delicious," the voice said. "You're a lucky man to have a wife who's such a good cook."

From behind the duct tape on his mouth, Coltrane's grandfather made a sound that might have been "Please."

"Six hours of torturing them like this?" Coltrane's emotions tore him apart.

"I'm afraid so," Nolan said. "I told you this would be rough. I think it would be best if I turned it off."

"Give me the remote control."

Coltrane aimed it toward the video player and pushed a button that fast-forwarded the tape while still allowing him to see the image. The picture quality became more grainy. Streaks ran through it. But Coltrane was still able to see his grandparents. What disturbed him was that normally, when a tape was fast-forwarded, the motions of the people on the screen became frantic and jerky. In this case, there was virtually no movement at all. His grandparents were struggling to stand perfectly still on their toes.

The counter on the tape machine showed that the elapsed time was forty-six minutes. Coltrane released the button on the remote control. The picture returned to normal, if that word could possibly be applied to what Coltrane was seeing. At first, nothing seemed to have changed, but as he looked closer, concentrating on his grandparents' feet, he could see that their heels were lower. The effort of standing in that position, combined with the pain of arthritis, had weakened his grandparents. They were lowering their weight, and as they did, the rope that stretched from their necks to the rafter became tighter. Not taut. Not yet. Ilkovic had made sure to leave enough slack that the process would be prolonged.

In dismay, Coltrane fast-forwarded the tape again. Except for the increased grain and the streaks, nothing seemed to change on the screen. At an elapsed time of one hour and forty-eight minutes, he again released the button.

Now his grandparents were standing flat on their feet and the rope was tighter and their breathing was more labored. But by comparison with the fast-forwarded image, everything seemed to be in torturous slow motion. Coltrane could barely imagine what the passage of time must have felt like to his grandparents. An eternity. The force of the rope made their eyes bulge. Their faces, which had been gray with fear, were now red from the pressure around their throats.

"Mr. Coltrane, I really think," McCoy started to say.

"Shut up." Coltrane pressed the fast-forward button. When the indicator on the tape machine showed two hours and fifty-one minutes, he returned the tape to normal speed and saw a urine stain on his grandfather's pajamas.

McCoy left the room.

On the tape, the guttural voice said, "Well, accidents happen."

Their knees began sagging.

After three more fast-forwards, Coltrane saw his grandmother's chest stop moving at an elapsed time of 4:07. His grandfather managed to last until four forty-nine.

"Photographer," the guttural voice said. "This is nothing compared to what I'm going to do to you."

Coltrane's scream brought McCoy rushing back into the room.

"I'm going to kill him!" Coltrane screamed. "I'm going to get my hands around his throat and—"

Other officers rushed in. By then, Coltrane had hurled the remote control at the television screen and was trying to pick up the TV so he could throw it across the room.

6

He's going to be at the cemetery today." Coltrane quivered from the rage that consumed him. His voice was strained, his vocal cords raw. "He'll need to check out the area before he risks showing up there to look for me tomorrow."

Nolan and McCoy glanced at each other.

"Then we have a second chance to grab him," McCoy said. "We have a team at the cemetery right now."

"*Now?*" Coltrane said.

"They're inspecting it so we know where to place our men tomorrow."

"No! Get your men away from there."

"What?"

"Don't you understand? If Ilkovic sees your men there today, he'll realize you're anticipating him to be there tomorrow. He'll back off and go to ground. God only knows when he'll decide to make another move."

"But there's no other way for us to do this. We have to be able to protect you tomorrow," Nolan said.

"Not tomorrow. It's going to be *today*."

"What the hell are you talking about?"

"Call your men off," Coltrane said. "What time is it? Jesus, one o'clock. It might be too late. When is Daniel's funeral tomorrow?"

"The same time as now," Nolan said.

"Which means the burial will be around two-thirty." Nerves in turmoil, Coltrane rushed to stand. "If I hurry, I can get there by then."

"I still don't understand what you're talking about," McCoy said.

"Ilkovic will want to check out the area today at the same time the burial will happen tomorrow," Coltrane said. "It doesn't make any sense for him to see what it's like at ten in the morning if the patterns in the area are likely to be different by midafternoon. If I can get there by two-thirty, there's a good chance he'll see me."

"It's still the same deal," McCoy said. "When he tries to follow you, we grab him. Nothing's changed, except that we've moved the schedule up twenty-four hours."

"It's *not* the same deal," Coltrane said. "If you were Ilkovic, would *you* try to follow your target if you saw law-enforcement officers in the area?"

"But how's Ilkovic going to know who they are?" Nolan raised his hands, frustrated. "They're not wearing uniforms. They're not going around staring at everybody. These men are trained to blend in. They look like they're mourners. They look like they're groundskeepers. Ilkovic isn't going to spot them."

"The way they look isn't what bothers me," Coltrane said.

"What do you mean?"

"Ilkovic is an electronics freak. He likes to play with microphones. He doesn't need to *see* your men. All he needs to do is *listen* to them."

"Listen?"

"Your men have to stay in contact with one another, right?" Coltrane asked. "They're wearing miniature earphones. They've got button-sized microphones on their sleeves or their lapels."

"Of course," McCoy said.

"Well, how hard do you think it would be for someone as clever as Ilkovic to get his hands on one of those units, set it to the same frequency, and overhear what you're planning?"

"He's right," Nolan murmured.

"Tell them to turn the damned things off and get out of there," Coltrane said. "*Now.*"

"Then how are we going to protect you?" McCoy demanded.

"You'll be waiting somewhere else. *Where I lead him.*"

7

You have to promise me," Nolan said. "If you have even the slightest suspicion that Ilkovic knows what you're trying to do, get away from there."

They were hurrying through the police building's parking garage.

"There'll be unmarked cars two blocks in every direction," Nolan said. "That's as far back as we can put them and still hope to give you backup. For God sake, don't take any chances. Drive straight to where we'll be waiting for him."

"I still don't like this," McCoy said. "Endangering a civilian."

"I'm volunteering," Coltrane said.

"But it isn't bureau policy," McCoy said. "I don't have time to clear this with my superiors. I want to go on record—this isn't sanctioned by the FBI."

"I'm glad you told me that." Coltrane stopped where he'd parked his car. "For a while, I was beginning to think I'd misjudged you, that you weren't the self-serving jerk I first thought you were."

McCoy's eyes widened.

Coltrane turned to Jennifer. "Take Sergeant Nolan and the SWAT team to Packard's house. Explain the layout. They won't have time to size up everything on their own before I get back there."

"I hope to heaven Ilkovic doesn't move against you before then," Jennifer said. "Be careful."

"Count on it." Coltrane kissed her. "Just keep reminding your-self—by tonight, this will all be over."

Hugging herself, Jennifer glanced toward the police cars in the garage. "I've forgotten what it feels like to be safe."

Nolan handed him a walkie-talkie. "Take this. Just in case. If you need backup in a hurry, it won't matter if Ilkovic can overhear."

Coltrane was setting out from downtown Los Angeles. When he glanced at the Saturn's dashboard clock and saw that the time was 1:31, he realized that he had less than an hour to get to the valley. All he could do was hope that the Golden State Freeway wouldn't be congested.

His thoughts in a frenzy, he accessed the freeway, relieved when he saw that traffic was moving easily. Now that he was on his own, he couldn't get over his eagerness. Instead of being afraid, he was filled with anticipation. For a moment, it puzzled him.

Do you miss dodging bullets in places like Bosnia and Chechyna so much that you can't wait to put yourself in danger again?

What I can't wait for is this to end. In fact, I'm going to make sure it ends.

I'm going to kill him.

There, Coltrane thought. I've put it in words again.

What he had screamed after seeing the videotape of what Ilkovic had done to his grandparents was exactly what he hoped to do. Nolan and McCoy had seemed to think that he was exaggerating, that he was merely venting his rage. They had cautioned him about losing control. They had warned him about taking the law into his hands, and he had told them yes, that he was sorry for overreacting.

It had all been a lie. He couldn't recall ever having been so seized by an emotion. Not fear. He was absolutely released from fear. The rage within him as he watched the tape of what Ilkovic had done to his grandparents negated his fear. It made him feel liberated. Eager? He was so eager that he trembled. For what Ilkovic had done to Daniel, Greg, and his grandparents, he was going to make Ilkovic pay. He was going to trick Ilkovic into following him. He was going to make Ilkovic think he had taken Coltrane by surprise. He was going to see the big smile on Ilkovic's face, then the frown of confusion when Ilkovic realized that Coltrane had caught *him* by surprise.

8

It wasn't until Coltrane heard the roar of arriving and departing jets that he realized Everlasting Gardens was near the commotion of the Burbank airport.

As he steered through the cemetery's entrance, he became viscerally aware of entering Ilkovic's territory. The hairs on his neck bristled like antenna, his survival instincts possessing him. To get even with Ilkovic, he warned himself, he had to be as cautious as he had ever been in any of the war zones he had photographed. He couldn't take anything for granted.

Driving past tombstones, noticing mourners gathered around a casket at an open grave site, seeing groundskeepers trimming hedges and mowing grass, he wondered if Nolan had kept his end of the bargain. He thought about the officers who had come here to check the cemetery in preparation for tomorrow's surveillance. What if some of them hadn't left? What if Ilkovic had seen them and snuck away and Coltrane was wasting his time? Or what if they *had* left and it was Ilkovic who was pretending to be one of those mourners?

One thing was certain: Coltrane couldn't make it obvious that he was searching the area. The result would be the same as if Ilkovic realized that there were police officers in the area. He would suspect a trap and leave. It had to seem the most natural thing in the world that Coltrane would be at this cemetery today, and Coltrane knew exactly what his reason for coming here would be. He followed a lane around the treed cemetery, eventually coming back to where he had entered, making it seem that he was trying to orient himself, which was actually the truth. He passed a solemn-looking building that resembled a church but that didn't have any symbols and would be suitable for services in any religion. Or perhaps it's a mausoleum, Coltrane thought. When he felt that the movement was natural, he glanced around, appearing to assess his surroundings, all the while alert for anyone who paid attention to him. No one did.

His muscles tight, Coltrane stopped at a building that reminded him of a cottage. It had sheds and a three-stall garage in back, the open doors revealing large riding lawn mowers and other maintenance equipment. He locked his car and again glanced around in apparent assessment of his surroundings—still no one unusual. Sprinklers watered a section of the cemetery, casting a fragrance in his direction. As a jet roared overhead, he opened a screen door and knocked on a wooden one.

He knocked again, then studied a sign that read OFFICE HOURS: 9–5. He tried the knob. The door wasn't locked. Easing it open, he peered into a compact, well-lit office and asked, "Anybody here?"

Apparently not.

"Hello?" he called.

What in God's name am I doing? he thought. For all I know, Ilkovic is in there. He stepped quickly back into the sunlit air, only to jolt against someone.

He spun, startled.

It wasn't Ilkovic. The dignified gray-haired man was tall and thin. He wore a somber suit and touched Coltrane's arm. "I'm sorry."

"It's not your fault." Coltrane tried not to seem uneasy. "I wasn't looking where I was going."

"I just stepped out of the office for a moment. Is there something I can help you with?"

"Yes, I'm looking for a grave site."

The somber man nodded. "It's always wise to plan ahead. Step into my office and I'll explain our services."

"Excuse me?" Coltrane suddenly realized that he had misunderstood, that the man was actually asking him if he had come here to *buy* a grave site. "No, what I meant was, a friend of mine is going to be buried here tomorrow."

"Ah." The man now realized that *he* had misunderstood.

"I can't come to the burial," Coltrane said, "but I thought, if I found out where his plot was, I could drop by later and pay my respects without having to ask someone from his family to come and show me where he is."

"Of course," the man said. "Please accept my condolences about your friend."

"Thank you," Coltrane said. "Believe me, it wasn't his time."

"If you'll tell me what your friend's name is . . ." The man started toward his office.

"Daniel Gibson."

"Oh." The man stopped.

"Is something the matter?"

"Not at all. But I don't need to look up your friend's name in my records. Earlier this morning, someone else asked me where his plot is. I distinctly remember the location."

"Someone else?"

"Yes. A phone call. Like you, he said he was a friend who couldn't attend the burial but wanted to know where the grave would be so he could pay his respects later."

"I think I might know him. Did he happen to have an Eastern European accent? Slavic?"

The man thought a moment. "I really can't remember. I was too busy concentrating on the deceased's name and his plot number."

"Sure. Maybe I'll see him here later."

"Possibly. One never knows. Your friend's grave site is . . ." The long-legged man walked onto the lane and pointed toward the middle of the cemetery, toward activity beyond various gravestones, two lanes over. "Our maintenance staff is preparing it."

Across the distance, Coltrane saw the descending claw of a yellow backhoe and heard the rumble of an engine.

"You might want to reconsider going over there. We discourage the bereaved from seeing this part of the procedure. It might seem unfeeling."

"But it has to be done," Coltrane said.

"Exactly."

"I understand practicality," Coltrane said. "Thanks for your concern."

"If there's anything else I can do for you . . ."

"I'll definitely remember how helpful you were."

As the man stepped into the cottagelike building and closed the door, Coltrane stared beyond the various grave markers toward the rumbling backhoe in the distance. He got in his car and tried not to glance around as he drove down the lane. His stomach churned. His palms sweated, making his grip slick on the steering wheel. Had it been Ilkovic who phoned, wanting to know the location of Daniel's grave? Ilkovic would need that information. He would have to find out which section of the cemetery to watch. Around this time tomorrow, Daniel's hearse would arrive. His mourners would walk along this lane and gather among the tombstones, directing their mournful gazes toward the coffin supported on braces above the open grave. Of course, the mourners wouldn't actually see the open grave, Coltrane thought as he stopped his car near the clank and rumble of the backhoe. There would be a sash of some sort covering the pit; probably it would be colored green, just as imitation grass would cover the nearby pile of earth that now grew larger as the backhoe deposited another clawful.

Coltrane's tear ducts ached as he got out of the car and locked it. Come on, Ilkovic, get a good look at me. I know you're here. It's two-thirty. It's dress-rehearsal time. You want to find out where the best view is for tomorrow. I bet you're surprised to see me here. You're looking sharply around to find out if anybody else is with me—like the police. You're ready to run at the first sign of trouble, but you're hesitating—because you don't see anybody who's a threat and you can't believe your luck that I showed up, and you wonder what I'm doing here. But in a minute, it'll be obvious, and then you *really* won't believe how lucky you are.

The workman on the backhoe glanced with puzzlement toward Coltrane as he maneuvered the machine's controls and the claw dropped back into the grave-sized trench, digging up more earth. A bitter cloud of exhaust floated from the engine, irritating Coltrane's throat. He had never felt so exposed and threatened, totally certain that Ilkovic was somewhere close watching him, but at the same time absolutely confident that for as long as he stood next to Daniel's grave, he was safe. Ilkovic didn't want to shoot him. He wanted to *torture* him. For that, Ilkovic needed privacy and leisure.

He certainly isn't going to try to rush up, grab me, and drag me to his car, Coltrane thought. Not in plain sight. Not when I have a chance of fighting back. He'll watch and follow. He'll make his move when he has every advantage. But he's still suspicious, wondering if he should run.

Coltrane folded his hands in prayer, so immersed in sorrow that it took him a moment to realize that his gesture was exactly what was required to make Ilkovic understand why he had supposedly come here. Ilkovic would conclude that Coltrane feared it would be too risky to show up at the cemetery the next day, that he felt compelled to come a day early to pay his respects and participate in his own private ceremony.

When he lowered his gaze from the sky, the backhoe's claw slammed into the trench again, gouging up earth. Unnerved, Coltrane seemed to be back in his gravelike pit on the slope above the mass grave in Bosnia, staring through a telephoto lens at an identical yellow backhoe, except that it wasn't gouging up earth, but skulls and teeth and rib cages and shattered leg bones. The overlapping of the past on the present was so powerful that he shuddered and feared for his sanity. He watched the backhoe drop its burden, a welter of bones onto . . .

A pile of earth. It was only a pile of earth. And the trench was apparently now deep enough, for the driver didn't drop the claw back into the trench. Instead, he directed it into a neutral position and drove from the grave, rumbling along the lane. Later, Coltrane knew, someone would come around with a winch to lower a concrete sleeve into the grave, to shore up the sides and prevent earth from falling in. Eyes stinging, Coltrane stepped between other graves, plucked up a few blades of grass, and came back, dropping the blades into the grave, watching them flutter to the bottom.

I won't forget you, Daniel.

When he stepped away, he made no attempt to look around as he returned to the car. Either Ilkovic was here or he wasn't. Either Ilkovic would follow or he wouldn't. Unlocking his car, he had the sense that events were controlling him, not the other way around. When he got in and started the car, he was surprised to see that the dashboard clock showed 3:06. He had been standing there, grieving, far longer than he had thought. I can't let that happen again. I can't let myself lose track of time like that. I have to pay attention to what I'm doing. But then, in a sense, that was exactly what had happened—he had been paying attention to his grief.

Now it was time to pay attention to his rage.

9

THE PLAN HE AND NOLAN HAD AGREED UPON WAS THAT HE would lead Ilkovic to Packard's house, where Nolan and a SWAT team would be waiting. Jennifer would come out of the house as Coltrane arrived. Ilkovic would see the two of them and conclude that Coltrane hadn't wanted Jennifer to go with him to the cemetery, that he'd needed to be alone. With Jennifer's absence explained and with Coltrane's hiding place now discovered, Ilkovic would take time to reconnoiter the area, to assure himself that the police weren't around (they would be in the house, but Ilkovic wouldn't know that until it was too late). He would plan his entry onto the property, presumably through the back. He would make his move at night, after the house lights had been turned off and his targets had plenty of time to drift off to sleep. As soon as he was in the house, the police would spring their trap.

It's a perfectly feasible plan, Coltrane thought as he drove across the valley. It was simple. It had the merit of surprise. It had only one flaw. Ilkovic might be captured instead of killed. The UN tribunal might sentence him to life imprisonment instead of having him executed.

That's not good enough. I know another way, Coltrane thought. He accessed the San Diego Freeway and drove south, grateful for the congested traffic, needing a reason to drive slowly so that Ilkovic wouldn't have trouble keeping him in sight. He exited onto Sunset Boulevard, where traffic was only slightly less congested, and headed toward the Pacific Coast Highway. There, he proceeded north. He had always enjoyed this drive, the majesty of the Palisades on his right, the allure of the ocean on his left, the glinting waves, the gliding sailboats. But not this time. The only thing that occupied his attention was a plan that he rehearsed. Past Malibu, just when he began to fear that he wouldn't find the road he was looking for, he saw it on the right, next to a weathered wooden sign that read MAYNARD RANCH. The road hadn't changed since the first time he had used it three months previously. It was unpaved and narrow, and it led him up into the Santa Monica Mountains.

Since the cemetery, everything around him had seemed out of focus, in a haze. But now his perception sharpened. He had the sensation of seeing everything with the intensity of peering through a zoom lens. Every detail of his surroundings seemed magnified. He was struck by an overwhelming sense of the buckthorn, greasewood, and other scrub brush on the hills into which he drove. December rains had caused the chaparral to turn green, in contrast with the sand color of the desert soil, and under other circumstances, he would have stopped to photograph the differences in color and texture. But as he bitterly reminded himself, in place of a camera, he had brought a shotgun.

Near the highway, there had been service stations, restaurants, and motels. Along the base of the hills, there were occasional dilapidated ranch houses. But once the road twisted up into the hills, he had the impression of entering another time, of experiencing the solitary beauty of what Southern California had been like 150 years ago.

Just before steering over a ridge that cut off his view of the sloping land behind him, Coltrane checked his rearview mirror and thought he saw the dust of a following car. It was hard to be sure. The dust might merely have been nudged up by a breeze. Or it might have been the remnants of dust that he himself had raised. Or if the dust *had been* raised by someone else's car, there was no certainty that the car belonged to Ilkovic. Someone who lived in one of the ranch houses might be returning home from an errand.

But Coltrane didn't think so. Soon, he told himself. This is going to end soon. He kept seeing a mental image of his grandparents standing on tiptoes on the bench, with their arms tied behind them, duct tape across their lips, and a noose around their necks. He kept remembering the way his grandfather struggled to plead through the duct tape and how his asthmatic grandmother's chest heaved. He had never wanted to get even with someone so much.

The road made a dogleg turn to the right, taking him higher and deeper into the brush-covered hills. But Coltrane knew that shortly the landscape would change from a faint December green to an appalling blackness. The section of hills that he drove through had escaped a raging brush fire three months earlier. A valley on the other side of these hills hadn't been so lucky. Once owned by the western star Ken Maynard and used as the location for numerous cowboy movies in the thirties and forties as well as several western TV series, including *Rawhide*, during the late fifties and early sixties, the area had been devastated by the fire, which destroyed a replica of a western town that had doubled countlessly as Tombstone, Dodge City, and Abilene, and along whose streets everyone from Randolph Scott to Gary Cooper had walked.

Coltrane knew about the place because, just after the fire, *Premiere* magazine had asked him to go there and take photographs of the destroyed set, which the editor planned to juxtapose with stills from the famous movies that the set had been used in. With a fondness for some of the classics in which the valley and its set had been featured, Coltrane had turned down an important assignment in the Philippines. He had walked the ash-covered land, climbed burnt-over bluffs, and studied debris-filled streambeds, identifying many of the vistas with scenes he recalled from favorite movies.

The area fit all of his requirements. It was remote. It was abandoned. Equally important, it was familiar. Once he photographed a place, it became part of him.

As the road crested a ridge and the valley lay below him, spindly black skeletons of scrub brush punctuated the thick black ash that stretched in all directions. With the scorched timbers of the town in the distance, it was as thorough a wasteland as many war zones he had photographed.

Minus the corpses, he thought.

But if he had his way, there would definitely be one corpse here by nightfall.

10

JUST MAKE SURE THE CORPSE ISN'T YOURS, Coltrane thought.

At the bottom of the slope, the ash made the road hard to distinguish. He did his best to follow it, sometimes jouncing over rocks at the side. The ash wasn't powdery. Rain had dissolved it into a paste, which hardened when the sun came out. Crusty, like dried black mud, it made a crunching sound as he drove over it. Glancing at his rearview mirror, he saw the tracks that his tires had made. Then his rearview mirror showed him something else: the bluff behind him, where a car appeared, stopping as its driver surveyed the barren landscape through which Coltrane proceeded.

That barrenness was another reason Coltrane had selected the area. There was only one set of tracks heading toward the blackened town, and those tracks belonged to Coltrane. If other people were in the area—a team of policemen, for example—their presence would be easily detectable because there was no place to conceal them. Their movements would have left scars in the ash, giving them away. Ilkovic would at first be on guard. But as the sterile nature of the site became manifest to him, his confidence would return.

The car, tiny in Coltrane's rearview mirror, started down the slope.

Coltrane tried to put himself in Ilkovic's place. What would Ilkovic be thinking? For certain, he'd wonder what Coltrane was doing here. It wouldn't take him long to suspect that Coltrane might have lead him here. But for what purpose? To invite a confrontation? Apparently, Ilkovic found that notion appealing. Otherwise, he wouldn't be descending into the valley, following Coltrane's tire marks through the ash.

Coltrane slowed, letting the car, a dark sedan, gain on him. Ahead, the road dipped into a deep trough, then crossed a shallow stream, the site for innumerable movie ambushes. From those movies and from photographs that Coltrane had taken of the area, he knew that his car would be out of sight in the trough. He wanted Ilkovic to think that he was lying in wait for him down there. What he intended to do, though, was something else. The instant he reached the bottom of the embankment, he rushed from the car, opened the back door, and grabbed his shotgun from where he had hidden it under a sleeping bag before leaving Packard's house. He raced toward a gully where another stream joined this one at a right angle. That second stream paralleled the road along which he had driven. Its bed was low enough that if he stooped, he couldn't be seen as he ran along it.

Breathing hard, sweating, stretching his legs to their maximum, he charged along, avoiding a channel of water so that he wouldn't make a splashing noise that would alert Ilkovic if his windows were open. Ilkovic would be wondering why Coltrane's car hadn't reappeared. Ilkovic would be slowing, then stopping, waiting until he knew where Coltrane's car had gone. He wouldn't go forward again unless he assured himself that he wouldn't be entering a trap. Meanwhile, Coltrane sprinted closer, so close that he could now hear Ilkovic's car, the faint drone of its motor. Flash floods had scoured the gully free of ash. There wasn't any crust that his footsteps could break and cause noise. The only sounds he made were his labored breathing, which he struggled to restrain, and the brittle but subdued scrape of his shoes over gravel and rocks, which lessened when he reduced his pace, hearing Ilkovic's car thirty yards to his left.

The engine stopped. A door opened. Footsteps crunched on the ash. Ilkovic had evidently decided to circle the trough where Coltrane's car had disappeared. He was coming at it from an angle, which was leading him toward the gully in which Coltrane aimed the pump-action shotgun.

The footsteps crunched closer. Coltrane's finger tightened on the shotgun's trigger. Lining up the sights, focusing along the barrel toward the sound of Ilkovic's approaching footsteps, Coltrane had an unholy sensation that he was concentrating through a viewfinder, about to press a shutter button, when a face appeared above him, so startling that Coltrane was barely able to jerk the barrel away, recognizing the surprised, lean, thin-lipped features of FBI Special Agent James McCoy.

11

JESUS CHRIST!" McCoy gaped at the shotgun barrel and lurched back. His feet slipped from under him, his momentum throwing him to the ashy ground. He landed with a groan. "Damn it, put that thing down!"

By the time Coltrane scrambled to the top of the gully, McCoy was squirming to sit up. His blue suit was covered with black ash. He stood awkwardly and swatted at his clothes, belatedly realizing that he was only spreading the grit. He stared at his hands, which were totally black. His face was smudged. He recoiled when he saw that Coltrane still held the shotgun. "I told you, put that thing down!"

His surprise deepening, Coltrane obeyed.

"Look at this suit!" McCoy said. "Look what you've done to—"

"What are you doing here?"

"What are *you* doing here? As if it isn't obvious!" McCoy stepped angrily closer. "You might have fooled Nolan and your girlfriend, but this self-serving jerk, as you called me, didn't believe for a second that you were going to try to make Ilkovic follow you back to the house where you were hiding."

Coltrane didn't flinch.

"Not to the house!" McCoy emphasized. "Somewhere else. I saw that look in your eye. I could tell you had something else in mind. In case you haven't noticed, you wandered a little off track—about ninety minutes from where you're supposed to be meeting Nolan in the Hollywood Hills."

"You were at the cemetery?"

"Hell, yes. You were so convinced Ilkovic was going to be there, I thought I'd be criminally stupid if I didn't show up, on the chance I'd spot him."

"The police surveillance team?"

"Were never called off. Did you really think we'd let you go in there without support?" McCoy demanded. "For sure, *that* would have been criminally stupid."

Coltrane was sickened. "You ruined my chance."

"Hey, he wasn't there, Coltrane. He never showed up. We'd have seen him."

"Did you at least tell your surveillance team to shut off their radios?"

"Listen to me. Pay attention. You're a civilian. You don't tell law-enforcement officers what to do."

"Answer me. *Did they shut off their radios?*"

"Yes! For all the good it—"

"Then there's still a chance."

"To do *what?* This entire operation's a mess. Thanks to you! If there was ever a chance to trap Ilkovic today, you blew it when you didn't go back to where Nolan had a team waiting at the house."

"No, *you* blew it when you followed me here. If Ilkovic sees you, he'll suspect a trap and back off."

"Hey, I know my job. I watched for anybody else following you. Nobody. Zilch. Both of us took a ride in the country for nothing. Ilkovic isn't—"

McCoy's black-smudged blue suit suddenly had red on it. The next instant, Coltrane realized that the red was blood bursting from McCoy's right shoulder. The echo of a gunshot rolled over them, about the same time that McCoy's face turned gray. As the special agent groaned and dropped, Coltrane grabbed him before his face would have struck a rock. He tugged him backward. At once, a second bullet ricocheted close to McCoy, dirt and ash flying, the gunshot echoing. Frantic, Coltrane felt his right shoe slip over the gully's rim. He dropped to his knees, lowered himself into the streambed, and dragged McCoy down out of sight after him. A surge of adrenaline made his hands and feet turn numb as blood rushed to his chest and muscles.

"How bad are you hit?"

"Don't know." McCoy lay among rocks beside the trickling stream. He shuddered, as if he was freezing. "Don't feel anything."

"You're going into shock."

"Did you figure that out"—McCoy shuddered harder—"all by yourself?"

Coltrane stared toward blood pulsing from a jagged exit hole in McCoy's right shoulder. "I have to stop the bleeding."

"Another bulletin."

But how am I going to do it? Coltrane thought. He had reached the limit of his first-aid abilities when he had used a tourniquet and a pressure bandage to stop the young girl's arm from bleeding after the explosion that killed Greg. This wound was much worse. He tried to remember every makeshift treatment he had ever seen a battlefield doctor use on a wounded soldier.

In a frenzy, he groped in McCoy's pockets and found a handkerchief. He also found a key chain pocketknife, which he used to cut wide patches from the bottom of McCoy's suit coat.

McCoy groaned when Coltrane tilted him to press a half dozen of these makeshift bandages against the entrance wound in the back of his shoulder. Coltrane set a similar wedge of cloth in front against the exit wound. Rushing, he pulled off McCoy's belt, cinched it around his shoulder, and tightened it.

The pressure made McCoy groan again.

"We have to get out of here," Coltrane said.

"Still more bulletins."

"My car's about a hundred yards down this gully. Do you think you can stand?"

McCoy winced. "One way to find out."

"I have to do something first."

Coltrane turned toward the gully's rim. His stomach was so gripped with fear, he was sure he was going to throw up. What he did instead, the fiercest he had ever moved, was scurry up the slope, dive over the top, grab the shotgun where he had set it down, and roll back into the gully. As he dropped from sight, a richocheting bullet sprayed dirt across the back of his neck. The gunshot echoed.

Coltrane rolled to a painful stop, bumping his right side against a rock next to McCoy.

"Sounds like a rifle," the special agent murmured.

"It also sounds closer."

Struggling, Coltrane put an arm around McCoy's waist and gripped his uninjured left arm, lifting. With a gasp, McCoy braced his legs and stood, leaning heavily against Coltrane.

"Hang on to me," Coltrane said. "I need a hand free to hold the shotgun."

They staggered along the gully. McCoy's legs buckled, but he cursed himself and stayed upright, lurching farther along the stream.

The Saturn came into view. Staggering toward it, Coltrane scanned the top of the embankment down which he had driven. Ilkovic might have reached here by now, he thought furiously. He might suddenly appear, aiming at us. Have to hurry.

Coltrane leaned the shotgun against the car, yanked open the back door, and eased McCoy inside.

"Cold," McCoy said.

"Stretch out on the backseat. I'll cover you with this sleeping bag. Prop your feet up against the door. Keep them higher than your head."

"My fault."

Coltrane grabbed the shotgun and aimed toward the top of the embankment.

"My fault," McCoy repeated. "I shouldn't have—"

"No! It's *my* fault." Coltrane shoved the shotgun into the front seat, scrambled behind the steering wheel, rammed the car into gear, and roared out of the trough. The car bucked as it reached the crest, causing McCoy to scream in pain. Coltrane stomped his foot on the accelerator, racing along the barely defined road toward the charred ruins of the western town, throwing up a cloud of ash that he hoped would give them cover.

"I should never have tried this! I should never have come here!" The rage that had brought Coltrane here was now the faintest of memories. His obsession with revenge had completely drained from him. In its place was an overpowering fear that surged through every portion of his body. It completely controlled him. "Who did I think I was? Going up against Ilkovic—what was I thinking?"

The dust cloud of ash that the Saturn threw up behind it didn't provide as much cover as Coltrane had hoped. A chunk burst from the rear window. As safety glass disintegrated into pellets, a bullet slammed through the passenger seat and walloped into the lower part of the dashboard. McCoy moaned.

Sweating, Coltrane pressed the accelerator harder. The car sped to the crest of an incline and soared from the road, slamming down, Coltrane's stomach dropping, McCoy groaning from the impact, toppling onto the floor. The chassis screeched. As Coltrane fought to control his steering, another bullet burst through the remnant of the rear window. It struck closer to Coltrane, shattering the radio.

"McCoy?" Coltrane shouted to the back.

"Don't worry about me! Drive!"

The Saturn left the road again, crashed down, veered, regained its traction, and sped closer to the charred remnants of the movie set. Needing to concentrate on his driving, Coltrane nonetheless risked a glance at the rearview mirror, seeing only a cloud of black dust behind him. He heard a metallic whack, a bullet striking the Saturn's trunk. Or the gas tank, Coltrane thought.

"The more shots Ilkovic fires . . ." McCoy's voice was strained. "Someone will hear." He gasped for a breath. "Maybe call the police."

"I don't think so," Coltrane said, the Saturn jolting over a bump as he urged the car closer to the scorched ruin. "This used to be a movie set for westerns."

"Westerns?"

161

"The few people who live in the area used to hear shots in this valley all the time. They'll probably think another movie's being made."

"We're screwed."

The road curved to the left. As Coltrane changed direction, he felt chillingly exposed, the dust cloud no longer providing conceal-ment from where Ilkovic was shooting. Abruptly the Saturn lurched, as if it had struck another bump. But instead of jouncing off the ground, it leaned. The steering felt mushy. Distraught, Coltrane struggled to keep the car on the road.

"I think he shot the front left tire!"

The Saturn's back end fishtailed, then leaned more sharply to the left as another jolt shook the car, this time from the *rear* left tire.

"I'm afraid we're going to—"

Coltrane couldn't control the car. He stomped on the brake pedal, fighting the steering wheel, feeling the Saturn tilt even farther to the left. With a savage leftward twist on the steering, he forced the front wheels into a ninety-degree angle with the car, held his breath as the back end swung to the right, felt time stop as the car threatened to crash onto its side, and breathed out as the car slammed down flat.

12

THE CAR WAS TURNED SIDEWAYS ON THE ROAD. The driver's door faced the direction from which Ilkovic had been shooting. Move! Coltrane thought, a welter of impulses rocketing along his nerves. He grabbed the shotgun, slid across the passenger seat, shoved that door open, and leapt onto the ash-covered road, the Saturn giving him cover. A bullet blew a hole in the driver's window, safety glass exploding into pellets that sprayed him. As he huddled next to the car, sweat streamed down his face and stuck his shirt to his chest. His hands wouldn't stop shaking.

McCoy groaned from where he had fallen onto the back floor. Coughing from black dust that drifted over him, Coltrane yanked open the rear door and peered apprehensively inside. McCoy's blue suit coat was soaked crimson. His lips were thinner, his face narrower, squeezed by pain. His face was more slick with sweat than Coltrane's. His eyes were scrunched shut. At first, Coltrane thought he had passed out, but then McCoy squirmed awkwardly onto his uninjured left side, slowly opened his eyes, and with effort tilted his head toward Coltrane.

"I think you missed a few bumps," McCoy said.

"You're going to feel more of them. I have to get you out of there."

A bullet burst through the far side window, hurling glass over McCoy.

"Yeah, get me out of here," McCoy said.

Coltrane gripped his uninjured arm and shoulder, pulling as McCoy shoved against the floor with his feet, doing what he could to help. As gently as possible, Coltrane lowered him to the ashy road.

McCoy whimpered.

"Sorry."

". . . Thirsty."

"The nearest water's back at the stream where you got shot."

"I'd probably throw it up anyhow."

A bullet shattered the remnants of the driver's window.

"He took out two tires with two shots," Coltrane said. "That good a marksman . . . If he wanted to, he could have killed you back at the stream."

"Occurred to me."

"Or he could have shot *me* instead of the tires."

"Toying with us," McCoy said.

"Save your strength."

Coltrane hadn't shut the front passenger door when he leapt out. Glancing inside, he felt his heart swell as he saw the walkie-talkie that Nolan had given him at police headquarters.

He grabbed it. "I don't know what kind of range this thing has."

His voice shook. He was almost afraid to hope. "But we might be able to contact the state police with this thing."

McCoy nodded, guarded optimism showing through his pain.

Coltrane examined the walkie-talkie. It was black, the size of a cellular telephone. He pressed a switch marked ON/OFF, held the unit to his ear, and heard a reassuring hiss. "This must be set to the frequency Nolan's men are using. Otherwise, he wouldn't have given it to me."

McCoy spoke with difficulty. "But that doesn't mean . . ."

Coltrane knew the nervous-making thought that McCoy was struggling to complete. "Right, it doesn't mean it's set to a frequency the police *up here* are using."

His pulse lurched as a bullet shattered more of the back window. It took him a moment to realize the implication. The back window? With the car sideways on the road, Ilkovic had been shooting at the *side* windows. He must have changed position. He was circling.

Finger unsteady, Coltrane held down the talk button. "Can anybody hear me? Please, if you hear me, answer! This is a police emergency! An FBI agent has been shot! We need help!"

Shaking, Coltrane took his finger off the talk button, the release automatically switching the unit to its receive mode. He pressed the unit tensely against his ears. His spirit sank when he heard only static.

"Lousy . . ." McCoy murmured.

"What?"

". . . technique. . . . Supposed to say, 'Do you read me?' " McCoy groaned. "And 'Over.' " His face was alarmingly pale.

"And *you're* supposed to save your strength." Coltrane again pressed the talk button. "*Does anybody read me?* This is an emergency! An FBI agent has been shot! We need help! Over!"

"There you go," McCoy murmured.

"But nobody's answering." Disheartened, Coltrane listened to the relentless static. "Maybe we're too far into the hills. Maybe those bluffs cut off the signal to—"

"Photographer, I can barely hear you." A guttural voice crackled faintly from the walkie-talkie.

Coltrane felt as if a fist was squeezing his heart.

"There must be something wrong with your radio," the faint, deep Slavic voice said. "Your signal's so weak, no one outside this valley will receive it."

"How the hell—" Coltrane's voice dropped. Immediately he knew the answer. "He must have a police scanner in the car he's using!"

"I warned you, photographer." The gravelly voice was almost a whisper. Coltrane had to press the walkie-talkie hard against his ear. "What I did to your doctor friend . . . what I did to your grandparents . . . that was quick compared to what I'm going to do to you."

"Listen to me, you bastard." But Coltrane had forgotten to press the talk button. Ilkovic couldn't hear him.

Besides, Ilkovic had not yet released the talk button on his own unit. His gruff voice continued to whisper. "I've been promising myself this pleasure for a long time. I'll be sure to take pictures."

Furious, Coltrane pressed the transmit button. "My friends didn't do anything to you! My grandparents didn't! You didn't need to kill them!"

Suddenly his voice box didn't want to work. He seemed to have been struck mute, straining to listen for Ilkovic's response.

Nothing.

"The button." McCoy groaned. "You've still got your finger on . . ."

As if the button was on fire, Coltrane released it.

"Photographer, you didn't say 'Over,'" Ilkovic taunted.

You son of a bitch, Coltrane thought.

"No, your friends didn't do anything to hurt me," Ilkovic said. "Your grandparents didn't. But *you* did, didn't you? It's *your* fault for prying and meddling and taking pictures of things that aren't your concern."

"His voice sounds . . ." McCoy took a painful breath, struggling to complete his agitated thought.

"Louder. My God, he must be coming closer." Coltrane glanced frantically around the car. "We can't stay here. We're protected only on one side. We have to . . ."

His vision focused on the charred ruins down the road behind him. He had intended to drive past them and up into the hills on the valley's far side. The road continued beyond them—to where, Coltrane had no idea, but he had hoped to find a town or a highway. Now the only town available to him was a jumble of fallen burned-out timbers.

Fifty yards away. The distance could as easily have been fifty miles.

"McCoy, do you think you can stand again?"

"No choice."

In alarm, Coltrane saw a pool of blood when he gripped McCoy's uninjured left shoulder and worked to lift him. Despite his trim body, McCoy seemed heavier, his body less responsive.

"Here." Coltrane shoved the walkie-talkie into a pocket in McCoy's suit coat. "Hang on." Coltrane grabbed the shotgun. "I hope you're good at the fifty-yard dash."

It was more like a fifty-yard crawl. McCoy wavered. Coltrane lost his balance under McCoy's awkward weight. The two of them collapsed on their knees, the sudden awkward movement preventing one of them from getting hit as a bullet zipped past at shoulder level, sounding like a bumblebee, the gunshot echoing. But Coltrane was absolutely certain that whomever the bullet would have struck would not have been killed. Ilkovic had been vividly clear about his determination to prolong this.

That might work in our favor, Coltrane thought.

"Leave me," McCoy said.

"No."

"Save yourself."

"Not without you," Coltrane said.

Their first effort had taken them about ten yards. They staggered another five before McCoy collapsed again. Sprawling onto the ashy road, Coltrane tried his best to absorb McCoy's fall. Another bullet zipped over their heads.

"Photographer." The guttural voice came faintly, eerily, from the walkie-talkie in McCoy's pocket. "I see you."

166

"Come on," Coltrane urged McCoy, dragging him to his feet. "He can't aim a rifle if he's holding a radio."

Staggering, they managed another ten yards before a bullet nicked the left elbow of Coltrane's denim shirt. He felt its hot tug and pushed McCoy flat.

"He's shooting lower," Coltrane said.

"Photographer," the gravelly voice said in a singsong imitation of a child playing a game of hide-and-seek. "I see you. I aimed slightly to your left, but you twisted in that direction. I hope I didn't hit you. Did I? Is it serious? I don't want to spoil this."

Coltrane groped along his left arm, feeling the nick in his shirt, fearing he would touch blood. He became weak with relief when he didn't find any. The weakness lasted barely a second—only until Ilkovic's deep voice again sounded from the walkie-talkie in McCoy's pocket.

"Answer me, photographer! *How bad are you hit?* Describe the pain!"

Coltrane tugged McCoy forward, urged him upright, and lurched forward with him. They were halfway to the jumble of scorched timbers. Two-thirds. Closer. The collapsed buildings loomed, filling Coltrane's frantic vision. He had the disorienting sensation of seeing them through a lens. The illusion ended when McCoy stumbled and took Coltrane with him. Toppling forward, Coltrane tried to cushion McCoy as they fell over a tangle of blackened beams and crashed among scorched boards. He feared he would cough his lungs out from the thick layer of ash into which he landed. Feeling smothered, he thrashed to get onto his back. He coughed deeper. His eyes stung, watering.

Panicked, he saw McCoy facedown in a pile of ash and grabbed him, twisting him, directing his soot-covered face to the sky. Each time McCoy coughed, he groaned, shuddering from pain. His blood was stark against the blackness.

13

THEY WERE IN A CHARCOAL-FILLED CRATER that was formed by the collapsed walls of an incinerated building.

The shotgun, Coltrane thought. Where is it? I dropped it.

Groping among the brittle burnt ruins, he saw an unscorched chunk of wood protruding from a blackened pile and grabbed the shotgun's stock, tugging it free. He squirmed in a frenzy toward the crater's rim, peering warily above it, ready to shoot if he saw Ilkovic coming.

McCoy coughed behind him, straining to say something. ". . . arrel."

"What?"

"Barrel. Ash in it."

Coltrane's stomach convulsed when he realized what McCoy was trying to tell him. The shotgun had fallen barrel-first among the burnt timbers. Ash and chunks of grit would have been wedged up the barrel. If Coltrane pulled the trigger, the plug might be tight enough to make the weapon backfire. Imagining an explosion of buckshot into his face, he hurriedly reversed the weapon and tensed when he saw that the barrel was indeed jammed.

Hands shaking, he opened the pocketknife he had taken from McCoy and shoved the blade into the plugged barrel—only to flinch when he realized, What am I doing? I'm staring down the barrel of a loaded gun.

Desperate, he put on the safety catch. But he still felt nervous about peering down the barrel, and he racked the pump slide under the barrel, ejecting shells without firing them.

Now! he told himself. After peering urgently toward the valley to make sure Ilkovic wasn't in view, he raised the pocketknife to free the jammed grit from the barrel.

A ballpoint pen appeared before him, McCoy's left hand trembling as he offered it.

Coltrane understood. The plastic pen would go deeper.

As he pried a thumb-sized chunk of charcoal from the barrel, he marveled at McCoy's determination. The wounded man shakily withdrew his revolver from the shoulder holster under his suit coat and aimed it toward the valley.

Coltrane was equally shaky. Staring intermittently toward the wasteland beyond where they had abandoned the car, he freed the barrel, wiped each shell before he shoved it into the weapon, and pushed the safety catch to the off position. Feeling a surge of triumph, he aimed toward his unseen target.

"Pump it," McCoy forced himself to say.

"What?"

"You need to rack a shell into . . ."

Coltrane's surge of triumph dissipated. In its place, he felt a dismaying humility. He had forgotten that after loading the shotgun, he had to work its pump to insert a shell into the firing chamber. Otherwise, the weapon was useless.

"Right." Pulling toward him on the handgrip beneath the barrel, Coltrane heard the satisfying snick of a shell being seated in the firing chamber. "Good to have you along."

"Wouldn't have missed it."

Coltrane aimed toward the wasteland, reminding himself that a shotgun was a short-distance weapon. Ilkovic would have to come within fifty yards before Coltrane's gun would be effective. In the meantime, Ilkovic's rifle gave him the advantage.

"Where *is* he?" Coltrane demanded.

"Maybe . . ." With tremendous effort, McCoy finished his sentence. ". . . coming behind us."

A shadow loomed, but when Coltrane whirled, he saw only a continuation of the wasteland. The shadow had been caused by clouds—*dark* clouds. Throughout his effort to reach the scant cover the ruin provided, Coltrane had paid no attention to the roiling clouds drifting from the west. The ground, not the sky, had been what concerned him. But now the sky was definitely a concern. It was going to rain.

Hearing something scrape behind him, he whirled again. And

again he saw nothing. The sound had been caused by a breeze against two charred boards.

The breeze turned into a wind. The clouds darkened.

"The storm will keep us from seeing him." Coltrane kept glancing nervously toward the area behind him. "Do you have the strength to watch this side while I watch over there?"

"No." McCoy's barely audible answer made Coltrane's scalp prickle.

"Dizzy." McCoy lowered his head.

"Feel strange." McCoy dropped his revolver and sank onto his chest.

Alarmed, Coltrane saw that the belt had slipped off McCoy's shoulder. The blood-soaked pressure bandages had fallen loose. Grabbing the knife, he cut off the left sleeve on McCoy's coat, slashed it apart at four-inch intervals, made two equal wads of the bandages, and eased them against McCoy's entrance and exit wounds. He found the belt where it had slipped down McCoy's right arm. Breathing hard, he again cinched it tightly around McCoy's right shoulder, pressing the bandages against the wounds, hoping to stop the blood.

McCoy made no response. His only movement was from his chest as it raspingly took in air.

"Don't die on me," Coltrane said. "I'll get you out of here. I promise."

Sporadic drops of water pelted Coltrane's face.

Get you out of here? Coltrane thought. *How?*

The drizzle intensified. Staring toward the dimming wasteland, Coltrane watched the drops hit the ash, raising puffs. Apart from that and the seething of the clouds, he detected no other movement.

"Photographer," Ilkovic said.

Coltrane whirled, although an agitated part of him knew that he was only hearing a voice crackle from the walkie-talkie.

"It's too bad you didn't bring rain gear," Ilkovic said. "This morning, you should have listened to the weather report as *I* did. A military surplus shop sold me an excellent camouflage rain slicker. I know that getting wet will be only a minor discomfort for you compared to what I intend to do, but every little bit counts."

The deep, raspy voice was louder than it had been during Ilkovic's last transmission. He was getting closer.

But from which direction?

The drizzle became a downpour. Soaked, his clothes sticking to him, his hair pasted to his scalp and his neck, Coltrane peered around uselessly, his vision so severely reduced that a gray wavering curtain seemed to surround him. He couldn't see twenty feet away from him.

Ilkovic could be *anywhere*.

Immediately a corollary occurred to him. But if I can't see Ilkovic . . .

He can't see *me*.

McCoy's car. While Ilkovic stalks toward these ruins, I can head for the car. I can get help.

As the warmth of hope fought the chill of the rain, Coltrane braced his legs to crawl out of the crater, then stopped instantly. No, I can't leave McCoy.

But I can't take him with me. I've got to move as fast as I can.

Coltrane surveyed the crater, squinting toward a jumble of charred beams behind him, to his left. They seemed to be a collapsed section of the roof. Dragging McCoy toward them, he came close enough to see a hollow underneath. Fearful that Ilkovic would find him as he worked, he tugged at one of the beams and created an opening. Despite his efforts to be gentle, he was dismayed by McCoy's moan as he shoved the unconscious man into the hollow. He rearranged the beams, protecting McCoy from the rain, blocking him from view.

There were two things he did before shoving McCoy in there: He removed McCoy's car key from his pants and the walkie-talkie from his coat, careful to shut if off. Slipping in the muck that the rain created, black from head to toe, he returned to the rim of the crater, where he grabbed McCoy's revolver. Mindful of the mistake that he had made with the shotgun, he took care that the revolver's hammer wasn't cocked before he shoved the weapon under his belt. Try to think the way McCoy would, he told himself. He picked up the pocketknife, folded its blade, and put the knife in his jeans. He gripped the shotgun in one hand, the walkie-talkie in the other, and concentrated on the downpour. The slime of ash on him was so greasy that it wouldn't wash off. He imagined he looked as if he'd risen from hell. Unable to detect any motion beyond the gray curtain of water, he told himself that he might as well die trying to do something instead of hiding.

He crept from the ruins.

14

THEN HE RAN, unable to tell if he shivered from fear or the cold rain lancing against him. His wet clothes sticking to his skin, he felt exposed, naked. His rib cage tightened in anticipation of a bullet that would blast his chest. But a frantic part of his mind tried to assure him that Ilkovic wouldn't shoot him in so vital a spot. The impact would probably be in an arm or a leg, disabling him, rather than killing him, so that Ilkovic could have his fun. *That's some consolation,* Coltrane told himself. *Don't think about it. Move.*

But as he tried to hurry through the cloak of the storm, his mind wouldn't stop working. He kept wondering if he'd made a good choice by heading straight from the ruins in the direction from which he had come. Maybe he should have snuck away on an angle. But wouldn't Ilkovic be more likely to suspect that he'd try something indirect? Perhaps heading straight out from the ruins was so obvious that it wasn't obvious at all. For that matter, would Ilkovic even suspect that Coltrane would abandon McCoy and try to sneak away? The possible guesses and counterguesses were maddening.

A dark shape loomed before him. Coltrane dropped the walkie-talkie and aimed the shotgun, or tried to. Rain blurred his vision. His water-heavy eyelids blinked repeatedly as he struggled to peer along the barrel. If his first shot didn't hit Ilkovic, he would give away his position and make himself a target. He had only one chance to—

The shape wasn't moving. The shape didn't resemble a man. It's my car, Coltrane realized.

But that didn't mean Ilkovic wasn't hiding behind it. Retrieving the walkie-talkie, Coltrane backed away, simultaneously veering to his right, wanting to take a wide arc around the disabled vehicle. When he was far enough away that he couldn't see it anymore, he increased speed, once more running in a crouch.

The air became darker. This time of year, sunset was around five. Soon it would be night.

And if this storm keeps on, I won't be able to see a thing, Coltrane thought. He raced harder, knowing that he would eventually reach the gully that bisected the valley. A noise louder than the rain, the rush of water along the streambed, alerted him that he was getting closer. He stopped as the sound from the streambed intensified.

Peering down, he saw white-capped water churning along the gully. Not a flash flood. But if the storm persisted, the stream could easily turn into one. Even at its present strength, the flow of water looked dangerous. The problem was that to get to where McCoy's car was on the other side, Coltrane would eventually have to cross it. But not here. The bank was too steep, the channel too narrow. The water would have too much strength.

Concerned that the bank might give way, he stepped back, then hurried along it. Although wary of Ilkovic, he couldn't keep glancing around him. He had to concentrate on the stream. He had to find a shallow section where he could cross. But as he searched, he couldn't help thinking of McCoy back at the ruin. Will he stay alive long enough for me to bring help? Maybe I shouldn't have left him. What if Ilkovic searches the ruins and finds where I hid him? What if—

Coltrane tripped over a rock and landed on his shoulder. No! Rolling through a thick layer of mud, he banged against another rock and shivered from the chill of a puddle. He spat out gritty water. He restrained the impulse to cough, almost choking on fluid in his throat. He had no idea how much noise he had made when he fell, but he knew without doubt that he couldn't risk making *further* noise, especially something so distinctive as a deep lung-clearing cough. Distraught that he had dropped the shotgun and the walkie-talkie, he crawled, pawing among the muddy puddles through which he had rolled. What if I can't find—

His left hand trembled when he grasped the walkie-talkie. His right knee grazed the shotgun. Had they been damaged when they fell? Had the mud clogged them? In the darkening rain, he brushed them off. He fingered mud from the shotgun's barrel. As for the firing mechanism, he had no way to check it.

Keep moving! If the stream gets higher . . .

Stumbling along the gully, he reached where it curved. Ahead, in the shadows, the embankment was less pronounced. Puddles filled what seemed to be wheel tracks coming out of it. Coltrane tingled as he told himself that he had reached where the road descended into the trough and then rose from the stream.

He started down. Near the bottom, the churning stream tugged at his calves. He waded farther, determined, feeling the rushing water strengthen. He lost his footing, regained it, willed his legs to move harder, felt the mushy ground tilt upward, and reached the other side.

He had only a hundred yards to go before he would reach McCoy's car. His pulse swelling his veins, he anticipated the excitement of scrambling into McCoy's car, starting it, and fleeing back to the Pacific Coast Highway to get help. By the time Ilkovic realized what was happening, it would be too late for him to do anything. If I can find a police car quickly enough, Coltrane told himself, the authorities might even be able to trap Ilkovic in the valley.

Hurry.

But just before he crested the slippery embankment, his body moved less willingly, a dark suspicion holding him back. From the distance of the ruins, it had seemed a good idea to come here. But now that Coltrane was actually close, doubts seized him. Wasn't

McCoy's car an obvious target? Wouldn't Ilkovic assume that if Coltrane got the chance, he would head for it, the only means of escape? Rather than risk getting shot stalking toward the ruins, wouldn't Ilkovic want to wait at McCoy's car and shoot Coltrane when *he* stalked toward the vehicle?

He felt paralyzed, unable to decide what to do. He wouldn't accomplish anything by returning to the ruins. But he couldn't stay where he was. A sense of déjà vu again possessed him. He was taken back to when he had driven into this valley, hidden his car in this trough, and crept toward McCoy's car, although at the time he had thought that it was Ilkovic's car. He had followed a stream that connected with this one at a right angle. That other stream paralleled the road on which McCoy's car was parked. The stream and the road were thirty yards away from each other. Retreating from the crest of the trough, heading to the right, Coltrane approached the other stream as he had done earlier—with the major differences that now dusk was setting in and the stream's gully was swollen with rain. This time, he couldn't hurry along the bottom. He had to ease up the side and shift along the muddy incline.

He unbuttoned his soaked shirt, shoved the walkie-talkie under it, and rebuttoned the shirt. With his left hand free, he could now better balance himself and hold the shotgun as he proceeded cautiously along the side of the gully.

The rising stream licked at his mud-caked sneakers. His feet felt cold, the tips of his fingers numb. Inching higher to get away from the stream, reaching the limit of where he could crouch and still not be seen from McCoy's car, he counted his steps, trying to calculate when he had gone a hundred yards. Just to be certain, he went a little farther, but his mounting sense of urgency finally compelled him to stop and peer over the top of the gully.

He couldn't see the car. As the rain increased and the air became grayer, he wiped water from his eyes and stared harder, but he still couldn't see it. Is it farther away than I guessed? Did I go too far?

Easing over the rim, pressing himself flat, he crawled through mud, using his elbows for traction, keeping his hands and the shotgun they held out of the water. The revolver under his belt and the

175

walkie-talkie under his shirt gouged against his stomach, but he hardly noticed the pain, too intent on what was before him.

After squirming forward for what he estimated was ten yards, he saw a vague hulking shape in the wavering curtain of the storm. McCoy's car. To his left. He had indeed gone past it while he made his way along the gully. Adjusting his direction, trying not to make noise in the mud, he crawled toward it.

He stopped as the vehicle became more distinct. He was about fifteen yards from the car's left-rear fender. There wasn't any sign of Ilkovic behind the car or on this side. But that didn't mean he wasn't on the *other* side.

Changing direction, Coltrane kept a distance and warily maneuvered around the back of the vehicle. All the while, he strained to see beneath it. If Ilkovic was hiding on the other side, his legs might be visible through the gap underneath. But the myriad splashes of rain made it impossible for Coltrane to see anything that close to the ground. Cautious, he reached a place where he had a view of the opposite side of the car. Still no sign of Ilkovic.

Coltrane dared to hope.

But what if Ilkovic is *inside* the car? I can't just keep lying in the rain. McCoy needs help. Rising to a crouch, he braced himself to run toward the car. When he reached the rear window, he planned to aim the shotgun and blast the backseat, spraying it with buckshot. If Ilkovic was inside, that would be his likely hiding place. If he *wasn't* in the car, the blast from the shotgun would bring him running, but not before Coltrane could rush into the car, start it, and escape.

Mustering his nerve, Coltrane couldn't help worrying that the car wouldn't be able to get traction in the mud. He never got the chance to find out.

The car burst into flames.

15

IT DIDN'T SO MUCH EXPLODE AS ERUPT, fire spewing from the gas tank, engulfing the car. With a grotesque *whooshing* sound, a wall of heat struck Coltrane and thrust him backward, the flames so powerful that the storm was powerless to extinguish them.

No! Coltrane's mind wailed. Stumbling farther back, he turned his singed face from the fire, desperate for the rain to cool his skin. The flames turned dusk into day. The fire exposed him. He had to race for cover, to reach the protection of the gully. Scrambling into it, almost sliding into the raging stream, he pressed his stomach against the mud and peered over the gully's rim.

From somewhere beyond the fire and the curtain of rain, Ilkovic's laughter rumbled toward him. "Photographer, did you honestly think I'd let you get away with something so obvious? Do you think I'm that stupid?"

Where *is* he? Coltrane thought desperately.

The car's metal hissed as rain poured through the flames.

"Did you think this would end so easily?" Ilkovic shouted. "You have no idea how many ways I can prolong this! By the time I'm finished, you're going to beg me to kill you!"

Coltrane concentrated to hear where the shouts were coming from. Ilkovic seemed to be moving from the area behind the burning car to somewhere on the right.

The car's metal hissed more loudly, the rain subduing the flames.

"I tried to reach you on your walkie-talkie! Have you switched it off?"

Coltrane felt it pressing against his stomach.

"Turn it back on, photographer! So we don't have to shout at each other!"

But I'm not the one who's shouting, Coltrane thought. What's he up to? Is he trying to distract me?

Except for the impact of the rain, the rush of the stream behind him, and the diminishing hiss of the car as the flames lessened, Coltrane heard nothing. Ilkovic's last shout had come from the right. *Is he trying to trick me into thinking he's headed in that direction? Now that he quit shouting, is he going to reverse direction and come at me from the left?*

The flames were completely out. Smoke from the gutted car contributed to the deepening dusk. The stench of gasoline, melted plastic, and scorched metal flared Coltrane's nostrils.

Which direction will he use? Coltrane repeated to himself. *Right or left?* Fear made him feel so helpless that he could understand why an animal, caught in the glare of swiftly approaching headlights, didn't flee from the tire that crushed it.

Which way? he demanded. He aimed quickly to the left and then the right. *I can't just wait here until he makes his move!*

Choosing what he hoped was the least likely direction in which Ilkovic would expect him to go, Coltrane squirmed from the gully and headed straight ahead toward the cover of the burned-out car. Toward the camouflage of its smoke. The closer he got, the more he felt the lingering heat from the extinguished fire. The smoke had been dispersed somewhat by the rain, but not enough to stop irritating his nostrils. As he entered it, he tried to keep his face down and breathe shallowly.

Throughout, the walkie-talkie continued to gouge at his stomach. Stopping near the gutted car, he unbuttoned his shirt, pulled out the walkie-talkie, and switched it on. A faint crackle told him that the battering it had received hadn't damaged it. He pressed the transmit button. "Ilkovic, let's end this face-to-face. Let's do it now!"

He released the transmit button, set the walkie-talkie near the gutted car, and backed away.

"Photographer." Ilkovic's guttural voice crackled from the walkie-talkie. "You keep forgetting to say 'Over.'"

Coltrane continued to crawl away.

"You want me to break your body with my fists? Is that the punishment you think you deserve? Your lack of imagination disappoints me. I have so many more inventive methods in mind."

Coltrane was far enough that he could no longer see the walkie-talkie. In the gathering gloom, the static-ridden voice was almost ghostly.

At once, it fell silent.

Coltrane slithered into a depression filled with water. The ground had been so seared by the brush fire that it had formed a nonabsorbent shell. The rain was filling it. Immersing himself in the greasy pool, he allowed only his arms and head to be exposed. Resting the shotgun on a rock, he aimed toward where he had left the walkie-talkie.

Static crackled.

Ilkovic can use that sound to figure out where I'm hiding. That's why he wanted me to keep the walkie-talkie on.

Coltrane eased his right index finger into the shotgun's trigger guard.

Static crackled.

He must be pressing the transmit button on and off, creating noise without giving his own position away by speaking.

Coltrane braced his finger against the shotgun's trigger. From the force of the rain, the smoke had now completely dispersed. But the burned-out car remained obscured, the storm darkening, the wind intensifying. As the pool in which Coltrane lay deepened, he ignored the pressure of the rising water and focused his attention on where he had set the walkie-talkie near the gutted car. Every murky detail appeared magnified. Soon Ilkovic's shadowy figure would creep into view and—

Static crackled.

That's it, Ilkovic. Keep listening for that sound. Get closer. Surprise me where you think I'm hiding next to the car.

The shock of surprise was total. From behind, powerful hands grabbed him, yanking him from the pool. Coltrane was so overwhelmed that his finger jerked on the shotgun's trigger, discharging the weapon, spewing a blast of buckshot harmlessly into the storm. The hands, which had grabbed his shoulders, released him for the fraction of an instant Ilkovic needed to reach under Coltrane's armpits and across his chest, the hands grasping each other, muscular arms squeezing against Coltrane's rib cage.

Coltrane's feet were off the ground. He struggled to breathe. The fierce noise of the shot had battered his eardrums. A terrible ringing in them added to his confusion, but he was still able to hear Ilkovic's labored grunting as he squeezed harder against Coltrane's chest.

"Is that what you had in mind, photographer?" Ilkovic murmured against Coltrane's right ear, his breath so close that Coltrane felt it on his skin.

Coltrane fought for air. His vision became gray, spots of red dancing.

"This is only the start," Ilkovic murmured intimately against Coltrane's neck. "I'll take you close to death a hundred times before you finally bore me."

Grunting harder, he increased the pressure against Coltrane's ribs.

I'm going to pass out, Coltrane thought in dismay. He had kept his grip on the shotgun, but the weapon was useless unless he worked the pump to eject the used shell and chamber a fresh one. He tried. He didn't have the leverage. His arms no longer had the strength. Even if he did manage to pump a fresh shell into the firing chamber, he wouldn't be able to aim at Ilkovic behind him.

Dropping the shotgun, Coltrane gripped his hands over Ilkovic's and strained to pry them free, but Ilkovic's thick fingers were like steel bands welded together. Coltrane couldn't budge them. More red dots swirled in his vision as Ilkovic's relentless arms tightened.

No! Coltrane jerked his head back as hard as he could, hoping that the rear of his skull would strike Ilkovic's face with enough force to stun him and make him loosen his grip. But Coltrane was the one who was stunned. Instead of striking flesh and bone, his skull hit something metallic that had two round surfaces, its sharp edges gouging his scalp. He moaned in pain. A mask? His panicked thoughts weren't able to identify the object. As his strength drained, he kicked his heels behind him toward Ilkovic's legs, but they hit a slippery rubber rain slicker that Ilkovic was wearing, the impact absorbed.

McCoy's revolver. Frenzied, Coltrane drew it from beneath his belt. Feeling the mud that covered it, hoping that it wouldn't be jammed, that it wouldn't backfire, he raised it, aimed it over his left shoulder, and felt it fly from his awkward grasp as Ilkovic released his left hand and yanked the weapon away, throwing it into the mud. Throughout, Ilkovic's right arm was so powerful that he continued to maintain his suffocating grip on Coltrane's chest.

But not completely. For an instant, while Ilkovic's left hand was occupied with the revolver, the pressure lessened just enough for Coltrane to manage a gasp of air. It was one of the most purifying sensations he had ever known, erasing the spots in his vision, clearing his thoughts enough for him to remember he had another weapon. As Ilkovic's left arm snapped back into position around Coltrane's chest, Coltrane lowered his left hand, fumbled in his jeans pocket, took out McCoy's knife, used his weakening right hand to open the blade, and mustered his remaining energy to stab the backs of Ilkovic's interlocked hands again and again. The blade slashed and tore and shredded. Hot liquid spewed over Coltrane's plunging fist.

Ilkovic screamed. Releasing his grip, he stumbled back, wailing. Coltrane dropped to the mud. Landing on his knees, he gasped to fill his lungs. His crushed ribs didn't want to respond. He couldn't inhale fast enough to replenish his strength.

Howling, Ilkovic grasped his mangled hands and cursed. At last, Coltrane was able to see him. But the top of Ilkovic's face was covered not with a mask, but with a device that resembled the eyes of a giant insect. Night-vision goggles. Ilkovic had been using them to track Coltrane in the gathering gloom. With the hood of his camouflage rain slicker pulled up over his head and with the huge twin lenses of the goggles projecting from beneath the hood's drooping folds, Ilkovic looked monstrous. Furious, he charged.

Coltrane dove to the side a moment before Ilkovic's heavy-soled shoe would have collided with his groin. Rolling through the mud, Coltrane tried to keep the knife's blade away from his own body, the weapon suddenly feeling puny against the massive force raging toward him. Coltrane's photographs had shown how imposingly solid Ilkovic looked. But in person, he exuded a raw power that was awesome.

As Ilkovic kicked again, Coltrane scrambled to avoid the blow, feeling the rush of Ilkovic's shoe barely miss him. He almost tripped over the shotgun, grabbed it, spun, and found Ilkovic straightening from where he had picked up McCoy's revolver.

Coltrane aimed the shotgun and pulled the trigger. Nothing happened.

"You didn't pump a shell into the chamber, photographer." Ilkovic aimed toward Coltrane's left shoulder.

Helpless, Coltrane watched him pull the trigger.

But the revolver was jammed with mud.

Instead of firing, it blew apart.

Ilkovic stood as if paralyzed, staring through his grotesque goggles at his explosion-mangled hand. Mouth stretched open in a silent wail, he looked dumbfounded.

Coltrane moved as deliberately as if he had been adjusting the focus and shutter speed of a camera prior to taking a photograph. He racked a shell into the chamber, checked that the shotgun's barrel wasn't clogged, aimed, and blew Ilkovic's head off.

SEVEN

I

A CHAOS OF EMOTIONS THREATENED TO TEAR COLTRANE APART: relief, horror, triumph, dismay, victory, revulsion. Sinking to his knees, staring down in shock toward the headless torso that had been Ilkovic, he had a terrible sense that the corpse was actually that of his father. But this time, his father hadn't blown his brains out— Coltrane had done it for him.

"Thank God," he murmured. Tears mixed with the rain on his cheeks. "Thank God."

Immediately, fear reinvaded him. He had to get help for McCoy. But with McCoy's car destroyed, there wasn't any way to drive back to the Pacific Coast Highway. He would have to do it on foot. Ten miles away along a mud-slogged road. It would take hours. McCoy would bleed to death by then.

Despite his exhaustion, Coltrane struggled to his feet, but no sooner did he start to run toward the storm-obscured hills than he lurched to a halt, a sudden thought seizing him. There *was* a way to drive for help. He had forgotten there was another vehicle— Ilkovic's. If he could find where . . .

Coltrane stared toward the headless corpse. Something rose in his throat as he took one hesitant step after another. Stooping, afraid that Ilkovic's mangled hands would thrust up and clutch his throat, Coltrane trembled and pulled up Ilkovic's rain slicker. He had been convinced that the worst was over, that there couldn't be anything more horrifying than what he had just endured, but now he realized how wrong he had been. Touching Ilkovic's warm corpse, fumbling in his pants pockets, feeling his spongy flesh beneath his wet garment, Coltrane became so light-headed, his mind reeling, that he feared he was going to pass out. His quivering fingers brushed against a set of keys. He tightened his grip and pulled his hand free, squeezing the keys rigidly in his palm lest he lose them as he slumped onto his hips, fighting not to throw up.

Slowly, he wiped his mouth and straightened. Find the car, he urged himself. Where would Ilkovic have left it? Coltrane had heard McCoy drive into the valley—but he hadn't heard *Ilkovic's* car. Did that mean Ilkovic had left it on the ridge above the valley? The trajectory of his bullets had indicated that at the start he was shooting from up there. Had he abandoned his vehicle and come down on foot?

Go! Coltrane inwardly shouted. You have to get help for McCoy!

Running through the dark rain, doing his best to follow the road, he felt the muddy ground angle upward, his lungs heaving, his legs straining. The effort of his ordeal had so drained him that he wavered as he reached the top. Where would Ilkovic have left the car? Not on the ridge, not where Coltrane could have seen it from below. Farther beyond the ridge. Near the road. Ilkovic wouldn't have wanted to get too far from his escape route.

Coltrane slammed into the hood of the vehicle before he saw it. The startling impact shocked him backward, his knees, thighs, and lower abdomen in pain. But he didn't have time to let his further injuries slow him down. His thoughts were totally on McCoy. Grabbing the driver's door of what he now recognized was a dark van, he tugged, cursed when the door didn't budge, fumbled to unlock it, and finally scrambled up behind the steering wheel. It took his shaking right hand three tries to fit the key into the ignition switch. Starting the van, putting it into gear, he warned himself to go slowly. Don't get stuck in the mud. He put on the headlights and made a slow, gentle turn, praying as he felt the tires slip in the wet earth. But they gained traction, and he exhaled when the van completed its arc. Starting back through the hills toward the Pacific Coast Highway, he pawed at the levers on the steering wheel and found how to activate the windshield wipers. Throughout, he was conscious of a terrible odor, but with so many activities occupying his attention, it was only when he was on his way that the rank stench in the van fully struck him. It reminded him of rotten meat, and he suddenly knew, his soul frozen, that the rear of the van was where Ilkovic had butchered Daniel.

2

POLICE RADIOS SQUAWKED. The headlights of numerous emergency vehicles pierced the night gloom of the valley, their crisscross pattern creating a sense of being in a maze. The storm had diminished to a drizzle, its din no longer muffling the drone of idling police cars. Although Coltrane had warned the state trooper whose cruiser he had nearly run off the highway that the stream would be too high and fast for an ambulance to get across, the officer had radioed for one, regardless. Now its white outline, haloed by the glare of headlights, stayed fifty yards behind McCoy's gutted car, amid the other emergency vehicles, all of them trying to remain far enough away that they wouldn't contaminate the crime scene.

On the opposite side of the stream, across which Coltrane had again made his way no matter the risk, a medevac helicopter hovered, its whirling rotors creating a high-pitched whine, its searchlights aimed toward the charred ruins of the western town. Those lights forced Coltrane to shield his eyes as he sat in a puddle among jumbled scorched timbers, cradling McCoy's listless body where he had pulled it gently from its makeshift hiding place. McCoy's body was cold; Coltrane wrapped his arms around him, desperate to warm him. "You're going to be all right. They're going to take care of you."

McCoy made no response. His only motion was a slight rise and fall of his chest.

"Don't die on me, McCoy. You've got help now. You're going to be fine."

The young state policeman, who had at first tried to keep Coltrane from entering the swollen stream and who had in the end followed him, waved to the helicopter, motioning for it to set down next to the ruins. The reflection of the chopper's searchlights gleamed off the red cross on the side of the white fuselage.

Coltrane hugged McCoy, doing his best to transfer his body heat. The medevac attendants jumped out, stooped to avoid the whirling rotors, and ran toward the ruins, mud splashing their white uniforms. In less than two minutes, while Coltrane described the gunshot, they rigged up an IV line and an oxygen mask. As much as Coltrane was eager for McCoy to be rushed to a hospital, he felt an odd sense of separation when the attendants eased McCoy onto a stretcher and hurried with him to the chopper. The noise of the rotors changed from a whine to a roar as the chopper lifted off. Coltrane stared upward, waiting until the chopper's searchlights were extinguished and he could barely hear the receding *whump-whump-whump* before he turned to the state policeman, who told him yet again that there were many people with an awful lot of questions for him.

By then, the police had rigged safety lines across the swollen stream, allowing investigators to cross toward the ruins. The peripheral glare from their flashlights revealed their stark wet faces, their annoyance about their useless rain gear changing to bewilderment and then astonishment as Coltrane explained what had happened. A part of him warned that he ought to wait until he had the advice of an attorney, but he told himself that he didn't have anything to hide. Requesting an attorney would only make it seem that he *did* have something to hide. If Coltrane's original plan had worked and he had managed to ambush Ilkovic, that would have been another matter, he knew. But McCoy's presence had changed everything. Coltrane couldn't imagine any law-enforcement officer or district attorney wanting to arrest and prosecute someone who had risked his life defending a wounded FBI agent. So, their amazement growing, Coltrane walked them through it, showing them his disabled car and the tires that Ilkovic had shot out. He showed them where he had hidden McCoy among the charred timbers. He took them back to and across the stream, to where McCoy had been shot and where Ilkovic had later set off an incendiary device in McCoy's car. All the while, the investigators were trying to preserve the crime scene, keeping a distance from the already-existing foot marks in the mud. As cameras flashed repeatedly, Coltrane couldn't help thinking that everything was twisted around—*he* should be taking the photographs; he shouldn't be the reason the photographs were being taken.

"Who *was* he?" A state police lieutenant pointed toward the body.

"Dragan Ilkovic." Coltrane explained about Bosnia, about Daniel, Greg, and Coltrane's grandparents.

"This guy killed an LAPD detective?"

"I hope his fingerprints are on record somewhere," one of the medical examiner's team said in the background. "It's going to be hard as hell to identify him without a . . ."

Then the photographers were finished, and somebody set down planks so the investigators could get closer to Ilkovic's body without making new tracks in the mud. Coltrane wasn't sure when Nolan and Jennifer had arrived. As he turned from answering more questions, he suddenly saw them making their way through the glare of headlights and flashlights. He prepared to start reexplaining, but the first thing Nolan did was introduce himself to the officer in charge, and the first thing Jennifer did was peer from Coltrane toward Ilkovic's corpse and take a shocked step backward.

At once, Nolan was gripping Coltrane's arm, tugging him away. Nolan's burly shoulders were rigid with anger. "Looks like you got a little lost, forgot where the house was. *Where you were supposed to meet us.* Just what the hell are you doing here?"

"There was a slight change of plan," Coltrane said.

"You led Ilkovic out here to try to kill him."

"Did I?"

"You think a grand jury's going to believe you didn't set this up?"

Coltrane shrugged wearily. "You're right. I did come out here to kill him."

"You admit it?"

"But then McCoy showed up, and we talked about it, and he convinced me I was wrong. But I never got the chance to leave—because that's when Ilkovic shot McCoy. After that, it was self-defense."

Nolan stared at him for the longest while. "That's your story."

"That's my story."

"You better hope McCoy pulls through to verify what you just told me."

"I hope he pulls through, no matter what."

"Just the right tone of sincerity. It might work. I think you might actually get away with this."

"I'm not getting away with anything," Coltrane said. "That son of a bitch shot McCoy. If not for me, McCoy would have died out here."

"If not for you, my friend, McCoy wouldn't have been here at all."

Coltrane didn't have an answer for that.

The state police lieutenant interrupted. "We're going to have to take you back to headquarters and get your statement."

Coltrane nodded. "Can I have a minute to talk to . . ." He pointed toward Jennifer, who was glancing around in dismay, totally disoriented.

The lieutenant didn't look happy. "I don't want you talking to anybody who isn't associated with this investigation—not until we're finished. If she's involved in this, you're not the only one who wants to talk to her."

The next thing, Coltrane was getting into one cruiser and a policeman was escorting Jennifer to another. The vehicles, followed by Nolan's, struggled up the muddy slope, tires slipping, drizzle glistening in the gleam of headlights.

3

AT 2:00 A.M., after five hours of questions, the state police finally told Coltrane that he could go home. "But keep us informed about anyplace you might be, and don't leave the Los Angeles area."

They had replaced Coltrane's soaked, filthy, blood-covered clothes with a pair of coveralls.

"I'll get these back to you," he said.

"You'll have plenty of opportunity. You'll be seeing us often enough."

Outside the interrogation room, Coltrane found Jennifer on a wooden bench in the hallway. Her short blond hair, still wet from the rain, was pressed against her head. Her discouraged gaze was directed toward the gray-tiled floor. She glanced up and barely nodded as he came out.

"Ready to go?" he asked.

"Yeah, they told me it would be okay." Dejected, Jennifer stood. "Sergeant Nolan's around here somewhere. He said he'd give us a ride back to Los Angeles . . . Mitch . . ."

"What?"

"Why in God's name did you . . ."

Nolan came down the hallway.

Most of the hour drive back was in silence.

"You're lucky. They told me they're probably going to buy what you're selling," Nolan finally said.

"I'm not selling anything."

"As long as McCoy backs you up, which you're lucky about also, because the word from the hospital is that he's going to pull through."

Thank heaven, Coltrane thought.

"Of course, you'll still have to convince the grand jury," Nolan said. "But for the time being, you've got a break from the state police. Not you and I, though. We're not finished. If I wasn't so tired, I'd take you over to the Threat Management office right now. Tomorrow, you're going to come over and explain to me why you think you're so damned much better than me that you can jerk me around."

"I'm sorry. That wasn't my intention."

"Save it for tomorrow."

"There's something I have to do first. After that, I'm all yours."

"Something you have to do? Put it off. Believe me, there's nothing more important than—"

"Yes, there is. Daniel's funeral."

The car became silent again.

"Yeah, go to the funeral," Nolan said. "I'll see you there. Greg's is the day after. I'll see you there, too. Not that there's anything left of Greg to bury."

"My grandparents' funeral will probably be the day after that."

"Maybe we ought to give you a medal for shooting the son of a bitch."

They drove another mile in silence.

"Where do I drop you? Your place or Packard's?" Nolan asked.

"The airport."

Nolan visibly tensed. "You're not supposed to leave the area."

"The America West parking garage. I left my car there Saturday night."

In the middle of the night, the access to the airport was almost deserted. Nolan stopped outside the parking garage.

Coltrane opened his door. "I'll meet you at your office at four."

"I know you will."

Coltrane waited for Jennifer to get out with him.

She didn't.

"Something the matter?" Coltrane asked.

"Sergeant, since we're in the neighborhood, would you take me to my apartment in Marina del Rey?"

Nolan frowned toward her and then at Coltrane.

4

AT ALMOST 4:00 A.M., Coltrane's street was quiet, his Westwood town house in darkness. His headlights reflected off puddles. Reluctant to be closed in by the garage, he parked at the curb and climbed the wet steps to his concrete patio. The air was cool enough to make him shiver. He kept telling himself that Ilkovic was really dead, that the police had checked his town house for explosives, that he had nothing to be afraid of. All the same, as he inserted his key in the front door, he felt uneasy.

He reached inside and flicked a light switch, illuminating the living room before he entered. The furniture was in disarray from the bomb squad's search, but the disorder that troubled him was the empty bottle of chardonnay on the coffee table, as well as three wineglasses, two of them half-full, on the counter next to the telephone. They were from Saturday afternoon, when he had celebrated with Jennifer and Daniel, showing them his photographs—just before Ilkovic's phone call had forced them to set down their glasses. Saturday afternoon. It seemed impossible that Daniel had been killed since then.

Coltrane locked the door and stepped hesitantly toward one of the wineglasses, the one that was empty, remembering that Daniel had finished his before he and Jennifer finished theirs. The once-sparkly glass had a film of dried liquid. Reverentially, Coltrane picked it up, careful not to touch Daniel's faintly visible fingerprints. He stared at them for the longest time. At last, he set down the glass, went to a cupboard in the kitchen, pulled out a bottle of Wild Turkey, and drank three long swallows straight from the bottle's mouth. Gasping, he set it down, the fire in his throat and stomach not strong enough to distract him from his emotions.

He climbed the stairs to his bedroom, which was also in disarray because of the bomb squad. After stripping off the coveralls, he went into the bathroom and took the longest shower he could ever recall, repeatedly soaping his hair and body, rinsing, soaping, scouring himself, trying to rid himself of the lingering feel of death. Despite the bruises on his legs, chest, and arms, he toweled himself roughly until his skin was raw. He had come here to get extra clothes and other things he would need for Packard's house. But all of a sudden he felt too exhausted to go there. He stripped the covers from the bed, intensely aware that Ilkovic had been in this room and touched them. He dragged a sheet and blanket from a hallway closet and spread them over the bare mattress. He programmed his bedside clock to wake him at 9:00 A.M., turned off the lights, crawled wearily between the sheet and the blanket, and tried to sleep.

5

THE JANGLE OF THE TELEPHONE ROUSED HIM FROM A RESTLESS, anxious semiconsciousness in which arms seemed to squeeze his chest and rain had the color of blood. Dazed, he directed his bleary vision toward the bedside clock. A little after six. He decided it must be Jennifer or Nolan or the state police.

"Hello?"

"Mr. Coltrane?"

Coltrane didn't recognize the voice. "Who wants to know?"

"I'm a reporter for the *L.A. Times.* I'd like to—"

No sooner had Coltrane hung up than the phone rang again.

The next reporter was from the Associated Press.

Coltrane unplugged the phone in the bedroom, but the phone downstairs rang almost immediately, and by the time Coltrane got downstairs to unplug that one, he heard a man's voice on the answering machine identifying himself as a reporter for *Newsweek*, asking him to describe details about—

Coltrane pulled the plug.

He knew what was coming. Fighting his cramped muscles and his exhaustion, he hurried upstairs, put on a navy blazer and gray slacks, packed two suitcases with clothes, slung a camera bag over his shoulder, and managed to get outside, to drive away a few seconds before a TV news truck sped past him. In his rearview mirror, he saw it pull up in front of his town house.

There were *three* TV news trucks at the church in Burbank when he got there a little before one. Keeping a distance from each other, identical-looking, attractive, stern-eyed women wearing business suits spoke into microphones, their backs to the church while cameramen recorded the mourners filing in. Coltrane couldn't help wondering if any photographs he had taken had ever interfered with someone's grief. Now he knew what it felt like to be on the other side. After parking his car in a lot behind the church, he debated whether to risk going in, then decided that the TV news team couldn't know what he looked like—to the best of his knowledge, no photograph of him had ever been published.

So he took the chance. Jennifer was already in the church when he entered. She wore a black dress and veil. The latter didn't quite conceal how weary her features were. Sitting next to her, apparently surprising her, Coltrane nodded. She nodded somberly back, looked as if she was about to say something, then turned toward the pallbearers carrying Daniel's coffin down the center aisle toward the altar. Daniel's ex-wife, supported by an elderly man who might have been her father, sobbed and followed the coffin, her footsteps unsteady. After the coffin was set on a bier and Daniel's ex-wife took her place in a front pew, a priest accompanied by altar boys came out to begin the Mass for the Dead. Coltrane couldn't help remembering the mournful classical music that Ilkovic had repeatedly left on his answering machine: Verdi's Requiem.

The day of wrath, the day of anger,
will dissolve the world in ashes. . . .
How horrid a trembling there will be
when the judge appears
and all things are scattered.

Well, Ilkovic, damn you, you're the one being judged now.

The priest gave a eulogy in which he alluded to Milton's *Paradise Lost* and how one of the hardest acts of faith was to justify God's ways to human beings. "When something this incomprehensible occurs, we find ourselves powerless and adrift. What kind of God would permit such savagery? What kind of universe presents the conditions in which something this horrid can happen? We are tested to our utmost limits. Tested," the priest emphasized. "If we are to persevere, we must not turn our backs on God. We must not turn our backs on the world. What we must hate and turn our backs on is the evil that we were put on earth to overcome."

Turn our backs? Coltrane thought. I don't think so. Daniel, I got even for you.

After the service, Coltrane accompanied Jennifer from the church. "Can you wait here a minute?" He went over to Daniel's ex-wife, embraced her, and explained how sorry he was. Perhaps on medication, she didn't seem to hear. Nolan, who evidently had been in the back of the church, watched from the side of the steps. After exchanging glances with him, Coltrane made his way back through the mourners, most of whom he recognized from various times when he had visited Daniel at the hospital.

"Are you okay?" he asked Jennifer.

"No."

"I'm sorry," Coltrane said.

"For what? *You* didn't kill Daniel."

"For what you had to go through."

"What *I'm* sorry about," Jennifer said, "is that you didn't tell me what you were planning to do. You shut me out."

"I didn't want to put you in danger."

"You still shut me out. You didn't trust me enough to tell me what you were doing. You treated me like a stranger. But *you're* a stranger. I would never have believed you were capable of . . ."

Coltrane glanced away, self-conscious.

"I'm a stranger to *myself*," Jennifer said.

"What do you mean?"

"That argument we had about guns. Now that Ilkovic is dead, I feel like a coward."

"I don't understand."

"I wish *I'd* had the chance to blow the bastard's head off."

Coltrane was shocked.

"I've never been this confused," Jennifer said.

Coltrane touched her arm. "After we go to the grave site, do you want to get some lunch and talk about it?"

"No."

"You want a little time alone?"

"Yes. These past few days, we've been together a lot. Sometimes it's possible to have too much of a good thing. Different, huh? *Me* wanting to be alone?"

Coltrane spread his hands in a gesture of futility. Abruptly he was

194

distracted by a commotion at the edge of the crowd. Evidently someone had identified him to the news teams, because they were swarming in his direction.

Pursued by cameramen, he barely reached the parking lot ahead of them.

6

FIFTEEN MINUTES FROM THE CEMETERY, Coltrane swerved into yet another narrow alley, checking his rearview mirror, satisfying himself that the TV news trucks no longer followed him.

He drove to where he had waited throughout the morning until it was time to go to Daniel's funeral, to where he felt confident that the news teams wouldn't be able to find him—because *Ilkovic* hadn't been able to find him there. In the maze of streets in the Hollywood Hills, cresting a tree-lined slope, he peered down at his sanctuary. After everything he had been through, the house's castlelike appearance made him feel secure. The green-tinted copper on the garage door reminded him even more of a fortress, as did the two upper levels, each with a parapet.

Because the garage door's remote control was in the disabled rental car that he had abandoned the night before, he parked at the curb. It was an odd sensation to feel free to leave his vehicle in the open and not be afraid that someone would try to kill him. Exhausted, he secured the front door behind him, peered up the stairs toward the sun-bright living room, then moved in the opposite direction, down toward the vault.

It was where he had gone when he had arrived earlier, where he had spent the morning waiting to go to Daniel's funeral. After what he had been through, the vault no longer seemed repellent. Indeed, he wondered why it had ever seemed that way to begin with. Needing something to occupy him, he knew without doubt what that something would be. Determined to shut out his nightmares, he un-locked the vault and passed the gray metal shelves, reaching the far left corner. The glaring overhead lights no longer seemed harsh. The fifty-five-degree air no longer made him shiver. The concrete walls no longer seemed to close in on him. He reached toward the back of the shelving, freed the catches on each side, and pulled out the wall.

Again, the incredibly beautiful face gazed out at him. The vault's light spilled into the hidden chamber, casting a glow over the pic-ture, making the woman seem alive. He stepped closer, admiring the perfect geometry of her face, the elegant chin, curved lips, high cheeks, and almond-shaped eyes. Her lush black hair framed her features alluringly. Her brilliant white shawl made her dark eyes magical.

His mouth dry, Coltrane picked up one of the boxes and carried it out to the shelves. After removing the lid, he carefully took out one eight-by-ten photograph after another, studying them, setting them along the shelves, picking up new ones. He lingered over a close-up in which her eyes gazed so directly into his that she gave the allusion of being in the present. He couldn't tell what filled him with greater awe: Packard's genius or his subject. He had never seen any woman so entrancing.

"Mitch?"

The voice came from beyond the vault.

Coltrane flinched.

"Mitch, it's Duncan Reynolds."

In a rush, Coltrane crossed toward the open door.

"Mitch?"

He heard Duncan coming down the steps, and he left the vault, closing the door a moment before Duncan could have peered in. That was when Coltrane realized he had no intention of telling Duncan about the photographs.

7

I SAW YOUR CAR OUTSIDE." Duncan put away his key. "I'm surprised I caught up to you. I brought this for you, but I expected I'd have to leave it here, rather than be able to give it to you in person."

Wondering about the box he was handed, Coltrane tried not to look uneasy about his departure from the vault. He didn't want Duncan to suspect that he was hiding something. "A telephone with a built-in answering machine?"

"The service is still hooked up. Now I won't have so hard a time getting in touch with you about the details of buying this house."

"Well, I've been a little busy," Coltrane said.

"So I found out when I turned on the television this morning. You certainly did a good job of hiding your nerves when I met you here on Sunday. Are you hurt?"

"Cuts and bruises."

"The television news made it seem like a nightmare, and *you* seemed like a hero."

"More like a damned fool. I almost got myself killed. I don't want to think about it."

"Yes, the strain shows on your face. I'm sorry for intruding. I've got the purchase agreements for the house and the furniture. We can talk about them another time." Duncan opened his briefcase, handing him documents. "You asked me to find out more about the history of the place."

"Yes?" Coltrane leaned forward.

"I did a title search and learned that in addition to the movie producer who first owned the property—"

"Winston Case." Coltrane remembered the name from a biography about Packard that included background about some of the houses he had photographed.

"That's right. He owned the property from 1931 until 1933, the year Randolph photographed it. Then, from '33 until '35, it was owned by a woman named Rebecca Chance."

"Who?"

"I don't know anything about her. She's a name on a document. She was the only other owner. In the fall of '35, Randolph took possession of the house, buying it through a corporation owned by a corporation owned by a corporation that Randolph inherited from his parents. That sort of secrecy was customary with him. He used the same method to purchase an estate in Mexico, for example, and was equally concerned about maintaining his privacy there. As far as this house is concerned, to my knowledge he never actually lived here."

"And no one else ever occupied it?"

"That's correct, which explains its superb condition. Since no one was here to wear it down, it didn't require much repair. With the exception of the installation of the vault and the darkroom, the house remains the same as when it was built in the thirties."

"Exactly. That's why I'm buying it."

8

IN PHOTOGRAPHY, when unfocused rays of light reflect off an object and strike a negative, they create overlapping blurs known as "circles of confusion." That was how Coltrane felt, trapped in circles of confusion. What are you doing? he asked himself. As he drove through frustratingly dense traffic toward the police administration building in downtown L.A., his mind—no matter how weary— wouldn't let him have any peace. Do you think that if you put yourself in a time frame that goes back far enough, you'll be able to feel as if nobody you love has died?

He thought of the most important object in his life—the photograph of his mother pushing him in the swing at the trailer park.

It was impossible to count the hours that he had spent, both as a child and an adult, staring at that photograph, projecting himself into it, imagining that he was there. Always, the effort had been frustrating, because the woman and the boy in that picture remained frozen in time, whereas *he* continued to get older. He wasn't a participant. He was an observer. He and that boy were no longer the same. And yet the woman was always his mother.

Do you think that if you live in Packard's house the way it was in the thirties, you'll trick yourself into feeling remote from the present, less traumatized by what Ilkovic did to your grandparents and Daniel and Greg? Your problems won't go away. They'll be the same in the past as the present. But the past will raise different problems, intruding on the present.

9

"HAVE YOU ANY IDEA HOW I CAN FIND INFORMATION ABOUT A woman who lived in Los Angeles in the thirties?" Coltrane asked.

Nolan wasn't prepared for a change in topic.

"She owned the house I'm buying," Coltrane explained. "I'm trying to find out some history about the property."

"Haven't you been listening to me?" Nolan asked. "You're barely going to scrape through this and stay out of prison. If I were you, I'd keep my mind on what to tell the grand jury."

"If I keep thinking about Ilkovic, I'll go crazy."

"Well, you're not going to get much of a break from talking about him. The state police want you to drive back up there. They want another heart-to-heart. At six-thirty." Nolan glanced at his watch. "Which gives you ninety minutes."

"They're working late."

"You're a popular guy."

Coltrane rubbed his raw eyes and stood.

"The library has city directories," Nolan said.

"What?"

"For the thirties. She owned the house how long?"

"From '33 until '35."

"Follow her through the directories. Where did she move after she left the house you're buying? See if she's in the '36 listing. Same thing with the phone book. Eventually she'll disappear from the listings—either because she moved to another city or she died. If she died, there'll most likely be an obituary in the *L.A. Times.* Of course, it'll take awhile for you to check all the copies of the newspaper for the year when she no longer appears in the listings, but if it's important to you . . ."

"The house has a colorful past. I'd like to know more about it," Coltrane said.

"With all the problems you have—"

"It's better than thinking about the last few days."

"Can't argue there. What you need is a private investigator." Nolan pulled a business card from a drawer. "Try this guy. He'll need whatever you've got on her, including a photograph."

"I don't have one," Coltrane lied.

10

RETURNING TO PACKARD'S HOUSE NEAR MIDNIGHT, he was so exhausted he could barely keep his eyes open. A glance in his rearview mirror showed him that his second lengthy conversation with the state police had etched deep fatigue lines into his face, as had his insistence that if they had more questions, they were going to have to wait: He was leaving the next day to go to Connecticut for his grandparents' funeral.

He put the car in the garage, locked the house's front door behind him, and finally took halting, weary steps into the living room.

There, he accomplished the monumental task of removing the gray slacks and navy blazer that he had worn to Daniel's funeral so long ago this morning. Tired to the point of dizziness, he sank onto his sleeping bag.

But his mind wouldn't let him rest. Half-formed nightmares made him twitch. The mangled hands of Ilkovic's headless corpse seemed to reach up to choke him. Jerking awake, he strained to see the luminous dial on his watch and exhaled in despair when he discovered that the time was only twenty-five after three. Just keep lying here, he told himself. Close your eyes. You'll soon be asleep again. But his ravaged nervous system refused to obey. Before he left for New Haven, he had to make plane reservations and contact his lawyer about the documents that Duncan had given him. He had to arrange for his accountant to send escrow checks. He had to—

He got up and proceeded through darkness into the dining room and then the kitchen. After turning on a light beneath one of the counters, he found the documents where he had set them next to the stove. He read them and felt that they were straightforward. Had it not been that he wanted to be certain of gaining unquestioned title to the property, he would have signed them right away, without bothering to wait for his lawyer's opinion. Negotiation wasn't an issue. At all costs, he intended to gain possession of this house.

Next to the refrigerator, a blinking red light caught his attention: the combination telephone/answering machine Duncan had given him. Coltrane hoped that it was Jennifer who had called. He regretted the way their conversation had ended at the funeral. He wanted to settle their differences. But then he realized that Jennifer couldn't possibly know the phone number here. It wasn't listed. He himself hadn't known until Duncan gave it to him at the end of today's conversation.

Coltrane pressed the play button. For a moment, he had the irrational fear that Verdi's Requiem would start playing, that Ilkovic's guttural voice would again threaten him, that last night hadn't happened, that his waking nightmare hadn't really ended. But what he heard instead was almost as troubling.

No message at all. Just silence. Then a click.

Only a wrong number, he told himself.

Sure.

He poured water into a glass, but instead of drinking it, he found himself leaving the kitchen. That was how he perceived his action. He didn't choose to leave so much as he discovered that he was doing so. The moment he started, however, he knew where he was going.

It took him no time at all to unlock the vault, pull out the section of shelves, and enter the hidden chamber. After Duncan's visit, he had been careful to put the photographs back and close the wall, lest Duncan—perhaps wondering about what Coltrane had been doing in the vault—might come back to satisfy his curiosity. Again, Coltrane removed the box and took out photograph after photograph, arranging them on shelves, admiring the woman.

When he finally put them away and left the vault, he was surprised to find that the sun had been up for several hours.

11

NEW HAVEN WAS A FOOT OF SNOW, a bitingly cold wind, and a funeral to which almost no one came because most of Coltrane's grandparents' friends had died before them. After listening to the minister's final prayers, he put his gloved hands on each of the coffins and whispered, "Good-bye."

Back at his grandparents' house, he began the long, heart-sinking process of disposing of the accumulation of a lifetime. The telephone rang as he sorted through a shoe box full of receipts.

"How are you feeling?" Jennifer asked.

"About what you'd expect." Snow lancing against the living room window made Coltrane look in that direction.

"I thought I'd call to try to cheer you up."

"I'm glad you did." Coltrane thought he heard Jennifer exhale in what might have been nervous relief.

"A lot of memories to deal with, I bet," Jennifer said.

Coltrane slumped into his grandfather's rocking chair. "I lived here until I was eighteen, until I moved out to Los Angeles to go to college. Last night, I slept upstairs in my old bedroom. The furniture's still the same. In fact, it's even in the same position. The only spot I haven't . . . I keep wanting to go down to where I used to hide in the basement when I was a kid—where I used to think about my mother. But I can't bring myself to look at where"—he could hardly say it—"Ilkovic killed them."

"Are you going to sell the house?"

"No. I ran into some seniors who were friends of my grandparents. One old couple had their rent raised, and they can't afford to live in their apartment anymore. I'm going to let them stay here for free. They said they didn't want charity, so I told them they'd be doing me a favor—that I needed somebody to take care of the place."

"Nice."

"Well"—Coltrane looked at the big Christmas tree in the corner of the living room—"it's that time of year."

"Will you be back for the holiday?"

"I don't think I can manage by then."

"Oh." Jennifer's voice dropped. "I was hoping . . . I'm still having trouble about . . . I don't want to have anything hanging between us. I'm sorry about what I said after Daniel's funeral."

"There's nothing wrong with wanting some time to yourself."

"But I could have picked a better time to say it. I'm still confused, but . . ."

"You're not the only one."

"Maybe I'm ready to talk about it now."

"We'll do that when I get back," Coltrane said.

"Yes. Not on the phone."

"Not on the phone. Have a good holiday."

"Same to you. At least as good as you can. Mitch, I haven't forgotten about the special edition of the magazine. The photographs are still at Packard's house. When you come back . . ."

"I'll make sure you get them."

The snow lanced harder against the front window as Coltrane hung up. He walked to the window and watched dusk thicken. Cars struggled through deepening drifts.

His photographs—they had completely slipped from his mind. It was a measure of how severely things had changed. A week ago, he had been elated about the new direction that his life was taking. He had felt reborn. And now he could barely recall the sense of renewal that had made him excited. Out of habit, he had brought a camera with him, but it remained in one of his suitcases, along with shirts that he hadn't unpacked.

Going into the front hallway, smelling must, he started up the oak staircase. The banister felt wobbly. Or maybe *I* am, he thought. In his bedroom, he opened his suitcase, took out his camera, set it aside, and removed a large manila envelope that he had reinforced with stiff cardboard to make sure that it didn't bend.

The envelope contained a dozen photographs from the chamber in Packard's vault. He spread them out on the bed and stared down at them, directing his gaze from left to right. Dizzily returning to the first, he began again.

And again. The haunting woman looked back at him.

12

She was an actress."

It was four days after Christmas. Coltrane was back in Los Angeles, sitting in the uncluttered office of the private investigator he had hired before going to New Haven.

The man's name was Roberto Rodriguez. Short and slender, with silver sideburns, wearing spectacles and a conservative suit, he looked more like an attorney than a private detective.

"This is a photocopy of the police file. You can keep it."

"Police file?" Coltrane worked to steady his right hand as he opened the file. A faint blotched image on a Xerox of a photograph peered up at him, making him tingle. As imprecise as it was, the image left no doubt. That lush dark hair. Those expressive lips and almond-shaped eyes. He was looking at the woman in Packard's photographs.

He turned the page and frowned at typescript that was hard to read, faded by age and what incomplete portions of characters suggested was an overused typewriter ribbon. "Missing persons department?"

"The complaint was filed by her agent back in 1934," Rodriguez said. "She had a five-year contract with Universal. Nothing major. She certainly wasn't a star, although judging from the photo I used to make that Xerox, she could have been. When she didn't show up for the start of a picture, the studio grumbled to her agent, and the agent realized that he hadn't heard from her in over three months. Which tells you how close they were."

"And?"

"There isn't an 'and.' She was never found."

Coltrane felt a sinking sensation. "But how could Randolph Packard have purchased the house from her if she was never located?"

"Who knows? Maybe after a year she was assumed dead and her parents got permission to put it on the market. Somewhere in that file there's a summary of a telephone interview with them. The detective in charge of the investigation wanted to know if she had ever shown up where they lived in Texas. They claimed they hadn't seen her in four years. Which tells you how close the family was."

Coltrane turned more pages, shaking his head, baffled.

"The detective notes that the family didn't have a phone. The interview took place at the local police station," Rodriguez said. "Add the abundance of *ain'ts* and double negatives, and you get the impression of a down-on-his-luck, undereducated farmer. But his last name isn't Chance. It's Chavez. *The daughter's* first name isn't Rebecca. It's Juanita."

"She changed her name to disguise her Hispanic origins?"

"I love old movies. I love to read about them," Rodriguez said.

"Back in the twenties and thirties, you get *male* stars with ethnic names. Rudolph Valentino and Ramon Novarro come to mind. The studios played up their sultry appearance. But I can't think of more than a few *female* stars—I'm talking major—who didn't have a white-bread appearance and name. That doesn't mean they *were* white-bread. Several of them had ethnic backgrounds, but they hid it. Had to. Rita Hayworth's a good example. She didn't become famous until the forties, but her career started in the thirties. She was Hispanic. Her real name was Margarita Cansino. She had dark hair and a widow's peak that made her look very Spanish at a time when there was a growing prejudice against Mexicans. So she dyed her hair auburn and plucked out her widow's peak to make her hairline look symmetrical. She added some voice lessons to get rid of her accent, changed her name, and managed to assimilate herself. It looks to me like Rebecca Chance did the same."

13

HERE." The reference librarian, a petite young woman in braids, escorted Coltrane into a Spartan room that had several microfilm machines. "When you're finished, please bring the film back to my desk."

"Thanks," Coltrane said.

It had been years since he had used this kind of machine, but his familiarity with it soon came back. After attaching the roll to a spindle on the right at the bottom, he fed the film through the machine and linked it to a spindle on the left. By twisting a knob, he could forward the film past the light that projected and magnified the small print onto the screen. The roll was for all the issues of the *L.A. Times* that had been published during the last quarter of 1934, which, according to the police report Coltrane had brought with him, was when Rebecca Chance, born Juanita Chavez, had disappeared—specifically, during the second week of October. The missing persons' report had been filed on October tenth, two days after she failed to show up for work. That meant Coltrane had only nine issues of the newspaper to spin through before he got to the period of time that interested him, but to give himself some context and to avoid missing any seemingly innocent reference to her earlier, he made an effort not to speed ahead but, rather, to take his time and do the job right.

The headline for the October first issue was about Franklin Roosevelt and the President's efforts to deal with the Depression. A related story described the worsening economic conditions in Los Angeles. International news about fears of a war in Europe were next to a report of a local fire in which five children and two adults had burned to death. If you weren't in a bad mood when you woke up, Coltrane thought, you would be after reading all this.

As the machine's fan whirred, preventing the heat of the bulb from burning the microfilm, Coltrane spooled further on. He paid close attention to the entertainment section in each issue but failed to find any mention of Rebecca Chance. Even when he got to October tenth, the day the police had been told that she was missing, he still didn't find any mention of her. Was the studio keeping her disappearance quiet in order to avoid a scandal? If so, what kind of scandal?

On page eighteen, two days later, October twelfth, he finally found it, "Actress Missing," a story only six inches long that basically summarized what was in the police report. She had failed to report for work at Universal. The studio had grumbled to her agent. The agent had tried to phone her and then had gone to her home, where no one answered. A neighbor said that he hadn't seen any sign of activity in the house, including lights, for at least a week. When police searched the house, they found nothing that appeared to have been disturbed or missing. An assistant director at the studio said that she was always on time and knew her lines—it wasn't like her to fail to be punctual. There weren't any gaps in her clothes closet to indicate that she had packed and gone on an unannounced trip. Foul play was suspected.

A photograph accompanied the article, and Coltrane had the impression that the article might not have been printed at all if Rebecca Chance hadn't been so beautiful. Although the photograph, obviously a studio still, didn't do her the justice that Coltrane knew was possible, he had trouble taking his eyes away from it. The tone of the article wasn't reverential. It didn't treat her as a star. That the small piece was buried in the middle of the newspaper reinforced the impression that this was being considered more a crime story than a show-business one. *Up-and-coming* and *promising* were the words used to describe her. At the end of the article, Coltrane wrote down two titles, the films she had most recently appeared in: *Jamaica Wind* and *The Trailblazer*.

Finishing the issue for October twelfth, he continued to the next day, and the day after that. On page twenty of the latter, Rebecca's photograph, another studio still, immediately caught his attention. It, too, couldn't compare to Packard's amazing depictions of her. Nonetheless, her gaze held his own. When he finally broke away and read the article, he learned that the only hint of progress in the investigation was that an actress friend at Universal had told the police about crank phone calls and obsessive fan mail Rebecca had complained about. The calls and the letters all seemed to have come from the same person, and they were all about the same thing: vows of eternal love. "The 'eternal' part sounded creepy," the actress friend said. Rebecca had apparently thrown the letters away—when the police went back to search her house again, they couldn't find them. The police were speaking to other actresses who might have received similar letters. Other than that, there weren't any leads.

Coltrane leaned back in his rigid wooden chair and rubbed his forehead. The copy of the police report that Rodriguez had given him made no mention of an overinsistent fan. Did that mean the file was incomplete, or did it mean that the police had put no credence in the story the actress friend had told? Perhaps the actress friend hadn't been such a close friend after all; perhaps her only motivation had been to get her name in the newspaper. If the police discounted her claims, would they have mentioned them in their report? This wasn't the only discrepancy Coltrane had noted. The first article had listed Rebecca's age as twenty-two, while the missing persons' file had given her age as twenty-five, a figure supplied by her parents. At the same time, it had *not* mentioned Rebecca Chance's real name. Ohio, and not Texas, was now her home state. All of this suggested to Coltrane that the newspaper hadn't gotten a look at the police report but had received its information through an intermediary, what seemed to Coltrane like a studio publicist who was protecting the studio's investment in her, persisting in its white-bread image of her.

The effort had worked. Coltrane scanned the bold print at the start of every article in every issue on the microfilm, continuing through to the end of the year, feeling an odd sense of time overlapping when he reached December twenty-ninth, the same date as when he now examined the microfilm. There were no further references to the disappearance of Rebecca Chance. He rubbed his eyes, which felt as if sand had fallen into them. Stretching his arms, he glanced at his watch and blinked with shock. A few minutes before six o'clock. He had been here seven hours.

14

"JAMAICA WIND?"

"Yes."

"*The Trailblazer?*"

Coltrane nodded.

"Never heard of them." The purple-haired clerk was about twenty. Videotapes crammed the shelves behind him.

"I'm not surprised. They never heard of them over at Tower Video, either. But they told me that if anybody *would* know how to get a copy of them, it'd be you."

The clerk, who also had a ring through his left nostril, straightened a little, his pride engaged. He pulled Leonard Maltin's *Movie and Video Guide* from beneath the counter and started to leaf through it.

"They had a copy of Maltin's book over at Tower," Coltrane said.

"These movies aren't in it?"

Coltrane shook his head.

"Well, if Maltin doesn't list them, it's a pretty good sign these things have never been shown on TV."

"Except maybe since that edition of the book came out," Coltrane said. "And Maltin himself admits that his book doesn't include every minor film that ever had only a couple of showings at midnight forty years ago."

The clerk, who was wearing an *Edward Scissorhands* T-shirt, pulled another reference book from beneath the desk. This one was called *A Worldwide Filmography*. It was oversized, battered, and thick. He looked through the pages. "*Jamaica Wind*. Yep, it exists."

"I never doubted that."

"Universal, 1934."

"Right."

"Guy Kibbee, William Gargan, Beulah Bondi, Walter Catlett, Rebecca Chance."

Coltrane felt his pulse increase.

"Sounds like a remake of *Rain*," the clerk said.

"What?"

"This is almost the same cast as *Rain*, but without Joan Crawford."

"You really do know your movies."

The clerk, who wore a Mickey Mouse wristwatch, straightened with greater pride. "I try. But I have to tell you—I never heard of this actress here at the end: Rebecca Chance."

"She had a short career."

"What else was she in?"

"That other movie I'm trying to find."

"*The Trailblazer?* Let's have a look." The clerk flipped to near the back of the book. "Yep. Same company. Same year. Bruce Cabot, Hugh Buckler, Heather Angel, Tully Marshall, and . . ." The clerk made a drumroll with his hands. "Rebecca Chance. Now we're getting somewhere. The picture was directed by George B. Seitz."

"Who?"

"A couple of years later, Seitz did *The Last of the Mohicans*. Matter of fact, some of these actors were in that movie."

"You continue to amaze me."

"In this case, it's not so amazing."

The clerk pointed toward a row of film posters above the shelves of videos on the opposite side of the long room. One of them, tinted orange, faded, announced THE LAST OF THE MOHICANS—STAR-RING RANDOLPH SCOTT. Scott, incredibly young, was seen in profile. He held a flintlock rifle and wore a buckskin jacket as well as a coonskin cap. Two Indians fought each other in the background. At the bottom, bold letters proclaimed DIRECTED BY GEORGE B. SEITZ.

"A friend of mine's a George B. Seitz fanatic. He gave me that poster to put up. Personally, I don't get what's so special about Seitz's work. He's sure not Orson Welles. But my friend's an expert. He's the guy to ask."

15

THE FRAIL, distinguished-looking, white-haired, elderly gentleman had a Vandyke beard and a cane. Bundled in a thick brown cardigan sweater, he was waiting at the metal gate of his home in Sherman Oaks when Coltrane parked in front. The expansive Tudor house was high in the hills, the glinting lights of the valley spread out below.

"I didn't realize how late it was," Coltrane said after he shook hands and introduced himself. A cool breeze tugged at his hair. "If I'd thought about it, I never would have let the guy in the video store call you."

The elderly man made a "think nothing of it" gesture. His voice was reedy. "Sidney knows I don't go to bed until two or three in the morning. Anybody who wants to talk about the work of George B. Seitz is welcome anytime."

"Actually, Seitz isn't why I'm here."

The elderly man looked confused.

"What I'm really interested in is an actress he directed in *The Trailblazer.*"

"Which actress?"

"Rebecca Chance."

The elderly man nodded.

"You *know* about her?" Coltrane asked.

"*About* her? Not in the least."

Coltrane felt something deflate inside him. "I guess I've bothered you for nothing. I'm sorry. I won't take up any more of your time."

"But I've seen her work."

Coltrane froze in the act of turning toward his car.

"You came to talk to me about *The Trailblazer.* Don't you think it would be more satisfying if you watched it?"

"*Watched* it?"

"I don't have every picture Seitz made. Many of the silents were on film stock that disintegrated before they could be preserved, although I do have copies of the most famous ones, such as *The Perils of Pauline,* which he wrote before he became a director. The sound pictures he directed are another matter. From *Black Magic* in '29 to *Andy Hardy's Blonde Trouble* in '44, the year Seitz died, I've managed to track down a print of every film Seitz made."

The dignified gentleman, who introduced himself as Vincent Toler, escorted Coltrane into his house, the living room of which had a screen behind retractable oak panels at one end and a projection room adjacent to the opposite end, the two rooms linked via a space behind an Andrew Wyeth painting that slid to the side.

Toler, Coltrane learned, was a widower, a retired neurosurgeon who lived alone. He had hated being a neurosurgeon, he explained. "I never wanted to enter medicine, but my father, who was a doctor, bullied me into doing so. What I really wanted was to work in the movies. In what capacity, I had no idea. I just knew that was what I loved, but my father wouldn't hear of it, and I wasn't brave enough to stand up to him." After Toler retired, he had happened to see an Andy Hardy movie on the American Movie Classics channel, had remembered the delight with which he had watched it as a boy, had reexperienced the same delight, and had noticed when viewing the movie on its next AMC showing that the director was George B. Seitz.

That name had meant nothing to him, but when he asked the clerk at a video store he frequented (the same video store to which Coltrane had gone) to find other movies that Seitz had directed, Toler had been delighted to discover that Seitz had directed almost all the Andy Hardy movies and many other movies that Toler recalled fondly from his youth. "I started collecting videos, but some of Seitz's movies weren't available on video, so the next step was . . ." Toler indicated the reel of film that he was attaching to the projector. "It's been an interesting hobby. You could say that I'm collecting my youth."

As he finished setting up, Toler explained that Seitz had invented the cliffhanger serial in 1914 and had eventually switched to feature films in 1925, making westerns, mysteries, crime melodramas, and comedies. "He was a professional. His pictures were on schedule and underbudget. More important, he knew how to entertain."

Settling into a plush chair, Coltrane was surprised that his anticipation of seeing Rebecca Chance move and speak was making him uneasy. After Toler turned off the lights and then turned on the projector, tinny epical music, evocative of rivers, plains, and mountains, obscured the projector's whir. Simultaneously, a beam of light hit the screen, showing a brilliant black-and-white image of a hand that opened a book and revealed the title, *The Trailblazer*, with Seitz's "directed by" credit below the title. Coltrane gripped the upholstered arms of his chair as the cast list appeared. There wasn't any separate card for the star; rather, all the actors' names appeared together on a list, with the star's name at the top. Rebecca Chance's was the sixth name down. Seeing it made Coltrane lean forward.

Writers. Cameraman. As the hand continued to turn pages, the music built to a dramatic peak, and all at once, Coltrane was startled by the last of the credits.

"Produced by Winston Case?" Coltrane said in shock.

"You recognize the name?" Toler asked from the darkness behind Coltrane.

Good Lord, Coltrane thought. Rebecca Chance hadn't only bought Case's house, she had worked with him. They were connected. "Do you know anything about him?"

"Not a lot. This is the only picture he produced for Seitz."

"What about Rebecca Chance? Was she in any other of Seitz's movies?"

"No."

While they spoke, the screen showed a wagon train making its way across a prairie. A lean, tall man in buckskin, Bruce Cabot, was leading the pioneers. The vista was impressive, as was the multilayered sound track—the creak of wagon wheels, the plod of hooves, the jangle of harnesses. The dramatic use of sound was amazing, given the limitations of recording devices then in use. But Coltrane didn't care about that. All he did care about as he watched intently, scanning the crowd of pioneers, was a glimpse of . . .

"I did a little research on Case," Toler's disembodied voice said. "He started producing in 1928, just as sound was coming in. Except for *The Trailblazer* and one other film, he wasn't associated with anything I've heard of."

"That other picture wouldn't be *Jamaica Wind*, would it?"

"How did you know?"

"That's the other picture I'm looking for. Rebecca Chance is in that one also.'"

Coltrane kept staring at the wagon train. It entered a canyon, where Cabot frowned toward smoke rising from a hollow. He told the wagon train to wait while he and one of the pioneers investigated.

"But you've never seen her act?" Toler asked.

"I've only seen stills."

"What made you interested in her?"

Avoiding the question, Coltrane asked, "When does she appear?"

"Soon."

In the hollow, Cabot galloped to the burning wreckage of a Conestoga wagon. He found a dead dog with an arrow through it, dismounted next to a middle-aged man and woman who were sprawled on the ground, and checked to see if they were still alive. His scowl toward their heads, which were discreetly out of camera view, made clear that they had been scalped. The pioneer who had come with him heard a noise, pulled out his handgun, crept toward a stream, and shouted for Cabot to come running.

Movement behind reeds against the bank of the stream revealed a terrified figure emerging from a hiding place. The figure was a woman, and Coltrane became even more attentive, trying to identify Rebecca Chance's features. But despite her disheveled hair and grimy face, it was instantly clear that she wasn't Rebecca.

"I keep forgetting she's only a supporting player."

"But she has an important part," Toler said.

After the woman had been helped to the wagon train and cared for, introducing herself as Mary Beecham, Coltrane understood. There had been someone else in their party, she told Cabot, sobbing—her sister, Amy. The Indians who had attacked their wagon had taken her with them.

Because the attack had happened only a few hours earlier, there was still a chance to get Amy back if a rescue party set out immediately, but that would leave the wagon train undermanned and vulnerable. The pioneers had to make a moral choice—whether to forget about Amy, look after themselves, and keep going, or whether to jeopardize the good of the many for the possible good of one person. Cabot's doe-eyed looks at Mary made clear that he had fallen instantly in love with her. He told the pioneers that they could do what they wanted but that *he* was going to rescue Mary's sister. Coltrane had the strong suspicion that Cabot was motivated less by wanting to rescue Amy than he was by wanting to impress Mary. In a dramatically staged scene, Cabot galloped off with six men, following the raiding party's tracks, while the wagon train proceeded in a different direction.

Coltrane felt light-headed as the scene shifted and he saw Rebecca secured by a rope, stumbling next to the raiding party, who jeered at her from their horses. She, too, had disheveled hair and grimy features, but nothing could obscure her riveting beauty. Her blouse had been torn, revealing more of her right shoulder, almost to her upper breast, than he had realized was permitted by censors

215

back then. Similarly, her skirt was torn up to her knees, exposing her stockings, the tantalizing sight of which seemed more sensual than bare flesh would have been. The animal quality suggested by her lush, tangled hair, the insolence in her dark eyes, the defiance in her full lips made for as erotic a combination as he had ever seen.

"My God," he whispered.

"Yes," Toler said, "she could have been a star. But I never saw her in another movie."

"This was her last. She disappeared."

Coltrane watched, awestruck as a member of the raiding party tugged the rope and made her stumble, a movement that she accomplished with the grace of a dancer while still making it look like a stumble. In fact, all of her actions had similar grace. Her body had a sensual fluidness that caused every gesture, no matter how trivial, to be impossible to look away from. When she spoke, Coltrane wasn't prepared for how wonderfully full-throated and sonorous her voice was. Whatever Hispanic accent she had brought to Hollywood, she had worked hard to eliminate. She had re-created herself, and yet there remained the slightest hint of the origins she was trying to disguise.

Coltrane was so enthralled that he had trouble concentrating when other actors were featured in the story. Bruce Cabot pursued the raiding party, overcoming brush fires, thunderstorms, swollen rivers, buffalo stampedes, avalanches, and ambushes in his determined effort to save the sister of the woman he loved (the structure of the film was obviously indebted to the cliffhanger serials that Seitz had directed in his youth). Meanwhile, the wagon train overcame similar obstacles. A young man had taken over Bruce Cabot's role as expedition leader and was proving himself to be such a hero that Mary, praying for Cabot to come back with her sister, had fallen in love with Cabot's substitute. Seitz crosscut between the two sets of adventures. To build suspense as to whether Rebecca's character was still alive, her screen time was reduced after an Indian, angered by her insolence, grabbed her long black hair and wielded a knife to cut it off.

Watching Cabot scale a cliff and race through a forest, Coltrane waited with mounting frustration for Rebecca to reappear, and when she finally did, the Indian was hurling her off a cliff into a river. The fight between Cabot and the Indian was suspenseful, but all Coltrane cared about was another glimpse of Rebecca, who made him inhale sharply when he saw her wading from the river, her wet clothes sticking to her, her soaked dark hair slicked back against her head and hanging down her back. Every curve of her body was emphasized. It was as if she were one with the water, her body gathering substance as she emerged from it, retaining the fluid grace of the waves. She was Venus rising from the water. With her head tilted back, every magnificent detail of her face was pronounced, and if it had earlier seemed questionable that Bruce Cabot would instantly fall in love with Mary Beecham, there was no strain of credulity at all when he triumphed over the Indian and hurried to help Rebecca, only to see her wading from the sensuous waters and to be overcome with attraction.

In the end, he brought Rebecca back to the wagon train, where he announced that he and Rebecca were going to be married. But Rebecca's sister had a surprise of her own—*she* was going to be married to the man who had taken Bruce Cabot's place. Hugs and kisses. A good laugh all around, no hint whatsoever of the sexual complexities embedded in the story. As the camera panned to the snow-capped mountains, the music reached a crescendo. *The End* appeared. The screen went black.

In the darkness, Coltrane heard the camera whirring. He heard a chair creak as Vincent stood in the darkness, presumably to go into the projection room and shut off the machine.

"You said Rebecca Chance disappeared after making this movie?" Vincent's disembodied voice asked.

Coltrane was so enraptured by what he had seen that he had to force himself to speak. "That's right."

"When I told you I didn't know much about Winston Case, I neglected to tell you all of what I *did* know," Vincent said.

"Oh?"

"This was *his* last picture, too. He disappeared after producing it."

16

COLTRANE RETURNED TO PACKARD'S HOUSE AT TWO IN THE morning. His circles of confusion not only had come back but were more severe than ever. His mind was filled with a welter of overlapping blurs. Surely the police would have known that Rebecca Chance wasn't the only person associated with *The Trailblazer* to disappear. Why hadn't Winston Case's disappearance *also* been noted in the newspaper? The two incidents would have reinforced each other and made a good story. Had the studio covered it up? Or had Winston Case's "disappearance" been merely a retreat from the movie business, which would have been the same as vanishing from the face of the earth, as far as Hollywood was concerned.

In his kitchen, the red light on his answering machine was blinking.

Uneasy, he pressed the play button.

"Mitch, are you . . . I'm beginning to worry." Jennifer sounded as if she'd just walked swiftly from somewhere or was having trouble restraining her emotions. "Have we got a problem? Duncan Reynolds phoned me at the magazine to ask when he could expect the issue that features your collaboration with Packard. He happened to mention that you'd talked to him from New Haven the day before and that you'd be back in Los Angeles last night. That was certainly news to me. Without him, I wouldn't even have known that you have a telephone and an answering machine over there and what your number is. If you don't want to see me, fine. I have no intention of crowding you. But whatever's going on, we still have to work together. I need those photographs. You don't have to bring them over. Just FedEx them. But for heaven's sake, do *something*."

17

"I APOLOGIZE," Coltrane said the next morning.

Jennifer motioned him toward a chair in front of her desk, then closed the door to her office.

"Things have been a little hectic," he continued. "I had to meet with Nolan. Then I went to see McCoy in the hospital."

Jennifer's stern blue eyes assessed him. "How is he?"

"In pain, but feisty as ever. If he keeps improving, his doctor's going to release him in a couple of days."

"Good," she said flatly.

"And it looks as if the district attorney isn't going to make trouble for me."

"Excellent," Jennifer said without inflection. "And sometime during the rest of the day, couldn't you have found a chance to let me know about all these good things that were happening?"

"Well . . ."

"Maybe I'm not looking at this properly. Maybe I was foolish to think that it wasn't just you but the two of us who ran from Ilkovic, that I had a right to hear what you just told me. As it happens, I already know about McCoy—because I went to see him. And I know about the district attorney—because I phoned Nolan."

Coltrane raised his hands in a gesture of defeat. "I could have done this better. In New Haven, I got so involved in my memories about my grandparents that I felt too low to talk to anybody. When I got back . . . I've been trying to sort some things out and . . . Here are the photographs." He set the portfolio on the desk.

"Thank you."

"I feel as if somebody else took them."

"But the fact is, *you* did, and they're wonderful. A lot of terrible things have happened, Mitch, but that doesn't mean you have to turn your back on the *good* things."

Coltrane sighed. "Look, I know I was wrong not to keep in

touch. I don't want any tension between us. What do you say we go to dinner tonight? We'll have that talk we said we were going to have. And maybe I'll show you a surprise."

18

As COLTRANE HEADED UP A SHADOWY, tree-lined, curving street in Sherman Oaks, Jennifer looked at him, baffled. "Where are we going?"

"To the movies."

"Up here?"

"It's an out-of-the-way theater."

"Well, you did say this was going to be a surprise. I might as well lie back and enjoy the ride."

"That's the spirit."

Dinner had been at a place called the Natural Food Café—low-fat foods, no pesticides, no preservatives—a welcome change from Coltrane's recent fast-food dietary assaults on his body. The grilled salmon, wild rice, and steamed vegetables had tasted wholesome and soothing.

His conversation with Jennifer had also been soothing, a lot of issues having been settled: his confusion about himself, *her* confusion about *him*.

"When I saw you that night—covered with mud and ashes and what looked like blood—when I saw what you had done to Ilkovic, I couldn't . . . I felt as if I didn't know you anymore."

"I didn't know myself."

"And then I couldn't get over that you'd misled me, that you hadn't told me what you were planning to do."

"I'm not sure I realized what I was planning until I was actually doing it. There's a lot to be confused about." He touched her hand.

"The best thing I can suggest is that we share our confusion and try to move on together."

Jennifer studied him for the longest time. "Yes."

He stopped in front of the Tudor house on the street above the glinting valley. As Jennifer got out of the car, tightening her shawl against a chill evening breeze, she shook her head. "What are we doing here?"

Vincent Toler, wearing a blue cashmere pullover, emerged from the house, his cane clicking on the concrete walkway.

Jennifer looked increasingly bewildered.

"Good evening, Mitch." The elderly man sounded cheerful.

"Good evening, Vincent."

"And this is Jennifer?" Vincent offered his wizened hand. "Welcome."

Jennifer shook his hand, not sure what was going on. "Thank you. Vincent . . ."

"Toler. I understand you're a movie fan."

Jennifer turned toward Coltrane, her eyes twinkling with amusement. "You mean we really *are* going to see a movie? You're coming with us, Vincent?"

"No, the two of you are coming with *me*."

Jennifer immediately looked baffled again as Vincent guided them toward the house.

"I collect old movies," Vincent explained. "Last night, Mitchell watched *The Trailblazer* with me."

"I'm beginning to understand. Over dinner, I heard about . . ." Jennifer looked at Coltrane. "So this is where you saw it. Why didn't you tell me?"

"I didn't want to be predictable and boring."

"You're definitely not that."

They entered Vincent's living room, which he explained had been converted into a screening area for a once-famous director who had owned the house in the fifties.

"What was his name?" Jennifer asked. When Vincent told her, she shook her head. "I don't think I ever heard of him."

"His specialty was comedies. His sense of humor fell out of fashion. *Sic transit gloria.*" Vincent's tone was filled with melancholy. "At least George B. Seitz died before *he* fell out of fashion."

"Mitch told me how much he enjoyed *The Trailblazer*. He made me wish I'd seen it with him. Now that I know the movie we're going to watch, I can't wait."

"Oh," Vincent said. His Vandyke beard emphasized the drop of his chin. "I hope I'm not going to disappoint you."

"Disappoint me?'"

"You won't be seeing *The Trailblazer*."

Coltrane frowned. "We won't? But I thought—"

"I know many collectors of vintage films. I made some phone calls this morning and managed to track down the other movie you're interested in."

"You're kidding." Coltrane sat forward. "You're telling me you actually found a copy of—"

"*Jamaica Wind.*"

19

THE PROJECTOR WHIRRED, the screen glinted with a black-and-white drawing of palm trees, and South Seas music started playing. Beneath the title, the director's name appeared.

"Never heard of this man, either," Jennifer said.

"For good reason, I'm told." In the darkness, Vincent came back from the projection booth. "The collector friend who loaned me these reels says that this director didn't have a quarter of the skills that Seitz had."

"Apparently not," Jennifer said. "Hawaiian music in Jamaica? God help us."

Coltrane gripped his chair when Rebecca Chance's name appeared.

Cameraman.

Screenwriters.

Produced by . . .

"Winston Case?" Jennifer sounded surprised. "Wasn't he the first owner of . . ."

"Packard's house." Coltrane kept his gaze fixed on the screen. "Rebecca bought it from him. And Packard bought it from *her*."

"And took thousands of pictures of her," Jennifer said. "What on earth was going on?"

"I'm hoping this movie will help us find out."

When Coltrane had developed his prints updating Packard's series about L.A. houses, he had gone over each of them with a magnifying glass, searching for the slightest imperfection in the darkroom process: a bubble in the emulsion, a water spot. His concentration had been intense. But it didn't equal the intensity with which he now stared at the images before him. Vincent was right: The direction of *Jamaica Wind* was clumsy compared with Seitz's work on *The Trailblazer*. Coltrane didn't care. The movie's faults didn't matter. Rebecca Chance was in this movie. *That* was what mattered.

The plot was about English pirates fighting to unseat a corrupt British governor-general. The lean, dashing, mustached hero alternated sword fighting with kissing the heroine, the daughter of the governor-general's aide.

"This is terrible," Jennifer said.

Coltrane concentrated harder on the screen.

"Look at that beach," Jennifer said. "It obviously isn't in Jamaica. It looks more like Santa Monica. I think I see the curve of Malibu in the background."

The camera kept whirring, images glinting.

"But wait a minute," Jennifer said. "Now it's a different beach. That tropical foliage isn't just a bunch of ferns and palm trees they stuck in the ground. They're *real*. Where do you suppose . . . I bet they went down to Mexico."

"There she is." Coltrane sat up.

Rebecca Chance emerged from a cluster of vines and totally dominated the screen. She turned a piece of junk into a work of art. She made the director's clumsiness become insignificant.

Coltrane felt as if a hand pressed upon his chest, but the sensation wasn't threatening—it was stimulating. Rebecca Chance wore a flower-patterned sarong that exposed about the same amount of cleavage as the heroine's, but the heroine looked like a boy compared to her. Rebecca's lush dark hair hung down to her bare shoulders. Her left leg was exposed to her exquisite knee. Her feet were splendidly bare. It turned out that she, too, was in love with the hero and was spying for him. A chase through a tropical forest reached a climax when Rebecca found herself trapped on a cliff above the sea and escaped by making a spectacular dive into the ocean. Later, when she waded from the ocean, Coltrane inwardly gasped at the parallel between this scene and the scene in *The Trailblazer* where she was thrown from a cliff and waded from a river. Both scenes were similar to some of the photographs that Packard had taken of her rising from the ocean, the same erotic association with water and waves. In the end, she was killed when she showed the hero and his men an underwater passage into the fortress. The hero and his men displayed appropriate grief and anger, pressed on with their assault, defeated the governor-general, and freed his prisoners, one of whom was the heroine. Hugs and kisses. Sad words about Rebecca's passing. Homilies about freedom. Music up. Fade out.

"What junk," Jennifer said.

"What a beautiful woman," Coltrane whispered.

"I'm sorry, Mitch. I didn't hear you."

"I said, she has incredible screen presence."

"No question. She could have been a star."

As Coltrane continued to stare at the blank screen, Vincent turned on the lights, then excused himself. "I'll go make some coffee."

The moment he was out of earshot, Jennifer told Coltrane, "But we didn't learn anything to help us understand why Packard took so many pictures of her, then hid them."

"We didn't learn that, but we did learn something. Did you recognize the cliff she dove from?"

"Should I have?"

"It's the same cliff she stood on when Packard photographed her," Coltrane said.

"One cliff's pretty much the same as—"

"No, this one has a distinct rock formation farther along its edge. It reminds me of a cat arching its back."

"I didn't notice any rock formation in any of the photographs of her on the cliff."

"I guess I've had more time to study them."

Jennifer frowned. "You saw a similar rock formation on the cliff in this movie? *You watched it that closely?*"

"To make sure, I'll ask Vincent to replay the scene."

"Yes," Jennifer said without enthusiasm, "by all means, ask him to replay it."

20

I HAD A GOOD TIME," Coltrane said. To go to dinner, he had picked Jennifer up at the *Southern California* offices on Melrose. Now he stopped next to Jennifer's BMW in the almost-deserted parking area behind the building. "I'm glad we finally had a chance to talk."

"We need to talk more," she said.

"I know what you mean. What Ilkovic put us through, I don't think we'll ever get over."

"The person I had in mind was Rebecca Chance. We need to talk more about your interest in her."

"How about tomorrow night?" Coltrane asked. "New Year's Eve."

"I was wondering if you were going to suggest doing anything."

"An appropriate night. The end of the past. The start of the future."

"But what about the present?"

They studied each other.

Coltrane leaned close, kissing her gently on the lips, feeling the brush of his skin against hers. When he eased back, he gazed into her eyes, assessing her reaction, wondering if he'd done the right thing.

"That's something else we haven't done in a long time," Jennifer said.

When he kissed her a second time, her mouth opened. Her tongue found his. With her body against him, he felt a tingle flood through him.

"Anything special you'd like to do tomorrow night?" he asked.

"More of what we're doing now."

"That can be arranged."

"Maybe I'll even distract you from Rebecca Chance."

"Jealous of her?"

"You talked an awful lot about her tonight," Jennifer said.

"The photographs of her don't make you curious?"

"The only person I'm curious about is you."

They kissed again, hungrily.

Jennifer broke away, breathless. "What time tomorrow?"

"I'm suddenly thinking about right now."

"Can't." Jennifer inhaled. "The end of the year or not, I have an eight o'clock breakfast with my most important advertiser. I have to look alert."

"Six tomorrow night?" Coltrane asked. "Come over to my place. I'll make my famous marinara sauce."

"Which place is that?"

"I don't understand."

"Your town house or . . ."

"Oh." Coltrane realized what she was getting at. "Packard's. The furniture's going to be delivered tomorrow. I thought you'd like to see it."

"Yes and no. Packard's house has unpleasant associations for me."

"That's another reason we have to use New Year's Eve to put the past behind us."

22

COLTRANE WAITED UNTIL JENNIFER GOT INTO HER CAR AND drove away, her red taillights disappearing around a corner. He thought for a moment, then picked up his car phone and pressed numbers.

"Vincent, I'm sorry to call you this late, but I remembered that you told me you didn't go to bed until two or three in the morning. I was wondering if you'd do me a favor. I'd be glad to pay for any expenses it involves. I don't care what it costs. Before you return *Jamaica Wind* to your collector friend, would you ask him if we could take it to a duplicating studio and have it transferred onto videotape? It would be a way of protecting the movie. Also, would *you* mind doing the same with your copy of *The Trailblazer?* I'd very much like to have copies of them."

EIGHT

I

STIEGLITZ.

When Coltrane returned to Packard's house, he went straight to the vault and for the first time ignored the life-size face of Rebecca Chance gazing at him from the darkness of her sanctuary. He was too compelled. Pivoting toward the shelves on the right, he picked up stack after stack of boxes and carried them out to the shelves in the vault.

Stieglitz, he thought again.

Driving home, he had been unable to stop marveling about how unique it was for a photographer of Packard's genius to have devoted so much of his output to a single person. Indeed, he could think of only one other photographer who had done so: the most influential in the medium, Alfred Stieglitz, who during 1918 and 1919 had obsessively taken pictures of his lover and eventual wife, the painter Georgia O'Keeffe. These photographs and others taken in later years amounted to more than three hundred, although there were rumors that after Stieglitz's death, O'Keeffe had prevented the release of many others, perhaps even destroying them.

Randolph Packard had been infamous for his arrogance, but he had been humble in his appreciation of genius and, like every other great photographer during Stieglitz's lifetime, he had made a pilgrimage to New York to learn from the master. Packard's first meeting with Stieglitz had been at Stieglitz's celebrated gallery, An American Place, in 1931, two years before he took the photograph of Rebecca Chance's house and twelve years after Stieglitz had taken the bulk of his passionate photographs of Georgia O'Keeffe. Had Stieglitz shown Packard the O'Keeffe portraits? Had the idea of a pictorial monument to Rebecca Chance occurred to Packard because of Stieglitz's influence? If so, some of the photographs would have been . . .

Pausing only long enough to verify that the humped rock formation in the photographs of Rebecca on the cliff was in fact the same as the formation on the cliff she had leapt from in *Jamaica Wind*, Coltrane hurriedly set aside the boxes he had previously looked at. Each night when he had responded helplessly to the urge to come down here, he had been eager to sort through the entire collection but had never gotten past three of the boxes. To have rushed through such an abundance of beauty would have been gluttony.

But now rushing was exactly what Coltrane did, opening box after box, sorting through their contents as quickly as he could without risking damage to the images. The late hour and the glare of the overhead lights made his head pound. His hands trembled with apprehension that he was wrong, with anticipation that he was right. His emotions twisted and tugged. Five boxes. Eight. Twelve. Their contents occupied shelf after shelf. Photographs of Rebecca Chance on horseback, on a sailboat, on a diving board, a forest path, a garden terrace, a stone staircase, a sun-bathed balcony. Fifteen. Eighteen. Of Rebecca Chance in evening clothes, in slacks and a blouse, in jodhpurs, a swimming suit, a gardening dress, a flower-patterned skirt, a white top, and an even whiter shawl.

The full impact of the amount of photographs that Packard had taken of Rebecca Chance was stunning. These many pictures—no wonder Packard hadn't produced many new photographs. He wouldn't have had the opportunity. Developing so many photographs (and Packard *always* developed his own work) would have taken a lifetime.

Although Coltrane was fervently convinced that his logic was correct, his hands trembled with despondency as he reached the final box and fumbled to lift its lid, expecting disappointment. As a consequence, he wasn't prepared. The first nude photograph rendered him powerless. His legs became rigid. His body turned to stone. His breathing stopped.

The most arousing photograph he had ever seen showed Rebecca

Chance naked and yet covered, draped with the chromium beads that hung on the walls of the dining room upstairs. She leaned with her customary natural grace against the blackness of the wall beyond the beads. She was angled slightly to the left, her head and body almost in profile but not quite, both of her eyes visible, directed unashamedly toward the camera. Light came from the left, contributing a sheen to her lush black hair, making her dusky skin seem to glow and her dark eyes seem to have something burning within them. At the same time, the light reflected off the strings of chromium beads, causing them to gleam with the simultaneous evocation of ice and fire. The image had so tactile an illusion that Coltrane could feel those cold/hot beads on his own skin. They seemed to caress him, all the while promising to move and expose more of Rebecca Chance's magnificent body, the gleaming beads contrasting with the large dark nipples that projected from among them, as well as with the even darker silken pubic hair past which they dangled.

Coltrane's penis hardened. The unwilled motion broke his paralysis, causing strength to return to his legs. His hands, frozen in the act of setting the box's lid to the side, resumed their activity, trembling as he placed the lid on the shelf. His breath returned, air coursing into him, filling his lungs, reducing the light-headedness that had increasingly overtaken him while he stared at the picture. But his dizziness was only partially abated, for he felt he was falling into the photograph.

His erection became harder. Conscious of his body as much as he was of hers, he thought, I was right. Stieglitz had shown the way. Of the hundreds of photographs that Stieglitz had taken of Georgia O'Keeffe, an astonishing number of them were the most meticulous, loving nude shots that any man had ever taken of any woman. Sometimes it seemed that Stieglitz had commemorated every inch of O'Keeffe's body, her expressive hands, yes, and her breasts and her eyes, but also her elbows and knees, the cleft in her hips and the soles of her feet, the curve of her shoulder blades, parts of her that, to Coltrane's knowledge, had never been the subject of a close-up portrait but that Stieglitz's amazingly intimate photographs evoked.

One critic had been almost frightened by the power of Stieglitz's portraits of O'Keeffe, describing them as primal, implying that Stieglitz thought of O'Keeffe as the great Earth Mother.

But in Packard's naked depiction of Rebecca Chance, she wasn't the mother but the *lover* of us all, Coltrane thought. Overwhelmed, he turned to the other photographs in the box, finding more nude portraits, each more candid and beautiful than the one before. None was as artistically staged as the one he had first seen, but each was a work of art because Rebecca Chance was a work of art. Her unclothed body, its smooth curves, indentations, and ridges, was mysterious, at the same time daunting, so powerful in its frank presentation of sexual womanhood that it caused Coltrane to react not only with desire but also with awe. Rebecca Chance didn't pose so much as present herself before the camera, allowing herself to be photographed. Gazing unabashedly into the lens, she was so at home with her female nature that Coltrane had to fight feeling embarrassed about his sexual reaction to her.

He examined more photographs and came to a remarkable sequence in which Packard had done what Stieglitz only hinted at with Georgia O'Keeffe, photographing literally every inch of Rebecca Chance's body, her ears, the top of her head, the nape of her neck, the area beneath her arms, the inside of her thighs, the backs of her knees. There was no area so commonplace or private that Packard had not taken a picture of in close-up. What made the sequence so moving was the devotion with which Packard had recorded the separate parts of the object of his obsession, as if in the thoroughness of his subdivision of her he could multiply her beauty.

Coltrane reached the last of the nude photographs and felt emotionally exhausted. Bracing himself against a shelf, he closed his eyes, inhaled deeply, and mustered the energy to begin putting all the photographs back into their boxes. His hands felt numb. His heart pounded. Despite his closed eyes, he continued to see Rebecca Chance, naked, gazing at him. Raising his eyelids, he took one more look at the final nude photograph before him, then managed to put all of them away.

Upstairs, on the sleeping bag next to the increasingly pathetic-looking artificial Christmas tree in the living room, Coltrane fell into a black doze almost immediately. On previous nights, Ilkovic had haunted his dreams, turning them into nightmares, but tonight, it was Rebecca Chance's arms that reached for him, her naked body pressing against him.

2

CAREFUL," the paunchy foreman told the two young men who were working with him. They all wore blue shirts that had the same logo as was on the side of the blue semitruck: PACIFIC MOVERS. They opened the back of the truck, the right and left hatches slamming against each side. After securing the hatches, they pulled out a ramp from a slot beneath the truck, the ramp making a scraping sound that grated against Coltrane's nerves. While the workers hooked the ramp into place, Coltrane walked toward the open rear and saw stacks of furniture hidden by generous amounts of protective blankets.

"Careful," the paunchy foreman repeated, and now Coltrane realized that the man was talking to *him*, not his young coworkers. "You'd better stay out of the way. Sometimes stuff falls, or one of these guys might trip."

"I hope not."

"The last thing we want is a client to get hurt."

"I'm not worried about *me*. Don't let anything happen to the furniture."

"No problem there. I've been doing this for twenty years."

But the young men obviously hadn't—they looked barely older than twenty. Uneasy, Coltrane backed away, watching them mount the ramp and begin undraping blankets from the first layer of furniture.

His chest felt warm when he saw a glimmer of metal. He was suddenly looking at a chair. But he had never seen any furniture like it—so simple and yet so aesthetically pleasing. The chair's legs and sides were composed of steel tubes, the gray hue of which was polished to a sheen. The seat and back had clean, straight lines, black suede over a padded reinforcing material. It invited being touched, which Coltrane almost did as one of the young men carried the chair past him at the bottom of the ramp. The second young man followed with another chair.

"Where do you want them?" the foreman asked, looking up from a clipboard.

"In the dining room."

Coltrane led the way into the house. In the living room, the miniature Christmas tree and the sleeping bags were no longer in evidence. "The dining room's to the left."

"Nice house."

"Thanks."

"I've never seen anything like it." The foreman turned to the young men. "Okay, put the chairs against the dining room wall so they won't get in the way. Hold it. Those walls are . . ."

"Covered with strings of chromium beads," Coltrane said.

"I definitely haven't seen anything like *that*."

And so it went, the young men unloading furniture while the foreman didn't do anything but make check marks on his clipboard, then follow his helpers into the house to be certain that nothing was damaged.

Four more dining room chairs. Then the dining table itself: glass-topped, rectangular, with rounded corners, a steel frame supporting the glass top, and steel legs.

The foreman used a soft cloth to wipe smudges of dust from the glass top. "Not a scratch." He looked at Coltrane for confirmation.

The living room furniture was framed by aluminum tubes that were coated a shiny black. The tubes were arranged horizontally, eight inches apart, forming low cages with high backs. The effect was vaguely industrial, a glorification of mechanization that had been prevalent back in the late twenties and early thirties, but the design was so harmonious that it felt liberating. Thick, wide cushions were set into the frames and against the backs. The material was red satin. Three chairs and an L-shaped sofa filled the living room. Glass-topped side tables, coffee tables, and wall tables filled more of the space, as did a chromium cabinet. So much glass and polished metal made the living room gleam.

Standing in a corner, telling the young men where he wanted them to set the pieces, Coltrane began to feel tugged toward the past. Oddly, though, the past seemed the present. The furniture had been designed so long ago that it seemed new and fresh.

"Mister, I've been hauling furniture half my life," the foreman said. "I gotta tell you—this stuff is definitely different."

"But do you like it?"

"What's not to like? The junk I sometimes have to deliver . . . But this is solid. Look at the sweat on these kids' faces from lifting all this metal. Nothing flimsy here. No danger of *this* stuff falling apart. Style. Reminds me of a real old movie I saw on cable the other night. It had furniture like this. I'm not a dress-up kind of guy, but being here makes me feel we ought to be wearing tuxedos and drinking martinis. Hey." He turned to his helpers. "We're supposed to be movers. Let's get a move on."

Coltrane turned to watch them go for more furniture, and he wasn't prepared to find that Duncan Reynolds had come through the open front door.

Duncan looked more surprised than Coltrane was. In fact, he seemed startled. His usually florid face was pale, emphasizing the numerous colors on his sport coat. His mouth hung open.

"Duncan? What's the matter? Are you all right?"

"I came to see your reaction when the furniture was . . ." Eyes wide, Duncan surveyed the living room. "To find out if you were satisfied with . . ." Shocked, he pointed toward the sofa, then the chairs, then the end tables. "How did . . ."

"What's wrong?"

"Nothing. That's the problem. Nothing's wrong. Everything's just as I remember it. *Exactly* as I remember it. But that can't . . . How could you possibly have . . ."

"What are you talking about?"

"The furniture's in the same places where Randolph preferred it. Twenty-five years ago, a few months after I started working for him, the day he first showed me this house, the furniture was positioned exactly as it is now. Randolph told me it had been that way when he bought it, that he had never varied it, that he never wanted it to be varied. It never was. Until it was taken away to be auctioned. And now you've arranged it so it looks precisely as when I first saw it. I almost expect to see Randolph stroll upstairs from working in the darkroom. How did . . . How could you have known where to . . ."

"I had help from some photographs."

Duncan's mystification deepened.

"I've been doing research," Coltrane said.

Duncan stepped nearer, anxious for an explanation.

"I figured a house designed by Lloyd Wright would have attracted attention when it was built. Yesterday I went to the library to see what I could learn about it. The reference librarian showed me a yearly subject index for every article that was published in every major magazine. So I started in 1931, when this house was built. I looked under Lloyd Wright's name in the index, and I got a reference to him right away, an article about him in an architectural magazine that isn't published anymore but was fairly trendy back in the thirties—*Architectural Views*. Excellent library that we have in L.A., the periodical department has every issue of that magazine on microfilm. So I had a look. Turns out this house received a lot of attention when it was built. The article had an analysis of Lloyd Wright's design. It also had photographs: interiors as well as exteriors. Each room. Including the furniture." Coltrane gestured toward the living room. "All I did was imitate the arrangement of the furniture as it was shown in the photographs."

"You don't suppose Randolph took the photographs?"

"That's what *I* wondered," Coltrane said. "But I didn't have to look at each photograph for more than a second to decide that the images were so uncomposed and poorly lit that they couldn't possibly be his work. I strained my eyes a little trying to read the fine print on the microfilm. The photo credit went to someone whose name I didn't recognize."

Duncan calmed himself. "For a moment, I thought you might have discovered some Randolph Packard photographs that no one knew about."

"Wouldn't that have been something if I had."

"Coming through." The overweight supervisor led the way for his two young assistants, who were carrying more black metal tubes. "I don't know what this is, but I'm guessing it's a bed frame."

"King-size or regular?"

"When we get all these pieces assembled, I'm betting it's a king."

"Master bedroom. Top floor."

"You heard the man," the foreman said to his helpers.

The troop disappeared, trudging upward.

Duncan watched in a daze.

"Duncan?"

"Uh, what?" Duncan turned, blinking.

"The other day, you mentioned that Randolph owned an estate in Mexico."

Duncan's face didn't change expression, but something in his eyes did, becoming wary.

"You said that Randolph used various shell corporations when he was buying property, so that no one would know the true buyer. You said Randolph bought *this* house that way—and a place in Mexico."

"Now that I think about it, I suppose I did mention something about that."

"I was wondering where the estate was."

Duncan's gaze remained guarded. "What makes you ask?"

"Just curious. Randolph had such a unique way of viewing things, I thought the hacienda might be as dramatic as this house. It might be worth going down to Mexico to have a look."

Duncan answered too quickly: "I wouldn't know."

From upstairs, Coltrane heard the faint clang of metal tubes being bolted together.

"Careful," he heard the foreman say.

"You wouldn't know if I'd find it interesting to visit the estate?" Coltrane asked.

"I wouldn't know where it is. I was never there." Duncan looked

236

up the stairs toward the metallic sounds. "Randolph never told me. Some place in Baja California, I think he might have mentioned."

"That's too bad."

"Sorry I can't be more helpful."

"It probably doesn't matter. For all I know, it isn't as unique as this house, or it hasn't been preserved the way this place has. Did Randolph still own it when he died?"

Duncan looked away. "Years ago, he mentioned something about selling a property in Mexico."

"Well," Coltrane said, "it was just a thought."

"Careful," the foreman repeated.

3

I'D LIKE TO SPEAK TO MR. BLAINE," Coltrane said into the telephone.

"May I tell him who's calling?" the receptionist replied.

Coltrane gave his name. "I've been having some discussions with him about the estate of a deceased client of his. Randolph Packard."

The receptionist's voice came to attention. "Randolph Packard?"

"I'm buying a house he owned, and I need some further information. I know it's New Year's Eve afternoon." Coltrane tried to sound self-deprecating. He chuckled. "Or whatever today is called."

The receptionist sounded amused. "Yes, I've been having the same problem."

"Anyway, Mr. Blaine probably has a ton of work he still needs to finish, but I was hoping he could spare a few minutes for me."

In death as in life, Packard's name got results. Twenty seconds later, an unctuous baritone was on the line. "Mr. Coltrane, I trust that your arrangements are proceeding satisfactorily."

"Totally. In fact, I'm so pleased that I was wondering if another property Mr. Packard owned might be available for sale."

"If you're referring to the house in Newport Beach, it was given to his assistant. You'd have to speak with him about that."

"No, I was thinking of a property in Mexico."

"Mexico?"

"I believe it's in Baja California."

The baritone sounded confused. "No, I'm not familiar with it."

Coltrane glanced down in disappointment, his suspicions having proven groundless. "I guess it must have been sold years ago."

"The only property I'm familiar with that Randolph Packard owned in Mexico isn't in Baja."

"Excuse me?"

"It's on the western main coast of Mexico, much farther south than Baja. Below Acapulco, in fact. Near a town called . . . I can't remember it in Spanish, but in English it's very distinctive. The spine of the cat."

"What?"

"That's the name of the town."

"Espalda del Gato?" Coltrane asked.

"I'm impressed. Your Spanish is very good."

"I spent a lot of time in Spanish-speaking countries. If there's a way for me to see the place, if it's still in Mr. Packard's name, maybe I'd be interested in buying *it* also," Coltrane said.

"I can't help you with that. It's out of my hands. The hacienda was a bequest in Mr. Packard's will. The title was transferred a week ago."

Coltrane couldn't hide his frustration. "To whom? Can you tell me?"

"Against my advice, Mr. Packard didn't transfer all of his assets to a trust. The hacienda in Mexico was one of the items that he neglected to include. If he *had* included it, the bequest could have been handled privately, without involving a California court. But because the hacienda was included in a will, it has to go through probate. It'll be a matter of public record. I could put you through the inconvenience of going to the court house. I don't see why that's necessary, however. Mr. Packard gave the Mexican property to someone named Natasha Adler."

"Natasha Adler?"

"I have no association with the woman. I can't tell you a thing about her."

"Do you have her address and phone number?"

"*That* information was *not* included in the will. I had to hire a private investigator to find her. I'm afraid I'd be violating her privacy if I told you where she lived."

Damn it, Coltrane thought.

"Now if there's nothing else I can help you with," Blaine said.

"Maybe one thing."

The baritone had a hint of impatience in his voice. "Yes?"

"Would you mind telling me the name of the investigator you used?"

4

"CHEERS."

"Cheers."

Coltrane and Jennifer clicked glasses of Absolut and tonic.

Jennifer sipped from hers and wrinkled her nose. "It's like with champagne—the bubbles are ticklish."

"Maybe you need more vodka and less tonic," Coltrane said.

"Then the *rest* of me would be ticklish." Jennifer wore a black Armani dress, the hem of which came up just above the knee. Its top ended where her breasts began. Pearl earrings and a matching necklace couldn't compete with her smile.

Taking another sip, she surveyed the living room. "I expected the furniture to look striking, but not *this* much. It's really—I don't know what word to use—fantastic. I feel as if I'm in that wing of the Museum of Modern Art, the one where they have furniture that's considered art."

"Does that mean you feel the house has changed enough for you to give it another chance? You don't still associate it with Ilkovic?"

"It feels different now."

"Good."

"As if I'm in the 1930s."

"That's the illusion I want to create. I want this to be a haven from the present."

"It seems to me that the present's still here, though." Before Coltrane could ask what she meant, she added, "Is it safe to sit on this stuff?"

"Of course." Coltrane laughed.

Tentatively, Jennifer lowered herself onto the red velvet cushion of a black tube–enclosed chair. "So far so good. It didn't collapse."

"The man in charge of the crew who delivered it assured me that this stuff was made to last."

"It certainly has. After all these years, it's as shiny as new." Jennifer took a long sip of vodka and tonic. "You're certain Duncan lied to you about the place in Mexico?"

"It wasn't so much what he said. He told me he had a vague memory that it had been sold some time ago, that maybe it was in Baja. No big deal. But there was a nervous look behind his eyes."

"Maybe he just needed a drink. Not everything's a mystery."

"I phoned the private investigator Packard's attorney uses. I got lucky and caught him in. For five hundred dollars, he looked in his files and told me that Natasha Adler, the woman who inherited the estate, lives up in Malibu. Her number's unlisted, but he gave me that, too."

Jennifer raised her glass to her lips. The drink did nothing to relax her increasingly troubled expression. "I don't see what you hope to accomplish."

"I'd like to know why Packard gave it to her."

"Maybe she was a friend or a business acquaintance."

"Fine. But if she knows the estate, maybe she can tell me something about it."

"Such as?"

240

"Whether parts of *Jamaica Wind* were filmed there and whether she's ever heard of Rebecca Chance."

Jennifer shook her head.

"Aren't *you* curious?" Coltrane asked.

"Professionally, sure. Those photographs are a major discovery. It's important to learn when they were taken, who the subject was, what sort of relationship Packard had with her. That information doesn't make the photographs any more brilliant than they already are, but as a magazine publisher, I can tell you human interest adds incalculable monetary value. That raises the question of when you're going to tell Packard's estate about them. Without being specific, I did some checking with an attorney. As I understand it, you have a claim to own the photographs, but the right to reproduce them belongs to Packard's trustees. You're going to have to come to an arrangement with them."

"When I'm ready." Coltrane bit his lower lip. "You said 'professionally.' "

"Excuse me?"

"You told me that *professionally* you were interested in the photographs. You emphasized the word, implying, I suppose, that you weren't interested personally."

"Not the way *you* are. The way you talk about Rebecca Chance, it's like she's a living, breathing person. Last night, you asked me if I was jealous of her. Maybe I am a little. It's almost as if . . ."

"What?"

"You're falling in love with her."

Coltrane didn't comment.

Jennifer finished her drink.

"Time for a refill?"

"You bet. It's New Year's Eve, after all."

"And if we're not going to starve, I'd better start the marinara sauce." Coltrane walked with her through the dining room and into the kitchen.

A smaller version of the glass-topped, steel-rimmed dining table was against a wall.

"I guess I shouldn't be too hard on Duncan about possibly lying to me. I wasn't exactly honest with him, either."

"Oh?"

Coltrane refilled Jennifer's glass, adding a lime wedge and ice cubes. "I told him I knew how the furniture was supposed to be arranged because I had seen the layout in an old architectural magazine. Not true."

"Then if you didn't find out from a magazine . . ."

"The photographs we found in the vault. By now, I've had a chance to go through all of them. It turns out that several of the pictures of Rebecca Chance were taken in this house, and as you might expect from anything Packard did, those photographs are as clear and crisp as can be. I had no trouble using them as a guide to arrange the tables and chairs and things."

Jennifer studied him.

"I also found some interesting photos of a different sort," Coltrane said.

Jennifer studied him harder.

"Nudes."

The moment Coltrane said it, he wished that he hadn't.

"Nudes," Jennifer said flatly.

"You know, the type of thing Stieglitz took of Georgia O'Keeffe."

"Yes, I know exactly the type you mean. Show them to me."

5

CROSSING THE VAULT, Jennifer said, "No shivers anymore?"

Coltrane furrowed his brow in puzzlement.

"This vault used to give you the creeps," Jennifer said. "It made you claustrophobic."

"Oh, that. Well, I guess I've been coming down here enough that I got used to it."

"Yes, you definitely did get used to it. It's cool enough in here to give *me* the shivers." Jennifer rubbed her bare arms.

"Here." Coltrane took off his sport coat and draped it around her shoulders.

"Thanks."

"Better?" His hands lingered on her shoulders.

"Much."

Jennifer turned to him, spreading her palms against his shirt. His nipples reacted. A gentle kiss lengthened, becoming forceful.

They held each other.

"So where are these nude photographs?" Jennifer asked.

"You haven't changed your mind?"

"Maybe I've got a kinky streak."

Taking his arms from around her, Coltrane released the catches that held the wall in place.

When he pulled the section free, Jennifer stared at Rebecca Chance's life-size features. The harsh light from the vault dispelled the darkness of the chamber. The photograph's eyes reflected the illumination.

"She's much more beautiful here than in the movie I saw," Jennifer said.

Coltrane had left the box containing the nude photographs on top of the others. He carried it out to one of the shelves and took off the lid.

Stepping forward, Jennifer stared down at the image of Rebecca Chance in the dining room upstairs, the strings of chromium beads draped over her naked body.

Slowly, she turned to the next photograph, and the next. The room was so still that the only sounds Coltrane heard were the subtle scrape of the photographs and Jennifer's tense breathing. She kept turning the pictures.

At last, she was finished.

"Well?"

"Her nipples," Jennifer said.

Coltrane had no idea what reaction to have expected from her, but this certainly was not one that he could have predicted.

"The nipples and the aureoles around them," Jennifer said.

"I don't understand."

"Mine are different from hers."

Coltrane found himself blushing. "I wasn't trying to imply that . . ."

"That hers are more attractive than mine? They are. Rebecca Chance was an astonishingly beautiful woman. She was blessed by nature. But that's not what I'm getting at. My nipples are small, the width of the tip of my little finger. Rebecca Chance's are as wide as the tip of my index finger. The aureoles around *my* breasts aren't pronounced the way Rebecca Chance's are."

"And?"

"I could get my nipples and aureoles to start looking like hers, however."

"You're talking about surgery?"

"If I got pregnant."

Coltrane's heartbeat lurched. "You think she was pregnant?"

"I suspect it was her first time. I don't see any stretch marks to indicate that she previously had had a baby. I'd say she was about three months along, still able to keep her stomach flat. But she couldn't keep her breasts from getting fuller and the nipples larger as the photographs progressed. The glow on her face and the luster on her skin make me think that some powerful hormones had started to kick in."

"Pregnant," Coltrane said with wonder, then looked with new eyes at the photographs.

"So the obvious questions are: Who was the father? Was he Packard? And, assuming that the child was born, whatever happened to it?"

6

COLTRANE ARCHED HIS BACK AND TILTED HIS HEAD UPWARD, a surge of pleasure seizing his body. Moving slowly, he tried not to disrupt the delicate balance between immediate need and exquisite postponement. Jennifer kissed him, thrusting against him: "Don't hold back." Moving faster, he felt her urgent rhythm match his own. Climaxing, he felt as if the present stretched on forever. Too soon, time became separate moments, and he eased out of Jennifer, settling next to her. Neither moved. Streetlights glinted through the bedroom's open blinds. A breeze made tree branches sway, casting wavering shadows across the darkened room.

She turned onto her side, facing him. "It's been a long time."

"*Too* long."

"We'll have to catch up."

"The spirit is willing, but the flesh might be weak."

"I'll see what I can do to put some strength back into it."

"Some food might help, too. If I don't start making that marinara sauce pretty soon . . ."

"No." Jennifer touched his cheek. "Lie there awhile longer."

"It's a great way to end what in other respects was an awfully bad year," Coltrane said.

"In one respect, it wasn't such a bad year. You took some wonderful photographs. You found a new direction for your work."

Coltrane shrugged.

"Your work still doesn't seem important to you?"

"Not compared to everything that happened."

They lapsed into silence.

Jennifer was the first to speak. "When you were making love to me, did it occur to you that Rebecca Chance and Randolph Packard might have made love in this bed?"

". . . No."

245

"It did to me. I imagined that she and I had changed places. Did the nude photographs of her excite you?"

"A little."

"Did they make you more eager to have sex?"

"I suppose."

Jennifer lowered her hand from his face and drew it along his body, fondling him.

"Like *this* excites you?"

"Yes."

"Good."

When Jennifer kissed him, he tasted the salt of a tear on her cheek.

"Because I can't compete with her, Mitch. I'm not a goddess. I'm only a woman."

7

ALTHOUGH THE MORNING WAS BRIGHT AND THE SKY CLEAR, a cold breeze, at least by Southern California standards, made Coltrane retreat from the patio outside his bedroom. "Brrr," he said, cinching his robe tighter, turning toward Jennifer, who still lay in his bed. "I was hoping we could have coffee out there, but I'm afraid it would have to be *iced* coffee."

"It's nicer in here anyhow," Jennifer said. She raised the covers, giving him a glimpse of her breasts, her inward-curved tummy, and her light-colored pubic hair, gesturing for him to crawl under and join her.

"That's the best offer I've had all day."

"And the day's young yet," Jennifer said.

"You're going to wear me out."

"As long as I didn't wear *this* guy out."

She pointed toward the erection that he showed when he slipped off his robe.

"Since when did you like talking dirty?" He eased under the covers, feeling her warmth.

"You call that talking dirty?"

"At the very least, I'd call it suggestive."

"And what do you call this?"

"I'm a little distracted at the moment. Maybe the word will come to me if you do it again."

"*Something* better come."

"And the day's young yet," Jennifer had said. But she was wrong about implying that there would be more opportunities in the day for them to make love, for after they collapsed into each other's arms, after they nestled against each other, got up to take turns showering, and finally dressed, Jennifer told him that she was expected at her parents' house around one o'clock. "You remember from last year," Jennifer said, "it's a tradition. I always go over and help Dad watch his marathon of New Year's Day football games. You want to come with me? He and Mom will be glad to see you, and there'll be more than enough food. You seemed to enjoy yourself last time."

"I did. It was fun. But I'm afraid I'm going to have to beg off."

"Oh?" Jennifer's voice was frail with disappointment.

"Yes. I promised Greg's widow that I'd come over and spend some time with her and the kids."

"Oh." The inflection was now one of understanding. "I didn't know you'd spoken with her."

"I guess it slipped my mind."

"I've never met her, but please tell her I'm very sorry about her husband."

"I will."

"That coffee you mentioned would sure taste good right now."

The kitchen was a mess from the marinara and meatball dinner that Coltrane had made, the dishes having been left in the sink while they finished a bottle of champagne and watched a TV celebrity narrate the countdown in Times Square. Coltrane had only a dim memory of the two of them stumbling up to his bedroom.

"Ouch," Jennifer said, surveying the damage. "I'm going to need that coffee to brace myself to help with this."

"Forget it," Coltrane said. "Come on. We'll go out for breakfast."

When they got back at twelve-thirty, they lingered in front of the house.

"If your visit with Greg's widow ends early, come over to my parents," Jennifer said.

"I will," Coltrane said. "Wish them a happy New Year for me."

Jennifer looked uncertain about something. "Would you do me a favor?"

"What?"

"Get a camera and take my picture?"

"Take your picture?"

"It's a new year," Jennifer said. "A new beginning. It would make me happy to see you taking photographs again."

"If it would make *you* happy, it would make *me* happy."

A minute later, he was back with his Nikon, positioning Jennifer against the ivy-looking greenish blue copper trim on the corner of the house.

"The background makes you look even more blond," Coltrane said. "In fact, you look radiant."

As her eyes brightened the way he had hoped they would in response to his compliment, Coltrane snapped the picture.

NINE

1

GREG'S WIDOW TURNED OUT TO HAVE A HOUSE FULL OF company: her parents, her sister, friends from where she worked at an insurance company, friends from the police department, not to mention neighbors. Paying their respects, they came and went. Although Greg's widow looked as if she hadn't been getting much sleep, she was making an effort to cook a turkey for the holiday, but it was clear that there wouldn't be enough to feed everyone, and Coltrane stayed only an hour, leaving well before dinner.

Hollow, he decided not to return to Packard's house but instead to take Jennifer up on her offer and go over to her parents' historic Victorian near Echo Park. The quickest way to get there from Venice was to take the Santa Monica Freeway east until it merged with the Golden State Freeway, eventually reaching the east end of Sunset Boulevard, which wasn't far from Echo Park. He was surprised, then, when he went in the opposite direction, taking the Santa Monica Freeway *west* to the Pacific Coast Highway. He finally admitted to himself that his destination was Malibu.

2

WHEN COLTRANE HAD FIRST ARRIVED IN LOS ANGELES seventeen years earlier, feeling a compulsion to learn as much as he could about the area, he had been intrigued to learn that Malibu—for

249

him, the name had mythic overtones—was actually many different places: the Commune, where upper-echelon show-business personalities lived within a guarded, gated community; the beachfront, where narrow two-story town houses abutted one another for what seemed miles, a narrow road in front, the ocean in back; a long string of gas stations, motels, and quick-food restaurants along the PCH; and, farther north, where the ocean and the highway diverged, a rustic community of expensive homes on large wooded lots reached by mazelike meandering roads that for the most part did not have an ocean view. Coltrane could smell the salt breeze. He had the sensation of being near water. Apart from that, he could have been in an exclusive section of the San Fernando Valley.

It was along one of these meandering roads that Coltrane now drove. Pausing occasionally to check a map that he had bought at a service station on the Pacific Coast Highway before turning off it, he continued west, or as much as he could in that general direction, sometimes having to retreat because of errors he made due to unmarked streets, other times reaching a dead end where the map made it seem that the road he was on connected with another. In frustration, he finally stopped where a wall of scrub brush blocked his way. A path led through it. As much as he could tell, the road he wanted lay beyond it.

Glancing at his watch, seeing that the time was already almost three o'clock and that he was close to wasting the day, he calculated that it might take him another twenty minutes to backtrack and get over to the road he wanted. That was assuming the road would be marked and he wouldn't have more difficulty finding it. Why bother when his destination was practically before him? Jennifer's request that he take her photograph had produced the effect she intended. Responding to old habits, he had brought his camera with him. Now he slung it around his neck. After getting out of his car and locking it, he buttoned his sport coat against the increasing chill of the day and pushed his way through the crackling branches of the scrub brush.

He heard the pounding of surf before he saw the ocean below him. He was on a steep ridge that looked down on the road he wanted, a line of impressive homes hugging the coast, no one in sight. In contrast with Malibu's famous beaches, the shoreline here was almost entirely gray rock. Intrigued by the whitecaps hitting those rocks, as well as by the red tile roofs on some of the homes, Coltrane raised his camera, chose a fast shutter speed to freeze the waves, and took several photographs.

Then he made his way carefully down a zigzag path on the bluff, some of which had been eroded by the recent heavy rains. He grasped an exposed tree root to help lower himself, clawed at clumps of grass, dug his heels firmly into the soft soil, and finally reached the bottom, where concrete barriers had been put up to protect against mud slides.

The surf pounded louder, and yet he was terribly conscious of the noise of his breathing. It's just from the exertion of coming down the slope, he told himself. Sure. When he reached a mission-style home, he saw that the number on the mailbox was 38, but he was looking for 24, so he proceeded farther along, too preoccupied to pay attention to the *cree-cree-cree* of seagulls floating overhead.

Yesterday, after he had obtained Natasha Adler's address and telephone number from the private investigator that Packard's attorney used, he had called that number and been frustrated when a computerized voice had told him that the number was no longer in service. Had the investigator given him the wrong information, or had Natasha Adler moved? Maybe she's living in the estate in Mexico now, Coltrane thought.

Continuing along the road, he passed another mission-style home, then a Spanish colonial. But his gaze was directed toward a house farther along, which his count of the remaining mailboxes told him was the address he wanted. It was substantial, sprawling, modernistic, an assemblage of two-story all-white blocks silhouetted against the stark blue sky, tinted by the lowering sun.

Struck by the geometry of the image, he again raised his camera. The contrast of light and shadow might be hard to capture, he knew, so he adjusted his exposure to favor the middle shadows of the image and took the photograph. As a precaution, he made two further exposures, the first favoring darker elements of the image, the second favoring lighter ones. The technique, known as "bracket-ing," would give him a choice of contrasts.

Having pressed the shutter button a final time, he lowered the camera and felt as if he had been away for a moment. It was a feel-ing that he hadn't experienced since the day he had come upon Packard's house and taken the last photographs in his update on Packard's series. He began to realize how truly numbed he had been by the intervening horrors. A new year, a new start, he thought, re-calling Jennifer's encouragement before they had separated earlier in the day.

Then what am I doing here?

3

LIKE MOST MALIBU SHORELINE HOMES, the house was close to the road. On the right, a tall metal fence enclosed a small garden. On the left, a red Porsche was parked in the short driveway, the closed doors of a two-car garage beyond it. Otherwise, no vehicles were in sight. At least someone's home, Coltrane thought. He verified that the number on the mailbox was what he wanted: 24.

And now what? he asked himself. Are you going to knock on the door in the middle of the afternoon on New Year's Day? That'll cer-tainly make an impression.

He peered through the metal fence toward the front windows, looking for movement in the house, some indication that a family gathering was in progress. The windows were blank eyes. The rooms were still. Maybe I wouldn't be interrupting anything, he thought. Maybe knocking on the door wouldn't be as inappropriate as I first thought. If I come back and knock on the door tomorrow or the day after, I'll still be intruding.

Barely aware of the ornate shrubs in the garden, he approached the front door. Instead of knocking, he pushed the doorbell and heard it ring hollowly inside. After waiting a moment, he pushed it again, the echoing doorbell making the place seem deserted. He rang it a third time, holding it a little longer. Someone has to be home, he thought. Otherwise, why would the Porsche be in the driveway? Whoever lives here wouldn't have gone on a trip and left an expensive sports car in the open. He switched from ringing the bell to knocking on the door, but still no one answered.

Maybe a couple are making love in there, he thought. Maybe if I keep ringing this bell and they finally do open the door, they'll be very explicit about how much I've annoyed them. I'm here to get some questions answered, not to antagonize the person I need to answer those questions.

Self-conscious, he hesitated, his finger an inch away from the doorbell. Yeah, tomorrow's better. Except maybe no one will answer the door then, either. If only the phone was in service.

Retreating to the road, Coltrane scanned the front windows to see if anyone was peering out at him, and finally he decided to give up. I should have gone with Jennifer, he thought. But as he prepared to walk back the way he had come, he suddenly realized that there was a perfectly reasonable explanation for the presence of the car and the failure of anyone to come to the door when he rang the bell.

Whoever's here is outside walking along the ocean.

He moved toward the left side of the house, intending to use the space between this house and the next to give him access to the shore. A wall blocked his way. On the right side, a similar wall stopped him. His excitement changing to frustration, he noticed that all the other homes had barriers, preventing outsiders from intruding on the beach.

When he walked past the remaining properties, he discovered a fence that went down to the waterline. The *cree-cree-cree* of the gulls became more pronounced. The crash of waves intensified as he stepped around the end of the fence, his shoes getting wet. It's one thing to ring a doorbell and disturb someone on New Year's Day, but it's quite another if I come across someone taking a walk, he thought. It would be natural for us to say hello. It wouldn't seem as intrusive for me to explain who I am and to ask a few questions.

Approaching the rear of the house, he saw a white deck perched over shelves of uneven gray rock that led down to the ocean. Stretching in both directions, the shelves of rock glistened as the spray from waves drifted over them.

But no one walked along those rocks. The shore was deserted.

Coltrane shook his head. Forced to admit that, for today at least, he truly had wasted his time, he began to turn to go back to the road, then stopped as movement among the rocks attracted his attention. Narrowing his eyes against the glare of the lowering sun (how could the sun be so bright and the air so shiveringly cool?), he thought he was hallucinating, for the movement wasn't just among the rocks—it *was* the rocks. One of them was rising from the others.

His skin prickled. He shivered harder, but no longer from the cold. The gray hump of rock rose higher, emerging from the shelf. *What am I seeing?* Coltrane asked himself, compelled to step forward. At once, something equally startling happened, for as the hump of rock rose high enough to detach itself from the shelf, Coltrane saw that the rock had an oval of white within the gray—a face. Gray arms detached themselves, one of them reaching up toward what had become a head and neck. A gray hand pulled at the gray on the head and, to Coltrane's amazement, peeled it off as if it were skin, revealing lush dark hair that clung wetly to the head of an amazingly beautiful woman. What he had been seeing, Coltrane realized, was a woman in a wet suit emerging from the ocean. The gray rubber of the suit was the same color as the shelves of rock. Rising from the waves, she had seemed to be born from them.

Immediately, he raised his camera, opened the aperture so that the waves would be indistinct behind her, and pressed the button as the woman emerged from the ocean. Her pose was so familiar that he felt he had to be hallucinating. He took another photograph, then another, each time stepping closer. Noticing him, the woman paused, one leg in front of the other, the knee slightly bent, about to transfer her weight from her back leg to her front. She wasn't wearing a scuba tank or a mask. She hadn't been diving, only swimming, using the insulation of the wet suit to keep her warm in the cold water. Her hands were covered with gray rubber gloves, one of which she had used to peel off the cowl of her suit. With the other gloved hand, she now brushed back her wet hair, and Coltrane had seen *that* pose before also. He pressed the shutter button again, catching her in midmotion. If it hadn't been for the wet suit, Coltrane would have been shaken by the most powerful déjà vu he had ever experienced. Even *with* the wet suit, the parallels were so striking that Coltrane didn't know if he could keep his hands steady as he continued taking photographs. The suit clung to the woman like skin. Its wet slickness enhanced the sinuous movement of her legs, the fluid motion of her body, the sensuous contours of her hips, her waist, her breasts, her . . .

He lowered the camera, his dazed mind demanding to know how it was possible that he could be looking at Rebecca Chance.

4

As he took another step, a look of fear crossed the woman's face. She stumbled backward, lost her balance, and slipped to her knees in the waves.

"No!" he told her. "You don't need to be afraid! I'm not here to hurt you!"

He raised his hands, causing her to raise her own gloved hands as if to protect herself.

"Please!" he said. "I didn't mean to startle you! All I want is to ask you some questions! I'm not going to hurt you!"

The slap of waves against the rocks wasn't loud enough to mute the sudden noises behind him: doors banging open, shouting, shoes scrabbling over rocks. Pivoting to look behind him, Coltrane was astonished to see a half dozen men racing toward him, two from the house, two from hiding places under the deck, one from shrubs on each side of the house.

"Stop right there!" one of them yelled, his face twisted with anger. "Don't move!"

As fast as he could, Coltrane turned and ran.

"You son of a bitch! Stay where you are, or I'll—"

Coltrane didn't hear the rest, the noise of the waves and his frenzied breathing blocking it out. His shoes slipped on the wet rocks, but he managed not to fall as he strained to increase speed, all the while hearing barked curses behind him. Without warning, ahead of him a man lunged from the side of another house, shoving out a hand, yelling at Coltrane to stop. Just when it seemed that he and the man would collide, Coltrane changed direction, veering around him, charging away from the shore, but two of the men racing behind him had anticipated that move and were running parallel to him, ready to grab him.

He changed direction yet again, hurrying back toward the shore. The man who had appeared from the side of the house had assumed that Coltrane would continue to rush inland. As a consequence, the man had left his strategic position and was racing inland, as well. Coltrane outmaneuvered him, continuing to charge along the shore.

"Damn it!" someone yelled.

Coltrane avoided a difficult shelf of rock and felt something twist in his stomach when he saw that the shore curved inward. To avoid the waves facing him, he would have to go inland again. His pursuers racing closer, he hurried around the half circle of the shore.

As one of the men darted at him from the side, Coltrane recalled how he had used his cameras to defend himself in Bosnia. He pulled the camera from around his neck, gripped its cord, and reached back to swing the camera toward the head of the attacking man.

"Hey!" The man lurched back.

Simultaneously, Coltrane lurched also, the backward motion of his arm causing him to lose his balance. His feet slipped out from under him. The next thing, all he saw was the sky as his body arched backward. The shock of cold water took the remainder of his breath away.

Not that it mattered. He couldn't breathe anyhow. He was submerged in a hollow among the rocks, flailing to reach the surface.

The current of a wave gripped him. Thrashing with cold-cramped arms, he heard a roaring in his ears. When he broke through the surface, the sun was almost blinding. Buffeted by another wave, he gasped and fought to inhale. Swallowing water, he coughed and tasted salt, then struggled against the weight of his water-filled shoes and soaked clothes and pawed toward a shelf of rock.

"Let him drown," a man said.

Peering up through water-bleared eyes, he saw the men standing along the shore, just beyond the reach of the waves, their faces as craggy as the shelves of rock. They wore sneakers, jeans, and windbreakers, and looked like the only thing they had wanted for Christmas was a renewal of their exercise-club memberships.

"Yeah, let's do the world a favor," another said.

"Sure," a third said. "He ran. He fell. We couldn't get him out before he drowned."

"But think about the lousy paperwork."

Coltrane's right hand gripped the shelf of rock. A wave thrust him toward it but as quickly tugged him away. His numbed hand lost its hold.

"The paperwork's worth it," the first man said. "Can you think of any better way to spend New Year's than watch this prick drown?"

"Not me," the fourth man said.

Aching from the cold, Coltrane got another grip on the rocks and strained to pull himself up. A wave knocked him against the shelf, making him groan. But despite the undertow, he mustered the strength to grip the shelf harder, pulling himself higher.

"Hold it." The first man stepped forward and pressed the sole of his sneaker against the back of Coltrane's right hand.

Coltrane winced.

"You didn't ask, 'May I?' " the man said.

"What do you think, Carl?" The second man turned toward someone approaching. "Do we let this jerk drown or pull his sorry ass out?"

Coltrane struggled as another wave splashed over him, his numbness worsening. He coughed and fought for air. Despite the bleariness in his salt-irritated eyes, he peered helplessly upward and

managed to get a look at the person joining them, a man in sneakers, jeans, and a windbreaker similar to what the others wore, a man
whose brown hair was trimmed to almost-military shortness and
whose matching brown eyes had a no-nonsense steadiness, showing
no reaction as he gazed down at Coltrane.

"Pull him out."

"What kind a fun is that? At least let's watch him splash around
a little longer."

"No, pull him out. This isn't the guy we want."

"How can you be sure."

"I know him."

"*What?*"

"He's a photographer named Mitch Coltrane. He lives in Los
Angeles, and believe me, he was otherwise occupied when all of this
started. We've got the wrong man."

The man who pressed his sneaker against Coltrane's hand took a
quick step backward.

Coltrane strained to get out of the water. The newcomer quickly
grabbed him, raising him dripping from the waves.

"Are you all right?" the man who had saved him asked.

"Frozen." Coltrane's teeth chattered. "I didn't know your first
name was Carl."

"That's because I wanted you to think that my first name was
Sergeant."

"What are you doing here?"

"That's exactly what I was going to ask *you*," Nolan said. "And I
can't wait to hear your answer."

5

YOU CAN SEE WHERE WE WOULD HAVE GOTTEN THE WRONG IDEA."
The first man gestured apologetically.

A blanket wrapped around him, Coltrane didn't respond, only kept shivering as he sat in a white wooden chair in an all-white living room. The back wall was composed entirely of glass, providing a panoramic view of the ocean. The late-afternoon sun blazed in but didn't warm him.

"You were peeking in her windows," the second man said.

"Give me a break. I was checking the house from the road, trying to see if it looked like anybody was at home."

"And taking pictures of the place," the third man said.

"I'm a professional photographer. That's what I do, take pictures."

"Including of a woman you claim you've never seen before, while you're trespassing?" the fourth man asked.

"Yeah, how come you were sneaking up on the house?"

"*Sneaking up?*" Coltrane asked.

"I suppose you're going to tell us you walked all the way here from L.A. Where's your car?"

Anger raised Coltrane's temperature as he told them where he had left his car.

"Okay, okay, that explains why you were on foot. But you weren't just sight-seeing. You didn't just happen to pick this house. What are you doing here?"

"I could have hit my head and been killed. You threatened to let me drown. I'm not answering any more questions until I find out who you are and what the hell's going on."

The group lapsed into an uncomfortable silence.

For the first time since entering the house, Nolan spoke. He had been standing in the background, shaking his head unhappily. "I think you already have a pretty good idea who the rest of these men are."

"The same as you—police officers."

"Not quite the same." In deference to the all-white decor, Nolan and everyone else had taken off their shoes. His socks whispered on the thick wall-to-wall carpet. "Malibu doesn't have a police department. Walt and Lyle here are with the local sheriff's department. Pete and Sam are with the state police. The rest of these men are LAPD."

"And how did *you* get involved?" Coltrane asked. "Since when do L.A. policemen work in Malibu?"

"They don't," Nolan said. "Unless it's their day off and they're here unofficially, doing somebody a favor."

"Me," the first man said. Nolan had introduced him as Walt. "I'm the one he was doing a favor."

"It's a stalker situation." Nolan gestured wearily, having dealt with crimes of this sort too many times before. "The woman living here has been harassed for the past three weeks by someone who seems to know everything she does. Until a while ago, he phoned her constantly. Even though she changed her number five times and none of them was ever listed, he still managed to find out what the new ones were and keep calling her. Finally, she had the phone taken out of service."

"That explains the computerized voice I heard when I tried to call yesterday."

"So you did try to call," the second man, Lyle, said. "I was going to ask you why you didn't phone instead of paying an unexpected visit on New Year's Day."

"You still think I'm lying?"

"Just crossing the *t*'s."

"Meanwhile," Nolan interrupted, "she started getting photographs."

Coltrane straightened.

The men studied him—he had never been looked at so directly.

"Photographs." Coltrane understood. "So when I showed up with a camera and started taking her picture, you assumed . . ."

"The photographs she receives—there are hundreds—have been taken wherever she goes," Nolan said. "No matter what she does, somebody manages to shoot pictures of her."

Coltrane felt a return of the bone-cold sensation of having been in the water, except that in this case he was frozen because he remembered how violated he had felt when he learned that Ilkovic had followed and photographed *him.*

"And that doesn't include the bouquets of flowers that are delivered to her a half dozen times a day. Not always when she's at home.

She's been getting them at restaurants, at her dentist's, once even at her gynecologist's. A note read, 'Thinking of you,' " Nolan said. "Love letters on the windshield of her car. Special-delivery proposals of marriage."

"So, naturally, she got worried enough to call the sheriff's department," Walt said. He had a brush cut, a squarish face, a sand-colored mustache, and a slight scar above his right eyebrow. "I'm the one who came out and interviewed her. We're not a big department. We don't have a lot of staff and resources, but that's what we were going to need, I knew, because right away it was obvious that the complainant needed surveillance, and not just in Malibu. *We* might care about jurisdictions, but the guy we're after is free to roam as he pleases. The complainant has business in Los Angeles. She goes there often. So I decided to call the LAPD Threat Management Unit and see if they had any advice."

"Which is where I come in," Nolan said. "Walt and I went to the Police Academy together. For a time, he was with the LAPD Robbery Division, but eventually he moved up here."

"For the peace and quiet," Walt said, as if peace and quiet were not what he had found.

"He asked for me," Nolan said, "and we discussed the obvious problem, which is that, strictly speaking, this ardent admirer hadn't broken the law."

Coltrane cocked his head in confusion.

"The problem is that, in addition to a pattern of harassment, there has to be an element of threat," Nolan said. "To you or me, it might be common sense that someone who pesters a woman night and day with professions of love is trying to intimidate her. But the district attorney's office might not see it that way. They might worry that a jury will figure this guy is more a nuisance than a threat. I once had a case where a stalker sent chocolates to a woman all the time, boxes and boxes. Phoned her constantly. Wrote hundreds of letters. She felt threatened and wanted him stopped. A restraining order didn't do any good. So I arrested him, and the case actually went to trial. But the jury couldn't decide if he was guilty of anything. This happened around Valentine's Day. One woman on the jury later said she thought sending all those chocolates was 'quaint.' Honest to God. Anyway, after the hung jury, the guy showed up at the woman's house one night and shot her in the head. Said he got tired of waiting for her to marry him. Said if *he* couldn't have her, nobody would. How's *that* for true love?"

"But in this case, we got lucky," Lyle said.

"If you want to call a threat lucky," Walt added. "The ardent admirer sent our complainant a funeral wreath with a ribbon across it that read, 'Till death do us part.' That's not the most explicit threat I ever heard of, but the ten-pound heart that came with the wreath certainly was. It turned out to be a bull's. It had an arrow through it, and a note attached to the arrow. 'Be mine. You're wounding my heart. Don't make me wound yours.' Tender, don't you think?"

"And enough to make a jury put him away," Coltrane said.

"Maybe not for long. But hey, the complainant would breathe easier for a while at least. Hell, maybe this jerk would use the time to reconsider how he shows affection."

"You don't have any idea who he is?"

"No, and neither does the complainant. The obvious temptation is to suspect he's someone she knows. But that's not always the way these things work. He might be someone she met five years ago and doesn't remember. Maybe he's a clerk at the bank she uses. Sometimes it takes only one look for a creep like this to get fixated on someone. We do know he orders the flowers by sending a letter of instructions along with cash to various flower shops. The wreath and the bull's heart were delivered by a parcel service. The return address on the packages was bogus. While the phone was still working, the guy frequently left his voice on the complainant's answering machine, but she doesn't recognize it."

"The best tactic we could think of," Walt said, "was to try to entrap him."

Lyle explained further. "Before the complainant had her phone disconnected, we told her to tell this guy when he called that it was time to put up or shut up, that she'd be waiting for him here this afternoon. She made certain he understood how angry she was with him and that she wanted to see him face-to-face to guarantee he got the point that she wanted nothing at all to do with him."

"It was an ultimatum we hoped he couldn't refuse," Nolan said. "Especially because, when the phone was disconnected yesterday, the creep had no way to get in touch with her to try to renegotiate the terms of the meeting."

"Then we sent for the cavalry," Walt said. "Lyle and I are officially on duty. These other guys are friends helping out."

"On New Year's Day. I'm impressed," Coltrane said. "Friends wouldn't normally give up New Year's Day to—"

"The complainant's generous," one of the other men said.

The rest of the group looked at the man as if he had said too much.

"There's nothing wrong with it," Walt said. "When we're off duty, she hires us to be her protection. One or the other of us goes into L.A. with her."

"Speaking of . . ." One of the state troopers glanced around nervously. "Where *is* Tash?"

The group tensed.

"Jesus." Walt snapped to attention. "What happened to her? The last time I saw her, she was coming out of the water and we were chasing—"

6

I NEEDED TO GET INTO SOMETHING DRY," a voice said from above, on Coltrane's right.

He turned toward a stairway, seeing a bare foot appear on the landing. The voice was full-throated, making Coltrane think of similar-voiced actresses in films from the thirties and forties. In his memory, they were always in a sparkling evening gown, standing next to a piano in a nightclub, exchanging repartee with a handsome hero in a white dinner jacket.

But the woman who descended the white carpeting on the stairway wasn't wearing an evening gown. She wore a cotton sweatsuit, the raspberry color of which enhanced her tan face, dark eyes, and even darker hair. Although the exercise suit was oversized, a dramatic opposite to the tight wet suit she had worn a little while ago, her present outfit was nonetheless almost as revealing. The loose seat suggested the trim firmness of the hips it concealed. The similarly loose top moved up and down in the front and suggested that the woman had not put on a bra.

Everyone watched as she reached the bottom. Coltrane had the sense that the men liked to see her bare feet touch the plush carpeting, but his own attention was directed toward her face: the broad forehead, high cheekbones, almond-shaped eyes, slender nose, curved lips, angular chin, and narrow jaw that were the elements of classical beauty and that Rebecca Chance had been blessed with. But a catalog of her features couldn't communicate the animation of those features. Even in a sweatsuit, this woman had come down the stairs with the same fluid ease that Rebecca Chance had shown descending a staircase, wearing a sarong in *Jamaica Wind*. Her hair, still wet from having been in the ocean, was pushed back, clinging to her head, the way Rebecca Chance had pushed it back as she waded out of a river in *The Trailblazer*. That pose coming out of the river had been the same as the pose in Randolph Packard's photographs of Rebecca Chance stepping out of the ocean, the same pose that *this* woman had assumed as she came out of the ocean onto the rocks not long ago.

Coltrane's mind was aswirl.

"Hello." She approached Coltrane, her gaze locked intimately on his as she held out her hand. "I'm Tash Adler, and I'm sorry about the misunderstanding."

Coltrane felt a spark when their hands touched. Only static electricity from the carpet, he told himself. And yet . . .

"I hope you aren't hurt."

"No, I'm fine." Coltrane suddenly felt foolish holding the blanket around him. "A little cold is all." He eased the blanket off him. "Nothing serious." He repressed another shiver, his wet clothes clinging to him. "Tash?"

"It's short for Natasha. You should get into something dry before you catch pneumonia." The concern in her voice made him feel that at that particular moment he was the most important person in the world to her. "But where am I going to find dry clothes for you? I don't think you'll fit into one of my bathrobes."

The fact was, she was only about three inches shorter than Coltrane's six-foot height, and he might indeed have fitted into one of her bathrobes.

"I know," Tash said. "Why don't you go into the bathroom down the hall, take off your wet clothes, and give them to me. I'll put them in the dryer."

"I . . ."

"It'll take only fifteen minutes," Tash said. "We'll leave the door ajar so you can be part of the conversation and not feel you're in limbo. I'll make a pot of strong hot coffee for everybody and hand a cup in to you."

Coltrane's face felt warm, only partly because his cheeks were losing their numbness from the cold water. "Sure."

"This way."

Tash gripped his arm, the feeling intimate, guiding him past the white stairway, down a white corridor, to the open door of a white bathroom. A white kitchen was farther along the corridor.

"I'll wait," Tash said.

Self-conscious, Coltrane entered the bathroom and shut the door. For a moment, his automatic impulse was to lock it, but he stopped himself, imagining how ridiculous the snap of the lock would sound, as if he was afraid she would barge in on him while he was undressing. He peeled off his wet sport coat, shirt, pants, and socks, took his belt, wallet, keys, and comb from his pants, hesitated, then decided that he didn't want her to have to deal with his underwear. Even as things were, he didn't feel comfortable that she would have to touch his wet clothes. He solved the problem by wrapping them in a towel. Despite the underwear he kept on, he didn't think he had ever felt quite so naked as when he stood behind the door and opened it a foot, peering out at her.

"I'm sorry to put you through the inconvenience," he said.

"Nonsense." Tash's eyes crinkled with amusement. "I'm hoping that if I'm nice to you, you won't sue me."

Coltrane couldn't help smiling.

"Be back in a jiff." She carried his towel-wrapped clothes down the corridor.

Coltrane took another towel from the rack, dried himself, then sponged the towel against his wet underwear. That done, he combed his hair, folded his sport coat over the toilet seat, rubbed his arms to try to get warmth into them, and was surprised to hear Tash's voice behind him.

"Maybe this will fit you after all."

Turning, he saw her hand projecting through the gap he had left in the doorway. She was offering a white terry-cloth bathrobe.

"Thanks, but I'm sure I'll be fine," Coltrane said.

Instead of replying, Tash leaned in far enough to drape the bathrobe over the side of the tub, her head turned away from him. The next thing, her arm was gone, and her footsteps receded along the hallway.

Coltrane looked at the robe a long time before picking it up and putting it on. Tash was right. Although a little snug, it did fit him. The fragrance on it was possibly from perfume and not laundry soap.

7

EVEN WITH THE DOOR AJAR, Coltrane couldn't hear what Tash and the men were talking about in the living room. Their voices blended. An echo distorted them. Frustrated, he waited, tensing as heavy footsteps came along the corridor. What'll it look like if one of those guys comes in and sees me crammed into this robe? he wondered.

"Do you want a beer instead of the coffee?" Nolan's voice asked.

"Yeah, with a straw."

Nolan chuckled. By the time he returned, handing a Budweiser into the bathroom, Coltrane had gotten out of the robe and hung it on a hook. Nolan had indeed put a straw into the open can of beer. Coltrane shook his head in amusement, took out the straw, tilted the can to his lips, and drank half of it.

The indistinguishable voices in the living room filled him with increasing frustration. The hands on his watch didn't seem to move. To distract himself, he looked for a magazine, didn't find any, and examined the pump containers of hand soap and lotion that were on the counter. Curious, he reached to open the medicine cabinet.

"All done." Tash startled him.

Turning in embarrassment, he saw her hand offering him dried clothes through the gap in the door.

"Thanks."

When Coltrane took them, their hands happened to brush. He felt another crackle of electricity.

"Sorry," she said from the other side of the door. "The air must be dry in here or something. I didn't mean to shock you."

"I barely noticed."

"*I* did. I've been doing it a lot lately. I even took off my socks so I wouldn't generate static. No difference. It makes me self-conscious."

"There's no need to be."

"It's in my nature."

"To give off static electricity?"

"To be self-conscious. See you in a few minutes."

"Right." Coltrane looked at the side of his hand where the crackling sensation lingered.

As quickly as possible, he slipped into his pants, shirt, and socks, enjoying their warmth, grateful to be dressed again. He tried to look natural when he entered the living room, the men looking up at him from the sofa and various chairs.

Walt and Lyle, the two officers officially on duty, were drinking coffee. The others each had a beer. Tash leaned against a wall, holding a glass of white wine. The crimson of the soon-to-set sun filled the white room, the combination of colors so intriguing that Coltrane wished he still had his camera.

An object on the coffee table caught his attention.

"*My Nikon?* I thought I'd lost it in the water."

"No, you dropped it on the rocks," Walt said. "In all the commotion, I didn't have a chance to go back and get it until a few minutes ago."

"I owe you. This camera and I have been through a lot." Coltrane examined it, unhappy to see that the lens was shattered and the body more scratched than it had previously been, but it didn't appear that the case had been cracked—the negative of the images he had taken of Tash might not have been exposed to light. Even so, with its lens cracked, the camera was temporarily useless to him.

"We told you ours. Now you tell us yours," Nolan said.

"Excuse me?"

"Your story. You didn't just happen to show up here. Why did you come?"

So you're still not sure about me, Coltrane thought. "My timing wasn't the greatest. I hope this doesn't sound presumptuous." He looked at Tash. "I'm curious about . . . You inherited some property recently from a man named Randolph Packard."

Tash straightened against the wall. "That's right."

Except for Nolan, the men looked puzzled by the reference. Coltrane told them who Packard was.

"I met him toward the end of November," Coltrane said to Tash. "In fact, I collaborated on a project with him, although he died before I could get much input from him. Not that it mattered—from the beginning of my career, he had tremendous influence on me. And especially lately, I guess you could say he changed my life. Anyway, I decided to buy a house he owned. When I heard about another property he owned, one in Mexico, I was tempted to buy it also, but then I discovered that the property had been given to you, so I . . ." Coltrane's sentence hung in the air.

"You came here to ask me if I'd be interested in selling it?" Sounding almost relieved, Tash leaned away from the wall.

"Something like that," Coltrane said.

"*That's* what this is all about?" Walt sounded annoyed. "You came here to buy real estate?"

"Basically," Coltrane lied.

"Well, for God sake," one of the state policemen said. "I waited around to hear *that*? I was sure there had to be a fancy explanation for the coincidence."

"Sorry."

Shaking their heads, several men stood. "I've got to be going," one of the state troopers said.

"Me, too," Lyle said. "My wife's got a pot roast in the oven. There's no point in all of us hanging around anymore. The man we were trying to catch was probably studying the house. When we tipped our hand too soon because of . . ." He gestured toward Coltrane.

"Yeah." Walt sounded disgusted. "The creep's long gone by now. We started our surveillance in the middle of the night, presumably before he started his own surveillance." Weariness strained his face. "But now that he knows we were waiting for him, we'll have a hard time setting another trap. The good news is, tonight will probably be quiet. You guys go ahead. Enjoy what's left of your New Year's. I'll hold down the fort."

"No, that's all right," Tash said. "You go ahead, too."

"But . . ."

"As you said, tonight will probably be quiet. Cross fingers that whoever it is left the area for now. The sheriff's department has more people to protect than just me."

"But not all of them *need* protecting," Walt said. "I don't feel comfortable leaving you alone."

"I appreciate your concern," Tash said. "I won't be alone, though."

Walt looked puzzled.

"Mr. Coltrane is going to stay for a while. We're going to discuss real estate."

Coltrane must have looked surprised.

"If that's convenient," Tash said to him. "Perhaps you have somewhere else you need to be. I just thought that since you came all this way to talk to me . . ."

"No," Coltrane said. "No, there's nowhere else I have to be."

8

THE TIME WAS JUST AFTER FIVE IN THE AFTERNOON, the air turning from crimson to gray, the breeze increasing, becoming cooler as the men stepped outside the front door and put on their sneakers. Tash opened the twin garage doors, revealing two large four-wheel-drive vehicles, an Explorer and a Mountaineer. As some of the men got into them, Tash eased into her Porsche and backed it out of the driveway, allowing the Mountaineer that she had been blocking to get out of the garage. The moment the stall was free, she pulled into it.

Coltrane couldn't help noticing that for the brief time she was away, the men who hadn't yet gotten into the vehicles stopped talking and watched her.

"Remember, if you have even the slightest hint of trouble, don't think twice—call us," Lyle told her.

"Don't worry. I'm a coward at heart. When I'm by myself, I don't go anywhere without carrying the phone."

Coltrane frowned. "Phone? But I thought it was out of service."

"It is," Walt said. "We're talking about a cellular phone I bought for Tash and had activated in *my* name. Whoever this creep is, he keeps managing to find out the new numbers she gets in *her* name. But so far, he doesn't know anything about this number."

"Good idea," Coltrane said.

"Let's hope it *stays* a good idea. Tash, if you need anything, let me know."

She touched his arm in a gesture of thanks.

"While you guys are still here . . ." Coltrane said.

They looked at him, wondering what he was leading up to.

"Can you wait another few minutes while I get my car? I don't want to stumble around looking for it after dark. This way, Tash won't be alone while I'm gone."

"Yeah, I can stick around a little longer," Lyle said.

"And I'll make it quicker by driving you to your car." Nolan motioned for Coltrane to follow him to the garage and the Explorer that remained in the stall next to Tash's Porsche.

One of the policemen was in the passenger seat. Another policeman and one of the state troopers was in the back. While Nolan got behind the steering wheel, Coltrane climbed into the back. He saw Walt and Lyle talking to Tash in front of the house while Nolan left the garage, reached the road, and drove away.

"Our cars are parked behind a service station on the highway," the policeman in the front seat explained. "That way, it didn't look like we were having a convention at Tash's place while we were waiting for him to show up."

"You set it up well."

"Too bad the wrong guy showed up."

Uncomfortable, Coltrane changed the subject. "I'm on a street on that bluff."

"You certainly had yourself lost," Nolan said.

By the time Coltrane got back, it was dark. Lights glowed warmly in the house. The officers in the Mountaineer had gotten out and joined Walt and Lyle, speaking with Tash in her front hallway.

Tash smiled at Coltrane in welcome.

"Just as a precaution," Lyle told him, "better put your car in the garage, where nothing will happen to it."

"Right."

Then Walt, Lyle, and the others said good-bye and drove away. As the gleam of taillights receded, the road became dark except for the pinpoints of lights in a house farther along.

Finally Coltrane and Tash were alone.

9

SHE BROKE THE SILENCE. "Would you like another beer?"

"Sounds good." Coltrane had all kinds of questions, but he didn't want to overwhelm her. Take it slow and easy, he thought.

She locked the front door, then opened the inside garage door and pressed a button that closed each stall. After that, she secured the inside garage door, too.

"Before I get you that beer, would you help me walk the picket line? You know, check the security?"

"Officer Coltrane reporting for duty." He hoped it sounded like a joke, which apparently it did, because she looked amused as she started down the hallway.

"Carl and the others already locked up, but I feel more comfortable if I double-check," she said. Past the stairway, they entered the living room and crossed to the sliding glass doors that led onto the deck. There, Tash tried to open the door. "Definitely secure."

Pensive, she looked out past the white deck toward the darkness on the rocks and the whitecaps on the waves in the black ocean. "I used to love sitting out there, even when it's cold like this, watching the waves hit the shore, listening to them. Sometimes I can see a freighter on the horizon, its lights moving, heading to mysterious places. 'So we beat on, boats against the current . . . ' "

" '. . . borne back ceaselessly into the past.' "

She turned to him, surprised. "You know *Gatsby*?"

Coltrane shrugged. "When I was at USC, one of my photography instructors insisted I take a few literature classes. For some reason, *The Great Gatsby* really stayed with me, that final image. Randolph Packard had an image like that in one of his photographs. The lights of a freighter on the horizon."

"Heading to mysterious places," Tash echoed. She had sounded melancholy, but now she mocked herself. "Probably only to Long Beach. Anyway, for a while, those nights are over."

She pressed a button on the wall to the right. A faint rumble puzzled Coltrane until he saw metal shutters descending, blocking off the all-glass wall at the back of the living room.

"It makes me feel like I'm in a castle," Tash said, "except I'm lowering the shutters instead of raising the drawbridge."

Coltrane followed her into the kitchen, where she turned on an overhead light that reflected off white countertops, creating a pleasant luster. After confirming that a side door was locked, she leaned against a counter, stared down, shook her head, then roused herself. "Almost forgot that beer."

There were several in the refrigerator. Presumably for the men helping her, Coltrane thought.

"Don't bother about a glass. The can is fine," he said.

"You sure?" She poured Chablis into a glass and touched it against the beer can she had given him. "Cheers."

"Cheers."

"It doesn't seem much like New Year's, does it?"

"I have a friend who keeps emphasizing that it's a matter of attitude," Coltrane said, "that we should think of it as a chance for a new beginning."

"Yeah." Troubled, Tash sipped her wine. "The question is, a new beginning of *what?* The start of the *really* bad times?"

"I don't think that's the attitude my friend had in mind."

Leaning against the counter opposite her, Coltrane had a dizzying sense of unreality. Tash Adler even *spoke* like Rebecca Chance, her full-throated voice and engaging cadences the same as Rebecca Chance's in *The Trailblazer* and *Jamaica Wind.* She seemed to be in her mid-twenties, the same age Rebecca Chance had been when she disappeared.

"Is something the matter?" Tash asked. "You're looking at me as if . . . Have I got something caught in my teeth?"

He laughed. "Not at all. Sorry. I didn't mean to stare. It's a photographer's habit. I can't help imagining how I would take someone's picture."

"Is that what you want to do? Take my photograph?"

273

"There's something about the way you're leaning against that counter."

"Oh?" She looked puzzled.

Coltrane realized that a compliment about her looks might sound as if he was coming on to her. The last thing he wanted was to alienate her. "The raspberry of the exercise suit you're wearing is the only bright color in the room. Otherwise, everything's white. Well, not totally. Those knives in that container have black handles. So do the handles on that toaster and the knobs on the stove."

"I added those touches of black deliberately," Tash said. "Without contrast, white isn't effective."

"That's what intrigued me. Your suit makes this room a black-and-white photograph in color."

Tash considered him. "You're very observant."

Coltrane made a modest gesture. "It comes from taking a lot of photographs."

"No, I suspect taking photographs didn't make you observant. The other way around. But I also suspect you often see more than you ever wanted to. Not everything's beautiful."

Coltrane remembered sighting through his telephoto lens as Ilkovic directed his men to grind up the bones of the corpses that the backhoe had dredged up from the mass grave in Bosnia. "Yes, not everything's beautiful."

"I need to ask you something."

Coltrane inwardly came to attention.

"The reason I asked you to stay."

Coltrane waited.

"I didn't want to talk about this in front of the others," Tash said. "You seem to know an awful lot about Randolph Packard."

"Since my late teens, I've been trying to learn everything I can about him."

"Then maybe you could tell me something. Do you have any idea at all why he would have included me in his will?"

It took Coltrane several seconds to recover. "You don't know?"

"I was absolutely mystified when his attorney got in touch with me. Sure, I know who Randolph Packard was, but for the life of me,

I can't figure out why he would have given me that estate in Mexico. It's like he picked my name out of a hat or something. Totally unexpected. I asked his attorney. What's his name? Blaine?"

"Yes."

"I asked Blaine if *he* knew why Packard had chosen me, but Blaine told me he hadn't the faintest idea."

"From what Blaine told *me*, that seems to be the truth."

"I didn't know who besides Blaine to ask," Tash said, "and by then, I was deep in this mess with whoever . . ." She gestured toward a wall and whatever lurked beyond it. "I've had a lot of things on my mind. So when, out of nowhere, I heard you mention Packard and the estate in Mexico, you could have knocked me over."

"I have to be honest about something."

Tash's dark eyes narrowed, as if she was afraid of what he was going to say.

"I haven't been entirely open with you," Coltrane said.

She looked more uneasy.

"The reason I came here wasn't just to find out if you'd be interested in selling the Mexican estate. I've never seen it. Who knows how it'll strike me if I ever do see it? What I really came here for was to ask you the same question *you* asked *me*."

"Why Randolph Packard gave me the Mexican estate?"

"Yes."

Tash shook her head in exhaustion. "Please. I have all the mysteries I can handle."

"But maybe the answer to mine will help solve one of yours. Have you ever heard of an up-and-coming movie actress in the thirties named Rebecca Chance?"

Baffled, Tash considered the name. "No."

"I'm not surprised. She disappeared before she had the chance to become a star."

"But what does she have to do with—"

"She was being stalked. The same pattern of letters, gifts, and phone calls. Then one day she vanished."

"If you're trying to frighten me even more than I already am . . ."

"No," Coltrane said. "I'm trying to help you figure out why Randolph Packard put you in his will. Packard was desperately in love with her."

"Rebecca Chance."

"Yes." Coltrane paused, struck anew by the alluring features of the woman across from him and the uncanny situation in which he found himself. "And Rebecca Chance looked so much like you . . . *you* look so much like her . . . you might as well be the same woman."

"What in God's name are you talking about?"

Coltrane hesitated.

He told her everything.

"*Photographs?*"

"And movies that Rebecca Chance was featured in. But you're right to zero in on the photographs. They're what's truly important. Because Packard took them. Because he hid them."

"And Rebecca Chance is identical to me?"

"So much so that I thought I was hallucinating when I first saw you."

"This is . . . I can't . . ." She stared at him. "Show them to me."

Coltrane blinked in surprise. "What?"

"I want to see the photographs."

"But I don't have them with me. I can come back tomorrow and bring—"

"Now. I want to see them. *Take me to them.*"

Tash's emotion was so intense that for several moments Coltrane wasn't able to move or speak. He found himself saying hesitantly, "All right . . . sure . . . if that's what you . . ."

"I'll just need a second upstairs."

"We'll be going into L.A."

"You don't have to worry about driving me back. I'll follow you."

"I wouldn't mind driving you back. It's just that . . ." A misgiving nagged at him. It had nothing to do with showing Tash the photographs. If anybody had the right to see them, it seemed to him that *she* did. His uneasiness came from another source, something to do with the parallel between Rebecca Chance's stalker and Tash Adler's stalker and . . .

Mine. With a shudder, he realized that in order to help Tash, he had to be as cautious now as he had been when Ilkovic was hunting him. He had to put himself in her place, to imagine that *he* was the person in danger.

"It's better if I drive you," Coltrane said.

Tash paused on her way from the kitchen. She looked mystified.

"If someone *is* watching your house, he'll follow you when you follow me, and he wouldn't have much trouble. A Porsche isn't inconspicuous."

"That's what Walt said." Tash sounded disheartened. "Get rid of the Porsche, or at least rent something bland until this jerk is in prison. I've already reduced my movements until I'm practically living in a box." She shook her head stubbornly. "I'm not going to let that bastard take anything more away from me."

"But you don't have to drive the Porsche."

"What am I going to do, run behind you and bark at your tires?"

It sounded so unexpectedly humorous, they stared at each other and found themselves laughing.

"God, it feels good to do that," Tash said. "I can't remember the last time I truly laughed." It made her radiant.

"Honestly," Coltrane said, "I think I should drive you."

"But if he's out there, he'll still see the two of us in your car. He'll still follow."

"Not if you get in my car while the garage door is down. You lie on the back floor until we're a distance away. Since he won't know you're with me, he'll stay and watch the house. Have you got any timers for the lights?"

10

As THE GARAGE DOOR DESCENDED, Coltrane removed his hand from the remote control he had taken from the Porsche and continued backing onto the murky road. He turned on his headlights only after the door was sufficiently low that illumination into the garage wouldn't reveal that Tash wasn't in there and wasn't pressing the control on the wall to lower the door.

So far so good, Coltrane thought. But he knew that a couple of other tactics were required to make the ruse convincing. Pausing at the foot of the driveway, he turned on his car's interior lights and consulted a map, as if figuring out how to get back to the highway. Anyone watching the house would see that he was alone. Next, he shut off the interior lights and tapped his horn twice, two short blasts, evidently saying good-bye. As he proceeded along the road, his headlights probing the darkness, he glanced at his rearview mirror and saw a lamp go off in a window.

"The timer worked perfectly," he said.

"It looks like I'm still at home and turning off a few lights?" Tash asked from where she hid on the back floor.

"Yep. And there goes the second one," Coltrane said, watching his rearview mirror.

"Inspired," Tash's voice came muffled from the back.

"Not to be immodest, but I agree. Even so, stay down for a while. I want to watch for any headlights that start following us."

"Is this . . ."

Coltrane waited, but Tash didn't finish her question. "What?"

"Maybe you don't want to talk about it."

"How can I know until you tell me?"

"Is this what you had to do when you were running from Dragan Ilkovic?"

The reference caught Coltrane unawares, blunting the satisfaction he had felt in getting Tash out of the house. "How did you know about me and Ilkovic?"

"While you were in the bathroom waiting to get your clothes dried, Carl Nolan told me."

It felt odd to be having a conversation with someone Coltrane couldn't see. He made an effort not to tilt his head in Tash's direction and ruin the illusion that he was alone.

"I knew about what had happened at that movie ranch," Tash's voice continued below and behind him. "At the time, there wasn't much else in the newspapers or on the television news. But when I met you, your name didn't register. I didn't make the connection."

"That's encouraging. I hate to think that every time I introduce myself to someone new, I'll always be remembered as the man who shot Ilkovic. I prefer to be known for my photographs, not for killing someone—even if he did deserve it."

"I'm sorry for asking you to talk about it."

"No, it's fine. I can't pretend it didn't happen. I used to check for headlights behind me all the time. I used to drive around the block and down narrow alleys and one-way streets—anyplace that would make it unusual for someone to stay behind me. But the timers on the lamps, all that business in the garage, they weren't anything I'd tried before."

"It's reassuring to know you're inventive."

"Yeah, but it's not something I'm overjoyed to find out I'm inventive at. Keep staying down." Coltrane steered onto the Pacific Coast Highway and checked for any headlights that emerged onto the highway after him. "So far so good."

"Let's hope," Tash's muffled voice said.

"When you found out what I had done to Ilkovic, did it change the way you looked at me?"

"No."

"Why not?"

"As you put it, he deserved to be killed."

"That he did." Coltrane sighed bleakly. "That he did."

"People you know did change the way they related to you?"

"One in particular."

"Powerful emotions can be frightening." Coming from the darkness, Tash's disembodied voice sounded more faint, almost childlike. "Do you have nightmares?"

"Yes. I thought they'd go away, but they haven't. I keep dreaming that Ilkovic isn't dead, that he's still coming for me. I imagine his hands . . ."

"I have nightmares, too," Tash said. "Someone's reaching for me, but I can't see his face. Since I don't know what he looks like, it's natural that he'd be faceless, I suppose, but it's worse than that. It's almost as if he doesn't have a . . ."

"Head."

"Then you understand."

"That's in *my* nightmare also," Coltrane said.

"This'll sound odd, but I'm glad."

"What?"

"You're the first person I've been able to talk to about what I'm feeling and know that you understand. Walt, Lyle, Carl, and the others—I try to explain how alone and afraid I feel, and they tell me they know what I mean. But they *don't* know. How can they possibly? They're big men with badges and guns. Their lives are in control. They're not being stalked."

"We're in a limited club."

"Not you. Not any longer. But it's reassuring to know that you survived. I feel safe with you."

"I hope I don't let you down." Again, Coltrane checked his rearview mirror. "I didn't see any cars pull onto the highway after us. I think it's okay now for you to sit up."

"Since I'm feeling safe . . ."

Coltrane wondered what she meant to say.

"Why don't I stay down out of sight until we get to *your* place?"

"It's a long drive," Coltrane said.

"It won't be if we keep talking the way we are. Tell me about your photographs."

11

ALL CLEAR," Coltrane said as his garage door rumbled shut.

"Ouch," Tash said. "I'm going to need a couple of aerobics classes to get my back into shape after this." She rose, massaged her spine, and got out of the car. But it was obvious that she wasn't that creaky.

An upward stretch of her arms accentuated her trim body. She had changed from her loose-fitting sweatsuit to a pair of blue slacks, a gray turtleneck sweater, and a jacket whose color resembled the raspberry tint of what she had previously been wearing—obviously a favorite color; it added a depth to her dark eyes and hair. When she stretched, she turned modestly away, so as not to emphasize her breasts in front of him, Coltrane assumed. No matter, that upward stretch and a slight twist this way and then that were a pleasure to behold, her body assuming the dancer's grace she had exhibited when he first saw her, although Coltrane continued to have the uncanny feeling that he had first seen her long before that.

Watching in wonder, he suddenly found himself in darkness.

"What happened?" Tash asked in surprise.

"The garage opener's overhead light is supposed to stay on for a minute after the door goes down, but it's been cutting out much sooner. I'll go over and turn on the switch."

Footsteps scraping on concrete, he inched through the darkness and approached where he estimated the door to the house was. Reaching blindly, he touched the door and groped toward the switch on the right, all at once flinching from a shock, seeing a spark as a hand brushed past his and reached for the same switch.

"Oh my God," Tash said, "I'm sorry."

"Whoa. You really do give off static electricity."

"I thought you were having trouble finding the switch. I was looking in that direction when the lights went off, so I figured it would be easier for me to . . . I really am sorry."

When Coltrane turned on the light, he discovered he was startlingly close to her. Again, her beauty amazed him. Her subtle perfume filled his nostrils. Trying not to look flustered, he unlocked the door to the house and opened it, guiding her in. "Can I get you something?" He hoped that she wouldn't notice that his voice was slightly unsteady. "More wine? Coffee? Something to eat? It's close to dinnertime. I could make some—"

"The photographs." Tash ignored the house and its unique furnishings, fixing her gaze on him.

"Of course. They're the reason you're here, after all." He led the

281

way downstairs, unlocked the vault, and pushed open its metal door. Cool air cascaded over them.

Tash hugged herself.

"That's the way *I* felt at first," Coltrane said. "You'll get used to it."

"Will I?" Tash looked around at the austere shelves and blinked from the overhead glare.

Crossing the vault with her, he had never felt so aware of being alone with a woman.

En route, he had explained how he had happened to find the chamber. But she still wasn't prepared when he freed the catches and pulled out the section of shelves, and she certainly wasn't prepared when she entered the chamber and came face-to-face with her look-alike. It might have been the garish overhead lights that caused what happened next, but more likely, Coltrane thought, it was blood draining from Tash's face that made her look abruptly pale.

She wavered. Afraid that she was going to collapse, Coltrane reached to catch her, then stopped the impulse when she regained her composure, standing rigidly still. He could only imagine the turmoil she must be suffering. For his part, as he looked from Tash toward the wall before her and the life-sized features of Rebecca Chance, he suffered a sanity-threatening unbalance. The photograph was Tash. Tash was the photograph. But it *wasn't,* and *she* wasn't. The face in the photograph was almost two-thirds of a century old.

"I . . ." Tash swallowed as if something blocked her throat. Her voice thickened. "How on earth is this possible?"

"That's what I was hoping *you'd* tell *me.*"

With palpable effort, she turned from the photograph. "And you say there are *other* photographs?"

"Thousands of them. I was so absorbed by them that I never took the time to count them."

"Show me."

The distress in her eyes frightened him. "Are you sure you want to go through with this? This is more unsettling for you than I expected. Perhaps you should—"

"*I want to see them.*"

"Yes." Coltrane felt powerless. "Whatever you want."

He picked up the top box, suddenly remembered what was in it, set it aside, and picked up the next one, carrying it out to one of the shelves. Tash followed, stepping so close that he felt her shoulder against him as he opened the lid.

Rebecca Chance stepped out of waves onto a beach, just as Tash had stepped out of waves a few hours earlier.

Coltrane felt the air that Tash's forced breathing displaced. In her need to look at them, she would probably have pushed him aside if he hadn't stepped out of the way. Then the echo of his sideways movement dwindled, and the only sound in the vault was the smooth slide of photographs being hurriedly turned, one after the other after the other.

Totally preoccupied by *them*, Tash was equally oblivious to *him*. It gave him a chance to indulge his need to admire her.

"What's in the first box?"

"Excuse me?"

Tash had reached the last photograph in the box so quickly and pivoted toward him so unexpectedly that he had been caught staring at her.

"You set a box aside before you picked up *this* one."

"Did I? I don't remember. I—"

"Why didn't you want me to look inside it?"

"No special reason. The photographs in this one are more interesting is all. I—"

Tash reentered the vault. Before he could take a step to prevent her, she came determinedly back into view, carrying another box, and Coltrane had no doubt which box it was. The previous evening, after he had shown Jennifer the nudes of Rebecca Chance, he had put the box on top of the others rather than at the bottom, where he had found it.

Tash narrowed her eyes, as if she suspected he had tried to betray her. Then she opened the lid and straightened at the sight of Rebecca Chance's naked body, the glistening chromium beads draped over her. Tash didn't seem able to move. Slowly, with a manifest effort of will, she turned to the next photograph and the next. Because

there weren't any clothes, the thirties style of which would have identified the period during which the photographs had been taken,
these images could as easily have been taken now, and could as easily have been of Tash—if that was how Tash looked naked.

Again she seemed paralyzed. But this time, when she finally
moved, it was to look at Coltrane. "You were trying to protect my
modesty?"

"Something like that. I wasn't sure how comfortable you'd feel
with me in the room while you looked at photographs of a naked
woman, especially when that woman looks just like you."

Tash studied him.

"I thought it would be sort of like looking at . . ."

"Myself?" she asked.

"It's an awfully personal situation."

"Thank you for respecting my feelings."

Coltrane nodded, self-conscious.

She touched his hand. "Show me what's in the other boxes."

12

YOU KEEP EMPHASIZING THIS ROCK FORMATION. Why do you think
it's important?" Tash asked.

"Because it reminds me of a cat arching its back," Coltrane said.

"So?"

"The estate Packard gave you in his will is located near a town
south of Acapulco called—"

"Espalda del Gato. I know. The name was in the documents
Packard's attorney sent me."

"How's your Spanish?"

"I see what you mean. 'Spine of the cat.' But that doesn't prove the
rock formation we're looking at has anything to do with the village.
It's more likely a coincidence and this cliff along the ocean isn't any-

where near the estate I inherited. For all we know, this cliff is in Southern California."

"But it isn't," Coltrane said. "The other night I saw a movie Rebecca Chance was in. It's called *Jamaica Wind*, and some parts of it were filmed on what is recognizably the Santa Monica beach, with the cliff behind it. But then all of a sudden, the location switches to a lush semitropical cliff-rimmed area along an ocean."

"That description fits Acapulco," Tash said.

"The movie has several cliff scenes that show the same rock formation: a cat arching its back."

"You're not exaggerating?"

"I swear they're the same. A friend of mine who has access to *Jamaica Wind* is arranging to have a videotape made for me. When you see that tape, you'll understand why I'm so sure. Other photographs in this box show Rebecca Chance in semitropical gardens similar to the ones in the movie."

"Let me understand this. You're saying that these photographs were taken in the same area where the movie was shot and possibly at the same time."

"More than that. I'm saying I think the movie was shot at Espalda del Gato, on the estate Packard gave to you."

"But why would . . . In the early thirties, it wasn't common for movies to be shot on remote locations, was it?"

"Not at all," Coltrane said. "The production companies liked to stay close to Los Angeles. Taking a movie crew to Acapulco would have been prohibitively expensive."

"Then why . . ."

"Packard was an immensely wealthy man from a fortune he inherited at sixteen, when his parents died. These photographs make it obvious how fixated he was on Rebecca Chance. His total devotion to her can't be mistaken. Suppose he became impatient with the limited ambitions of a movie she was being featured in."

"*Jamaica Wind.*"

"Yes. Suppose he decided to become a secret financier for it. What if he hoped that an expensively mounted picture would at-

285

tract more attention and boost her chances of becoming a star? Let's assume he paid to transport a film crew to his Mexican estate."

"And while he and Rebecca Chance were there, Packard took some of these photographs? I don't know. That's a lot of 'what ifs.' "

"But it's the only explanation that makes sense to me," Coltrane said.

"It's a tempting theory, I'll give you that. Plus, it has the appeal of being romantic." Tash rubbed the back of her neck, exhausted. "But it still doesn't give me the answers I want. Why do Rebecca Chance and I . . ."

"There's another name I haven't mentioned. He's connected to this in a way I haven't been able to figure out. He produced Rebecca Chance's final two movies. Then he disappeared not long after she did. Have you ever heard of anyone named Winston Case?"

Tash's mouth opened in shock.

"You know the name?" Coltrane asked.

The dark of her eyes widened. "Winston Case?"

"Yes."

"He was my grandfather!"

13

COLTRANE WAS SO STUNNED THAT HE WAS SURE HE HADN'T heard correctly. *"Your grandfather?"*

"That's the name my mother told me. I never met him, so I have to take her word for it."

"The name?"

"When I was a child, I noticed that a lot of my friends had grandparents, but I didn't know what that meant. I asked my mother if I had grandparents, and she said, yes, everybody had grandparents but that mine weren't with us any longer. Naturally, I wondered what she meant, and she finally found a way to explain to me, without disturbing me, that they were dead."

"Winston Case."

Tash nodded. "I memorized the name so I could tell it to my friends. To prove to them *I* once had grandparents, too."

"But maybe you misremembered."

"No, as I got older, I asked my mother what he was like. The name she referred to was always the same: Winston Case."

"And who was your grandmother?"

"Esmeralda Gutiérrez."

"Did your mother ever describe Winston Case as having been a film producer?"

"According to her, he was a carpenter. She remembered the family moving around a lot as he went from job to job, although I guess the word *family* makes it sound bigger than it was. There were only the three of them."

"Where did this happen?" Coltrane asked.

"In Mexico."

"An American working as an itinerant carpenter in Mexico?"

"Why not?"

"Well, for starters, as an American citizen, he could have brought his wife and daughter into the United States without any immigration problems. Given the difference in the standard of living, he could have taken better care of them here."

"In the Depression?"

"You've got a point," Coltrane said. "But surely if Winston Case had the money to produce films, he could have managed to hang on to enough resources to be comfortable during the Depression. He wouldn't have had to go to Mexico and become a manual laborer."

"Then maybe we're not talking about the same Winston Case."

"The coincidence is too much for me to accept. There's got to be a connection between . . . Does your mother live in Los Angeles? I need to ask her about—"

"My mother's dead."

". . . Oh."

"She died from lung cancer three years ago."

Coltrane didn't speak for a moment. "I'm very sorry." He felt as if a door in his mind had been shut. He struggled to open another one. "Yes." Abruptly he reached for the box of nude photographs.

"*What are you doing?*" Tash asked.

He hurriedly opened the box and sorted through the naked images until he came to the first waist-up shot. Rebecca Chance's breasts were prominent.

"I'm not comfortable with this," Tash said.

"Does she look pregnant to you? I have a friend who's convinced that . . ." He glanced at Tash and saw embarrassment and confusion in her eyes. "I know this is awkward. We've just barely met, and . . . I promise I'm doing this for a reason. Please, trust me. My friend pointed out that Rebecca Chance's breasts aren't the same in every photograph. They get fuller. The nipples get larger. That made my friend think that Rebecca Chance was pregnant when some of these pictures were taken. She was in great shape to begin with and she watched her weight, and she was far enough along for the hormones to be kicking in, but not far enough along for her to be demonstrably pregnant in other ways. Maybe that's true. Hell, my friend's a woman, but she isn't a doctor. What do *I* know about this sort of thing? But suppose it's true. What if . . . Could the reason you look so much like Rebecca Chance be . . ."

"That I'm her *granddaughter?*" Tash's voice was a strained whisper.

"Look at the pictures again. Can you think of another explanation?"

"I don't know what to . . ." Tash hugged herself. "Take me out of here."

Before Coltrane knew what he was doing, he put an arm around her. "Yes, you've been through a lot. Let's get you upstairs where it's warm."

14

COLTRANE'S NEED TO HELP WAS SO GREAT THAT, unusual for him, he didn't take the time to put the photographs back into the chamber and secure its entrance. His arm still around her, feeling her shiver, he walked with her from the vault. Immediately, as they stepped outside, a jangling sound startled them.

From Tash's purse.

Coltrane had picked it up as they started across the vault. Tash was so preoccupied that she didn't at first seem to recognize the shrill insistence of her cellular telephone.

"Don't tell me he found out *this* number," Tash said.

The phone rang again.

"Would you like me to answer it for you?" Coltrane asked.

The phone rang a third time.

"No," Tash said. "If he hears a man's voice, it might make him do something more extreme."

The phone persisted.

"Then don't answer it at all," Coltrane said.

"But what if it's . . ." Apprehensive, Tash reached for the bag, fumbled inside it, pulled out the phone, opened it with an unsteady hand, and pressed the talk button.

"Hello?" Her voice was tentative, but as she listened, she visibly relaxed. "Walt? Thank heaven. I was afraid it'd be . . . No, I'm fine . . . I went out. Mitch had something he needed to show me about the estate I inherited. We drove into Los Angeles. . . . You've been trying to call me for the past hour? But I had the phone with me all the time. It never rang. I don't know why it . . ." Her dark eyes focused on the open door to the vault. "Wait a minute. I was in a storage area that had a lot of concrete around it. It must have shut out the signal. . . . Slow down, Walt. What's wrong? You sound . . . Jesus." Tensing again, she listened harder. "He did *what? Were you hurt? Was anybody* . . ." She stared at the wall across from her,

289

but her eyes seemed so black with despair that Coltrane had the sense she wasn't seeing anything except nightmarish visions in her mind. "I don't know what to do. . . . That's kind of you to offer, but I can't go back there tonight. I didn't bring my car. Mitch would have to drive me all the way to your place, and rather than have him do it, I'll check into a hotel around here. . . . Yes, I'm sure. . . . Of course I feel safe with him."

"Let me talk to him," Coltrane said.

"I don't know the address here. I wasn't looking when . . ."

"I need to ask him something." Coltrane held out his hand.

"Just a second, Walt." Tash gave him the phone.

Coltrane felt the heat from her hand on it. He smelled her lingering fragrance. "It's Mitch Coltrane."

A dead silence was followed by Walt's husky voice saying, "The son of a bitch poured gasoline through the metal bars in front of Tash's house and set fire to the garden."

Coltrane tensed.

"The fumes were everywhere. If I hadn't stopped by to see if everything was okay, the house would have been destroyed," Walt said. "I phoned the fire department and used a garden hose to wet down the house until help arrived. It was damned close for a while."

"*Gasoline?*"

"That tells you something?" Walt asked.

"I once helped put a stalker in jail by taking his photograph while he poured gasoline on a woman's lawn."

"Well, too bad you didn't stay here instead of driving to Los Angeles. You might have gotten his picture," Walt said sarcastically.

Coltrane ignored it.

"What's your address?" Walt asked. "I'll come get Tash and make sure she spends the night somewhere safe."

"Are you using a cellular phone?"

"As a matter of fact, yes. What difference does it—"

"A couple of years ago, in Beirut, a man who knows about these things told me never to say anything important on cellular phones. It's too easy to eavesdrop on conversations over them. I'll bring Tash back tomorrow morning. But thinking of Ilkovic reminds me of something else. Did you ever have Tash's house checked for hidden microphones?"

"What?"

"Ilkovic specialized in planting bugs. That was how he anticipated my movements, by overhearing my conversations," Coltrane said. "Do you suppose this jerk knows all about Tash's movements because he planted bugs in *her* house? That would be one way for him to learn her new telephone numbers—when the service person told her what they were, she wasn't the only one listening."

More dead silence. "Christ."

"You *didn't* check for bugs?" Coltrane asked.

"I'm sure as hell going to."

"And after that, I'll bring Tash back." He gave the phone to her.

But Tash didn't raise it to her ear. She just kept staring at Coltrane. "*Microphones? You honestly think there might be . . .*"

"Tash? Are you there?" Walt asked faintly from the phone.

Slowly, she raised it. "Walt, I don't feel up to talking right now. But thanks for everything. I'm really grateful. . . . No, stay there. I'll be fine. I'll talk to you tomorrow." She pressed a button on the phone and put the phone back into her bag.

Neither spoke for a moment.

"*Microphones in my house?*"

"It's a possibility. It has to be checked."

"But the house has an alarm system. How would he get in to plant the microphones?"

"Before this started, did you have any maintenance work done around the house?"

"The carpeting was put in recently. You don't suppose . . ."

Coltrane spread his hands.

"Jesus, I feel so . . . violated."

"I've been there. I know what you mean."

"Do you think he set the fire to pay me back for trying to trap him today? Or did he figure out I drove away with you and he was jealous?"

"I was sure he couldn't have known you were in the car," Coltrane said. "But . . ."

"What is it?"

"I'm a little late wondering about the possibility of hidden microphones. If your house is bugged, he would have overheard us planning how to hide you in the car. I'm sorry. I might have made a mistake."

"I'm not into blaming people. You did your best." Tash controlled a shudder. "On the positive side, he couldn't have followed us and at the same time have started the fire. So we know I'm safe for now." She looked at him. "Can you recommend a hotel in the area?"

"One."

She waited for the name.

"Right here," Coltrane said. "There's a guest bedroom. I've got plenty of spare toothbrushes. If I can fit into one of *your* robes, I know you can fit into one of mine."

"I couldn't impose."

"Why not? Because you barely know me?"

Tash shrugged.

"In the last few hours, I'd say we'd gotten to know each other fairly well." Coltrane locked the door to the vault.

"After going through those photographs? I suppose you're right."

They started up the stairs.

"Look, I made a killer marinara sauce last night," Coltrane said. "There was plenty left over. I can cook up more pasta and—"

Another shrill noise startled them. They froze at the top of the stairs into the living room.

But this time the sound wasn't from the phone in Tash's purse. It came from the doorbell.

Coltrane frowned. "Who would *that* be?"

"Are you expecting anyone?"

"No. Sometimes Randolph Packard's assistant drops by, but he has a key, and he usually just lets himself in. Maybe he's decided to be polite and ring the doorbell."

With the second jangle of the doorbell, Tash looked more uneasy.

"It'll be fine. No one knows you're here," Coltrane said.

But he himself did not feel assured. He went to the door, looked through its peephole, and felt something inside him contract when he saw who it was.

Oh no, he thought.

He was tempted not to open it, but he couldn't be certain that his and Tash's voice hadn't carried faintly to the person on the other side. Preparing himself, he gripped the dead bolt's knob, turned it, opened the door, and tried not to look self-conscious when he smiled at Jennifer.

15

"Hey, what a surprise," Coltrane said.

"Surprise?" Jennifer looked confused. She still wore her black Armani dress. The same pearl earrings and necklace highlighted it, glinting from the outdoor lights. "You didn't get the message I left on your answering machine?"

"I just came in awhile ago. I haven't had a chance to listen to my messages." Coltrane remained at the partially opened door. "What have you got there?"

She held a cardboard box that contained several Tupperware bowls, each covered with a plastic lid. "New Year's dinner. There was plenty of food left over at my parents' house, and I wasn't sure how much you would have gotten to eat when you visited Greg's widow this afternoon. So I thought I'd bring you a care package."

"That was really thoughtful."

"But it's getting heavy. You'd better move out of the way so I can bring it in."

"Ah . . . sure. I'm so surprised to . . . Here, let me help."

Coltrane reached to take the box from her. His movement opened the door wider, causing Jennifer's previous look of confusion to become one of concern as she glanced past him.

"Oh . . . I beg your pardon. I didn't know you had company."

Tash had remained standing at the top of the living room stairs.

"Well, a couple of things happened today, and . . ." Coltrane didn't know how to get out of the sentence. "Jennifer, I'd like you to meet Tash Adler."

"Hello." Jennifer had trouble saying the word.

"Tash, this is my friend Jennifer Lane."

"Pleased to meet you." Smiling, Tash came down the stairs.

By then, Coltrane had overcome his awkwardness enough to finish taking the box from Jennifer. Her hands were free, but she waited a moment before she gripped the hand Tash offered.

"You look awfully familiar," Jennifer said, then frowned toward Coltrane. "I don't understand."

"Familiar?" Tash looked puzzled.

"Jennifer knows about the photographs," Coltrane explained.

"You've seen them?" Tash asked.

"Yes."

"*All* of them?"

"Yes," Jennifer said.

Despite Tash's tan, the embarrassment that colored her cheeks was obvious. It was almost as if she felt the nude photos were of her and not of Rebecca Chance.

"Tash Adler?" Jennifer searched her memory. "Are you the person who inherited Randolph Packard's estate in Mexico?"

"Yes. How did you know?"

"Jennifer's been helping me do my research," Coltrane said. He felt awkward standing between the two women, holding the box of Tupperware containers. "Jennifer, after I visited Greg's widow, my curiosity got the better of me. I went up to Malibu to see if I could find where Tash lived."

"You've certainly had an eventful day."

"I brought Tash back here to see the photographs and try to figure out why she looked so much like Rebecca Chance."

Jennifer couldn't take her eyes away from Tash. "And did you come up with any answers?"

"We're beginning to suspect she might have been my grandmother," Tash said.

"There you are, Mitch. I'm impressed by the progress you're making." Jennifer looked uncomfortable in the doorway.

"But why are we standing here?" Coltrane made room. "Come in, and we'll—"

"No, that's all right," Jennifer said too quickly. "I just wanted to stop by and leave this food. I wasn't planning on staying. I have a lot of things to do at the office tomorrow. I planned on getting an early start."

"Can't you come in for a little while at least?" Coltrane asked. "I was going to open a bottle of wine and . . ."

"Yes," Tash said. "Stay and we'll talk. It's awfully nice of you to bring the food. I'm sure Mitch is glad not to have to eat leftovers. He was going to reheat some marinara sauce he made yesterday."

"Oh, I don't know." Jennifer's voice sounded a little choked. "He makes great marinara sauce." She backed away. "I really have to be going. It was a pleasure to meet you, Tash. I'll talk to you later, Mitch."

"But—"

"Happy New Year."

". . . Happy New Year." Conscious of the heavy box of Tupperware in his hands, Coltrane watched Jennifer walk to the curb, get in her BMW, and drive away. She didn't look back.

16

ONLY AFTER HER HEADLIGHTS VANISHED OVER THE HILL DID Coltrane nudge the door shut. "Lock this for me, will you?"

"Sure," Tash said. "I have the uneasy feeling I got in the way of something. Are the two of you . . ."

"It's complicated. We're trying to see if we can work things out again." He climbed the stairs toward the living room.

"This misunderstanding couldn't have helped any." Tash followed.

"Is she the friend you mentioned, the one who emphasized that this was the time of year to concentrate on new beginnings?"

"I'm afraid so." Coltrane felt terrible about what had happened. "I suspect this wasn't the kind of beginning she had in mind. I'll call her first thing tomorrow."

When they entered the dining room, Tash faltered. "These strings of beads on the walls . . ."

"Yes, they're unusual, aren't they?"

"But . . ." Tash shook her head, baffled. "They were in one of the photographs downstairs. One of the nudes."

"Rebecca Chance used to own this house."

"*What?*"

"After she disappeared, Randolph Packard bought the place and kept it exactly as it was when she lived here."

"What in God's name is going on?"

"That's what I was hoping you'd be able to tell me."

"Never mind the wine," Tash said abruptly. "Have you got any scotch?"

Worried about her manner, Coltrane poured it. "Do you want ice or—"

"No." Tash grabbed the glass and took two quick swallows. She closed her eyes, then opened them. "Now you can add ice and water."

"Are you okay?"

"No."

Coltrane waited.

"I'm scared."

Coltrane nodded.

"But I don't know what scares me more, the man who's stalking me or the photographs you showed me. I'm even afraid of this house."

"Why on earth—"

"It makes me feel like I'm being dragged back in time. Rebecca Chance is here. I can sense her. I also feel Randolph Packard."

"But he loved her. There's nothing to be afraid of."

"Hold me."

"What?"

"I've never felt so alone and scared. Please, hold me."

Momentarily, Coltrane found it impossible to move. Hoping that his trembling wouldn't betray him, he moved close, stopped face-to-face with her, and put his arms around her. He did it gently, not pressing himself against her, simply holding her. Closing his eyes, he felt her head sink against his left shoulder. He smelled sun and salt water in her hair. He tried to control his breathing as she raised her own arms and put them around his back. Then he couldn't subdue his trembling any longer, but it didn't matter, because Tash was trembling also, holding him tighter. They were pressed against each other. He felt the rise and fall of her chest. He started to become erect, afraid that she would notice. Then her shoulders heaved, and all at once she made a sound that might have been a sob. As his erection diminished, she gently pushed away from him, wiped a tear from her right cheek, and gave him the saddest smile he had ever seen.

"Thank you."

"There were a lot of times when *I* felt alone and afraid," Coltrane said. "Anytime you need a shoulder."

"It's strange. I met you only this afternoon, but already I feel you're a friend."

"Same here."

Tash leaned to kiss him on the cheek, but her stomach rumbled, and she looked down, abashed. Unexpectedly, she laughed.

So did Coltrane.

"That's twice," Tash said.

"Twice?"

"That I laughed today. Thanks to you."

Her stomach rumbled again, and she laughed again.

"We'd better get some food into you," Coltrane said.

Tash's smile was no longer sad.

As they heated food on the stove and in the microwave, Coltrane made a decision about an idea that he had been debating. "Have you got Walt's phone number?"

Tash looked up from gravy she was stirring. "Two. One at the sheriff's station and the other at his home. I have them memorized in case I need him in a hurry."

"This late, he's probably off duty. Give me his home number."

"Why?"

"I think I know a way to trap the man who's stalking you."

Tash looked mystified after she told him the number and he picked up the phone. For the first time, he noticed the flashing red light on the answering machine, presumably the message that Jennifer had said she left. Continuing to feel terrible about the misunderstanding, he pressed numbers.

Three rings later, a recognizable male voice answered. It sounded a little huskier, perhaps because of alcohol. "What's up?"

"This is Mitch Coltrane again."

"Swell." Immediately, a possible implication hit Walt. "Why? Has something happened to Tash?"

"She's fine. That's not why I'm calling. Are you on a cellular phone?"

"No."

"Good. There's less chance of anybody eavesdropping. When we spoke earlier, you said you were going to Tash's house tomorrow—to search for hidden microphones."

At the stove, Tash watched him, more confused.

"You should have mentioned those microphones when nobody else was with you," Walt said. "You made me sound as if I didn't know my job."

"That wasn't my intention."

"And what about now?"

"I don't understand."

"Is Tash listening now?"

"No, she's in the bathroom," Coltrane lied.

"So what about the microphones?"

"I've got an idea I'm still working out. Ideally, it would be better if you *didn't* search for the microphones. But in case somebody used a scanner to eavesdrop on the cellular phone you had earlier, you have to do what you said you were going to do. Otherwise, he'll get suspicious."

"What are you talking about?"

"If you do find hidden microphones, don't disconnect them all," Coltrane said. "Leave a few, as if you hadn't found them."

"Are you telling me how to do my job again?"

"Listen to me. The plan I'm trying to put together won't work unless whoever's after Tash overhears her talking about her travel schedule for the next few days."

"Another trap."

"Not quite. I haven't thought all of it through yet," Coltrane said. "When I see you tomorrow, we'll talk about it."

"When you see me tomorrow?" Walt asked. "Wow, that'll certainly give me a reason to wake up cheery."

Coltrane set down the phone.

"Why did you lie that I was in the bathroom?" Tash asked.

"Walt's manly feelings get hurt if I make suggestions when you're around."

"He means well," Tash said.

"Oh, I don't doubt he's determined to help."

Tash studied him. "You've got me curious about this plan you mentioned."

"A couple of years ago, I did a photo assignment for the LAPD Threat Management Unit. I hid outside the house of a woman who was being stalked. In the middle of the night, I managed to take a photograph of a man pouring gasoline on her lawn."

The reference to gasoline made Tash wince. "Yes, you mentioned that when you spoke to Walt earlier."

"The woman was able to identify the man from the photograph," Coltrane said. "He was someone she'd dated twice several years before. My photograph put him in jail."

"And?"

"Suppose there *are* microphones hidden in your house. If he's been overhearing you talk about your schedule, that explains how he's been able to follow you so closely and get pictures of you wherever you go. So tomorrow you'll talk about your schedule one more time—to someone on the phone or to Walt at your house or whomever," Coltrane said. "Then you'll go about your business, and we'll hope that he takes the bait. Because *this* time, there'll be another photographer wherever you go." Coltrane pointed at himself. "I'll stay back far enough to take pictures of anybody in the area, with emphasis on people with cameras. After a couple of locations, if the same face shows up in the photographs . . ."

"And if I recognize that face . . ."

Coltrane nodded. "The police will put the bastard in jail and you can sleep peacefully for a change."

"If only." Tash's shoulders slowly relaxed. "I want that to happen so much." She touched his arm. "Thank you. You've given me a reason to hope."

A bubbling sound made them turn toward the stove.

"Good Lord, the gravy."

The tension was broken. As ordinary life interrupted, Coltrane took pleasure from mundane chores, carrying bowls from the oven and setting them on heat-resistant pads. Tash arranged place settings.

"Be back in a moment." She left the kitchen.

Hearing the bathroom door click shut, Coltrane couldn't keep from glancing toward the flashing red light on his answering machine. He set down a bottle of fumé blanc that he'd been opening and pressed the play button.

"It's me," Jennifer's voice said. "Still at my parents'. Just a little cleanup left. I'll be heading out in a little while. In case you get back before I talk to you again, don't make anything for supper. Mom's put together a ton of leftovers for you. I'll take a chance that you'll be home and drive by."

Water ran in the bathroom. As the door opened, Coltrane pressed the stop button.

"Did I hear someone talking?" Tash asked.

"Just checking my messages."

"Anything you have to deal with?"

"Not tonight."

"In that case, are you ready?"

Tash ate heartily, but thinking of Jennifer, Coltrane felt so dispirited, it was all he could do to get through his meal.

17

DANIEL, Greg, and his grandparents stood before him while Ilkovic's headless corpse came up behind them. About to scream, Coltrane jerked awake. Sweating, he stared at the shadows of wind-blown trees rippling across the dark ceiling. Then he jerked a second time, realizing that one of the shadows was from something moving in his bedroom. But before he could roll out of bed and try to defend himself, his sleep-clouded mind cleared enough for him to understand that the shadow at the top of the stairs leading into his bedroom belonged to Tash.

She wore a white robe he had given her, part of it obscured by her dark hair hanging over her shoulders, her face invisible. "Did I scare you?"

"No. Not you." Coltrane wiped a hand across his clammy fore-head. "I was having a nightmare."

"I know. You were moaning. I heard you all the way in the guest bedroom downstairs. I came to see if you're okay."

"Thanks." Coltrane's rushing heart rate slowly subsided. "I'll be fine now. Sorry to wake you."

"You didn't." Tash paused. "I was already awake." Another pause. "I had a nightmare, too."

"How bad?"

"*Very* bad. Somewhere between fright and terror."

"Yeah, that definitely qualifies as a nightmare. Lord, I hope this isn't a pattern for the new year."

"Why should the new year be any different from the old?"

Coltrane propped himself up on his elbows. "I promise you, my plan's going to work. The police will catch this guy. The new year *will* be different."

"Isn't it nice to think so."

"Why don't I make us some coffee?"

"No," Tash said, "I'm going to try to get back to sleep."

"I hope it happens for you."

"It almost never does."

"Maybe this time will be different."

"I'm afraid to sleep alone."

In the darkness, the white robe moved toward the bed.

Coltrane felt the covers being pulled back, pressure on the side of the bed, Tash's warmth. Then she pulled the covers over both of them, and they were together.

"So tired," she said.

"Close your eyes. Try to sleep."

He touched her shoulder to calm her and was shocked again. Static electricity shot off her, off her bare skin, making him realize that she had dropped the robe. Before he could restrain himself, he kissed her lightly. Not even when Ilkovic had stalked him at the Maynard ranch had he felt so terrified. Dizzy from his hammering heartbeat, he became even dizzier when her mouth opened, her tongue finding his. His mind aswirl, he cupped a hand over a breast, feeling its nipple harden under his palm. She moaned, her arms encircling him. His light-headedness intensified. He had never felt skin so smooth, pubic hair so silken. His sensations whirling, he touched her moistness and groaned as she dug her fingernails into his chest. He flicked his tongue across her nipples. With frightening need, she put her hand on his penis, thrust herself up, and guided him into her, wrapping her legs around his waist. At once, her urgency abated. Gently, she rocked. He whimpered. He had never felt anything so smooth and moist and tight and sweet. Then he couldn't hold back. His short thrusts became longer. She moaned in unison with him, their hips locked in a frenzy. She screamed as she came, and his own release was so powerful that he felt it go all the way to the top of his head, which seemed to have exploded.

18

THEY LAY IN SILENCE.

"That static electricity you give off—I saw sparks in the darkness," Coltrane said.

"I *felt* sparks."

"I've never experienced anything like . . ."

"Yes."

He drew a hand along her smooth thigh, along her flat stomach, over each of her breasts. He had the sensation of worshiping. Now it was his turn to say "Yes."

"You've chased away the nightmares."

"I'll *always* chase them away," Coltrane said. He suddenly remembered that Randolph Packard and Rebecca Chance had probably made love in this very room on this very bed. So long ago. And now *he* had made love here with Rebecca Chance's look-alike, possibly with her granddaughter.

"Not alone," Tash murmured.

"That's right," Coltrane said. "You won't be alone any longer."

She sighed, snuggling against him, her weight settling, her body relaxing. Soon she drifted off to sleep, her breathing slow, steady, and faint.

But Coltrane didn't sleep for a long while. He was unable to adjust to her presence next to him, to the heart-swelling reality of what they had done.

TEN

I

HE AWOKE WITH A RISING FEAR THAT IT HAD ALL BEEN A DREAM, that Tash wouldn't be lying next to him.

But she was, her eyes flickering slowly open, focusing warmly on him.

"Hi." Her smile was welcoming.

"Hi."

She touched his cheek. "Sleep well?"

"When I got myself calmed down."

She chuckled.

"And you?" Coltrane asked. "How did *you* sleep?"

"For the first time in a long while, I'm not waking up more exhausted than when I went to bed. Heaven knows, I *ought* to feel exhausted after the workout we gave ourselves."

"Maybe we need a massage therapist."

Tash stretched, her breasts lifting, her naked body shifting next to him. "Oh, I think any aches we've got we can make feel better by ourselves."

Yes, everything is going to be fine, Coltrane thought. He had worried that she would wake up with remorse, telling him that it had all been a mistake, that they had to pretend it had never happened and just be friends, although she regretted that being friends would be almost impossible after what they had done, and maybe it would be better if they didn't see each other again.

But Tash was so at ease with their being in bed together that he felt joyous.

"What about you?" she asked. "Have you got any aches that need feeling better?"

"One."

"Show me."

"Here," Coltrane said.

"Oh, yes, I can see why that would ache."

"What do you suppose we should do about it?"

"Well, there's a remedy the natives in Bora Bora practice."

"You've been there?"

"No, but I took a correspondence course in their customs. Of course, there's nothing like hands-on experience. What I learned is that, when this kind of ache comes up, there's a particular spot that has to be massaged."

"Smart natives."

"Not there. Whatever are you thinking of?"

"I . . ."

"*Past* there. *Behind* it. Shall I explain what they discovered?"

"Absolutely. As long as you keep . . . I've got nothing else on my mind."

"Behind your testicles."

"Yes, I'm listening."

"In the crutch of your legs, there's a cord that leads from . . ."

"Yes, I feel it."

". . . your prostate to your testicles. And when I draw my index finger back and forth along that cord . . . So gently. With the flat of my finger. Are you sure I'm not boring you?"

"Definitely not."

"Because if I *am* boring you . . ."

"No, please, keep . . ."

"When I trace my index finger along this cord, you'll notice that it gets larger."

". . . Yes."

"And that your testicles compact."

". . . . . . Yes."

"And that the more I stroke this cord, your penis gets harder, your cord gets more swollen, your testicles get . . . What's the matter? The cat got your tongue?" Tash asked.

305

"Something's got something else of me. But the ache's getting worse."

"Then the treatment isn't working. I'd better stop."

"No. The treatment's going to work. I'm sure of it."

"I think it is, too. But I suddenly realized that I forgot the most important part. I have to position myself like this and lower myself down onto you like this and . . ."

"*Yes.*"

2

AFTERWARD, he lay spent, so relaxed that he didn't move until a few minutes after Tash went into the shower. A high-pitched noise made him turn toward Tash's purse. She had carried it up from the downstairs bedroom and left it on a chair outside the bathroom door. The cellular phone in the purse was making its unpleasant sound again.

"Hello?"

"Who's *this?*" a husky voice asked. "*Coltrane?* What the—"

"Good morning, Walt."

"What's wrong with Tash's phone? Last night, I tried for an hour to reach her. Now I've been trying for another hour. Nobody answers. She's supposed to keep the phone with her wherever she goes."

"And she has. I don't understand why it didn't . . ." Then Coltrane realized. "Until a while ago, her purse was in another part of the house. I guess we didn't hear it."

"House? She's at *your* place? I thought you were taking her to a hotel."

"Change of plan."

"Put her on."

"I can't."

"Why not?"

306

"She's in the shower."

Walt didn't say anything for a moment. His voice was thicker when he spoke again. "You were right about microphones being in her house. I just got back to the station after the tech crew finished its search. There were bugs in every room. The SOB's been listening to every word she said."

"And everything you and the other men said when you were over there planning how to trap him."

"We look like fools," Walt said.

"Did you do what I suggested? Did you leave some of the microphones?"

"I don't know what you think you're—"

"Did you?"

"One. In the living room."

"That'll be enough."

"But what's this about?"

"I'll explain when we get there. Two hours? The sheriff's station?"

The bathroom door swung open. Tash came out with a towel wrapped around her, her wet hair combed close to her head, her features sculpted. She raised her eyebrows. "Is it Walt?"

Coltrane nodded.

Tash took the phone. "Good morning," she said into it. Her voice was wonderful. She walked around Coltrane and pressed herself against his bare back. "No, it was a very quiet night. I went to bed early. I slept like the dead."

3

THE DAY AFTER NEW YEAR'S, the Beverly Center was teeming with shoppers. The cavernous multistoried building reverberated with the rumbling echo of innumerable voices and footsteps. Coltrane was surprised. He had expected the place to be semideserted, everyone tired of shopping for Christmas, but maybe people were returning unwanted presents or looking for sales. Whatever the reason for their presence, they made it both easier and harder for him to accomplish his task: easier because he had expected to have trouble concealing himself while he took photographs of Tash's progress through the mall, whereas the crowd gave him all the cover he needed; harder because the crowd also gave cover to his quarry, to anyone who followed Tash, showing undue interest in her and taking her picture.

He was on the third level of the massive shopping center, peering over a railing down toward the escalator that carried a steady stream of shoppers from the first level to the second and third. He was by no means the only one at the railing; otherwise, he would never have dared show himself. Across from him, several people drank coffee at a Starbucks concession. To his right, a group of teenagers leaned over, shouting down to friends. To his left, a middle-aged man leaned the other way, his back against the railing, sipping an Orange Julius while he waited for his wife to return from a dress shop that she had entered a few minutes after Coltrane got into position. Potted plants, pillars, and directional displays added further visual clutter, as did the continuous chaotic movement of shoppers just behind Coltrane. Anyone who suspected this might be a trap would take an awfully long while to spot Coltrane, and by then, Coltrane—or at least his camera—would have spotted *him.*

He glanced at his watch. Almost two o'clock. Any moment now, he thought, and lifted his camera from a shopping bag, adjusting its zoom lens. As if on cue, Tash stepped onto the escalator that led up from the first level to the second. Coltrane hadn't expected to have any trouble seeing her. Her magnetic presence would have distinguished her in any crowd. Nonetheless, he was amazed by how immediately he noticed her. By contrast, the two men with her were relatively inconspicuous, one in front, the other in back: Walt's partner, Lyle, and one of the state troopers whom Coltrane had met the previous afternoon. Both had the day off and had accepted the chance to earn more extra money as her bodyguards. They wore casual clothes and slightly oversized windbreakers that concealed the handguns they carried, their presence reassuring.

Coltrane returned his attention to Tash. Planning today's strategy, the group had debated whether she should wear something attention-getting to make her easier for him to spot, but they had dismissed the idea as one that would be likely to make her stalker suspicious. Obviously, a woman afraid of being followed wouldn't want to be conspicuous unless she was trying to bait a trap. Accordingly, they had agreed that she would wear something attractive without being ostentatious: camel slacks, a dark blue blazer, an ecru silk blouse, and modest silver earrings. But as Coltrane looked down at her from the railing of the third level, he now realized that it was impossible for her not to attract attention. Even from a distance, her beauty was manifest. With her hand on the railing of the escalator, her body turned sideways, she looked like a fashion model. As faces on the opposite, descending escalator pivoted in her direction, Coltrane started snapping pictures.

It wasn't likely that anyone on the descending escalator would be the man he was hunting, but Coltrane didn't want to take chances—there was no way of telling what he might inadvertently capture in the background. Three shots later, he raised his aim and got pictures of the crowd on both sides of where the escalator came up to the second level. Because he and Tash had verbally rehearsed her movements, Coltrane knew that she would turn toward the right. As a consequence, he moved simultaneously with her, but in the opposite direction, to the left, farther along the railing, able to snap several photographs of her shifting through the crowd below and across from him. A little farther along, he caught her entering a clothing boutique. Even with a zoom lens, it was hard to tell from this distance whether anyone gave her more than the usual admiring glances. No one seemed to be photographing her, but because he was looking mostly through the viewfinder, he couldn't be sure. The magnified photographs would tell the story.

He changed position, heading to the right this time, to the store above the clothing store that she had entered. From that vantage point, he could look across the huge open space between levels. He could peer down toward the stores opposite the one that Tash had entered. He could see if anyone showed unusual interest in that store. Staying back from the railing so he wouldn't be obvious, he made sure to change angles, getting as wide a variety of shots as possible.

Once more, he checked his watch. A half hour had passed. As he and Tash had planned, it was time for her to be coming out, so he shifted to the side opposite the door that she and her two bodyguards would be coming through. He caught photographs of the crowd on each side, of anyone who might be watching. Aware that she and her bodyguards would now head toward the down escalator, he reached a spot where he could take photographs of anyone watching from the first level as she and her escorts descended the escalator from the second level.

At the bottom, they moved out of his sight, heading along a corridor of stores toward an elevator that would take them to the parking garage. But by hurrying to the escalator and taking it three steps at a time down to the second level, Coltrane was able to get Tash in sight again and photograph the shoppers in the corridor below him. She entered the elevator. Its doors closed.

His camera clicked on the last exposure. As the rewind motor whirred, he lowered the camera. His back muscles slowly relaxed. But his tension was the result of exhilaration. Working a camera after so long had given him a rush, as had the clandestine nature of the photographs he was taking, the idea that he was trying to trap someone who wouldn't know that he was being photographed. He wondered if that was the same kind of rush that the stalker got, the power of observing without being observed, of capturing someone's soul without the target's being aware that the theft had occurred. Suddenly chilled, he remembered the vulnerability and nakedness he had suffered when he found the photographs that Dragan Ilkovic had taken of him.

4

As soon as the camera's rewind motor finished whirring, he quickly removed the exposed film and put in a new roll. All the while, he calculated. He had to hurry to his car and get to Tash's next destination, another clothing boutique, this one on the Third Street pedestrian shopping area in Santa Monica. After that, she would go to a similar store in Westwood and finally all the way down to yet another clothing boutique at the South Coast Plaza in Orange County. She owned all of them, he had learned. She also owned three more in San Diego and four in San Francisco.

"I have other investments, too," she had said while they drove to the Malibu sheriff's station that morning. "I try to stay out of their day-to-day affairs, but periodically I drop in just to let the managers know Big Sister is watching. In the case of the clothing boutiques, my interest is greater, so I pay visits more often. This afternoon and this evening would be a good time to make my rounds."

"Do you ever phone your managers to alert them when you're coming?"

"Always. Granted, it gives them a chance to hide anything that might be wrong, but it also makes me seem less adversarial than if I showed up unannounced, trying to catch them at something. I don't want the managers to be afraid of me. I want them to work hard for me."

"This morning, after you get back to your house, why don't you use the phone to make appointments at the various stores for this afternoon? Add enough time between stops so I can get to each one ahead of you."

"But what I say will be transmitted through the hidden microphone Walt left in the house. He'll know my timetable."

"Exactly," Coltrane had said. "And we'll know his."

With the first phase completed, Coltrane got on the escalator down to the Beverly Center's bottom level. The time was twenty-five

311

to three. Depending on traffic, Tash needed only a half hour to get to the store in Santa Monica, but since the plan required him to arrive ahead of her, she had added another half hour to the timetable, making a 3:30 appointment with the manager. Tash's stalker, who had presumably overheard the telephone conversation, wouldn't expect her until then. Meanwhile, Coltrane would be able to arrive in time to start shooting various angles of the crowd. Of course, Tash's stalker might decide not to show up at any of the—

5

A HAND SHOVED HIM FROM BEHIND, with such force that Coltrane lurched forward on the escalator and almost lost his balance. Startled, he grabbed the railing to keep from falling and spun toward the person who had shoved him. "Hey, watch where you're—"

Twice as startled, he found himself face-to-face with Carl Nolan.

The sergeant and he were about the same height, six feet, but Nolan was on a step higher than Coltrane and seemed to tower, his weight lifter's shoulders looking broader than usual.

Nolan jabbed him again, harder, jolting Coltrane's right shoulder.

Almost falling, Coltrane gripped the railing harder. "What are you—"

"Keep your hands off her."

People on the escalator couldn't help noticing. As distracted as Coltrane was, he sensed their agitation.

"For God's sake, have you lost your mind?"

Nolan jabbed him a third time. "Stay away from her."

"If you don't stop—"

"You're missing the point." Nolan gripped Coltrane's right arm with a force that made Coltrane wince. "This is about *you* stopping."

Coltrane suddenly felt off balance, the escalator no longer moving. With equal abruptness, he realized that he'd reached the bottom. The people who'd gotten off ahead of him scattered.

Nolan tightened his grip on Coltrane's arm. "You're not going to make a fuss. We're going to walk calmly over to that elevator. We're going to find a nice quiet spot in the parking garage where we can chat." Nolan squeezed so hard that he cut off the circulation in Coltrane's arm.

"Whatever you want."

"Right. That's a good beginning. Whatever I want."

Shoppers farther along hadn't noticed what was happening. Moving Coltrane steadily through the crowd, Nolan reached the elevator and pushed a button. When the doors opened, Nolan shoved him inside. For a moment, they bumped together, and Coltrane felt Nolan's handgun in its shoulder holster under his windbreaker. The doors rumbled shut, the elevator descending.

"Take it easy," Coltrane said. "I don't know what this is about, but—"

Nolan's eyes were wide with fury. "I already told you what this is about: you stopping."

An elderly couple in the elevator looked nervous.

The doors opened, and Nolan tugged Coltrane into the parking garage. Along a row of cars, Nolan glanced around to see if anyone was nearby, then shoved Coltrane between two minivans until Coltrane's back was against a concrete wall. The minivans blocked them from view. "You're never going near Tash again."

"Carl, think about what you're doing. You're risking your job. You can't assault me. You'll lose your badge."

"Who's going to tell? You? That I did *this*?" Nolan punched Coltrane in the stomach.

As air wheezed out of him, Coltrane doubled over and sank to his knees, his hands locked tightly to his stomach.

"Or that I did *this*?" Nolan rocketed the heel of the palm of his hand against the side of Coltrane's head. It knocked Coltrane to the floor. "Answer me. *Who's going to tell?*"

Sprawled on the concrete, Coltrane didn't know which hurt worse, his stomach or his head.

"If you'd let us bring you in and protect you, Greg would still be alive. If you'd done what you were supposed to, McCoy wouldn't be in the hospital. You treated me like a fool and kept me waiting at your place while you went off to be a hero. You had to show me you were smarter than me, that you knew better than anybody how to handle Ilkovic."

When Coltrane tried to stand, Nolan used the heel of his palm to slam his forehead and knock him onto the floor again. The martial-arts move protected Nolan's hand while carrying power and not leaving a mark. "Oh, I've tried to be a good sport and hide my feelings. I tried to tell myself I'm being too harsh, that you got the job done on Ilkovic, that you paid him back for Greg. Hell, I almost had myself convinced. But then you showed up at Tash's yesterday and made me and the other guys look like idiots. The next thing I know, she's asking you to stay, and the next thing after that, you're taking her to your house, and the next thing after *that*, she spends the night with you. Now if that isn't fast work, I don't know what is."

"Carl—"

"Shut up while I'm talking to you. The way this is going to work, you're never going to tell anyone about this conversation, and you're never going to see Tash again."

His vision blurry, Coltrane peered up at him. "You and Tash?"

"I told you to shut up!"

"What's going on?" a male voice demanded.

Coltrane shifted his gaze as Nolan pivoted toward the front of the minivans.

A uniformed security guard studied them nervously. He was in his early thirties, tense-faced, rail-thin compared to Nolan, and shorter. He drew a walkie-talkie from a holster on his belt. "I had a complaint about a disturbance." His voice was unsteady. "Break it up."

"LAPD." Nolan already had his police wallet out of his windbreaker, opening it, showing his badge. "I just apprehended a suspect. He tried to get away."

The security guard narrowed his eyes and assessed the badge.

"LAPD?" He looked relieved. "I wasn't sure what was . . . Do you need any help?"

"I've got everything under control," Nolan said. "You can go back to what you were doing. I'll handle this."

"Right." The guard stepped back. "I won't get in the way."

Nolan waited until the guard's footsteps receded to a faint echo, followed by the thump of a door closing.

He pointed rigidly at Coltrane. "That was smart of you not to contradict me."

Keeping a careful distance, Coltrane wavered to his feet. His head throbbed. "Why would I? This doesn't involve anybody but you and me."

"That's where you're wrong. It involves you and me and *Tash*. Don't go near her again or I'll put you in the hospital. Is that plain enough for you?"

"Totally."

"Then we understand each other." Nolan turned and walked away.

Propped against the concrete wall, Coltrane held his stomach. His chest heaved. He fought the impulse to be sick. He listened to Nolan's heavy footsteps, heard them stop, heard a car door, an engine, and tires squealing.

Slowly, he pushed away from the wall. His chest continued to heave, no longer because his breath had been knocked out—but because of anger.

6

Is there something you forgot to tell me about Carl Nolan?" Coltrane demanded.

It was ten to four. He was using a pay phone at the outdoor pedestrian mall on Third Street in Santa Monica. Despite his injuries, he had managed to get to the mall before Tash arrived. He had photographed the crowd from as many angles as he could without drawing attention to himself. From a discreet position, he had watched Tash and her escorts approach the clothing boutique and enter. He had crossed the promenade and gotten shots of the crowd on the opposite side. With all of his obligations taken care of, he had then done what he had been determined to do since Nolan had delivered his final warning and stormed away—phone Tash at the store and find out what in God's name was going on.

"Mitch? What are you talking about?" Tash's voice was taut with confusion.

"Nolan seems to think that you and he are an item. He did his best to beat the hell out of me to prove his point."

"He what? Oh my God."

Down the mall from the store, Coltrane warily studied the crowd. "For all I know, he's in the neighborhood, and he's going to beat the hell out of me again to make sure the lesson sticks. So if it isn't too damned much trouble, would you mind telling me what's going on?"

"This is terrible. I never imagined he'd . . . Are you hurt?"

"Not as much as I'm confused. *Do* you have a relationship with him?"

"No. . . . It's complicated. I can't talk about this on the phone."

"Well, you're going to have to talk to me about him *sometime.*"

"I will. Soon. I promise."

"Could *he* be your stalker?"

"Carl? No. He can't be. I didn't meet him until a week after I started getting the letters and phone calls. He didn't know me until then. He couldn't have started this."

"Then maybe he's *continuing* it, making himself indispensable. Maybe he's the one who bugged your house and started the fire last night. No." Coltrane immediately corrected himself. "If Nolan did those things, he wouldn't be stupid enough to come at me and risk drawing suspicion. But if he *isn't* your stalker and he *didn't* plant the microphones, how did he know I was going to be at the Beverly Center?"

"Walt told him."

"Walt?"

"After you dropped me off at the sheriff's station, Carl phoned and asked to be brought up-to-date. Walt explained the plan we were trying. There's nothing mysterious about how Carl knew where you'd be. It's not like he had to be listening to the microphone in my living room."

"I was sure . . ." Head pounding, Coltrane couldn't resist going back to the same insistent question. *"Why does he think I'm interfering with something you have going with him?"*

"Please." Tash sounded self-conscious. "There are people here. We have to meet so I can explain. It's not what you're thinking."

"I'm not sure *what* I'm thinking."

"It's innocent. You're going to have to take my word until we see each other."

"When? You won't be done at the South Coast Plaza until maybe eight o'clock. That means you won't get home until around eleven. I need to develop the photographs so you can study them and see if you recognize anybody. That's going to take until . . . Why don't you save time and come to *my* house?"

"Love to."

"Your bodyguards can leave you there and—"

"Hold it. Does Carl know where you live?"

"Yes." Coltrane remembered Nolan's long wait at Packard's house while he himself had gone to the Maynard ranch instead of leading Ilkovic to the trap that Nolan had prepared.

"He might watch your house in case I show up," Tash said. "I don't want any more trouble because of me."

"I can deal with—"

"It's my problem," Tash insisted. "I'll take care of it. I'll phone him as soon as I get home tonight. I'll settle this. Believe me, he won't bother you again."

"When you finish talking to him, phone *me.* I want to know what this is all about."

"I promise. You'll understand everything." Tash hesitated. "I can't wait to see you."

Frustrated, Coltrane listened to the click as she hung up. Slowly, he replaced the receiver. He took a deep breath, trying to clear his mind. Tash and her escorts would soon be coming out of the shop. He had to be ready to photograph the crowd as she appeared and walked toward the parking lot. He couldn't allow himself to be distracted.

7

PREOCCUPIED, he worked in Packard's darkroom, filling the time until Tash would phone him. Having purchased the necessary equipment and chemicals on his way back from the South Coast Plaza, he processed the negatives that he had taken at the clothing boutiques. The next step, that of making eight-by-ten enlargements, would be not only time-consuming but tedious. These were snapshots, after all, not composed artistic images. There wasn't any creative challenge in developing them or stimulation in debating how to manipulate and crop them for the maximum aesthetic impact. Just get the job done, he told himself.

In this case, a one-hour photo-processing company would probably have done as well, but following Randolph Packard's example, Coltrane had never used a photo-processing company in his career. Besides, there was always the chance that the film he surrendered would be lost or damaged somehow, and he was too impatient to see the results of today's effort to take that risk, not to mention be forced to have Tash go through today's dangerous charade for a second time.

His thought about Packard made him imagine the countless times that Packard had come into this darkroom and done what Coltrane was now doing, transferring prints from the developing tray to a tray filled with chemicals that stopped the development process. He gently agitated the stopping solution, careful to rotate the prints from top to bottom to make sure that the stopping chemicals touched them evenly. Then he shifted the prints to a tray filled with chemicals that fixed the image on the paper, making it permanent. He repeated the process of agitation and rotation, finally placing the prints in a tray filled with slowly running water that would wash the chemicals from them.

He imagined Packard standing in this same spot, lovingly developing the photographs that he had taken of Rebecca Chance. Indeed, he could almost sense Packard within him as he gave in to the irresistible urge to make prints from a different negative entirely, from the film that had been in the camera that he had taken to Tash's house the previous day. Had Packard felt what he now felt as he made an enlargement and carried the eight-by-ten-inch photographic paper to the developing tray, holding his breath as he gently agitated the solution? Had Packard exhaled as Rebecca Chance's features appeared before him, just as Tash's identical features now came to life before Coltrane?

The alluring posture of the two women as they emerged from the ocean was identical. True, Tash wore a formfitting diver's suit, whereas Rebecca Chance had a more revealing wet, clinging bathing suit. But for all that, they were the same, just as Coltrane felt eerily that he and Packard were the same. Both loving the same woman. Making love to the same woman—in the same bed.

The phone rang, its jangle startling. Despite his anticipation, Coltrane had become so absorbed in Tash's image that he had stopped thinking about when she would call. He jerked his head toward the phone that he had brought from the kitchen and plugged into a jack in the darkroom. As much as he wanted to grab it, he couldn't bear letting Tash's image be ruined by keeping it too long in the chemicals. Quickly, he removed it from the fixing solution, shook fluid off it, and set the print in the washing tray.

By then, the phone had rung two more times. In a rush, he picked it up.

"I've been waiting for your call. How did it go?" he asked.

The person on the other end didn't answer right away. The voice was faint. "Somehow I suspect I'm not the one whose call you've been waiting for."

"... Jennifer?"

"I told myself I wasn't going to do this."

Coltrane felt a weight in his stomach. "How are you?"

She swallowed, as if trying to suppress emotion. "How do you think?"

"I meant to phone you today."

"But you didn't," Jennifer said.

"I couldn't. Something interfered."

"I can imagine."

"I wanted to explain about the misunderstanding last night."

"Oh?" Jennifer's voice was strained. "What misunderstanding is that?"

"Why I was with Tash instead of with you at your parents' house."

"I'm not sure there *was* a misunderstanding. I think I understood very well."

"We have to talk."

"I don't like the sound of that."

"Jennifer . . ."

"Get it over with. Talk."

"I . . ."

"Or maybe this isn't a good time. Maybe I'm interrupting something."

"No. I'm alone."

"Then why don't you let me in? I'm using a car phone. I'm outside your house."

8

JENNIFER LOOKED SMALL IN THE DARKNESS. In place of last night's Armani dress, she was wearing faded jeans, an orange *Southern California Magazine* sweatshirt, and a matching baseball cap—the same outfit she had worn the day she set out with Coltrane to find Rudolph Valentino's Falcoln Lair. The memory made him ache.

"Hi."

". . . Hi."

"You're sure it's safe to come in?" Jennifer's eyes looked red, as if she'd been crying.

"The coast is clear."

She entered uneasily. The way she peered around made it seem that everything was strange to her, the house unfamiliar.

"Can I get you something?"

"Yeah, a little arsenic sounds good."

Coltrane didn't know what to say to that and used the motion of closing and locking the door to mask his awkwardness.

"I'll settle for scotch."

Coltrane couldn't help remembering that scotch was what Tash had wanted the previous night. Reaching the kitchen seemed to take forever. But at least it was motion; at least it, too, masked his awkwardness, as did preparing her drink.

"You're not going to have one with me?" Jennifer asked.

"No. I've got a lot of work to do in the darkroom, and I don't want to get sleepy."

"This is tough enough as it is. I'm not sure I can get through this if you make me drink alone."

Coltrane's heart went out to her. "Of course. Why not? Let's have a drink together." He got out another glass, poured the scotch, added ice, and put in some water, more motions for which he was grateful.

He raised his glass and clicked it against hers. "Cheers."

"I wouldn't go that far. Maybe 'Here's mud in your eye.' But definitely not 'Cheers.'" Jennifer took a long swallow, made a face, as if the drink was too strong, and looked at him. She was standing exactly where Tash had stood the previous night. "Talk."

"I'm not sure how to begin."

"As long as it's the truth, however you tell it will be fine. I'll make it easy for you. The way you looked at her last night—are you in love with her?"

Coltrane glanced at his hands.

Jennifer nodded in discouragement. "You fell in love with Rebecca Chance's photographs. Then you fell in love with Rebecca Chance's look-alike."

"It's more complicated than that."

"Of course. You're a complicated man. Is she really Rebecca Chance's granddaughter? Is that why she looks so uncannily like her?"

"That's my suspicion," Coltrane said. "That's what I'm trying to find out."

Jennifer took another long swallow and shuddered. "Well, as I told you on New Year's Eve, I can't compete with a woman who's that beautiful. Not with a ghost. Really, you should have called me today. You should have put me out of my misery."

"I never meant to . . . I had a good reason for not calling you."

"Make me believe you weren't planning to dump me without bothering to let me know."

"I . . . Can I show you some photographs?"

"I don't think I could bear to look at more pictures of her."

"It's not what you think," Coltrane said. "These are different. Trust me. You'll understand what I mean when you look at them."

"Trust you," Jennifer said hollowly.

9

COLTRANE ENTERED THE DARKROOM AHEAD OF JENNIFER. Before she could see the print of Tash in the diver's suit, he used tongs to turn the print upside down in the washing tray. He hoped that she hadn't noticed what he was doing, that her attention was directed toward where he pointed, toward prints that were attached by clamps to a nylon cord, drying.

He turned on the overhead lights.

"Crowd scenes?" Jennifer sounded puzzled.

"Those were taken at the Beverly Center."

"But . . ." Jennifer turned to him, more confused. "Why would you take them? So *many*. The compositions are clumsy. Chaotic."

"I wasn't trying for an aesthetic arrangement. I just shot what I saw."

"Is this some new direction you're taking? I hope not. These can't compare with the photographs you took after you met Packard, before all the trouble started."

"It's a different kind of project."

"Different?" Jennifer looked back at the enlargements, walking along, paying closer attention. "Oh." She had finally seen Tash among the chaos. "Even in a crowd, she stands out." Jennifer sounded puzzled. "But she doesn't seem aware she's being photographed. It's almost as if . . ." Frowning, she faced him again. "You were following her?"

"Actually, I've been ahead of her."

"I don't know what you're talking about."

"It's going to take awhile to explain."

When he finished, Jennifer shook her head in dismay. "Ilkovic wasn't enough for you? You have to get yourself involved in a similar situation?"

"It's not the same. This time, I'm not the one being stalked."

"Unless you count Nolan. The way you describe him, he's been dealing with stalkers so long that he became one."

"Nolan will calm down once Tash makes him understand there's nothing between them."

"But why did he think there was something between them in the first place?"

"I don't know yet," Coltrane said. "Tash told me she's going to explain."

Jennifer took one more look at the photographs, then another look at him. "I give up. I won't waste any more of your time."

"We've been through a lot together. I want to make sure everything's right between us."

"That isn't going to happen, Mitch. Just because I want some closure on this, that doesn't mean everything's going to be right between us. And don't you dare say 'I hope we can still be friends.' "

Coltrane nodded.

"She owns more stores in San Francisco and San Diego?" Jennifer said. "And that doesn't count the other investments she didn't specify. She's not only rich—she's drop-dead gorgeous? You certainly got lucky."

Coltrane shrugged, awkward.

"How did she get the money?"

"I don't know. Her mother died a couple of years ago. Maybe it was an inheritance."

"How did her mother get so much money?"

"I have no idea," Coltrane said. "I didn't feel it was any of my business."

"Well, the two of you are certainly going to have a lot to talk about. I won't say I hope it works out for you, because that's not the way I feel." Jennifer hesitated, mustering the strength to continue. "But I will say this—I hope you don't get hurt." She blinked, unsettled.

"Jennifer . . ."

"I'd better go home." A tear trickled down her cheek.

They walked upstairs to the front door.

"Good-bye."

"I'm sorry," Coltrane said.

"Not as much as I am." Jennifer wiped away another tear and stepped outside. It took her two tries to tell him, "As soon as the special edition of the magazine is ready, you'll get the first copy. They really are great photographs, Mitch." Her voice broke. "Regardless of everything that's happened, I'm proud that I was in your life when you took them."

Coltrane's throat felt squeezed.

Lingering in the open doorway, he watched her walk to the curb and get into her car. As on the previous night, she didn't look back when she drove away. Only after her headlights started to climb the hill away from his house did he move to step back into the house.

But he stopped himself, noticing her headlights pass a car parked near the murky crest.

10

IT WAS HARD TO TELL IN THE NIGHT AND AT A DISTANCE, but the vehicle might have been an Explorer, the kind of car Nolan drove. Someone was behind the steering wheel, looking in Coltrane's direction. Jennifer's headlights disappeared over the hill. The car became barely visible.

Nolan? Coltrane's stomach muscles were still sore from where he had been punched. Angry, he wanted to storm up the hill and find out if that *was* Nolan watching the house. But his fury was displaced by a despondency about Jennifer that made him too weary for a confrontation. He wished that there had been another way. He had never wanted to hurt her. I bet that's something else Jennifer would have been annoyed to hear me tell her, he thought. He stepped back into the house and locked the door. If it *was* Nolan out there, he was going to have a long, wasted night.

Mouth dry, Coltrane glanced at his watch, realizing that the time was almost midnight. Tash should have been home by now. She should have called by now.

Unless she was waiting to contact Nolan first and Nolan wasn't home.

Unless that was in fact Nolan in the car out there.

Get back to work, he told himself. It'll help distract you.

Descending to the darkroom, he shut off the overhead lights, switched on the dim amber safelight, and began making more prints from the negatives he had prepared. Then he remembered the print that he had turned upside down in the washing tray, took it out of the water, and was stunned anew by the beauty of Tash in her diving suit as she emerged from the ocean. Her eyes seemed to look directly into his.

What's happening to me? he thought. How could someone I've known since only yesterday make me feel this way?

He had never believed that love at first sight was possible. But then it *hadn't* been at first sight, had it? he reminded himself. He had seen Tash's face long before he had met her.

He remembered having read about the theory of soul mates—that souls who had been devoted to each other in a former life could never be fulfilled unless they found each other in a later life. Perhaps that explained the irresistible attraction that had overcome him. It was as if he had recognized Rebecca Chance the first time he had seen her photograph. It was as if he had been in love with her in another time and now had the chance to be in love with her again—with Tash.

Whatever you're feeling, it doesn't need an explanation, he told himself. You'll ruin it.

So far he had made prints only for the shots he had taken at the stores in the Beverly Center, Santa Monica, and Westwood. He still had to deal with the images of the crowd near the store in the South Coast Plaza. Uneasy that Tash hadn't called, beginning to worry that something had happened to her, he forced himself to go to the enlarger and put one of the processed negatives into the negative holder. After determining the correct focus, he put a sheet of eight-by-ten-inch printing paper into the easel, set the timer, and turned on the enlarger lamp, which was positioned above the negative and cast a beam through it, projecting the negative's image down through a magnifying lens and onto the paper.

If he had been preparing prints that were intended to be displayed, he would have done tests to determine the ideal length of time to expose the light-sensitive paper to the negative's enlarged image, using trial and error to achieve the perfect density of detail and contrast of lights and darks. But these prints were important only for their information, not their aesthetic appeal. He needed to get them done as soon as possible, so he didn't care about perfection, only whether the faces in the crowd were clear enough for Tash to be able to recognize any of them.

His experience with developing the previous prints had taught him that twenty seconds was an effective length of time to let the negative's projected image touch the paper. The instant the timer clicked, the enlarger lamp turned off automatically. He removed the paper and set it where the only illumination that could reach it would be from the dim amber safelight. When he had exposed half a dozen sheets of paper, he took them to the developing tray, set them in the solution, and gently agitated the tray, rotating the sheets, developing them evenly.

The magic happened. Feeling a surge of anticipation, Coltrane studied them, as he had the earlier prints. During his fifteen years as a professional photographer, he had trained himself to have a keen visual memory, so he could easily recall details from earlier prints. But now his surge of anticipation changed to a sinking feeling of disappointment, for he still had not seen any faces that recurred in various locations. His pride made him hope that he wouldn't have to admit to Tash that his plan had been a failure.

To make matters worse, the six prints in the developing tray had something wrong with them: The faces in the bottom-right corner of each print were overexposed, too dark to be distinguished. The faces in the rest of the area were perfectly acceptable, however. That contrast told him that although twenty seconds of exposure to the enlarger's light was sufficient for most of the area in these prints, their bottom-right corners needed only *fifteen* seconds.

The prints weren't usable. Muttering an expletive, he shoved them into a waste can and returned to the enlarger. He prepared to reexpose sheets of paper to the six negatives. For each one, he again set the timer for twenty seconds. But for this set of prints, when the timer reached fifteen seconds, he slowly waved his right hand between the paper and the negative, preventing the enlarger lamp from projecting onto the bottom-right corner of each print for the final five seconds. The movement of his hand reminded him of a magician's gesture, an apt comparison because he was, after all, performing darkroom magic. By lessening the exposure time on the lower-right corners, he was able to enhance that area and bring out details.

When the sheets were finally exposed, he set them into the developing tray. But this time when the images came to life, he opened his mouth in shock. The previously indistinct lower-right corners were now vivid. As at the Beverly Center, he had taken these shots from an upper level, aiming down at the crowd. On the first print in the sequence, he found himself staring at a man with a 35-mm camera raised to his face, aiming in the direction of where Tash and her bodyguards approached her store. The camera was a mask, preventing Coltrane from noting the man's features. The salt-and-pepper hair was an indication of middle age. That and the man's somewhat-hefty build were the only identifiers.

Feeling as if something sharp was caught in his throat, Coltrane turned to the next print in the sequence and saw that the man had pivoted slightly to the right. His camera remaining at eye level, his finger pressing the shutter button, he was taking a photograph of Tash as she walked along. The new angle of his mostly hidden face revealed a thick neck and the suggestion of a puffy cheek. Coltrane turned to the third print in the series, where the man had pivoted more to the right, continuing to take photographs of Tash. From this angle, Coltrane saw a hint of a jowl. He told himself that he had to be wrong, that his imagination was deceiving him. Hurrying, he flipped through the final three prints in the sequence and saw in stop action the man lower his camera to his chin, to his neck, to his chest, never removing his intense gaze from where Tash was walking. The man's profiled face was now fully in the open, and Coltrane felt nauseated as he was forced to admit that he hadn't been wrong, that his imagination hadn't deceived him. The man was Duncan Reynolds.

11

WHEN THE PHONE RANG, Coltrane had trouble getting his muscles to work. Only after two more rings was he able to avert his eyes from the prints and pick up the phone. Concerned that Jennifer might have broken her word and decided to call, he kept his voice neutral, or tried to. The stress of having identified Duncan Reynolds made him hoarse. "Hello."

"Not very enthusiastic." Tash sounded mischievous. "I thought you'd be a little more pleased to hear from me." Her tone was wonderfully sonorous.

" 'Pleased' is an understatement."

"Did I wake you?"

"No. I've been working." Coltrane frowned toward the prints. He continued to strain to adjust to what he had discovered.

"I'm sorry I took so long. I didn't want to phone you until after I talked to Carl, but I've been ringing his number for the past hour and all I get is his answering machine."

"That's because he's probably in a car up the street from me, watching my house."

"You're kidding."

"*Someone's* in a car up the street. It looks like the kind he drives."

"Jesus," Tash said. "I guess we were right to have me go home instead of to your place."

"Maybe not. This time, he wouldn't be catching me by surprise. Maybe I should go out there and—"

"No, there doesn't have to be more trouble," Tash said. "I think I can get him to calm down. I just need a chance to talk to him and make him understand that he got the wrong idea."

"That's something *I'd* like to understand, too," Coltrane said. "What wrong idea are you talking about?"

"I promised to tell you, and I'm going to."

"Then how about now?"

"No. Not like this. Not over the phone. I need to see your eyes. I need to make sure that *you* understand."

"It's that bad?"

"There's nothing bad at all. But this is going to take awhile, and I remembered what you said about not using the cellular phone. Lyle and the state trooper are still with me. I had them drive me to a pay phone at a gas station on the Pacific Coast Highway. I'm not exactly where I can talk about this."

"Tomorrow?"

"Yes. That's another reason I'm calling. Do you have anything you can't get away from for the next few days?"

"Only from seeing you."

She didn't say anything for a moment. "That gave me shivers."

"The good kind, I hope."

"In the right places. Can you meet me tomorrow morning at LAX?"

"LAX?" he asked in surprise.

"At the Delta counter? Nine-fifteen? That ought to give us enough time to buy our tickets and catch a ten-ten flight."

"To *where?*"

"Acapulco. The estate I inherited. I can't bear looking over my shoulder any longer. I want to get away to where no one knows who we are. Where no one can bother us—not Carl, not the creep who's after me, nobody. Where it's just the two of us. Where we can talk and swim and lie on the beach."

"Sounds good."

"Do other things."

"Sounds better."

"You'll go?"

"Twist my arm."

Tash laughed.

"I like it when you laugh," Coltrane said.

"The only time I laugh is when you make me. Maybe in Mexico I'll do more of it."

"Delta. Nine-fifteen. I'll bring the photographs I developed. I think I found something."

"What?" Tash asked quickly.

"I'm still not sure what it means. A face. I'm curious if you'll recognize it."

"*You think you found him?*"

"Maybe."

"That's the best news."

"I might be mistaken."

"No. I've got a good feeling."

12

COLTRANE TURNED OFF ALL THE LIGHTS IN THE HOUSE. Taking care that he couldn't be seen, he peered past the blinds in his living room and surveyed the darkness outside. On the hill, a streetlight cast a glow, illuminating the upper part of the slope. The car was gone.

He couldn't tell if he was relieved or more troubled.

ELEVEN

I

THE MOMENT THE DELTA AIRLINES 757 LIFTED OFF, its engines roaring, Tash said, "Let me see the photographs."

But when Coltrane tried to lean forward to pick up the carrying case in the storage compartment under his feet, his seat belt prevented him. He started to unbuckle it, then thought better as the jet continued its steep climb. From his right-hand window seat, he noticed that they were passing above the yachts and sailboats at Marina del Rey. He had a painful mental image of Jennifer's condominium down there. Saturday morning, she might be sitting on her balcony, drinking coffee, perhaps looking up at the jet flying over.

"I'd better wait until we level off," he said.

"I could barely sleep for worrying that I wouldn't be able to identify the face you're suspicious about."

"Identifying the face isn't the problem. I already know who he is. The question is, will he look familiar to you?"

"*You know who he is?*"

"It came as a big surprise. In the photographs, there's a man taking photographs of you. Randolph Packard's assistant, Duncan Reynolds. Does that name mean anything to you?"

"No." Confused, Tash searched her memory. "I don't understand. What does Packard's assistant have to do with me? Why would he single me out if I don't know him?"

"Maybe you'll soon have an answer."

Glancing out the window again, Coltrane saw the gleam of sails on the wave-scudded ocean. Then the jet banked inland, heading south over the smog-shrouded L.A. basin. To the right, in the distance, he saw the tiny outline of Santa Catalina Island and was reminded that Packard's mother and father had died in a sailing accident near there. Packard, then sixteen, had been the only survivor. According to his biographies, the family had just returned from a voyage to Mexico. Had they been to Acapulco, just as he and Tash were going there?

"The pilot isn't climbing so steeply now," Tash said.

His thoughts interrupted, Coltrane turned from the window and looked at her. Again, he was struck by her beauty. She had dressed casually: deck shoes, khaki pants, a yellow cotton pullover, and a linen jacket, it too khaki, the cuffs folded up. A turquoise necklace. Hardly any makeup, only subtle eyeliner that echoed something in the turquoise, and a touch of peach lipstick. But for all her casual appearance, she looked stunning.

"Yes." He unbuckled his seat belt, leaned forward, and picked up the black case. When he opened it and handed her some of the photographs, he had never seen a more intense expression on anyone's face.

"Which one?" Tash asked.

"I don't want to prejudice you. I'm going to start with the first exposure I made. We'll go through the locations in the order you visited them, starting with the Beverly Center."

As Tash examined each one, she pursed her lips in concentration. "I don't see anybody I recognize."

"Here's the next set."

Again, Tash concentrated. "Nobody I recognize here, either."

"No repeated faces?"

"None."

She went through the third set with the same result. "There's too much to pay attention to. I'm worried that I'm missing something."

"Keep trying. Here's the fourth set. We're almost finished."

Coltrane had put the photographs that troubled him into the middle, where they wouldn't be conspicuous.

"Nope. Nothing on this one, either. And not on this one. And . . ." Words catching in her throat, Tash raised the next photograph, then went back to the three previous ones. Tensing, she looked at several of the next ones. "Him. The one with the camera."

333

"I shouldn't have mentioned the camera. It prejudiced you."

"No. In fact, I went right by it. Your eyes for this are better than mine. But *this* man . . ." She tapped a face. "This man I recognize. He was with the attorney who came to my house and told me that Randolph Packard had included me in his will."

Coltrane stared.

"But the name he used wasn't Duncan Reynolds. It was William Butler. He said he worked for the attorney. What's going on? Why did he lie to me?"

"Maybe he didn't want you to know his connection with Packard. Obviously, if you knew who he was, you'd have asked him all kinds of questions about why Packard included you in his will."

"Questions he didn't want to answer."

"It's a reasonable guess."

"But *why* wouldn't he have wanted to answer my questions?" Tash's voice had become so strong with anxiety that an expensively dressed couple in the adjacent row frowned at her. She leaned close to Coltrane and lowered her voice. *"Why is he doing this to me?"*

"I told you I did a photo assignment for the LAPD Threat Management Unit," Coltrane said.

"Yes."

"It taught me a lot. People think that stalkers are either rejected husbands and boyfriends, or fans obsessed with celebrities and politicians. But there are other categories. I found out some stalkers have only a casual relationship with their victims. A checkout kid at a supermarket becomes obsessed with a beautiful woman who shops there. He stands close to her while she pays by check, and he gets a look at her name and address. He starts driving by her house. When that doesn't satisfy him, he watches the house at night. Then that's not enough, and he follows her. He phones the house, hoping to hear her voice. He sends her flowers and notes. He takes surreptitious photographs of her. He wants desperately to have a relationship with her, but he knows that's impossible, and as his frustration mounts, he gets angry. Finally he decides to punish her for being too good for him, so he gets a can of gasoline or a knife or a gun and . . ."

Tash shuddered. "You're suggesting Duncan Reynolds fits that profile?"

"I wouldn't have believed it without the evidence. To tell you the truth, I kind of like him. He doesn't seem the type," Coltrane said. "But then, what *is* the type? When neighbors find out the man living next door to them just went to where he works and shot five people, they always say, 'But he was so quiet. I never would have expected him to do anything like that.' Who knows what anybody's capable of?"

Tash shuddered again. "What you said about the knife is a little too vivid."

"Sorry. I didn't mean to upset you." Coltrane touched her hand to reassure her. A crackle of static electricity jumped from her.

They both stared at where it had happened.

"Maybe what I'm really giving off is fear." Tash reached for the telephone attached to the seat back in front of her.

"What are you doing?" Coltrane asked.

"I'm phoning Walt. Now that we finally know who's been threatening me, the police can arrest him. They can make the bastard admit he's been stalking me."

"No. Stop," Coltrane said.

"What's wrong?"

"Walt can't do anything without evidence. He'll want to see the photographs."

"Then we'll show them to him." A thought struck her. "Oh."

"You see what I'm getting at? You'll have to explain why you can't show him the photographs. A vague excuse about taking a brief trip first is only going to puzzle him. If your evidence is so convincing, why are you waiting a couple of days to bring it to him?"

"I'll seem like a flake."

"Unless you tell him the whole story," Coltrane said. "That you didn't see the photographs until you were on a jet to Acapulco. But once he knows where you're going, he'll ask why."

"And our quiet getaway becomes everybody's business." Tash exhaled in discouragement. "If Carl finds out, he might even come after us."

"Right."

Her hand unsteady, Tash returned the phone to the seat back. "Duncan Reynolds doesn't know where I am, either. For now, there are just the two of us."

"You're sure you weren't followed to the airport?"

"I used a taxi. I told the driver to drop me off at United. Once inside, I hurried over to Delta. What was anyone following me going to do? He couldn't just abandon his car in all that traffic at the departure doors. His car would be towed away while he was trying to find me in the terminal."

"Is everything all right?"

Coltrane and Tash looked up in surprise at a female flight attendant.

"We just realized we had some business we forgot to take care of before we left," Coltrane said. "I guess there's no good time to take a vacation."

"Well, the movie we're showing is a comedy. Maybe it'll help get you in a holiday mood."

"I certainly hope so."

2

IF THEY HADN'T BEEN SO PREOCCUPIED, the rest of the three-and-a-half-hour flight would have been a pleasure. The service was first-class, especially the Mexican lunch of sea bass with tomato sauce, olives, and sweet and hot peppers. The scenery was spectacular. Glancing out his window, Coltrane saw the blue of the Gulf of California, with the rugged coastal cliffs of Baja California on the right. Then Baja ended in a series of dramatic rock formations, and the Pacific Ocean was spread out before him, breathtaking, as the jet continued along its southeast route far down Mexico's coast toward Acapulco.

When Cortés's soldiers had discovered the area in 1521, it was obvious that the deep C-shaped bay would make one of the finest harbors in the world, an article in Delta's seat-pocket magazine said. For hundreds of years, it had been a major trading depot, but not until the 1920s had the sleepy village with its pristine beaches and impressive mountainous background become prized as a recreation area. Rich vacationers from Mexico City were soon followed by the powerful and famous from other countries. B. Traven, Malcolm Lowry, and Sherwood Anderson had been there, as had Tennessee Williams, whose *The Night of the Iguana* was set there. But from its zenith in the fifties and sixties, Acapulco's popularity had declined due to overbuilding and overpopulation. Only in the late eighties had the authorities made a major effort to refurbish the resort and return it to its former glory.

To get a good view, Tash and Coltrane had to leave their seats and shift over to the left windows as the pilot announced his descent past the city.

"I wasn't prepared for how big it is." Coltrane stared in wonder.

"The magazine article mentioned that more than a million people live down there," Tash said.

"Yeah, and I bet very few of them can afford to stay in those hotels."

Hundreds of them, huge and brilliant in the sun, rimmed the semicircular harbor or perched on tropical slopes beyond it. Coltrane took a mental photograph of the impressionistic display below him, the green of myriad palm trees blending with copper cliffs, coral roofs, golden sand, and the azure bay. Cruise ships waited near the mouth of the harbor while excursion boats streamed toward docks, passing speedboats, sailboats, and yachts.

"But it didn't look like this in 1934," Coltrane said. "There wasn't a telephone until two years later. Land could be bought for three cents an acre. Only three thousand people lived down there. As hard to get to as it was, this would have been Eden's outpost."

"And Packard's Eden, Espalda del Gato, was even smaller," Tash said. "I wonder how Rebecca Chance reacted when Packard took her there."

337

3

THEY HAD ONLY CARRY-ON LUGGAGE, so after obtaining their tourist cards and passing through immigration, they were able to leave the chaos of the hangarlike terminal sooner than they expected. An airport taxi drove them northward along a coast that had golf courses, beaches, and luxury hotels, one of which resembled an Aztec pyramid. After twenty minutes, the highway climbed to the rim of a hill, where the spectacle of Acapulco's harbor appeared before them.

Costera Miguel Alemán, a scenic avenue that paralleled the curve of the bay, took them past modern-looking high-rise buildings to the old part of the city, where the architecture was traditionally Mexican and where they got out at a small hotel called El Geranio Blanco, the White Geranium, which the driver recommended when he found out that they didn't have a place to stay. He had a relative who worked there, he said, and although January was one of Acapulco's busiest months, he was sure that a room could be obtained for a suitable price. And a suitable tip, Coltrane thought after the driver came back from speaking to his relative inside, announcing with a smile that everything had been arranged. The smile grew broader when Coltrane gave him fifty dollars. As the taxi pulled away, he and Tash peered up at the array of white geraniums on each of the hotel's wrought-iron balconies.

"Let's hope our driver was telling the truth about the relative he had inside," Coltrane said.

They looked questioningly at each other and suddenly found the idea that they might have been cheated inexplicably funny. As things turned out, a room had indeed been obtained for them—one so small that the bed practically filled it, with only one window, on the fifth floor, the uppermost in a hotel that didn't have an elevator, for a rate that Coltrane suspected was equal to that for the most luxurious in the building.

"What do you think? Should we go somewhere else?" Coltrane asked.

"From what our driver said, the town's packed. I vote for staying," Tash said. "Look on the bright side. At least we've got a bathroom."

"But we have to crawl over the bed to get to it."

"Details, details."

"And there's something else we have to do."

"Are you still referring to the bed?"

"Carl Nolan."

4

I MADE A MISTAKE," Tash said.

Coltrane inwardly squirmed. "How so?"

They sat at a small wooden table at an outdoor café in Old Acapulco's busy plaza. Both had margaritas. Neither had touched them.

"The first thing you have to understand," Tash said, "is the past few weeks, since my trouble started, Carl and I have been together a lot."

Coltrane felt a sinking sensation.

"Nothing happened," Tash said.

"Look, I feel terrible asking you about this. Your life is your own. This wouldn't be any of my business if he hadn't threatened me."

"No," Tash said. "I'd make it your business even if he *hadn't* threatened you. If we're going to have a future together, you have every right to know about my past."

The plaza was shaded by palm trees. Children played on a bandstand. A Moorish-looking church with yellow spires and an onion-shaped blue top dominated the far end.

Coltrane registered none of this. "Is that what you want—a future with me?"

Tash smiled warmly. "I feel more comfortable with you than with any man I've ever met. As if I've known you a long time. But of course I haven't, so I get to have all the fun of finding out about you."

Emotion made it impossible for Coltrane to speak.

"Carl and I spent time together," Tash said. "So did Lyle and I, Walt and I, the others. They're my bodyguards, after all. One or another is usually with me—in cars, at the house. We share meals. We talk."

Coltrane waited uneasily.

"When the package with the bull's heart was delivered to my house, there was so much blood. . . . It freaked me out. A lab crew came and took it. Then Carl showed up to see if there was anything he could do. Walt and Lyle were already there, but they couldn't stay—they had a break-in to investigate. But Carl told them not to worry, that he'd hang around for a while, so they left."

Coltrane leaned forward.

"I was so upset that I started sobbing," Tash said. "I reached out and held him. I can't tell you how tired I was of feeling frightened. When he started kissing me, I didn't resist. It was human contact. It was . . . But then his kisses became more forceful, and he was touching me and—"

"Stop. You don't need to put yourself through this," Coltrane said.

"No, if Carl ever tells you I led him on, I want to make sure you understand everything. I want to explain this now so I don't ever have to do it again."

On the other side of the crowded plaza, a mariachi band started playing.

Coltrane didn't hear it.

"I pushed Carl away," Tash said. "I told him that he had the wrong idea, that sex wasn't what I wanted, that all I needed was a little comfort. I told him my life was out of control as it was, without complicating things. He said he'd fallen in love with me. He wanted to know what was wrong with him that I didn't want him, and I told him that under the present circumstances I couldn't think about wanting *anybody*."

Fidgeting, Tash glanced toward the harbor, where excursion yachts and fishing boats were docking, but the faraway look in her eyes made clear that what she was seeing had happened weeks earlier.

"The truth is, I knew I could never have a relationship with him. But this is what went through my mind. I'm not proud of it. Even so, here it is. I was thinking that some nut was out there, probably planning to kill me, and I needed all the help I could get. So I wasn't firm in rejecting him. When Carl asked, 'Maybe not now, but what about later, after we find this creep and you don't have to worry anymore?' I didn't have the courage to be honest. Instead of telling him no, what I said was that I couldn't think about anything like that while I was jumping at shadows. Now I realize that the false hope he took from that conversation is all he's been thinking about. When you showed up at my house on New Year's Day, I could see his resentment when I asked you to stay and talk about the estate I'd inherited. I could feel his jealousy."

"So he decided to pay me a visit at the Beverly Center and make sure I understood that I wasn't welcome, that he had dibs on you," Coltrane said.

"I'm afraid that's how he sees it—that he has dibs on me."

Coltrane's cheek muscles hardened. "Well, when we get back to L.A., after we arrange for Duncan Reynolds to be arrested, I'll make sure Carl gets his mind straight."

"No, let the police handle it. I don't want you to get hurt."

"This time, he wouldn't be catching me by surprise."

"Please," Tash said. "It was my mistake. There's been enough trouble. Let's not start more."

Coltrane couldn't resist her plaintive tone. "All right." He worked to calm himself. "I'll let the police handle it."

"Thank you."

When he touched her hand, he was pleased that this time there wasn't any static electricity. "The main thing is, it's almost over."

"Almost over." Tash sounded wistful. "Something worth drinking to."

They picked up their margaritas, clicking glasses.

"In fact, if we hadn't decided to fly down here, it *would* be over,"

Coltrane said. "Do you want to go home tomorrow, settle everything, and come back for a *real* vacation?"

"A day longer isn't going to make a difference. I need to know why Randolph Packard put me in his will. If we can find the estate I inherited, it might give me some answers."

"Yes. From the moment I found Packard's photographs of Rebecca Chance, I've had the sense that the past and the present are connected." Coltrane set down his glass and picked up his camera. "Hold that pose."

Now that he was paying attention to the plaza, he realized that this wasn't the first time he had seen the Moorish-looking church behind Tash. Its onion-shaped top had been in one of the photographs in the vault. Rebecca Chance had been in this plaza. So had Randolph Packard.

Coltrane pressed the shutter button.

4

WHERE IT'S JUST THE TWO OF US. Where we can talk and swim and lie on the beach," Tash had said, describing some of the reasons she wanted to go to Acapulco. It was too late for the swim, but just the right time to take a stroll, hand in hand, up a shop-lined hill to the cliff above the harbor, and watch the crimson of the sunset tint the blue of the ocean. As Tash leaned her head against his shoulder, Coltrane put his arm around her. They peered out toward the sun sinking below the horizon, only a faint orange sliver visible.

"Watch for a green flash."

She turned to him, puzzled.

"No, don't look at me," Coltrane said. "Keep your eyes on the horizon. In a second, there's going to be a green flash."

"What are you talking about?"

"Packard wrote a book about photography. He called it *Sightings*, and in it, he claimed that during the instant the sun vanishes below the horizon, there's a green flash. He claimed to have seen it many times, something to do with a change in the spectrum of light, and he said it had been one of his career-long goals to capture a photograph of that flash, although he was never able to, because by the time he saw it and pressed the shutter button, the flash was over. He tried to anticipate it and press the shutter button just before he thought the flash was going to happen, but he never managed that, either. I've spent many evenings staring at sunsets, trying to see that flash, but I've never been able to."

"Was Packard telling the truth? Do you think the flash really happens?"

"Other photographers claim to have seen it. Ansel Adams used to take guests onto his porch and try to show it to them."

"But it's always eluded you."

"Yep."

"Then what makes you expect you'll see it tonight?"

"Because you're with me."

Tash didn't say anything for a moment. "That's the tenderest thing anybody ever told me."

"Will you please stop looking in my direction?"

Tash giggled.

"Keep your eyes on the horizon."

"Yes, sir." Tash giggled again.

She peered away from him, watching the last speck of the sun's faint orange vanish below the horizon, and inhaled sharply, for as black invaded the sky, a green flash shot amazingly up, like a mono-colored single beam from the aurora borealis. With equal abruptness, it vanished.

"I'm almost afraid to ask."

"I saw it, too." Coltrane felt pounding behind his ears.

"Holy God."

"Yes."

"I feel as if we're the only people in the world who saw it," Tash said.

"Yes."

"Our own private show."

Coltrane turned her toward him and brought his mouth to hers. As the cliff seemed to waver, he had a fleeting sense that it wasn't their bodies but their souls that were trying to merge. Maybe that's why this is called a "soul kiss," he thought. Then he was incapable of thought as they held each other tighter, kissing deeper.

6

THEIR HOTEL WAS ONLY A TEN-MINUTE STROLL AWAY, but Coltrane had no recollection of the restaurants and shops they passed, hurrying back, seeming to get there instantaneously, and yet he couldn't recall an occasion when a comparable amount of time had seemed to take so long.

They barely managed to lock the door to their room before they were all over each other, unable to get enough of each other. Their hands slid urgently under each other's clothes, their need so great that taking the time to undress would have been an unbearable post-ponement. Then it wasn't necessary to take the time to undress, for they were suddenly naked, their clothes scattered everywhere as they pressed against each other, chest-to-chest, stomach-to-stomach, groin-to-groin, their skin itself a powerful sexual organ that drove them to even greater urgency. His back pressed against the switch on the wall, activating the overhead light. They didn't care. The light didn't matter. They were too absorbed by each other to turn it off. When they sank to the bed, Coltrane felt he was falling, never to stop. He rolled and twisted, sliding sweat-slicked over her, *into* her, moaning, seeming to soar above himself as he thrust, to plunge into himself as he withdrew. His brain pattern flashed white, black, white, black. Then there was only white, and he lay disoriented beside her.

Gradually, his heart pumped slower, no longer threatening to burst. When he finally mustered strength, he glanced toward Tash, whose eyes were closed contentedly, her body glistening with sweat.

"Don't move."

"I wasn't planning to," she murmured.

"I want to take your photograph."

She didn't answer for what seemed a long while. "Yes."

When he stood and peered down, trying to decide what angle to use, he was so enthralled by the casual perfection of her unselfconscious nakedness that he almost forgot to reach for his camera. She was on her back, her arms spread with sensual exhaustion, her breasts at ease, gravity tucking her stomach in, her pubic hair a perfect triangle, her right leg straight, the left bent lazily.

He had never been with a woman who had so entranced him by the sheer fact of her being a woman. It was as if he felt attracted to her because of a subtle chemical signal that he was biologically programmed to find irresistible. But that didn't explain it, even though the after-sex musk smell from her—it filled the room—made him feel intoxicated. His attraction was more than that. He had fallen in love with her long before he had met her. He had known her before and had been searching for her ever since.

He raised the camera, adjusted it, then lovingly sighted through the viewfinder, which heightened the impression she created. Her small, distant, yet close image became intensified, idealized. When he pressed the shutter button, he knew that this would be one of the finest photographs he had ever made. He took a dozen images from various angles, some of which were full shots, others half shots, a few of which showed only Tash's breasts, one of which showed only her perfect dark triangle.

He knelt, easing his right hand onto her mound, luxuriating in its softness.

Tash placed her left hand over his. "That feels nice."

Coltrane heard the forceful pounding of his heart.

"Do you think the photographs will be good?" Tash asked.

"Yes," Coltrane managed to say.

"I'm surprised that I let you take them."

"Thank you for letting me."

"I trust you. I know you wouldn't do anything with those photographs that would cheapen me."

". . . Never," he said gently.

7

IN EYE-SQUINTING SUNLIGHT, the soldier, one of three at a roadblock between two Jeeps, held up his hand for Coltrane to stop. Coltrane was driving a five-year-old blue Ford station wagon with a crumpled fender and eighty thousand miles on it, the only vehicle that he had been able to find for rent. The car-rental agency had told him that the next day something better would be available, but Coltrane hadn't wanted to wait. So, after making sure to get a good map and buy plenty of Mexican car insurance, they had headed south from Acapulco. Forty minutes beyond the airport, the rain forest–lined road had long since become two lanes, and the soldiers blocked their way.

Coltrane nodded in what he hoped looked like respect, asking in Spanish if anything was wrong.

Instead of responding, the soldier scowled into the station wagon's backseat and rear compartment, both of which were empty except for an ice cooler on the back floor. The soldier lifted his right hand from his automatic weapon and motioned that he wanted the cooler opened. Tash bent over the backseat and complied, the two soldiers on her side of the car concentrating on her hips as she showed them that the cooler contained only soft drinks. With a dismissive gesture, the first soldier indicated that Coltrane could proceed.

"What was *that* about?" Tash asked.

"The man at the car-rental agency said the army's been checking vehicles for guns and drugs."

"They looked so sullen, God help anyone they decide to arrest."

"This heat can't have improved their humor."

The temperature was almost ninety. The car's air conditioning wasn't working, forcing them to drive with the windows open. Away from the ocean breeze, the humidity seemed to have increased. But at least the air wasn't hazed with automobile exhaust.

"If this map is accurate," Tash said, "Espalda del Gato is the third village ahead of us—another thirty miles."

"And if this road gets any worse," Coltrane said as the station wagon jounced over a series of deep potholes, "it'll take us all morning to get there."

Tash handed him an ice-beaded can of Coke.

They got there in an hour. The first two villages were dilapidated, causing Coltrane and Tash to assume the worst when they rounded a foliage-rimmed curve and stopped to peer down at their destination. Surprised, they saw neat-looking thatch-roofed houses and shops in a small cove that had cliffs on the north and south and an inviting beach in the middle.

"It's sort of a miniature Acapulco," Tash said. "The way I suppose Acapulco once was."

A few small boats were pulled up onto the beach. Other boats bobbed on waves beyond the cove's entrance.

"Looks like a fishing village."

"But not for long." Coltrane pointed toward a yacht in the harbor. "It's been discovered."

When Coltrane got out to take photographs, something on the cliff opposite him made him focus his zoom lens in that direction. "Check this."

He handed the camera to Tash, who peered through it toward a cluster of white structures on the cliff beyond the village. "Seems to be an estate."

"Aim the camera farther to the right," Coltrane said.

She did, then suddenly lowered it, turning toward him. "That rock formation up there."

"A cat arching its back. The same as in Packard's photograph. We found it."

Excited, they got back in the car, but despite their eagerness to

347

hurry into town, they were forced to drive slowly down a narrow switchback road. On the left, scarlet, pink, and white flowers thrived beneath a canopy of trees. On the right, a cliff dropped into the ocean. At last, the road leveled off, winding through rain forest. They passed a villager leading a burro laden with firewood. Several women carried baskets filled with bananas. The roadside activity increased. Rounding a bend, they came into the village, its picturesque buildings made of upright poles woven together, the palm-leaved roofs tied neatly, layered thickly. Locals glanced with curiosity toward the unfamiliar car and the two strangers inside it.

The plaza appeared, stalls set up for market day, villagers shopping, children scampering. A centuries-old church stood at one end. A stone well and a trough for watering animals occupied the middle. Coltrane parked outside a tavern called La Primorosa, the Beautiful Woman, and surveyed the activity. This far south, much of the population was Indian, their copper-colored narrow faces, sloped foreheads, and pointed chins looking especially strong in profile, reminding Coltrane of the sharp details on newly minted pennies. The men wore white cotton trousers and shirts, their large sombreros woven from what might have been strands of dried palm-tree leaves. The women wore ankle-length skirts and colorfully embroidered blouses. All were either barefoot or in sandals. Hoping that his camera wouldn't offend them, trying to conceal it, he took several photographs through his open window, the possibilities exciting him. If he could capture the textures before him . . .

"Assuming that *is* your estate up there," he said, "you live in a pretty good neighborhood."

A teenage girl went by, selling yellow gardenias nestled in a banana frond. He called her over, bought one of the flowers, and gave it to Tash. "A homecoming present."

"A little premature, but a lovely thought." Tash smelled the flower, enjoying its fragrance.

Puzzled, Coltrane noticed that the girl hadn't moved. What's the matter? he wondered. Does she want me to buy more? Didn't I pay enough? But the girl wasn't gazing at him—only at Tash. "You've got a fan."

Tash smiled at the girl, who looked startled by the attention, stepped back, and hurried into the crowd.

"You're going to have to tone down your smile," Coltrane said.

"Probably not used to outsiders."

They got out of the station wagon.

Coltrane assessed the Coca-Cola sign on the exterior of the tavern he had parked next to. "I suppose this is as good a place as any to ask if anybody knows about the estate up there."

But before he could enter, he paused for an elderly woman with waist-long braided hair who frowned as she approached them. Passing, she frowned back harder.

But not at Coltrane.

"First the flower seller. Now that woman. What's going on?" Tash said.

A bandy-legged gray-haired man carrying a chicken by its feet looked astonished when he noticed Tash.

"*What on earth?*" Tash asked.

"I don't get it, either," Coltrane said. "I'm the one who looks foreign. If you were wearing a long native skirt and your hair was braided, you'd fit right in. They should be staring at *me*."

Another woman stared.

"Come on. Let's get off the street," Tash said.

They crossed hard-packed earth, stepped under a canopy of palm leaves, and entered the tavern. Coltrane's eyes took a moment to adjust to the softer light. The place was clean. It had a plank floor, simple chairs, and trestle-style tables. A child petted a dog in a corner. Americans, presumably from the yacht, looked up with mild curiosity, nodding before redirecting their attention to bottles of Corona beer. Locals, however, set down their drinks and looked startled.

So it isn't just that we're outsiders, Coltrane thought. Trying to seem oblivious, he escorted Tash to the worn mahogany counter. But as he started to ask the bartender what he knew about the buildings on top of the cliff, a row of photographs on a warped shelf behind the bartender caught his attention.

Simultaneously, the gangly bartender glanced up from washing cups, got a look at Tash, and couldn't stop his mouth from hanging open.

"My God," Coltrane said. He pointed toward the photographs. They were old and yellowed—a dozen eight-by-tens. They all depicted a beautiful woman, hence the name of the tavern, La Primorosa. The face of the woman was the same in each photograph. In unconscious imitation of what the flower-selling teenager had done when Tash smiled at her, Coltrane gaped. "Rebecca Chance."

"They think it's me," Tash murmured.

"*Un fantasma*," the bartender managed to say.

"No," Coltrane said hurriedly in Spanish. "Not a ghost. My friend is the granddaughter of the woman in the photographs."

"*¿La nieta?*"

"*Sí*," Coltrane said. "*De Rebecca Chance.*"

"*¿Señorita?*" a frail voice asked.

They looked toward a stoop-shouldered, white-haired, white-bearded man in the doorway. Unlike the Indians in the village, he had a broader facial structure—of Spanish descent.

"*¿Quién es usted?*" Who *are* you? The old man seemed afraid to ask.

"*Mi nombre es Natasha Adler.*"

"*La nieta*," the bartender said. The granddaughter.

The old man stepped uneasily closer. Behind him, a crowd had gathered beneath the portal.

"*¿Es verdad?*" The old man paused before Tash, studying her. Is it true?

"*Sí.*"

"*Después de tanto tiempo.*" After so much time. The old man continued in Spanish: "You must speak with Esmeralda."

The name jolted into Coltrane's memory. Esmeralda had been the first name of the woman whom Tash's mother had said was Tash's grandmother. But she couldn't be. Rebecca Chance was Tash's grandmother.

"Esmeralda Gutiérrez?"

"*Sí. Mi esposa*," the old man said. My wife.

8

A SPLENDID FLOWER GARDEN SEPARATED THE SMALL COTTAGE from the rain forest. Sitting in chairs made of woven branches, with glazed cups of papaya juice on a table in front of them, Coltrane and Tash peered mystified toward a wizened, cinnamon-skinned, white-haired woman, who kept staring at Tash, shaking her head, and fingering her rosary.

"You look exactly like her," the old woman, Esmeralda, said in Spanish, pointing toward faded photographs of Rebecca Chance that her husband had brought from the house.

"My mother claimed that *you* were my grandmother," Tash replied in Spanish.

"No," Esmeralda said, "although I did take care of your mother." *How old must she be?* Coltrane wondered in dismay. *In her eighties?*

"Especially afterward."

"Afterward?"

"After your grandmother's death." Esmeralda's voice was whispery with age. Coltrane had to lean forward to hear what she said.

"Then why did my mother lie to me?"

"Why does anyone lie? To avoid the truth."

"Do *you* know the truth?"

The old woman nodded. "I regret so."

"Drink," Esmeralda's husband said. "This talking will make you thirsty."

Esmeralda dropped her rosary into her lap and used both hands, slightly atremble, to raise her cup of juice to her wrinkled lips, then set it back down. "Why have you come here?"

"Because of a man named Randolph Packard."

The old woman grimaced.

"You know of him?"

"Too well. If he sent you here—"

"No. He died recently."

351

Esmeralda's aged eyes narrowed. "Randolph Packard is dead?"

"A few months ago."

"Then the world is a better place, but I pity the poor souls in hell."

"I inherited some property from him. We think it's the estate on top of the cliff to the south of the village."

"Burn it."

"What?"

"Destroy it. It can only bring you harm."

"What are you talking about?"

The old woman shook her head in distress.

"Tell them," the old man said. "It was so long ago. If Randolph Packard is truly dead, you no longer have anything to fear." He looked at Tash and Coltrane for confirmation.

"I saw his ashes sprinkled into the ocean," Coltrane said.

Her hands more unsteady, the elderly woman again raised the earth-colored cup to her lips, drinking, then slowly setting it down.

9

WHEN SHE WAS SEVENTEEN, she said, the village was so isolated that Acapulco was a three-day trek along a snake-infested trail through the rain forest. Outsiders were unheard of. Then the first stranger she had ever met—and the first gringo—sailed into the harbor.

"He was amazingly tall. His leanness emphasized his height. But what I noticed most were his oddly handsome face, his shock of black hair, and his eyes, which never stopped searching."

"Randolph Packard," Coltrane said.

Esmeralda nodded. "He told us that he planned to live near the village, that he wanted to be a good neighbor, that he had brought us gifts of clothing, tools, and medicines. He would pay us generously to work for him, he said. So the corruption began. Each year after the rainy season, he returned. In the meantime, we built his estate up there, tended his gardens, kept everything clean and in repair, flowers in vases, fresh linen on the beds, ready on a moment's notice for when the sails of his sleek boat would reappear, approaching the harbor. We grew dependent on him. If he was late, we worried that he might not come at all. Without the money, goods, and medicines he brought, we knew we would suffer."

One year, Packard didn't come alone. He brought many other boats and an army of gringos who unloaded electrical generators, cameras, lights, sound equipment, sets, tents, an invasion of movie equipment that the locals knew nothing about and that caused chaos within the village. Along with the invasion came more money and luxuries than they had ever seen. The corruption worsened. Esmeralda hated all of it. With one exception—an actress, the most beautiful woman she had ever seen, to whom she was assigned as a maid.

Esmeralda's wrinkled gaze lingered on the face in the yellowed photographs on the table. She redirected it toward Tash, reverential, as if Rebecca Chance sat before her.

It soon became clear, she said, that the reason Packard had brought the movie company to the village was to ingratiate himself with Rebecca, to put her in debt to him for going to such extremes to advance her career. At the same time, it also became clear that Packard had a rival for Rebecca's affections—the film's producer, Winston Case.

The name brought Coltrane and Tash to greater attention.

Esmeralda learned about Rebecca's situation because the actress, who spoke Spanish, confided in her. Winston Case had produced Rebecca's previous three films. They had formed a close professional and personal relationship. Knowing her struggle to rise within the film industry, he had even given her a house that he owned in Los Angeles. She was indebted to him. But at the same time she was attracted to Randolph Packard, whom she had met one day when she discovered him photographing her house. A conversation had led to a dinner, then other dinners, then weekend outings. His flamboyance and wit had been irresistible.

Esmeralda felt helpless, watching the two men vie for Rebecca's attentions, seeing how Rebecca was torn between them. But Esmeralda wasn't the only one who noticed, for the film crew and the actors soon realized that their work was secondary to the greater drama developing behind the scenes. Several times, Winston Case and Randolph Packard exchanged angry words in front of the company. Packard wanted to take photographs of her whenever she wasn't working. Winston Case wanted her to spend every evening with him. Their persistence so wore her down that she finally demanded that they both leave her alone, and there the matter remained when the film was finished and the cast and crew returned to Los Angeles, including Rebecca, who accompanied Winston Case, while Packard followed her.

"I never expected to see Rebecca again," Esmeralda said, "but the boat came back in less than a year, Rebecca and Packard, no one else. To my delight, I was asked to be Rebecca's maid again, but my delight became worry when Rebecca told me that she had not come willingly, that Packard had invited her onto his boat for a weekend cruise and then had kept sailing, refusing to let her off. Escape through the snake-infested jungle was out of the question. But Rebecca vowed to get away and prayed for someone else's boat to enter the harbor."

Meanwhile, she pretended to be sympathetic to Randolph's attentions. To keep him from suspecting her plans, she let him photograph her. To further confuse him, she submitted to the indignity of agreeing to remove her clothes before his camera. But after a few weeks in which no opportunity for escape presented itself, a new source of tension afflicted her—because changes in her body made it obvious that she was pregnant.

Esmeralda's first thought was that Randolph had forced himself upon her, but Rebecca confessed that in a moment of weakness and passion she had given herself to Winston Case. It had been Packard's suspicion about their intimacy that had driven him to abduct her. Now the growing evidence of that intimacy made Rebecca fearful for the baby's safety, an apprehension that seemed justified when approaching sails made Randolph lock her away.

The boat that entered the harbor belonged to Winston Case, who had finally suspected where she was. But when he hurried up to the estate, he found that Packard had hired a dozen men from the village to guard the property and keep him from getting inside. Reduced to staying in the village, he gazed up longingly at the estate, his only consolation the messages that Esmeralda brought whenever Rebecca sent her on an errand into the village.

The rainy season arrived as Rebecca's pregnancy reached its term. Winston waited for Rebecca to regain her strength while the baby, a daughter, became strong enough to travel. Then, with Esmeralda's help in relaying messages, Winston used the cover of an evening storm to sneak past the guards. He hid until the storm cleared and the estate was in darkness, then used a club to overcome a guard sleeping outside Rebecca's room.

Immediately, Rebecca was at the window. She handed the baby to him, climbed out, and rushed after him through the darkness toward a path that zigzagged down from the cliff to the harbor. Winston had hidden a lantern behind the rock formation, but before he could light it, the baby started to cry, and Packard, who had not yet fallen asleep, burst from the house, shouting for help, racing toward the cries from the baby.

He caught them at the rock formation. Winston still held the baby, but either Packard didn't realize it or else he didn't care, because he kept shoving at Winston, causing Rebecca to scream in protest. She lunged between the two men and reached for the baby, but Packard kept shoving, and the next thing, Rebecca's scream was one of fright as she plummeted over the edge, vanishing into the darkness, her scream ending on the surf-pounded rocks far below.

Packard couldn't move. Anguished, he gaped downward for the longest time, then wailed. By the time the guards arrived, Winston had scrambled down the path with the baby.

10

Esmeralda's gaze returned from a faraway place. She cast another look at the yellowed photographs on the table in the flower garden, then shook her head and glanced toward Tash.

"I was waiting at the bottom. I asked where Rebecca was. He didn't answer, just kept urging me toward the rowboat that would take us out to his sailboat. While I held the baby, he pulled at the oars with a strength that I never would have dreamed he possessed. By the time we reached the sailboat, we heard Packard and his guards on the beach. They jumped into fishing boats to chase us. But Winston raised his sails and disappeared into the darkness before they came close."

Esmeralda's frail voice dwindled.

Her husband helped her to drink more juice, then told Coltrane and Tash, "You must leave now, so she can rest."

"We understand," Coltrane said. "Just one question. Señora, if you got ahead of Packard, you should have been able to escape to Los Angeles. But Tash's mother said that you and Winston and the child roamed from village to village here in Mexico, where he earned food by working as a carpenter. He was rich. Why didn't he take advantage of his wealth?"

"Winston said that if we went to Los Angeles, we would never be safe from so powerful a man as Randolph Packard. Our only way to disappear was by doing something that Randolph would never have dreamed of, by becoming poor. Only after several years did he think Randolph's anger would have cooled enough for him and the child to enter the United States."

"You didn't go with him?"

"Please," Esmeralda's husband objected, "no more questions for now."

"I would have given anything to continue to take care of Rebecca Chance's daughter," Esmeralda said, "but Winston insisted that I had my own life to lead, and he made me go back to the village. As soon as he returned home, he promised to send payment for my years of service. He kept his word. One day a messenger arrived with photographs of the child and more money than anyone in the village had ever seen."

"And now." Esmeralda's husband stood.

"Thank you, señora." Tash clasped her hands.

"No, I thank *you*. Seeing you is like seeing Rebecca again." A tear rolled down the old woman's cheek.

"May we come back after you've rested?"

"Please."

Coltrane and Tash followed the old man into the house. At the last moment, Coltrane looked back, seeing the old woman pick up one of the photographs.

"Where did you get those, señora?"

"Rebecca gave them to me. She's still alive as long as they exist. The more people who see them, the more she remains alive. I have put them throughout the village. Once a year, on the day of her death, a Mass is said for her. The village prays over her photographs." Esmeralda shook her head dismally. "But in this climate, the images decay."

"And Randolph Packard?"

"He abandoned the village, as I always knew he would."

11

THE ROAD UP TO THE ESTATE WAS SO OVERGROWN THAT Coltrane wasn't sure the rented car would make it to the top. Leaves blocked his windshield. Branches scraped the doors. As the Ford's wheels jounced over a fallen tree limb, sunlight gleamed, butterflies scattered, and the estate was spread out ahead.

What had seemed white from the distance of the village was now revealed as the gray of concrete from which stucco had fallen, a few surviving patches indicating that the original color had been coral. Some buildings had one level, others two. All had an elegant simplicity that reminded Coltrane of pueblo architecture. A jumble of fallen poles and decayed thatching visible through an open doorway showed where woven palm-leaf roofs supported by timbers—peaked as in the village—had long ago collapsed.

"Imagine how magnificent this place once looked," Tash said as they stopped outside a low vine-covered wall that enclosed the compound.

"And how everything went wrong." As Coltrane stepped from the car, he admired the gardens that had run wild, hibiscus, bougainvillea, and orchids seemingly everywhere. He raised his camera and took a photograph.

"I don't know what I expected to find here," Tash said. "The truth is down in the village. With Esmeralda."

"I'm not so sure. Some inconsistencies bother me."

Tash looked puzzled.

"If Randolph Packard killed Rebecca Chance, why did he keep hunting Winston Case? Revenge couldn't have been a factor. Rebecca's death was Packard's fault, not Case's."

"Maybe it wasn't Winston he was hunting. Maybe he wanted the child."

"Why? If the child was Winston's, as Esmeralda claims, why would Packard have wanted her?" Coltrane asked.

"Maybe he wanted to kill the child to get even with Winston."

"For what? For making Rebecca Chance pregnant? Packard had plenty of opportunity to hurt the child when it was born."

"And risk losing any hope of making Rebecca love him?" Tash said.

"True." Coltrane brooded about it. "But that still doesn't explain why Packard was so desperate to get the child *after* Rebecca was killed. Unless . . . Do you suppose he believed *he* was the father? He was trying to get his daughter back."

Tash raised a hand to her throat. "You're suggesting *Randolph Packard* is my grandfather?"

"It explains why he put you in his will. He spent most of his life trying to find his daughter. But she was dead by the time he did, and *he* was near death when he learned about *you*. He couldn't reveal his connection with you without incriminating himself. Still in love with the woman he had killed, all he could do was give you the place where she gave birth to your mother."

"A ruin."

"Fitting, given all the lives that were ruined in the name of love." For a moment, Coltrane couldn't help thinking of the ruin his own father had caused. But not me, Coltrane thought. He dismally surveyed the husks of the buildings. "Well, as long as we've come this far . . ." He walked along the wall, passing a gigantic aloe vera, approaching the back of the estate.

"Where are you going?"

"To see where your grandmother died."

Tall cacti stood like sentinels as Coltrane approached the cliff. Ignoring a lizard that scurried underfoot, he concentrated on the cat-like rock formation before him. "Definitely the formation in the photographs that Packard took of Rebecca Chance."

He paused a few careful steps from where the cliff fell away to the sea. The pounding of surf against rocks rumbled up, making him uneasy.

"The lantern was behind this rock formation," Tash said. "The path down the cliff is . . . over here, where the coastline curves toward the village, forming the bay. This is where Randolph Packard and Winston Case fought."

"And where Packard inadvertently pushed the love of his life over the cliff. He spent the rest of his days mourning for having killed the woman he worshiped. He couldn't let the world know what had happened, so he built a secret monument to her, where he achingly studied the photographs he had taken of her."

Although the day was hot, Tash hugged herself and shivered.

"Stay there for a moment. Just like that," Coltrane said.

He stepped back from her, moving farther along the ridge, putting the cliff on his left and Tash's profile ahead of him. As a breeze pushed her hair, he raised his camera, sighting through the viewfinder. Reality and his memory coincided. "Packard once stood on this very spot, taking a photograph of your grandmother on the spot where *you* are now, in that same pose."

Tash shivered again.

Coltrane pressed the shutter release. "If you were wearing a white shawl, the images would be virtually identical."

"This gives me the creeps."

"The height doesn't help much, either," Coltrane said.

"Good-bye." Tash peered down, as if addressing the soul of her grandmother.

"I warned you," a voice said from behind.

Spinning, Coltrane just had time to see the blur of a fist before it jolted him off his feet.

12

SPRAWLED NEAR THE ROCK FORMATION, Coltrane struggled numbly to raise his head. Blood streaming from his mouth, he stared up dizzily at the impossible towering presence of Carl Nolan.

"I gave you a fair chance." Nolan's face was livid, twisted with fury. "I told you nicely." The sergeant's powerful arms, his weight lifter's muscles bulging in a short-sleeved flower-patterned shirt, dragged Coltrane to his feet and shook him so hard that Coltrane's teeth snapped together. "But a smart guy like you just can't listen, can you? You always know better. Well, maybe you'll listen to *this*."

The second blow struck Coltrane harder. Ears ringing, his vision blurring, he landed hard, but his head seemed to be falling farther, and at once his consciousness cleared enough for him to realize that his head had indeed fallen farther. Half of him was hanging over the cliff.

"Or to *this*." Nolan kicked him another few inches over the cliff.

"I told you not to touch her again, but you went ahead and did it anyhow. You never take advice."

This time, when Nolan kicked him, the force was so great that it shocked Coltrane over the edge. A groan escaping him, stomach rising, he clawed at the rock wall, scrabbling to find an outcrop. With a strain that threatened to dislocate his arms, he jerked to a halt, his body dangling, his fingers clinging to a two-inch ledge ten feet below the top. A hundred feet farther down, the hungry, pounding surf waited for him.

"Still hanging around?" Nolan frowned over the edge. "What do I have to do, drop a rock on your head?"

Staring up helplessly, his ribs aching from where he'd been kicked, Coltrane opened his mouth to say . . . he didn't know what. Whatever it was came out as a hoarse inhuman croak.

Above him, Nolan looked around, presumably for the rock he meant to drop, then scowled at something behind him. "Hey, where the hell do you think you're going?" He charged away from the cliff.

Tash, Coltrane thought. She must be running for help. He's trying to stop her.

Despite the agony that racked his body, Coltrane scraped his shoes against the cliff. Unnerved by the thunder of the surf below him, he trembled, feeling a surge of hope when his right shoe found support in a crevice.

Do it! he mentally shouted. He lifted his left foot, taking three tries before he pressed his shoe onto a rock spur. His mind became gray. No! Clinging more fiercely, he inhaled deeply. His heart pounded faster. His consciousness focused, the gray dispersing. Move!

But his body didn't want to obey.

Then his reflexes took control when he heard Tash shouting. He reached up his right hand, wedged his fingers into a crack in the stone, lifted his right foot, scraped it against the cliff, planted it on an outcrop, and pulled himself higher. The camera around his neck snagged on something. He squirmed, fearful that his movements would dislodge him, imagining his plunge to the rocks.

Again Tash shouted. He freed the camera and stretched higher, lifting, pawing, groping. Then he couldn't find another handhold. His strength dwindling, he clawed at air, heard Tash shout a third time, and realized that the reason he couldn't find another handhold was that there weren't any to be found. His fingers were at the top. All he had to do was grip the edge, push himself up, and . . .

13

THE ROCK FORMATION CAME INTO VIEW. Squirming over the rim, he rolled onto his back, but he couldn't allow himself to rest, and he rolled again, onto his hands and knees. The next shout from Tash made him waver to his feet and charge in her direction.

Her cry came from somewhere among the ruins. Adrenaline giving him strength, he didn't waste time looking for a gate through the waist-high wall. He raced straight ahead, sending more lizards scurrying as he scrambled over the wall. Landing among a tangle of ferns and flowers, he heard Tash yell within the maze of buildings. His camera thumping against his chest, he charged past the shells of what might once have been guest houses and servants' quarters. Vines tugged at his ankles, threatening to topple him as he veered around a corner and saw Nolan push Tash against a wall, trying to kiss her.

This time, it was Nolan who was caught by surprise. Before he could register the noise behind him, Coltrane slammed against his back, driving him hard past Tash, ramming him against the wall. With a groan, Nolan sagged, then spun, only to double over from Coltrane's fist in his stomach.

But before Coltrane could strike again, Nolan rammed his head forward. Colliding with Coltrane's chest, he propelled both of them across a flower-choked courtyard, walloping Coltrane against the opposite wall.

Coltrane wheezed, his breath knocked out of him. He did his

best to punch Nolan, but his arms were weak from struggling up the cliff, and he had no effect on Nolan's solid body. Nolan's hands found his throat, gripped the camera strap around it, and twisted. Wheezing again, Coltrane fought to breathe, his face swelling as Nolan tightened the camera strap, cutting into Coltrane's neck.

Coltrane's strength failed. His vision dimming, he fumbled to try to peel Nolan's hands away. He brushed against the shutter button on the camera, unintentionally tripping it, the camera's whir barely audible, the last sound he might ever hear. No! Conscious of Tash's frightened presence, he told himself he had to save her. He rammed his knee into Nolan's groin. Again. *Again.* Nolan lurched back in pain.

It was the sweetest breath Coltrane had ever known. As he filled his lungs, Nolan kept stumbling away, needing to gain as much time as he could to recover from his pain. Then Nolan took one step back too far, tripped over vines, and toppled backward into the wreckage of a ruined building. Coltrane gaped. His eyes had to be playing tricks on him, he thought, for the decayed thatch of the collapsed roof suddenly came to life when Nolan landed, poles and twigs and strands of fiber thrashing into motion, snapping at Nolan, twisting, rippling over him, and—Oh, my God, Coltrane thought, those aren't poles and twigs and strands of fibers. Those are snakes.

Nolan barely got a shriek out before his body tensed and trembled, dying. Snakes that had made their home in the ruin slithered out of the doorway.

"Tash!"

Momentarily paralyzed, she snapped into motion and rushed toward Coltrane. As the snakes hissed and coiled, Tash and Coltrane raced from the chaos of the ruins, staring frantically around to make sure they weren't running into others. Every bush seemed a danger, every cluster of flowers a trap. They squirmed onto the wall, hesitating, afraid of what might be hiding beneath the shrubbery below them. The quick-legged scamper of a lizard made Tash cry out and jump down past ferns, racing toward the car.

Coltrane was only a few hurried strides behind. They scrambled into the car and yanked the door shut, breathing in a frenzy.

"Dear God," he managed to say. His chest wouldn't stop heaving. Sweat mixing with the blood from his swollen lips, he turned toward Tash, whose head was pressed exhaustedly against the back of the seat. Her eyes wide with panic, she stared at the ceiling.

"Are you . . ." Coltrane filled his oxygen-starved lungs.

"I think I'm . . ." Her chest rose and fell in alarming turmoil. "I think I'm all right. He had me trapped. If you hadn't climbed to the top . . ."

"How the hell did he know where we'd be?"

"He shouldn't have. We were careful."

"I don't understand. What did we do wrong?"

"Somehow he followed us."

"I can't believe I'm still alive."

Trembling, Tash held him.

"I was sure I was going to fall," Coltrane said.

"Alive." Tash held him tighter. "My God, I was so scared. I *am* scared." Her mouth was suddenly on his, and the pain of the pressure against his mangled lips was nothing compared to the life-affirming force of their embrace. Alive, Coltrane thought.

14

BUT HE COULDN'T STOP FEELING NUMB AND HOLLOW.

"Talk to me," Tash said.

He kept shaking his head, staring out the window.

"What are you thinking?"

The car seemed filled with the smell of fear and death.

"Get it out of you," Tash said.

"We can't leave him like this."

"We can't take him *with* us."

Coltrane frowned toward the ruins.

"All those snakes. You're not suggesting we go back there and get his body."

"Of course not," Coltrane said. "But we can't just drive away. Somebody has to be told."

"The police? No way."

"We don't have a choice."

"You bet we do," Tash said. "We can get back to the States as fast as we can. The Mexican police scare me to death. They have a different kind of law down here. It's based on the Napoleonic Code. You're not innocent until proven guilty, the way we're used to. The reverse. You're guilty until you prove you're innocent, and this might not look like self-defense to them. They might decide it's manslaughter. What if someone thinks you pushed him onto those snakes? Down here, they don't believe in the right to a speedy trial."

"But the village knows we went up here," Coltrane said. "It's a safe bet they're also aware of another stranger in the area, that Nolan went up here. So what are they going to think when you and I come down but Nolan doesn't? Some of them are going to get curious enough to hike up and look around. As soon as they find Nolan's body, the police will be looking for two outsiders in a car that fits this one's description. They'll be waiting for us at the airport. Because we tried to run, we really *will* look guilty. Don't you see that we have to go to the police before the police come to *us*?"

15

A RED PONTIAC WITH A RENTAL-CAR STICKER ON IT WAS PARKED among ferns at the bottom of the overgrown lane. Nolan must have left it there and hiked up, Coltrane thought. That's why we didn't hear him. The rumble of the surf muffled his footsteps as he walked up behind me.

About to turn left onto the jungle-lined road that led into the village, he had to wait for an exhaust-spewing yellow bus to rattle past. Out of the corner of his eye, he saw Tash fidgeting. Sweat stuck his back to the seat.

"Pull ahead of that bus and make it stop," Tash said.

"What for?"

"If the driver says it's going farther north to Acapulco, I'm getting on it."

"Getting on it?" Coltrane looked at her in astonishment.

"A woman with my features isn't going to have a pleasant time in a Mexican jail."

"There's no guarantee you'll spend *any* time in a Mexican jail."

"I'm not going to take the chance." Tash kept hugging herself. "I saw the way those soldiers looked at me when they were checking for drugs and guns."

"Tash, nothing's going to happen."

"You bet it isn't—because the Mexican and U.S. police are going to sort this out after I get home."

"But the local police will find out we were together."

"Not if you tell them you went up there alone, that I wasn't feeling well and took the bus back to Acapulco."

"Tash—"

"*Please.* I'm asking you. Pull ahead of that bus and make it stop."

16

THAT VINE IS WHERE HE TRIPPED," Coltrane said. His mouth throbbed where he had been punched. "Be careful. There were snakes inside that building the last time I was here."

"Yes, I see one in the corner."

"What?"

"An especially nasty type."

Coltrane's skin turned cold. He had needed all of his willpower to guide the policeman through ferns and flowers toward this spot. Now he needed even stronger willpower not to bolt back to the car.

"A team of medical experts will have to drive here from Acapulco to examine the body before they move it." The policeman, the only one in the village, was middle-aged and heavy, with a thick dark mustache and solemn eyes. "You say you had a fight."

"Yes."

Coltrane had considered inventing a story in which he had happened to find Nolan already dead, but he couldn't think of a way to explain his mangled lips, not to mention the bruises that the medical examiner would find on Nolan's groin.

"Over a woman," the policeman said.

"Yes."

"And this woman . . ."

"Isn't here. As I explained, she wasn't feeling well. She took a bus back to Acapulco while I came up here."

"But meanwhile, this man . . ."

"Came up here also."

"He followed you from Los Angeles."

"Yes. He was very angry about the woman. He and I had a similar argument about her back in Los Angeles."

"But this time, while you tried to defend yourself, he stumbled back and . . ." The policeman gestured toward motion inside the building.

"I never meant for that to happen."

"Of course."

"There's something else I have to tell you."

"Yes?"

"The dead man is a U.S. police officer."

17

IT TOOK A WEEK TO STRAIGHTEN THINGS OUT. Coltrane endured most of that time in a crowded, noxious-smelling cell, not in the village, which was too small to have a jail, but in Acapulco, where his belongings were brought from the hotel, and where he learned that Tash had flown to the United States the day Nolan died. In Los Angeles, she had hired an attorney to fly to Acapulco and consult with a Mexican attorney about gaining Coltrane's freedom. The Los Angeles Police Department was disturbed that another of its officers had died, and equally disturbed about Nolan's behavior. For the sake of public relations and morale, it was decided to say only that Nolan had been on vacation and had died by misadventure: snakebite. Privately, the policeman whom Coltrane had first spoken to expressed severe reservations about Tash's sudden departure from Mexico the day of the death—"She was extremely ill," Coltrane emphasized—but the Mexican attorney earned his substantial fee, and Coltrane was eventually on a plane to Los Angeles. He had suffered doubts about how soon he would be released. He had definitely suffered from the privations of a Mexican jail. But throughout he had kept his emotional strength.

Because Tash had not gone to jail.

TWELVE

1

"THE NUMBER YOU HAVE CALLED IS NO LONGER IN SERVICE," a computerized voice said.

In his kitchen, Coltrane set down the phone and frowned. His travel bag was at his feet. I must have rushed and pressed the wrong numbers, he thought. He picked up the phone and tried again.

"The number you have called is no longer in service."

This time, he knew that he hadn't made a mistake. What the . . . As soon as he had been released from jail in Acapulco, he had called Tash's cellular phone but had failed to get an answer. At LAX, he had phoned her again and had still not gotten an answer. Now, in the forty minutes it had taken a taxi to drive him home in the congestion of evening traffic, her phone had been disconnected. What on earth was going on?

At once, he realized that he had another way to try to contact Tash: Walt.

"The number you have called is no longer in service."

This is crazy, he thought.

He tried the Malibu sheriff's station. "I need to get in touch with Walt Halliday. Is he on duty tonight?"

"No, sir, and he won't be on duty tomorrow, either. He isn't with us anymore."

"Isn't with . . ."

"He resigned a couple of days ago."

Speechless, Coltrane set down the phone.

2

Except for a light over the front door and the garage, Tash's house was in darkness, its modernistic assemblage of cubes silhouetted against the moonlit sky. No lamp was on in any of the windows. That wouldn't have been unusual in the middle of the night, but the time was only ten after nine, and even if Tash had gone out, Coltrane would have expected her to do what most people did—leave a few lights on. There was absolutely no sign that anyone was at home. But there *was* a sign of a different sort. Leaving his headlights on, Coltrane got out of his car to study it: FOR SALE, OCEAN REALTY.

This can't be happening, he thought. He walked quickly to the front door, rang its doorbell, listened to the hollow echo from inside, and pounded on the door. "Tash!" he yelled. The front of the house was scorched from the fire that had been set on New Year's Day. Peering through the metal fence that enclosed the incinerated flower garden, he strained to get a view through a window. As his eyes adjusted to the darkness, he saw that the room was totally empty, its furniture removed. "Tash!" Dismayed, he ran to the end of the street and along the fence to the water, hurrying toward her house from the back. The deck light wasn't on. The only illumination was from the stars and moon. He tripped on the deck stairs but ignored the pain and scrambled the rest of the way up, his urgent footsteps reverberating as he ran to a window. The metal shutters had not been lowered. Staring in, straining to decipher the blackness, he realized that there wasn't any furniture in *this* room, either. *"Tash!"* Despite the chill of the ocean breeze, sweat poured off him, soaking his clothes.

3

I'M NOT COMFORTABLE GIVING OUT THAT INFORMATION," the severe-faced woman said. She was in her forties, had frosted hair and long red fingernails, and wore a black designer pantsuit with a blue silk scarf.

"But I'm a friend of hers. I didn't know she'd moved. I'm trying to get in touch with her." It was nine in the morning. Coltrane stood in one of the cubicles in the Ocean Realty office. Outside, trucks rumbled by on the Pacific Coast Highway. "Surely she gave you the phone number and the address where she moved."

"She also gave me strict instructions not to let anyone else know it." Behind her desk, the woman pressed her back rigidly against her chair, as if wanting to keep as much distance as possible between Coltrane and her. "She told me one of the reasons she was moving was that she'd been threatened by a stalker."

"I *know.* I helped identify the man who was doing it."

"Then I'm sure you can appreciate my dilemma."

"I don't understand."

"For all I know, *you're* the man who was stalking her. She instructed me not to give out her new phone number and address."

"For Christ sake."

The woman flinched.

"Okay," Coltrane said. "I understand your obligation to your client. But would it be violating any confidence if you phoned Tash, gave her my name, and told her I wanted to speak to her? I really am a close friend of hers."

"I happen to know she won't be in today. I'll phone her tomorrow and tell her you want her to get in touch with you."

Tomorrow? Coltrane mentally groaned.

4

Just in time, Coltrane steered from the PCH as Lyle came out of the coffee shop and approached his cruiser. After skidding to a stop, the squeal of his tires attracting Lyle's attention, Coltrane hurried from his car and reached the heavyset officer, whom he had never seen in uniform before and who seemed even more heavyset with all the equipment on his gun belt.

Lyle's hair was cut short, military-style. He looked as wary as the woman in the real estate office.

"The dispatcher at the station told me you usually have coffee here about this time," Coltrane said. "I'm glad I caught up to you."

For his part, Lyle didn't look glad at all. He just nodded and waited.

"Listen, I'm confused about a couple of things," Coltrane said. "I'm hoping you can help me."

Lyle shrugged, nothing relaxed about the gesture.

Coltrane had to raise his voice to be heard above the passing traffic. "I've been trying to find Tash Adler."

"She moved."

"I know that. Do you have any idea where?"

"No."

"Why did Walt Halliday resign from the sheriff's department?"

"He didn't tell me. We weren't really that close. I just assumed it was on account of the stress of the job."

"Well, maybe *he* knows where Tash moved. I tried phoning, but his number's out of service. Do you have any idea where he lives, so I can talk to him?"

"Lived."

"Excuse me?"

"The same day Walt resigned, he left town."

"*What?*"

"He said he needed a change of scene."

The asphalt of the parking lot seemed to ripple, threatening to swallow Coltrane. "I don't get it. What the hell is happening?"

"Seems obvious to *me*," Lyle said.

"How?"

"It's too big a coincidence, both of them making a sudden decision to move at the same time. I had a suspicion there was something between them."

"*What?*"

"Even if there wasn't, it isn't any mystery why *she* would have moved: the stress of being stalked."

"But that's *over*. Now that you know Duncan Reynolds was doing it."

"Excuse me?"

"Duncan Reynolds. Didn't Tash explain to you?"

"Who the hell is Duncan Reynolds?"

"She didn't show you the photographs?"

"*What* photographs?"

Perplexed, Coltrane did his best to organize his thoughts, explaining.

"And you found something in these photographs?" Lyle asked.

"A man taking pictures of her. Duncan Reynolds. I *know* him. Tash met him once, but he used a different name."

"So where are these pictures?"

"Tash has them." The briefcase containing them had not been with Coltrane's travel bag when the Acapulco police had brought his belongings from the hotel. He had assumed that Tash had gone to the hotel to get her things before she went to the airport, that she had taken the briefcase back to Los Angeles with her—to show the police and make sure Duncan Reynolds didn't threaten her anymore. "Or maybe . . ."

"What?"

"Maybe she *doesn't* have them. Maybe they were lost when the Mexican police brought my stuff from the hotel. *That* would explain why she didn't tell you. She forgot to bring them with her, so she decided to wait until I came back with the proof. In the meantime, Duncan Reynolds kept harassing her, and she moved."

"Without even a hint to us that she knew who was after her? Does that make sense?"

"No. Not when you put it that way."

"And *you* don't have the photographs, either?"

The asphalt beneath him seemed more unsteady. Instantly, he felt on solid footing. "I have the negatives at home. I can make others."

"Then make them and bring them to me. But I have to tell you, I think this is bullshit."

Coltrane blinked as if he'd been slapped.

"I heard about what you claim happened with Carl Nolan in Mexico. He was a damned fine police officer. If you expect me to believe he was jealous of you and flew down to Mexico to get even with you—"

"But that's the truth."

"Sure. Except Tash told me a different version. She said Carl went down to *rescue* her. From *you*."

Coltrane's mind reeled.

"She said she was moving because you were smothering her so much that she had to get away from you."

"That's impossible."

"Are you calling me a liar?"

The parking lot seemed to spin. "Jesus Christ, am I losing my mind?"

5

COLTRANE ALMOST DIDN'T CLOSE HIS FRONT DOOR, so great was his need to rush down to the vault, grab the negatives he had stored there, and hurry into the darkroom to make new prints of Duncan Reynolds spying on Tash.

But after unlocking and opening the vault, Coltrane stood frozen in place, his mouth agape. The envelope of negatives that should have been on the nearest shelf wasn't there. Telling himself that he must have forgotten which shelf he had put the negatives on, he charged into the vault and examined *every* shelf, but he still didn't find them. The darkroom, he thought. I must have left them in . . . He rushed to search it, but they were gone.

6

I'M SORRY TO BOTHER YOU." Hoping that his eyes didn't look as wild as he felt, Coltrane pointed toward Tash's house next door. "Your neighbor moved recently."

The spectacled gray-haired woman held an artist's brush, wore a painter's smock, and looked annoyed that Coltrane had rung her doorbell. "The day before yesterday. I saw the van."

"Did she happen to give you her new address? I'm supposed to deliver some legal documents to her and—"

"She lived next to me for six months and never said a word to me. I can't imagine why she'd bother to give me her address."

"You saw a van? I don't suppose you happened to notice the name on—"

7

YEAH, I REMEMBER YOU," the overweight man in the Pacific Movers work shirt said. "We delivered that load of unusual furniture to you. Tubular stuff. Metal."

"That's right."

"Just a minute." The foreman turned to his two young helpers as they came out of an apartment building in Santa Monica. "Make sure you put all those pads back in the truck." He looked back at Coltrane. "You say you've been looking for me?"

"Your dispatcher told me where you'd be. I've got five hundred dollars for you if you'll do me a favor."

"It must be a hell of a favor."

"Not really. All you have to do is go back to headquarters and look up the computer file on a customer named Natasha Adler."

"And?"

"She's an old girlfriend of mine."

"So?"

"I need to know her new address."

The man nodded conspiratorially.

8

As the road twisted higher into the San Bernardino Mountains, the slopes became more rugged. Pine trees fought for space among granite outcrops. The temperature dropped, making Coltrane turn up the car's heater and be grateful that he'd thought to bring a ski jacket along with a hat, scarf, and gloves. Although dawn had been a half hour earlier, dense gray clouds cast everything in twilight. Sporadic snow flecked his windshield and added to the roadside accumulation. Steering with one hand, he drank hot black coffee from a thermos and peered toward his rearview mirror. For a while after he had turned off the interstate to follow this secondary road into the mountains, he had been able to see the glow of San Bernardino behind him, but now all he saw were snow-covered boulders and fir trees, not even the headlights of a pickup truck that had followed him for about fifteen minutes and then veered off. It won't be long now, he promised himself.

What he had been given wasn't really an address, just a post-office box. Tash had evidently supplied directions to the van's driver but not his dispatcher. There wasn't even a telephone number. But a PO box will do just fine, Coltrane thought bitterly. BIG BEAR LAKE, a road marker indicated, 25 MILES. *Soon,* he vowed. Soon. Meanwhile, he had plenty to think about: nagging questions that wouldn't stop threatening to tear his mind apart. Tash!

9

THE COLD AIR PINCHED HIS NOSTRILS AND CAUSED HIS BREATH TO come out as vapor. After parking his car on a side street where it couldn't be seen from the main road, Coltrane walked past rustic-looking shops, ignoring their Alpine exteriors. Christmas decorations still hung in some windows, but he ignored those also, his waffle-soled hiking boots squeaking on new-fallen snow as he strode around a corner and saw Big Bear's post office across the street. In contrast with the mountain-resort appearance of many buildings in town, this was the usual antiseptic institutional-style building, with a fake redwood and stone exterior, a low-pitched roof, drop boxes for mail, and an unobscured parking lot in front.

He checked his watch: 8:25. Although the post office staff wouldn't be on duty until nine, a few people going in and out the front door made clear that the building had been opened earlier so that customers with PO boxes wouldn't have to wait to pick up their mail. That meant there was a slight chance Tash had already been here to check if she had any. But I doubt it, Coltrane thought. She'll be tired after shipping her furniture two days ago and then trying to sort through the chaos of boxes yesterday. She'll give herself a break this morning. She won't be up to speed for a while yet.

He entered a chalet-style House of Pancakes and asked the waitress for a table at the window.

"Coffee?" she asked.

377

"Yes. But I'm not sure what I want to eat. I might take a while to order."

"Take all the time you need."

Believe me, I intend to, Coltrane thought. Pretending to study the menu, he kept his attention on the post office across the street.

10

TWO HOURS LATER, after the slowest-eaten pancakes, eggs, and sausages of his life, after pretending to read a newspaper over yet another cup of coffee, he decided that he couldn't hang around any longer without attracting attention. Outside, the air remained gray and cold. He pretended to study merchandise in shop windows within view of the post office. He feigned taking photographs of the area, training his zoom lens on the post office.

By 12:30, the parking lot at the House of Pancakes was almost full. One more vehicle wouldn't be noticed. He moved his car from the side street, found an inconspicuous spot that gave him a good view of the post office, and settled in to wait. Periodically, he turned on the engine to get warm. A little after two, he went in for lunch. Snow started falling again. While he stalled over a hamburger, fries, and coleslaw, he prayed the weather wouldn't become so bad that he couldn't see the parking lot. Unable to put off going to the rest room, he did so as quickly as possible, afraid that Tash would pick up her mail while he was away. Returning to his table, he was tortured by the misgiving that he had failed to see her. At ten after four, standing to pay his bill, he needed all his self-control not to reveal his excitement when he saw Walt getting out of his Mountaineer over there.

"This ought to cover it," he told his waitress. "Keep the change."

"That's very generous."

"I guess I'm still in the Christmas spirit."

Outside, seeing Walt go into the post office, Coltrane raced through flurries to get to his car before Walt came out and drove away. He slipped on a patch of ice, struggled to keep his balance, and barely avoided a pickup truck that drove from the restaurant. Breathing rapidly, the cold air burning his throat, he unlocked his car, hurried in, and started it. He was troubled by how much his hands were shaking. Then he concentrated on Walt coming out of the post office, his mustached square face sullen, his gloved hands empty, his trip apparently fruitless.

But not mine, Coltrane thought. He let Walt get a half-block lead, three vehicles between them, before he pulled out to follow. Does Walt know my car? He saw it the night I first met Tash, but in the dark, he didn't get a good look at it, and anyway, it's different now— it's covered with snow.

Two of the cars took side streets. Then Big Bear's outskirts merged into postcard scenery, Walt's car, the car in the middle, and Coltrane's car proceeding along a partially cleared road that paralleled, on the left, the ice-rimmed, pine tree–bordered lake. Making Coltrane nervous, the flurries thickened. Dark clouds hung lower, obscuring the peaks. Ahead, Walt switched on his lights. So did the driver in the middle. Wanting to be invisible, Coltrane resisted. Then, slowing, its signal light flashing, the middle car turned to the right onto a plowed driveway that led to a cabin, and Coltrane found himself fifty yards behind Walt's Mountaineer.

He dropped back farther, hoping that the increasingly difficult driving conditions would make his sluggish pace seem appropriate. But Walt slowed also. Don't tell me he figured out who's behind him, Coltrane thought in alarm. Walt slowed more. Jesus. Then Walt's right signal light flashed, and the Mountaineer headed up a road. At first there were cottages, then only snow-laden pine trees. After a quarter mile, Walt steered to the left up a lane. By the time Coltrane reached the turnoff, the Mountaineer had disappeared.

He eased to a stop and stared out his driver's window toward the tracks leading up the lane, toward the curtain of snowflakes that prevented him from seeing past the trees. Is this where Walt was headed, or did he notice me and he's trying to lead me where there'll be only the two of us?

The falling snow made a hissing sound, beginning to fill the tracks. So what's it going to be? Coltrane brooded. If I wait too long, there won't be any tracks to follow. He shut off the car, put on his hat, gloves, and scarf, adjusted the neck strap on his camera so that the camera was under his ski jacket, then zipped up the jacket and got out of the car.

The cold had deepened. It didn't matter. Finding Tash mattered. Getting answers mattered. He followed the tracks along the tree-flanked road. The snow came up to his ankles, an inch away from the top of his thick leather hiking boots. The increasingly heavy flakes brushed against his eyelids, making him blink repeatedly. Wary, he studied the drift-covered undergrowth on each side in case Walt might be hiding there. Then the road reached a Y; the tracks headed to the right, and Coltrane followed them nervously.

Except for the hiss of the snow and the muffled tread of his footsteps, the late afternoon was totally silent. Dusk thickened. He went another fifty paces before he lurched to a stop, a huge shadow towering over him, lights punctuating it. This isn't a road, he realized with a start. I'm on a driveway. I've reached a house.

11

A CABIN, he corrected himself, although it certainly looked as sizable as a house: two stories, a roofed porch, a massive chimney. He barely took in these details before he ducked off the driveway into the cover of the pine trees and waited uneasily for any indication that he had been spotted. After a minute passed and the only sound was the intensifying hiss of the falling snow, he slowly rose and took a harder look at the cabin, or as much of it as he could see through the snowfall. The cabin's base was built from huge rocks held together by concrete. Mortared logs formed the rest of the structure, except for the chimney, and two others that now became apparent, all made from the same huge stones along the cabin's base. Solid, substantial.

Keeping to the trees, he eased along the edge of the clearing, all the while studying the cabin. The porch continued along the right side. A small balcony projected from the second story. The roof was sharply peaked. A small structure to the side had tire tracks leading into it.

I'm still too exposed, he thought. Even with the snow falling, if I can see the cabin, someone inside can see *me*.

So what? Now that you've found Tash, what difference does it make if you're seen? Go up on the porch and pound on the front door. Demand to know what's going on.

But I don't know for certain Tash is in there. Just because I saw Walt go into the post office, that doesn't mean he has the same PO box she does. She might be staying in town or at another cabin. If I barge in on Walt and he's all by himself, what's *that* going to look like?

A shadow moved beyond a window, prompting Coltrane to tense. He backed deeper into the forest and relaxed only when the falling snow prevented him from seeing the cabin. The time was a little before five. Dusk, intensified by the weather, became more pronounced. It would soon be dark. The thing to do is find a place to hole up and wait, he thought. It's not like I haven't been in snow in the mountains before.

Sure, in Bosnia.

The thought startled him. Where the hell did *that* come from? Pushing it away, he glanced around and saw a wooded slope behind him. From its top, he would have a vantage point on the cabin as soon as the weather lifted. A drift spilled over the tops of his hiking boots, but his wool socks kept most of it from chilling his ankles. Breathing rapidly from the unaccustomed altitude, he arrived on the bluff, assumed he was in line with the unseen cabin, and took shelter beneath the snow-laden boughs of a fir tree. Its limbs were bent over him in a tent shape.

Again, he had the feeling that he'd done this before.

In Bosnia.

I haven't come far, he dismally thought.

12

AT SIX, the weather moved on. Stars glistened. Moonlight sparkled off drifts, as did lights from the cabin, now visible below him. His cold-pinched nostrils were pinched even more by the smell of smoke that drifted from the biggest chimney. It was the only imperfection in the Norman Rockwell homeyness of what he saw.

Muscles compacting, he noticed someone move beyond the lamp glow in a window down there. Even though he was confident that the illumination in the house would make the windows like mirrors and prevent anyone from seeing him in the night-cloaked forest, he reflexively crouched behind a fir-tree branch, peering cautiously over its snow-covered needles. At a distance of what he judged to be a hundred yards, he couldn't make out who was at the window, so he hurriedly unzipped his ski jacket, pulled out his camera, and rezipped the jacket against the cold that attacked his chest. He fumbled with a gloved hand to remove the camera's lens cap, pocketing it. He peered through the viewfinder and simultaneously held his breath so that frost from his mouth wouldn't waft up and cloud his vision. Then he zoomed in on the window, adjusted the focus, and felt his chest turn cold again when he saw Walt facing the window, looking down at something, making a stirring motion.

Walt wore a red checked shirt. The magnification of the camera wasn't strong enough to reveal the slight scar above his right eyebrow, but the sand color of his mustache was readily discernible. Walt turned to his right, Coltrane's left, and spoke to someone. With the zoom lens at its maximum, Coltrane concentrated on Walt's lips but couldn't read them. Someone came into view at a sliding glass door farther to the left. Coltrane aimed the camera in that direction, and if he hadn't already held his breath to avoid clouding the viewfinder, he would have done so now, for what he saw made his soul ache.

Wearing jeans and a gray rag-wool sweater that accentuated her lush hair hanging loosely, framing her heartbreakingly beautiful features, Tash had both hands gripped around a coffee mug. Coltrane so projected himself within her that his hands could feel the heat from the mug. She looked out at the snow-covered porch, then turned to speak to Walt, who moved toward her, his imposing body close to her. She was tall, but he was taller. He placed his large hands on her shoulders in a gesture of domination. She returned his stare.

He kissed her.

Coltrane flinched, almost charged from cover, almost raced toward the porch. But shock overwhelmed him. He heard a click and whir, and discovered that he had taken a photograph. What am I seeing? he thought. Walt's hands remained on her shoulders. She made no effort to set down the coffee cup and embrace him. She didn't move her head to avoid his kiss, but she didn't accept it, either.

Walt studied her. He asked her a question. Whether Tash's response was one of rejection or affection, Coltrane couldn't tell.

I need to get closer. Not caring whether his tracks would be seen in the morning, Coltrane responded to his sense of urgency and headed down the slope. Failing to look down, he stumbled over a snow-covered log and barely managed not to fall. With a lurch that jarred him, he came to the bottom half-running and strained to avoid tree limbs he scraped past. Frantic, he took slower steps and at last came to a stop, alarmed by how forceful his breathing was, how fierce his heartbeat.

In the trees at the edge of the clearing, he was only a hundred feet from the cabin. He didn't need his zoom lens to see Tash and Walt beyond the sliding glass door. Walt continued to grip her shoulders. Tash continued to stare up at him.

Then Walt kissed her again, and this time, Tash set the mug on a table, raised both hands, and kissed him back. She held him tightly, receiving, giving, and Coltrane heard another click and whir as he took a second photograph. Then he heard something else—an un-willed sound that came from his throat, as if he was being choked.

13

STUNNED, he sank into a drift. With his back against the rough bark of a pine tree, he hugged himself but couldn't subdue the spasms shaking him. This can't be happening, he thought. He shook his head insistently from side to side. From where he was slumped, he could still see the sliding glass door, see them kissing. Walt's hands were under Tash's sweater. Her mouth was pressed against his. She fumbled at his belt, and Coltrane screamed.

Before he knew it, he was on his feet, surging from the trees. He raced across the clearing and charged onto the hollow-sounding wooden porch, seeing the startled look on their faces when he yanked at the sliding glass door. His shoulder felt a shock of pain as the door held firm.

"I want to talk to you!"

Tash stumbled back.

Walt lunged toward something on the right.

"You told me I meant something to you!" Coltrane yelled.

His belt still dangling, Walt reappeared, jabbed at the lock, and shoved the door open.

Coltrane tried to veer past him. *"Why did you lie to me?"*

Walt struck him.

Coltrane lurched back. Ignoring his bleeding mouth, the same spot where Nolan had struck him in Mexico, he again tried to get to Tash. *"Why did you make me think you loved me?"*

Walt knocked him off the porch. But the moment Coltrane landed in a drift, he scurried to try to stand, only to lose all power of movement when he saw the revolver six inches from his face, aimed between his eyes.

"I could blow your head off." Walt's breathing was hoarse.

"*Why did you lead me on?*" Coltrane screamed at Tash.

"With your history. With the two men you've already killed," Walt said.

"What?"

"Peeking through windows, taking pictures. Stalking a law-enforcement officer, trying to break into my home. There isn't a grand jury anywhere that would blame me for defending myself."

Tash backed away in fright.

"Especially if I put an unregistered pistol in your hand," Walt said, "and squeezed a shot through that glass door, so you'd have powder residue on your glove and there'd be no doubt about your intentions. So go ahead. Try to get past me. Give me a reason to pull this trigger."

"*Why did you lie to me?*"

"You just don't pay attention," Walt said.

The gunshot was deafening. The heat of the bullet sped past the left side of Coltrane's head, singeing his hair. He didn't hear the impact of the bullet behind him. Couldn't. Could hardly hear Walt shout in his face, "Get out of here! Before I think twice and aim where I should have! If I ever see you around here again, if I ever see you *anywhere*—"

Walt fired again, this time to the right side of Coltrane's head, and the agony of the assault on Coltrane's ears made him clutch them and fall back, writhing in the snow. Walt pulled Coltrane's hands away and grabbed his camera strap, yanking the camera over Coltrane's head, hurling it against the side of the cabin, smashing it. He dragged Coltrane to his feet and shoved him across the clearing, thrusting him out of the driveway and onto the road, where Coltrane fell in a daze, gripping his ears again, unable to stop the torturous disabling roar in them.

14

I NEED A ROOM."

The motel clerk straightened. "My God, what happened to you?"

Coltrane could barely hear him. "I had a skiing accident."

"Man, you look like you ran into a tree."

"Another skier."

"Does he look as messed up as you?"

"He never got a scratch."

15

THE ROOM WAS SPARTAN BUT CLEAN—a small bed, a nineteen-inch television, a plastic ice bucket. Coltrane barely noticed. All he cared about was locking the door behind him, going over to the window, opening the draperies, and satisfying himself that traffic was vividly close. The motel was on Big Bear's outskirts, close to the road that Walt would have to use to drive into town. With the glare of headlights, Coltrane knew that he had little chance of recognizing Walt's Mountaineer if it went past tonight, but tomorrow would be another matter.

He picked up the phone and called Big Bear information, his ears still ringing so badly that he had trouble hearing the operator. "Do you have a listing for Natasha Adler? . . . How about Walt Halliday?"

He used a pencil and notepad on the bedside table to write down the number.

The phone on the other end rang five times. Maybe they're out, he thought.

"Hello?" Tash's throaty voice made Coltrane feel pressure in his chest.

"Just help me understand! Tell me why—"

Click.

Coltrane frantically pressed the numbers again.

The phone was picked up halfway through the first ring.

"You're going to be very sorry about this," Walt said.

The connection was broken.

Coltrane pressed the numbers again, but this time, all he heard was the pulsing beep of a busy signal. He called every ten minutes and continued to hear it.

16

THE DAY WAS CLEAR AND BRIGHT. In his chair, Coltrane stared out the window, traffic close enough for him to read license plates. Wrappers from sandwiches that he had picked up the night before littered the floor around him. Using the television as radio, he heard the CNN anchors tell him about a famine in Africa, an explosion at a school in Northern Ireland, a mass murder in Germany, an oil spill in the Gulf of Mexico, and mysterious deformities in frogs all over the world. Yeah, things are tough, he thought, never taking his gaze from the window.

The Mountaineer passed Coltrane's window just after four in the afternoon, Walt's big-boned no-nonsense face behind the steering wheel, Tash next to him. Coltrane sprang to his feet and grabbed his ski jacket. His car was directly outside the door of his motel room. Thirty seconds later, staying far enough back to hide in traffic, he again had the Mountaineer in sight.

It parked at the post office, but both Tash and Walt went into the building, so Coltrane lost that chance to speak to Tash alone. They came out and drove to a hardware store, both entering. Another lost chance. They drove to the parking lot of a duplex movie theater, bought tickets, and went in. After giving them time to get settled, he bought a ticket for Meg Ryan's newest film, but when he sat in the back, he didn't see any profiles that resembled Tash's and Walt's, so he went out, pretended to use the bathroom, ducked into Tom Cruise's latest, and saw them almost at once.

They were on the aisle, about halfway down on his right. At this hour on a weekday, there were plenty of seats available. Choosing one in the middle at the back, Coltrane watched them watch the movie. They ate popcorn and sipped from straws in paper cups. They leaned toward each other and whispered. Totally focused on their silhouettes, Coltrane had no idea what was happening on the screen.

But despite his concentration on Tash, she almost caught him by surprise when she stood and came up the aisle. He slid down just in time to avoid being noticed. A light haloed her as she opened the door and went out to the lobby. Immediately, Coltrane exited through the door on the other aisle, but not in time to intercept her as she walked down a corridor next to the door she had used and entered a door at the end marked WOMEN.

Coltrane stalled by buying popcorn. He stalled longer by going into the corridor and lingering over a water fountain next to the men's room. He pretended to show interest in posters for coming attractions. He turned as the door to the women's room opened and Tash came out.

She froze.

"Just give me an explanation," Coltrane said.

She stepped back, trying to escape into the women's room, but Coltrane grabbed her arm. "What changed? Why did you—"

"Let go of me."

"*How can everything suddenly be so different?*"

"You're hurting my arm."

"Just tell me why—"

"You heard the lady," a gravelly voice said. "You're hurting her arm. Let go of it."

Coltrane swung toward the right, where a broad, burly man in a

San Bernardino County sheriff's uniform stood in the open door to the men's room. The man's face had the grain of weathered barn board. His hand was on his nightstick.

"I . . ."

"One more time—take your hand off her arm."

Coltrane did. Movement in the lobby attracted his attention, a door opening, Walt coming out. Walt stopped and crossed his arms, not at all surprised by the scene that faced him.

"This was a setup?" Coltrane pivoted toward Tash, raising his voice. "Christ, all you had to do was explain to me and—"

"Mr. Coltrane," the sheriff said. The use of the name eliminated any doubt that the sheriff was here by coincidence. "California's antistalking law—"

"*Antistalking law?* What are you talking about? I've got a right to speak to this woman. I've got a right to know why—"

"—stipulates that for a crime to be committed a victim must be willfully, maliciously, and repeatedly harassed. After your intrusion on Ms. Adler last night, your numerous unwelcome phone calls, and the behavior I just witnessed, I'd say that you're perilously close to inviting me to arrest you."

The theater's ticket taker and its popcorn seller peered nervously around a corner.

"But Ms. Adler is reluctant to take the matter to that level. She tells me she wants to avoid trouble. She won't make a formal complaint. I think she's wrong. I think she's already *got* trouble. I think you're the trouble she *had* when she was living in Malibu. I think the only way to *get rid of* that trouble is for me to put you under arrest. If the state of California leans on you, believe me, you'll wish to God you'd never leaned on this woman."

"But . . ." Coltrane felt light-headed with confusion. "I'm not a stalker."

Aren't you? a part of him thought. How else would you describe what you've been doing? You've become your father.

He felt sick.

"So this is the deal I'm going to offer you," the sheriff said. "Get out of Big Bear and never come back. If I see you here again, I'll arrest you for the assault I just witnessed. At a minimum. Because next time, I'm willing to bet, Ms. Adler won't be so generous about not pressing charges. Leave town. *Now.*"

Coltrane looked at Tash. "Okay, damn it, if you don't want me to have anything to do with you, I'm out of here. Forget about why you made me think there was something special between us. Forget about how you lied."

"Mr. Coltrane."

"Just tell me one thing. What happened to the photographs? How did the negatives disappear from my house?"

"*What* photographs? Negatives?" Tash shook her head. "I don't know what you mean."

"Of Duncan Reynolds."

"Who?"

"Jesus," Coltrane said, "you are some piece of work. I don't know what game you're playing, but I'm not going to be a part of it anymore."

"Mr. Coltrane." The sheriff's tone was filled with warning.

"Don't worry, I'm leaving. I finally got my mind straight. Go to hell, Tash. You're not worth it."

"Wrong," Walt said as Coltrane passed him. "She's the best thing that ever happened to me."

17

THE NEGATIVES OF DUNCAN REYNOLDS. How had they disappeared from the vault? The question kept nagging at Coltrane all the while he drove angrily down from the mountains. Darkness obscured the peaks, but he wouldn't have paid attention to them even if he *had* been able to see them. There was too much on his mind. When he had discovered that the negatives were missing, he hadn't thought clearly about the implications. He had taken for granted that someone had broken into his house and stolen them, and that their disappearance was related to *Tash's* disappearance. If he could find out what happened to Tash, he would find out what happened to the negatives, he had reasoned. Both were tied together, because Tash was the only person besides himself who knew that he had taken photographs of Duncan Reynolds spying on her. The logical conclusion, then, was that Tash had been responsible for their theft, but that explanation hadn't made sense. Why would Tash want to steal evidence that would help imprison the man who was stalking her?

Stalking. The memory of what he had been accused of sent a shock wave through his mind. The sheriff had even gone so far as to imply that Coltrane was the person who had stalked Tash in Malibu. *Dear God, what have I gotten myself involved in?* He felt he was being sucked into a spinning vortex, totally without balance and direction.

The dismaying sensation was reinforced by a sharp curve in the mountain road that his headlights didn't reveal in time for him to reduce his speed. He almost veered out of control and narrowly avoided careening into the trees at the side of the road. His palms sweating, he fought with the steering wheel, steadied the car past the curve, and sped onward through the night.

Tash. Because it had seemed improbable for her to steal evidence that would help her, Coltrane had automatically rejected the idea. With no other explanation, however, the mystery had been thought-jamming, another on Coltrane's list of many baffling questions that he needed to ask her. But not anymore. Now that Tash had denied any knowledge of the negatives *and* Duncan Reynolds, Coltrane's thoughts were no longer blocked. Without his bias in favor of Tash, he saw the problem in the direct way that it should have struck him at the start. His house had *not* been broken into; there had not been any sign of forced entry. So how could Tash have gotten past the locks and the intrusion detector? She couldn't have. But *someone else* could have—the one person who stood to benefit by the theft of the negatives: Duncan Reynolds.

Coltrane hadn't had time to change the locks—Duncan still had a key. Although Coltrane *had* changed the numerical code on the intrusion detector, most number pads could be programmed with *several* codes, and Duncan must have known about an existing one that Coltrane did *not* know. Motive and means. It was the only way to explain so clean a theft. The reason Coltrane hadn't suspected Duncan was that Duncan hadn't been aware of the incriminating photographs Coltrane had taken of him. Duncan wouldn't have had a reason to invade Coltrane's house and steal negatives that he didn't even know existed.

Unless Tash had warned him.

Why?

Coltrane shot around another curve and saw the glow of Riverside below him. But instead of taking Highway 10 northwest toward the Hollywood Hills and home, he headed west, toward Newport Beach.

18

THE RED-AND-BLUE FLASHING EMERGENCY LIGHTS STARTLED HIM as he rounded the corner. Outside the estate that Duncan had inherited from Packard, police cars blocked part of the exclusive street. An ambulance was in the open-gated driveway. An unmarked car with a flashing dome light pulled in behind it. Radios squawked. Policemen came and went along the driveway. Feeling as cold as when he had hiked through the snow to reach Walt's cabin at Big Bear, Coltrane parked far enough back that his car wouldn't be in the way, then got out in a daze, slowly approaching the commotion. Neighbors had left their houses and formed troubled groups on the sidewalk.

"What happened?" Coltrane asked numbly, reaching the nearest group.

The well-dressed neighbors eyed his battered lips with suspicion.

"Do you live around here?" a policeman asked.

"No." The flashing lights were oppressive as Coltrane watched an attendant open the back doors of the ambulance in Duncan's driveway.

"Then please get back in your car, sir, and——"

"I came to visit the man who lives in that house." Coltrane's voice sounded faint to him, far away.

"Duncan Reynolds?"

"Yes." Coltrane felt colder. "I haven't talked to him in awhile. I was in the area. I thought I'd see if he was home."

"When was the last time you spoke with him?"

"A couple of weeks. What happened here?"

"Was he depressed about anything? Money problems? Problems in a relationship? Problems with——"

"No money problems. His employer died in November. The will was generous."

"Did the death hit him hard?"

"What are you getting at?"

The policeman hesitated. "A gardener noticed a smell. He hadn't seen your friend in several days. All the doors were locked. He peered through a back window and saw a trouser leg projecting from behind a chair."

"Dear Lord." Coltrane's mouth was so dry that he had trouble forming the words.

"When we forced the door open—I'm sorry to have to tell you this—we found your friend's body."

"What caused——"

"I'm not the medical examiner, but the way it looks now, he shot himself."

19

COLTRANE'S THOUGHTS WERE SO DISJOINTED THAT DRIVING down the hill toward his house, he was slow to notice the car parked in front: a BMW. A minute earlier, he would have sworn that his emotions couldn't possibly have gotten more complicated. He would have been wrong. After pressing the garage-door opener, he steered into the driveway, stopped in the garage, and got out. On the street, the BMW's door opened and closed. High heels clicked on concrete, coming toward him.

Jennifer, wearing a blue business suit, her short blond hair glinting from the light above the garage, stopped in front of him.

He felt awkward, embarrassed—didn't know what to say.

She broke the silence. "I promised I wasn't going to bother you again."

"Actually, I'm glad to see you."

She went on as if she hadn't heard him. "I've got a speech prepared. I don't want to forget any of it."

"Then you'd better not stop."

"I vowed I wouldn't phone you. Not show up at your home. Not happen to cross paths with you the way I did the last time we broke up. But here I am. The fact is, I've been leaving messages on your machine for the last two days. When you didn't get back to me, I figured you were determined to avoid me."

"I didn't know about the messages. I've been away."

"So I had to break my word and show up here and wait for you."

"You might have had a long wait," Coltrane said.

"It already *has* been. As soon as I got off work, I drove over here. Three hours ago."

"Somehow, I get the feeling it's not because of my irresistible charm."

Jennifer nodded. "You pretty much wiped out your charm the last time we talked."

"Then . . ."

"Just because I'm furious at you, that doesn't mean I wouldn't feel terrible if something happened to you. Her real name isn't Natasha Adler."

"What?"

"And men have a habit of dying around her."

20

THEY SAT IN THE TUBULAR CHAIRS IN COLTRANE'S LIVING ROOM, two cans of diet Pepsi open, glasses filled, neither of them drinking.

"After you told me to get lost," Jennifer said.

"I hope I wasn't that blunt."

"Everything's a matter of perspective. From *my* perspective . . ." She took a long breath. "Anyway, let's just say I felt hurt. I felt used. I . . ."

Coltrane looked down at his hands.

"I'm not trying to throw this back at you," Jennifer said. "The only reason I'm going into this is to make you understand why I did what came next."

"After what I've been through the past couple of days, believe me, I understand what you felt. Throw it back at me. I deserve it."

"I felt angry. And confused. And deeply deeply troubled. Not just about our breakup, but about Tash Adler. Maybe *you* thought it was normal to fall in love with her on the spot. But given your usual reluctance to make an emotional commitment, I thought your sudden commitment to her was disturbing as hell."

Coltrane felt stung.

"Those photographs of Rebecca Chance," Jennifer said. "Tash Adler's uncanny resemblance to her. The whole business didn't only baffle me; it struck me as being unnatural. So I decided to try to make sense of it. Not because I thought I might find some dirt that would help get us back together. I had no hope of that. I still don't. It's not why I'm here. For all I know, you're going to tell me I'm making all this up so I can cause trouble between you and Tash. But I have to try. Because if something happened to you, I'd never forgive myself for not having warned you."

"Don't worry. You can't cause any more trouble between Tash and me than there already is," Coltrane said. Coming into the house, Jennifer had asked about the gashes on his mouth. He had told her what happened in Mexico and Big Bear.

"If I'm right, there could be a *lot* more trouble," Jennifer said. "I think you're in real danger."

"Keep talking."

"I wanted to find out just who this woman is that she could set your mind spinning the way she did."

"And? You said her real name isn't—"

"She was born Melinda Chance."

"How do you know?"

"I hired the same private detective *you* did when you wanted to find out where Natasha Adler lived. He didn't have much to go on, just what you'd told me about the stores she owns and her connection with Rebecca Chance. But that was enough. The stores aren't owned in her name. They're controlled by a corporation she runs, called Opportunity Inc. The private detective followed the trail of that corporation and worked backward, but I'm going to explain from the beginning and work forward." Jennifer opened a briefcase that she had brought with her. "Here's a copy of a birth certificate. Melinda Chance. Born April twenty-ninth, 1972, Fresno, California. Father unknown. Mother—Stephanie Chance."

"All that proves is that some woman had the same last name."

"Here's a copy of a page from a Fresno high school yearbook."

His stomach fluttering, Coltrane peered down at the copy she set before him. It was a good-quality photographic reproduction. He scanned the rows of students' faces and fixed almost at once on the features of a young woman gazing back at him. Her dark hair was a little shorter, and her features were more girlish than womanly, but she had the same smoldering coals in her eyes. Tash. Except that the name under the photograph was Melinda Chance.

"When was this yearbook issued?"

"When she was seventeen. Just before she left Fresno."

"What's this caption under her name? 'Destined to launch a thousand ships'?"

"A compliment about her looks. At first, it puzzled me, too, but it reminded me of a quotation from something, so I asked a reference librarian to track it down for me. 'Was this the face that launch'd a thousand ships . . . ?' It's from a Renaissance play by Christopher Marlowe. The face that's referred to is Helen of Troy's. I thought the allusion was a little fancy for a high school yearbook, but then I noticed that below the caption it says 'Favorite activity: the Drama Club.' Here's a photocopy of another page from the yearbook. These are the members of the Drama Club. Melinda Chance is easily the eye-catcher. As the caption indicates, among other things, the club practiced by reading scenes from classic plays. Must have been a tough teacher. Portions from Shakespeare's *Hamlet* and Marlowe's *Doctor Faustus*. That's the play with the 'thousand ships' quote. You can see the title on the cover of the book she's holding in this photograph. It's about a man who sells his soul to the Devil."

Coltrane felt a chill. "What are you getting at?"

"She never finished high school in Fresno. She and her mother left town. The reason they left is that Melinda Chance also enjoyed being on the football team's cheerleading squad. She gave two of the players quite a bit of extra encouragement. The quarterback killed a fullback because of her."

Coltrane's chill worsened.

"Stabbed him in a parking lot after the spring prom."

"My God."

"The killer was eighteen, old enough to be tried as an adult," Jennifer said. "His family didn't have any social position. But the boy who got stabbed was *sixteen*, and *his* father was a bank president. The jury found the older boy guilty. The sentence was ten years."

"And Melinda Chance moved on."

"To Sacramento. She finished high school there and went to college. But by then, her name was Vivian Breuer. B-r-e-u-e-r. It's a distinctive spelling. I'll get to why that's important. In college, she majored in drama, but the drama she was involved in didn't happen only on a stage. A young man she was dating fell from the ten-story-high balcony of her apartment. The police questioned another boyfriend of hers who was in her apartment at the time of the fall. That second young man was eventually arrested for harassing her. Meanwhile, the chairman of the Drama Department, a forty-six-year-old man with a wife and two children, shot himself to death after the final performance of the Drama Club's spring production. The play was Tennessee Williams's *Cat on a Hot Tin Roof.* You'll never guess who played Maggie, the character Elizabeth Taylor played in the movie, and you'll also never guess who was suspected of having had an affair with the professor."

"You can prove all this?"

"Here are photocopies of articles from the Sacramento newspaper. I've underlined Vivian Breuer's name. By now, she was smart enough not to allow herself to be photographed for the yearbook, but the private detective I hired tracked down cast members from that production of *Cat on a Hot Tin Roof,* and they identified Vivian Breuer from Melinda Chance's photos in the Fresno high school yearbook. They're also the ones who suspected she was having an affair with the professor who killed himself. These are the private detective's notes of the conversations he had with the cast members, and these are the tape recordings of the same conversations."

Coltrane looked with horror at the accumulating materials.

"She transferred to Humboldt State University in Arcata, California, still majoring in drama, but now she changed her name to Linda Erikson. That last name's important, too. I'll explain why in a little while. In Arcata, the lead actor in William Inge's *Picnic* beat his male costar to death in an argument after the production's dress rehearsal. Do you remember the movie of that play?"

"William Holden was the star."

"Right, and Cliff Robertson was the male costar, and the plot had to do with how Holden, playing a drifter, showed up in a small town in Kansas and stole Robertson's girlfriend. Kim Novak played the girl."

"And Tash had the Kim Novak role? You're suggesting that what happened in the play also happened in life?"

"Except that in the play, one of the male costars doesn't beat the other one to death. Here are copies of the Arcata newspaper articles about the murder. Note that Linda Erikson managed to avoid getting her photograph taken. The student actor admitted that he killed the other actor because he was jealous about Linda. For her part, Linda professed to be as shocked as everyone else. She said that she was too disturbed about what had happened to continue her studies, and she moved on as soon as she finished testifying at the trial. The student actor got eight years. Here are transcripts and tape recordings of conversations that my private investigator had with members of the *Picnic* cast whom he tracked down. He showed them Melinda Chance's high school yearbook photographs. They identified her as Linda Erikson."

Coltrane's feet and hands turned numb.

"Meanwhile, the young man who was arrested for harassing her in Sacramento set out to find her as soon as he got out of jail. His search took him to—guess where—Arcata, where his body washed up on the beach one morning. The medical examiner's report suggested that he had drank too much, gone swimming at night, passed out, and drowned. Here's a copy of it. You ready for more?"

"No, but I think I'd better hear it."

"The next place she showed up was San Francisco, but she wasn't interested in college any longer. She suddenly had the money to start half a dozen clothing boutiques, and now her name was Evelyn Young."

"I assume *that* last name's important, too," Coltrane said.

"Yes, but this time she's making a joke."

"I don't get it."

"You will."

"The money for the stores. Where did she—"

"From the Acapulco Venture Group."

The name had uncomfortable overtones and filled Coltrane with misgiving.

"A subsidiary of Orange Coast Investments," Jennifer said, "which is a division of Seaview Enterprises"—she paused—"which was owned by Randolph Packard."

Coltrane looked down at the table and saw double for a moment. "So she lied to me when she said she didn't know about Packard."

"One of the things my private investigator couldn't find out is why Packard would have given her money."

"Because Packard thought he was her grandfather." Coltrane explained what he had learned in Mexico.

"Maybe Packard *was* her grandfather," Jennifer said.

Coltrane shook his head and regretted it, aggravating a splitting pain. "No. Rebecca Chance told her servant that Winston Case was."

"Assuming Rebecca Chance told the truth."

Coltrane's blurred vision cleared as a terrible thought occurred to him. "She made each man think he was the father? She was trying to set Randolph Packard and Winston Case against each other? She wanted them to *fight* over her?"

"Like grandmother, like granddaughter."

"And a lifetime later, Packard finally found his daughter and a granddaughter he didn't know about, and he gave them money."

"Or maybe earlier. The fact that in Fresno her mother and she used the last name Chance suggests that maybe they *wanted* to be found. Maybe they *were* found in Fresno. From what the private detective was able to learn, they had a lot of money."

"What happened when she showed up in San Francisco?"

Jennifer shrugged fatalistically. "She changed her technique and joined a sailing club. Two prominent male members competed for her. All three went out on a boat for a weekend up the coast. Only she and one of the men came back. The inquest didn't dispute their story—that the other man went on deck during the night, lost his balance, and fell overboard. The body was never recovered."

"Something she did on the boat made the two men fight over her."

"Of course. Two months later, the man who'd survived was arrested for harassing her."

"Just like the student in Sacramento," Coltrane said.

"And just like that student, he drowned shortly after he was released from jail. In this case, he took a boat out by himself, and it capsized."

"Or maybe she arranged for him to have an accident so there'd be one less person who knew how she got her kicks," Coltrane said. "The survivors of love affairs with her don't have much luck."

"*You're* a survivor. Think about that while I tell you about San Diego," Jennifer said. "She changed her name to Donna Miller."

"Is that a significant last name, too?"

"You bet. You'll understand why in a minute. She opened more clothing boutiques, ran them for a while, then turned them over to a manager and left on a yearlong around-the-world vacation. That was six months ago."

"Six months?" The number nudged at something in Coltrane's memory. "A neighbor of hers told me that's when Tash showed up in Malibu."

"As much as the investigator could determine, nothing happened in San Diego. He thinks she's planning to keep it uncontaminated. A home base. But Malibu was another matter. Melinda Chance or Tash Adler or whatever you want to call her was up to her old tricks—with a new variation that added more excitement. She pretended to be stalked so she could have policemen around her, big men with big guns, whom she would manipulate to fight over her."

"Pretended to?" Coltrane said. "No, you don't understand. Duncan Reynolds was in fact stalking her. He—" Instantly, another piece of the puzzle slid horrifyingly into place. "Jesus, he *wasn't* stalking her. He was her *accomplice*. He was doing what Tash asked him to do so the police would believe she was being threatened and she could manipulate her bodyguards until they turned on one another. That explains how Duncan knew about the photographs I took of him. Tash is the only one who could have told him. She must have ordered him to take the evidence and cover her tracks. And then—"

"What's the matter?"

"What *else* was stolen?" Coltrane sprang to his feet.

21

As COLTRANE SCRAMBLED DOWN THE STAIRS, he heard Jennifer running after him. Frantic, he reached the vault, unlocked it, and charged inside. He flicked at the light switch without stopping, raced past the shelves, reached the false wall in the far left corner, and shivered from more than the vault's chill when he stooped to free the catches and pull out the wall.

Behind him, Jennifer's heels sounded urgently on the concrete floor, but his attention was totally directed toward the hidden chamber, the vault's glaring overhead lights making him squint toward the shadows in there.

"She's gone." His voice broke.

Rebecca Chance's face no longer peered out at him. The life-sized photograph of her haunting features no longer hung on the back wall of the chamber. He took a half step back, as if he'd been pushed, then moaned and lurched into the chamber, knowing what he wouldn't find but needing to search anyhow. The effort was worthless. The chamber was empty. Every box of photographs had been removed.

Coltrane spun toward Jennifer. "Duncan didn't know about this chamber. Tash must have told him. Jesus." Feeling off balance, he groped for a shelf. "When I confronted her in Big Bear, she denied knowing anything about the negatives *or* Duncan. It didn't make sense. Why would she lie? So I drove to Duncan's house in Newport Beach to confront *him.* Too late. Several days ago, he shot himself."

"Duncan?" Jennifer turned pale. "Why would he . . ."

"Maybe Tash helped him along, the way we assume she helped

two of her old boyfriends along. One less piece of evidence, one less person who knew the truth."

The implications reduced them to stunned silence.

"What about the last names she used? Tell me why they're significant," Coltrane said.

"Breuer. Erikson. Young. Miller. Adler. In college, before I got into graphic arts, I thought about a career in psychology. I took a lot of classes in it. The names Erikson and Adler had a lot of associations when I saw them together. That made me think about the other names. They all fit. Every one of them is a famous psychotherapist. Breuer and Adler were colleagues of Freud. Adler was one of his disciples."

"I never heard of a famous psychotherapist called Young."

"Spell it differently. J-u-n-g. She's making a joke. Or she chose the names without realizing the connection among them, a subconscious slip. My private investigator found out that, under each of these names, she went to a therapist in each of the cities she lived in."

"And what about Miller?"

"Alice Miller. The subtitle of one of her books is *Tracing Childhood Trauma in Creativity and Destructiveness.*"

Coltrane's voice was an uneasy whisper. "Childhood trauma?"

"There's one other thing I have to tell you."

"You mean it gets worse?"

"She told you her mother was dead. Well, she's batting a thousand, because that isn't true, either."

22

IN POINT-AND-SHOOT CAMERAS, the viewfinder and the lens have different openings. As a consequence, the image seen through the viewfinder is not quite the same as that received through the lens and recorded on film, making precise framing difficult. The difference between what the viewfinder sees and what the lens sees is known as the parallax effect, and that is what Coltrane suffered now. What he had thought was happening was so at odds with what had truly been happening that the parallax threatened to drive him insane.

At ten the next morning, after he and Jennifer had caught a 7:00 A.M. flight to Oakland, he walked apprehensively along a corridor in the Redwood Rest Facility. In room after room, aged men and women lay in beds. A recreation room revealed a dozen residents in wheelchairs watching a game show on television. In the hallway, a few residents managed to get around with the aid of walkers. Coltrane nodded respectively to them, then stopped where a white-uniformed male attendant waited outside a room.

The attendant was in his twenties, with wire-rim glasses and his hair tied back in a ponytail. "You'd better prepare yourselves. The odds are, she won't know you."

"I don't expect her to," Coltrane said. "It's been years since we met," he lied. "The last time I saw her was when we lived on the same street in Sacramento. But I have these photographs I took of her daughter." Coltrane held up a packet. "And when her daughter found out I was coming to Oakland for a photo assignment, she asked me to visit her mother and give these to her." The camera hanging from Coltrane's neck gave credence to his story.

"Sometimes her language can be a little frank."

"No problem. I admire elderly women who speak their mind," Jennifer said.

"Well, maybe *frank* isn't the right word," the attendant said.

Coltrane tilted his head in puzzlement.

"*Shocking* would be more accurate," the attendant said. "But who knows, you might get lucky and catch her in one of her occasional ladylike moods. The doctor said the photographs you're bringing might improve her mental outlook. Nothing else has, so let's hope." The attendant reached for the doorknob. "Just give me a minute to go in and see that she's presentable."

"Take all the time you need," Coltrane said. While the attendant went in, his apprehension swelled.

"So far so good. The story about the photographs worked," Jennifer said.

"I wish it hadn't. I don't want to go in there."

The photographs of Tash that Coltrane had brought were from the film he had exposed in Acapulco. He had developed the prints the night before, careful to shield Jennifer from the nudes but inadvertently processing an image that he hadn't even known he had taken. When Carl Nolan had tried to strangle him with the camera strap, Coltrane had fumbled to attempt to pry the hands away and had accidentally pressed the camera's shutter button. The resultant image, tilted on a forty-five-degree angle, showed the blur of what might have been the side of a hand on the right and the blur of what was possibly a shoulder on the left. Between them, Tash's face was distinct. Coltrane had never seen an expression of such animalistic delight. He had almost been embarrassed to look at it, so open was the sexual pleasure that she took from watching Carl and him fight because of her.

The door hissed open, the attendant stepping out. "I can't tell her mood, but she's ready to see you."

Am *I* ready, though? Coltrane asked himself.

After an uncertain glance toward Jennifer, he felt encouraged by the touch of her hand on his arm. He entered the room.

The rest home's administrator had given Coltrane a sense of what to expect. Even so, he was caught by surprise, faltering as Jennifer closed the door.

"There's been a mistake. We're in the wrong room."

"No mistake," Jennifer said.

"But . . ." Coltrane stared at the apparently sleeping woman on the bed. "Tash's mother was born in 1934. Depending on when her birthday is, she'd be sixty-three or sixty-four now. But this woman is—"

"What are you whispering about?" the woman on the bed complained. She sounded as if she had broken glass caught in her throat.

"Sorry," Coltrane said. "We thought you were asleep. We were trying to decide whether to wake you."

"You mean you were trying to decide if I was asleep so you could feel me up."

"Uh . . ." Coltrane lost the power of speech. The woman in the bed, who should have looked in her early sixties, seemed in her nineties: stringy, thinning white hair, rheumy red eyes, shriveled skin, a prematurely shrinking and collapsing body. A scar disfigured each of her cheeks. But the most disturbing aspect about her was that, in spite of all the ravages her body had endured—"From alcohol and drugs," the administrator had explained—she was recognizably Rebecca Chance's daughter and Tash's mother, as if this was how Rebecca Chance would have looked had she lived and led a hard life, or as if this was how Tash was destined to end.

"Go ahead. Feel me up. The attendants do it all the time." The prematurely old woman pawed at her spiderweb hair, as if combing it.

Coltrane looked at Jennifer, shocked and sickened.

"Stephanie?" Jennifer approached the bed.

"Who the hell are *you?*"

"My name's Jennifer. We'd like to ask you a few questions."

"No women allowed."

"We brought you some photographs of your daughter."

"No women allowed."

"If I leave, do you promise to talk to my friend?"

"Did he come here to . . ."

The suggestion she made turned Coltrane's stomach sour.

"I'm afraid the attendants wouldn't like him to do that," Jennifer said. "They might get angry."

"Good."

"They might start a fight."

"Yes."

"You enjoy that?"

"Make them fight. They deserve to be punished."

"Why?"

"For wanting me."

"Does your daughter like men to fight?"

"The little . . ." The next word was shocking.

406

"Why do you call her that?"

"Thought she was better than me. Took my men away from me."

"When she was in college?"

"Hah."

"In high school?"

"Hah. When I was asleep, she got a razor, snuck up, and did this to my cheeks. Couldn't stand her momma to get all the attention. Thought she could destroy the competition. Didn't work. I'm still as beautiful as ever." She gave Coltrane the most demanding look he had ever received. "Aren't I?"

"Yes."

"Then . . ."

What she said next made Coltrane look away.

"What good are you? Get yourself a new boyfriend, missy. This one can't cut it. Pictures? Did you say you brought pictures of my daughter?"

"Yes," Coltrane managed to say.

"Burn them. Send her to hell. And get out of here. Quit wasting my time. I've got men lined up waiting to—"

"You're right," Coltrane said. "We're wasting your time. I'm sorry we bothered you."

24

O N THE PILLARED STEPS OF THE REST HOME, Coltrane sank and put his head between his knees. It took him several deep breaths before his swirling sensation passed and his stomach became still. From the bay, a salt-laden breeze drifted over him, cooling the sweat on his brow.

Finally he was able to peer up at Jennifer. "You're the one who took all the psychology courses."

"It's called being a sexual predator," Jennifer said. "In women, it's very rare."

"But how did . . ."

"Heredity or environment. Take your pick."

"Or both. In other words, who knows," Coltrane said.

"My abnormal-psych prof said that emotional illness can be inherited." Jennifer eased down next to him, crossing her arms over the knees of her gray slacks. "We don't know anything about *Rebecca's* mother, but she and her daughter and her granddaughter are all beautiful women so obsessed with their beauty, so self-conscious and uncomfortable about it, that they feel self-worth only when men fight over them."

"Or they were all abused as children and they're so ambivalent about men, so bitter, that they want to punish men for finding them attractive," Coltrane said.

"Which takes us from heredity to environment. We don't know how that pathetic woman in there was raised. It could be Winston Case was a monster. But from what she said about the way Tash or Melinda or whatever you want to call her was raised, it's clear that even as a child, Tash felt jealous about all the men her mother had around her. She needed attention, but since she couldn't get it from her mother, she got it from her mother's boyfriends. The trouble is, she may have gotten more attention than she bargained for. If Tash was molested, I'm not surprised that she feels so angry at men now that she's grown up. On the one hand, she feels compelled to tempt them. On the other hand, she needs to punish them for wanting her. Having sex with her is unforgivable."

Coltrane felt his cheeks turn warm.

"I have a terrible feeling you're next on her list of get-evens," Jennifer said. "But even if you hadn't had sex with her, you know she was lying about the negatives and Duncan Reynolds. You see through her act, and that puts you in a position to make trouble for her. If she's true to form, she'll protect herself by finding a way to get rid of you."

"Just as she got rid of Duncan and her former boyfriends. That's what she's doing with Walt. She's setting him up to use him against me."

"We have to warn him."

25

Mr. Coltrane, this is Eliot Blaine," a concerned voice said from the speaker on Coltrane's car phone. As soon as he and Jennifer had gotten back to the Los Angeles airport, he had called his home to find out if he had any messages on his answering machine. A series of hang-up calls had troubled him, reminding him of Ilkovic, making him wonder if it was Walt. Then Blaine said, "I'm the attorney for Randolph Packard's estate. I don't know if you've heard this from another source. If not, forgive me for being the messenger of bad news. I know you spent time with Randolph's assistant, Duncan Reynolds. He confided to me that he was fond of his chats with you. I'm . . . There's no easy way to say this. You'll be as dismayed as *I* was to learn that Duncan's body was found at his home last evening. Apparently, he'd been dead for several days. The police seem to think he committed . . . It's more appropriate if we discuss this in person. Please call me at my office. About a week ago, Duncan came to me with a strange request. I respected his privacy and didn't question him about it, but it now seems obvious that he was taking care of personal matters before . . . I have a package he wanted me to give you in the event of his death."

26

"AN AUDIOCASSETTE?" Coltrane looked puzzled at the object he removed from the envelope.

Seated in a soft-looking brown leather chair behind a large glass desk, Blaine slid a signed letter in Coltrane's direction, his manicured fingernails glistening. "At the time, I thought it was a strange request, but in my profession, strange requests aren't unusual. Duncan's instructions to me were that you should listen to the tape in my presence. When you telephoned to say you were coming, I instructed my secretary to rearrange my schedule so that we could do so now."

"Thank you."

"I always made time for Duncan. He was more than a business associate."

"Yes, I thought of him as a friend, too."

Blaine was in his fifties, of medium height and weight, with cautious eyes. His hair was perfectly trimmed, his suit expensively tailored, his shoes so shiny that they looked as if they had just come out of their box.

He stood and put the cassette into a player on a stack of stereo components next to law books. As a soft hiss came from speakers at each end of the shelf, he returned to his chair, interlocked his fingers on his desk, and hardened his patrician jaw in concentration.

The hiss on the tape continued. Something made a hollow thumping noise, as if a microphone was being moved. The clinking of what sounded like ice cubes in a glass was followed by the gulp of a large mouthful of liquid being swallowed.

"This message is for Mitch Coltrane," Duncan's slurred voice said. "If you're listening to this tape, you know I'm dead." Another strained breath. "What an odd thing to hear myself say."

More clinking of ice cubes. More liquid being swallowed. Duncan didn't speak again for what seemed like fifteen seconds.

His breathing was forced. "I thought about running, but that would only make her decide I'm a greater liability than I suspect she already thinks I am. Besides, I can't stand to be away from her. What she lets me do to her . . . A man of my years, with my ordinary looks, with my physical limitations. I never dreamed I could know such . . . To be indulged by . . . Maybe she *doesn't* think I'm a liability. Maybe I don't have a reason to be afraid. Maybe things will go on as they are, and she'll continue to let me . . ."

"What on earth is he talking about?" Blaine asked.

Coltrane held up a hand for Blaine to be silent.

"If only you hadn't taken those photographs of me," Duncan said. "You weren't supposed to get to the South Coast Plaza. Melinda told Carl that you'd be at the first stop, at the Beverly Center, photographing the crowd, trying to find the stalker. She had Carl worked up to the point where she knew he'd use force to discourage you from seeing her again. We were certain that you'd be sufficiently disabled not to go on to the other stores. When the photographs I took of her at the South Coast Plaza arrived at her house in the mail, our assumption was that you'd realize how close you had come to getting an image of the stalker. You'd have become more determined. That would have made *Carl* more determined. Eventually . . ."

A labored breath. "But damn you, you had to keep going, and now, if you're still alive, you've figured out that she destroyed the photographs you took of me and that I'm the only one who had access to your house to steal the negatives. But that still leaves you and me. For the first time, someone knows my connection to her. How will she destroy *that* evidence?"

A bump led to unnerving silence, not even a hiss, as if the tape machine had been turned off. The tape's hiss resumed.

"I thought I heard her," Duncan said. "I keep expecting her footsteps to come down the hall. She'll smile and put her arms around me and tell me who she's going to be next and the next game she's going to play. But when she makes me a drink, will she put something in it? Or will she get me more drunk than usual and take me out to the dock for a moonlight stroll and push me underwater—

411

the way she did to that kid who managed to follow her from Sacramento to Arcata?"

"Would someone explain—" Blaine started to say.

"Quiet."

Duncan chuckled bitterly. "She certainly had that kid jumping through hoops. But then she had us *all* jumping through hoops. Randolph knew what she was. Knew what her mother was. Knew what Rebecca Chance was. But he was powerless to resist, the same as *I* am. Even after he got so angry with Rebecca that he pushed her off that cliff in Mexico, he couldn't get away from her spell. He had to spend years trying to find the daughter that he wasn't even sure was his, and when he finally found her and his granddaughter, he fell into the same trap. In the name of love, he excused the terrible things they did. Melinda was happy to take his money, but she never came to see him, never made the slightest effort to delude him into thinking he was loved. Poor Randolph. Such a lonely man. He wanted the comfort of a family, but I was the only one who provided it. He finally had his will amended so that she would inherit the place he most hated, where he killed the woman he never stopped loving, even though he hated her for having manipulated him."

Duncan's voice was unsteady. "I have to stop. I don't dare let her catch me with this tape recorder. I'd warn you right now in person, but what if I'm wrong? What if she hasn't turned against me? I can't give her up. And if I'm right to be suspicious about her? In that case, I'm dead. I've got nothing to lose. Make sure she doesn't destroy you the way she did me. Get even for me, even though I deserve whatever she might do to me. I have absolutely no loyalty to her. God help me, though, how I need her."

The tape hissed. Something made a scraping sound, possibly Duncan's hand setting down the microphone. Then the tape became silent, although Coltrane could see it continuing to turn in the tape deck.

"Now?" Blaine asked. "*Now* would you explain what this is about?"

27

WHEN JENNIFER FINISHED, Blaine leaned back from the documents she had spread on the desk.

"We have to take this to the police," Coltrane said.

Blaine shook his head. "I don't know what good it would do. These materials don't prove anything."

"What are you talking about?"

"A skillful defense attorney would have a case predicated on these flimsy connections dismissed before it went to trial. You're filling in blanks without any support for your conclusions. In the eyes of the law, the theory you're proposing is wildly circumstantial."

"But what about all the names she used?"

"To protect her privacy. The defense would argue that she's an unfortunate young woman who, through no fault of her own, has been plagued by men who want to dominate her. A chain of terrible consequences, for which she bears no responsibility, has forced her to keep changing her name and where she lives. You can't prove she manipulates men into fighting over her. You can't prove she arranges for the victors to have lethal accidents. The law deals with facts, not supposition."

"What about Duncan's tape?"

"The ravings of a man deranged enough to commit suicide. The defense would deny any sexual connection between her and Duncan. It would argue that Duncan was fantasizing. In my professional opinion, these materials are worthless."

"But they might convince the police to look more closely into Duncan's death. It's clear now that he didn't commit suicide. He was murdered."

"Clear to *you*. But if Melinda Chance is as calculating as you believe she is, I think it's highly unlikely that she left anything to incriminate herself."

Coltrane started to say something, then gestured in frustration.

"But my *personal* opinion is another matter," Blaine said. "I think this woman is dangerous. I think you should give this material to the police in the hopes that they might finally investigate her. Then I think you should run like hell."

28

I BOUGHT A REVOLVER AND A SHOTGUN HERE BEFORE CHRIST-mas."

The clerk at the gun shop nodded.

"But I couldn't take the handgun because of the five-day waiting period."

"You've come to pick it up?"

"Yes—and another shotgun."

29

JENNIFER'S FACE WAS STARK WITH DISMAY AS COLTRANE SET THE shotgun in the backseat along with the briefcaselike container that the revolver came in. "It's happening *again.*"

"I know how you feel about guns," he said. "But I don't see another choice. It's my fault I got into this mess. If I'd stayed away from her . . . You don't deserve to be at risk. You've already helped a great deal. I'm going to take you home and—"

"Like hell you are."

Coltrane blinked.

"She makes me furious," Jennifer said.

The force of her words made Coltrane study her in surprise.

"I'm furious at the way she used you," Jennifer said. "At the way she's threatening you. At what she did to *us*. So don't give me any bullshit about taking me home. I'm going to do my damnedest to help you stop her." Jennifer thought about her tone and started to laugh.

"What's funny?"

"Just like old times. Did you ever argue with . . ."

"Her?"

"Yes."

He shook his head.

Their laughter subsided.

"Never," he said.

Jennifer remained silent for a long, somber moment. "Maybe you and I just aren't a match."

"Because we disagree about some things? Hey, it's easy not to disagree when someone's playing a role and constantly lying the way Tash was."

"Maybe that's my problem. I always tell the truth," Jennifer said.

"I wouldn't call that a problem . . . If I know what's good for me, you said. I'll tell you what's good for me. *You* are."

Jennifer studied him. Studied her hands. "But how will you feel tomorrow?"

"The way I feel right now," Coltrane said. He couldn't help thinking, If we're still alive tomorrow.

30

HE HAD CHOSEN A REVOLVER BECAUSE HIS LACK OF EXPERIENCE with handguns warned him to get something simple. There wasn't any magazine to be loaded and inserted, any slide to be pulled back, any slight possibility of jamming, characteristics of a semiautomatic pistol. With the weapon he had chosen, a Colt .357 Python, all he had to do was press a lever on the left side of the frame, tilt out a cylinder, push six rounds into its chambers, and shove the cylinder back into place. As easy as that, it was ready to use, an important consideration for someone with Coltrane's inexperience. Granted, a semiautomatic in a similar caliber held more than twice as many rounds as the Python, but Coltrane had concluded that a weapon he didn't feel comfortable with was almost as bad as not having a weapon at all.

He explained this to Jennifer after he pulled into his garage, loaded the handgun, and shoved it under his sport coat. It gouged his skin.

"You're going to carry that with you?"

"If we need it, it's no use in a drawer." Coltrane loaded the shotgun. "You remember I showed you how to use this?"

"I swore I never would."

"That was then. What about now?"

"Yes, I remember how to use it."

Coltrane had closed the garage before loading the weapons. Now he held the shotgun in his left hand, used his right hand to unlock the garage's entrance into the house, and pushed the door open. Jennifer came behind him. She closed the door as he turned to disarm the intrusion detector, but a fidgety corner of his mind was already warning him that something was wrong. The detector should have let out a thirty-second beep, reminding him to deactivate the system before it went into full alarm mode.

But it wasn't beeping.

"No," Coltrane said.

Jennifer secured the dead bolt on the door. "What's wrong?"

The glowing words on the keypad chilled him: READY TO ARM.

He spun toward the murky stairs that went up and down, aiming the shotgun. "I turned on the alarm when I left, but now it's off. Somebody's in the house."

Jennifer bumped backward against the shadowy wall.

It had to be Tash, Coltrane thought. Duncan had known the secondary codes that disarmed the intrusion detector. She must have made him tell her the sequence.

"Coltrane." The man's voice was deep, hoarse with anger. It came from the right, from upstairs in the dark living room.

"Walt?"

Jesus, if he sees me with this shotgun, he might not give me a chance to talk, Coltrane thought. Sweating, he set the shotgun on the entryway's floor, close to the wall, where it might not be noticed. He buttoned his sport coat, concealing the revolver under his belt. "I'm glad you're here."

"The feeling's mutual." The husky voice was unsteady with greater anger.

Coltrane flicked a light switch near the front door, activating a lamp in the living room. "I'm coming up. I've got something to show you."

"What a coincidence. *I've* got something to show *you*."

Coltrane took a deep breath and started up the stairs. Jennifer followed, her briefcase tight in her hand.

One step.

Another.

Coltrane gradually came up to the living room and saw Walt diagonally across from him, farthest from the illuminated lamp at the top of the stairs. His face in shadow, Walt was seated in one of the black tubular chairs, his hands on his knees.

"If you'll give me a minute," Coltrane said, "I need to tell you something."

"You read my mind again."

"Oh?"

"Because I came here to tell *you* something."

"This is Jennifer."

"If she's smart, she'll get out of here."

"Let me explain. In her briefcase, she's got—"

"I don't give a damn about what's in her briefcase." Walt stood, his rigid body rising like sections of an unfolding machine. "What I do give a damn about—"

Coltrane winced when he saw that as Walt rose, he lifted something from beneath the chair.

A baseball bat.

Holding it in his right hand, patting its hitting surface against the palm of his left hand, Walt had never looked so tall and menacing.

"—is making sure you get my message this time." Walt stepped forward.

"For heaven sake, listen. Tash has done this before."

"I warned you to stay away from her."

"I *have* stayed away from her."

"You call following her everywhere yesterday staying away from her?" Walt came closer, patting the bat.

"I *didn't*. I've been in Oakland!"

"Sure."

"Ask Jennifer."

"He's right," Jennifer said quickly. "Mitch was with me in—"

"You're lying!" Walt smashed an Art Deco lamp, the impact ear-torturing, glass and beads flying.

Coltrane had never seen a more furious gaze.

"If the two of you were in Oakland, how could you have followed Tash and me to the stores she owns?" Walt demanded.

"Followed? But I didn't—"

Walt shattered a glass table, shards exploding.

"Every damned store we went to, the minute we entered, the phone rang, and it was for her. From you!"

"*Tash* is the one who's lying." Coltrane made a placating gesture, startled to see that when Walt raised his arms to swing, his leather windbreaker hiked up and revealed a semiautomatic pistol in a holster clipped to his belt.

Oh Jesus, if he realizes I'm wearing a handgun, too, he might drop the bat and reach for—Suddenly, buying the gun seemed a terrible idea.

"She must have somebody helping her," Coltrane said. "Maybe she phoned ahead and told somebody in each store to claim she had a phone call when the two of you walked in. Then she pretended the call was from me."

"Bullshit! Why would she—"

"To make you so mad that you'd come after me!"

418

"What are you talking about? You stalked her in Malibu. You're stalking her now. But I swear you'll never do it again!"

Walt swung, his body movement warning Coltrane just in time for him to jump back. The bat whistled past his head and walloped against the wall.

"She likes men to fight over her!" Coltrane shouted.

As Walt swung in the reverse direction, Coltrane dodged again, and Jennifer dove to the floor. The bat missed Coltrane by an inch, the fierce movement of air cooling the sweat on his brow.

"Listen to me!" Coltrane shouted. "She wasn't being stalked in Malibu! She was making it up! She had help!"

"You expect me to believe that crap?"

"But it's true!" Jennifer yelled from the floor. "I've got the proof in my briefcase. Her name isn't Natasha Adler. It's Melinda Chance. She's had half a dozen different identities and—"

"Lady, I warned you to stay out of this!"

"Men keep killing each other because of her!" Jennifer rose with her briefcase, offering it in a crouch. "Just let me open this and show you what I—"

"You asked for it!"

Walt put all his weight behind his swing, delivering the full force of the bat against the briefcase, jolting it out of Jennifer's hands. It burst open and flipped through the air. Documents flying, the briefcase rebounded off the wall and landed among the broken glass of the table. Simultaneously, Jennifer shrieked, falling back.

Walt was poised to reverse the swing of his bat, aiming at Jennifer as she raised her hands to protect her head. Walt balked, suddenly seeming to realize what he had become.

"I—"

Whatever he meant to say, it was too late. Coltrane charged. The terror in Jennifer's eyes had released a fury in him beyond anything he had ever felt. He struck Walt from the side and collided with the table upon which the only light in the room sat. Their combined weight slammed down onto it, buckling the table, breaking the lamp, sending the room into darkness. As they rolled, Walt had to release his grip on the bat to block Coltrane's punches. The hard edges of

Coltrane's revolver tore against his side, making him groan. Then the revolver slipped free, falling among the wreckage, and Coltrane struggled upward with Walt. Amid the roaring fury of his frantic breathing and his savage heartbeat, he heard Jennifer shouting, "No!"

She was pleading, wailing, "Stop! This is what she wants!"

But Coltrane was far beyond reason. With no doubt whatsoever that Walt meant to destroy him, he had to do to Walt what Walt meant to do to *him*. They lurched this way and that, striking each other, groaning, blood mixing with the sweat on their faces. Legs weakening, Coltrane charged with all his remaining might. His body hit Walt so hard that Walt jerked backward, but the force of Coltrane's attack propelled Coltrane with him, and they hurtled through a French door, glass bursting like a bomb going off.

Kept hurtling.

Struck the railing of a balcony.

And plummeted over.

31

FOR A MOMENT, Coltrane had the sensation of floating in darkness. Then his stomach rose. Air rushed past him, or the other way around, as he and Walt rushed through air, falling, twisting, locked in each other's arms. Their impact was shocking, cold black water engulfing them. They struck the pool so hard that their momentum took them all the way to the bottom, jolting against it. His breath knocked out of him, Coltrane gasped, inhaled water, and panicked, struggling toward the surface. He broke through, gulped air, and was thrown underwater again as Walt gripped his shoulders and pressed down. Lungs burning, Coltrane twisted free, braced his bent legs against the pool's bottom, and thrust himself upward, breaking the surface again, straining to breathe.

Lights came on all around him, in the living room, from which they had fallen, in the lower level that gave access to the pool, in the shrubs of the backyard, in the pool itself. Temporarily blinded, Coltrane splashed backward just in time to avoid Walt's hands around his throat.

"Stop!" Jennifer's pleading voice was close. She must have turned on the lights and run down to the pool, but Coltrane paid no attention, too busy avoiding Walt's attempts to push him under. As Walt lost his balance in the shoulder-high water, Coltrane dove beneath the surface, rocketed to the surface behind Walt, grabbed him from behind, and pushed *him* beneath the water.

"No!"

A pole banged against the back of Coltrane's neck. Feeling bristles on the end of it, Coltrane vaguely realized that Jennifer was using one of the pool-cleaning tools to try to stop them from fighting.

Walt wrestled free, gasped for air, spun, and came at Coltrane as Jennifer dropped the pole between them and threw a cushion from a deck chair.

"Stop!"

They had each other by the throat. Coltrane felt his face bulging as he tightened his grip and—

The shotgun blast was so startling that he jerked his hands away. Stumbling back, he lost his footing, went under, splashed to the surface, breathed frantically, saw that Walt had reacted much as he had, and was astonished to discover Jennifer at the side of the pool, holding the shotgun.

Down the street, a dog barked in alarm. Several houses away, a man yelled, "What was *that?*"

Her movements unpracticed, Jennifer awkwardly racked a fresh shell into the shotgun's firing chamber. The spent shell arced through the air, clattering onto concrete. "Look at yourselves! It's what she wants! Don't you understand you're being used? For God's sake, what do I have to do to make you stop?"

Jennifer looked so surprised, her eyes fierce, obviously uncomfortable with the shotgun, doing her best to keep it balanced in her hands, that Coltrane suddenly had a sense of how out of control he had become.

"She's right." He stared at Walt. "I don't want to—"

Laughter interrupted him.

From above. Deep-throated, sensuous laughter.

Baffled, he looked upward and saw Tash leaning over the balcony on the topmost level, her beautiful features radiant with amusement. Her laughter swelled until she had to throw her head back to release it.

"Tash?" Walt murmured.

"Do you understand *now*?" Coltrane asked.

Peering down from two stories above them, Tash wiped away tears of laughter.

"But . . ." Walt became speechless with bewilderment.

"Read the documents I had in my briefcase!" Jennifer said.

Tash shook her head in delight. "Make her shoot again! Make her jump in and try to stop you!"

"Tash," Walt said, this time with realization. "You—" The word sounded like a curse as he splashed through the water. He reached the side, pulled himself out, glared up, dripping, and suddenly broke into a run, charging toward the house.

As Walt disappeared into the bottom level, Coltrane forced his way to the side of the pool. He crawled out, ignored the cold air on his wet skin, and raced after him.

Jennifer hurried next to him, the two of them passing the darkroom and the vault, pounding up the stairs. Higher, Walt was shouting something, Tash continuing to laugh. Coltrane reached the living room and surveyed the wreckage, the incalculable damage that Walt had inflicted on the priceless furniture. He saw the revolver that he had lost during the fight, and he picked it up, but he didn't see Walt, although he did hear a commotion above him and raced higher. When he and Jennifer came to the third level and rushed into the bedroom, Coltrane was shocked. The bedroom was the only room on that level. A flower-rimmed balcony led along all four sides, and through the windows, Coltrane saw Tash gamboling from one section to the next, taunting Walt as he pursued her.

The effect was dizzying: Coltrane in the middle of his bedroom, turning, peering outward, watching Tash sprint from one section of the balcony to the next. Walt was slowing, his chest heaving. For her part, Tash seemed to have an endless reservoir of energy, skipping, spinning, evading Walt. She wore an all-white ankle-long cotton dress of a type that Coltrane had seen in Mexico. Loose, it flared provocatively as she skipped and spun. A red shawl was draped over her shoulders, tied at her cleavage. Watching her and Walt round another corner, Coltrane turned, dizzier, amazed at the sudden burst of speed that Walt mustered. Thrusting out a hand, Walt grabbed the back of Tash's shawl and jerked her up short, causing her to gasp, but before Walt could pull her toward him, she ducked her head and slipped free of the shawl's tied loop. He shot out another hand, clutching her arm as she started to run. When he spun her toward him, he tossed away the shawl and drew back his hand to strike her.

She stared defiantly.

He hesitated.

"What's the matter? Are you afraid to hit a woman?"

"You're not a woman."

"You sure thought I was three hours ago when I—"

"That doesn't make you a woman."

Tash laughed. "No? What *does* it make me?"

Walt said a word, the crudity of which was devastating.

The laughter halted.

"I don't know what I saw in you," Walt said. "I'm going to have to burn my clothes and scour myself with bleach to get rid of the slime you left on me."

Tash's eyes darkened.

"You're a cesspool." Walt turned to enter the bedroom.

"Hey," Tash said.

Seeing Walt come through the doorway, Coltrane was overwhelmed by the look of absolute revulsion on Walt's face.

"Where do you think you're going?" Tash demanded.

Walt came farther into the bedroom.

"I'm not through with you," Tash said.

"The important thing is, I'm through with *you.*" Walt kept cross-ing the bedroom, not bothering to look at her.

"Nobody walks away from me!"

"Watch."

"Come back here!"

"Go to hell."

"You first!" Tash grabbed a heavy pot from a row of flowers, rushed into the bedroom, and hurled it against the back of Walt's head.

For an instant, Coltrane thought that the cracking sound he heard was the pot breaking, but then the pot thudded intact onto the floor, and Coltrane realized that the sound had come from Walt's skull. The burly policeman staggered toward Coltrane, reached for support, but never got that far. His eyes rolled up. His body became a collapsing rag doll. When his face struck the carpeted floor, the back of his head had an indentation covered with blood.

"Oh," Tash said.

The room seemed to shrink.

"Now look what you've made me do."

32

COLTRANE WAS SO STARTLED THAT HE COULDN'T MOVE. Next to him, Jennifer gaped at Walt's unmoving body.

The next thing, Tash was hunkered next to Walt's body, fumbling through his pockets. "It's not supposed to happen this way." She glared up at Coltrane. "You'll pay for this."

For the first time, Coltrane noticed that her hands were shiny.

She was wearing plastic gloves.

From Walt's leather jacket, she pulled out a small black electronic object that resembled a miniature remote control. She picked up

Walt's left hand, wedged his fingers around the device, and used his thumb to press a button on it. "Make you pay."

"I'm calling the police," Coltrane said.

Starting toward the bedside phone, he saw Tash grope hurriedly beneath Walt's jacket, understood, and yelled to Jennifer, "Get back down the stairs!"

Immediately, Tash pulled Walt's semiautomatic free of its holster, pressed it into his right hand, inserted his index finger into the trigger guard, and squeezed the trigger. The gunshot was deafening, not as loud as the shotgun blast had been, but ear-slamming all the same. The unaimed bullet missed Coltrane by a wide margin, blasting into a wall, but he had the sense that the next bullet would be very deliberately aimed. He scrambled toward the stairs as Tash removed the weapon from Walt's hand and sighted expertly along it.

"Jesus." Diving, Coltrane heard the shot as he felt a bullet whiz by him. He hit the stairs on his side, winced, and tumbled to the landing, seeing the blurred figure of Jennifer racing down the continuation of the stairs.

He rolled, the next gunshot making his ears ring, plaster exploding from the wall, stinging his face. Jolting to a painful halt in the living room, he only then realized that he was still holding the revolver that he had picked up before climbing the stairs to the bedroom. Reflexively, he pointed it upward and pulled the trigger, his aim bad, missing Tash as she ducked back from the landing above him.

Her surprise at being shot at slowed her enough that Coltrane had time to race down to the front-door landing before Tash fired again. He collided with Jennifer, who was fumbling to unlock the front door. "No time!" he yelled, dragging her down the further continuation of the stairs an instant before two bullets whacked holes in the door.

They were on the bottom level now, but the overhead light exposed them, and Jennifer flicked switches, sending the bottom level of the pool area into darkness. The next moment, Tash appeared at the landing, fired three times into the shadows, and dove back out of sight. Before his eyes could tell his brain to stop the impulse,

Coltrane fired at the empty landing, the gun awkward in his hand, the recoil unnerving.

"Jennifer?"

"Here." Her voice was unsteady behind him.

"Are you hurt?"

"No."

Coltrane's heart pounded so hard that he feared his arteries would burst. Crouching behind a concrete pillar, he aimed up toward the landing.

"The garden." Jennifer's voice shook. "We can get away through the back."

"No, we'd be trapped. There's a wall around it. We'd only have bushes for cover. She could pick us off from the living room balcony. Tash!"

No answer.

"Tash!" Coltrane raised his voice louder.

Still no answer.

"Melinda!" Jennifer called.

"What?"

"The neighbors will have heard the shots! They'll have phoned the police!" Jennifer said. "It's finished!"

"Not yet !" Tash/Melinda said. "But it soon will be!"

What's she talking about? Coltrane wondered. She isn't stupid enough to hang around until the police come. *Why is she waiting?*

And why is she wearing plastic gloves?

So she won't leave fingerprints, he thought.

Then why did she press Walt's semiautomatic into his hand and use his finger to pull the trigger?

So his hand would have gunpowder residue. Isn't that what Walt said up in Big Bear? He threatened to shoot me, then put a pistol in my hand and squeeze off a shot. "So you'd have powder residue," Walt had said. So it would look like I'd shot at Walt and he was forced to defend himself.

That's what she's doing. She wants to make it look as if Walt did the shooting, not her.

But there'll be other evidence she can't hide, he thought. How does she plan to—

What was that remote control she pressed Walt's thumb on?

"Do you smell smoke?" Jennifer murmured.

Coltrane whirled. Even in the darkness, he could see thick gray smoke billowing behind him.

From the darkroom.

It wafted up his nose and made him bend over, coughing, his eyes watering, the smoke so dense that it cloaked the exit to the pool.

Walt must have planted an incendiary device among the chemicals in there. The remote control Tash pressed Walt's thumb on set off—

"Jennifer, get away from—"

The door to the darkroom exploded, flames bursting out, flashing across the corridor, whooshing toward the ceiling. But as loud as the eruption was, it didn't muffle Jennifer's scream as she sprinted toward the concrete pillar behind which Coltrane crouched.

Tash shot at her silhouette against the flames.

Coltrane shot back.

"Jesus, my hair." Jennifer pawed at it, brushing out sparks.

"*Now* it's almost over!" Tash said.

Coltrane cast a panicked glance toward the roaring wall of flames behind him.

"So I'll give you a choice!" Tash said. "You can burn to death, or you can let me shoot you."

"And then drag Walt's body down here to make it look like *he* killed us but got caught in the fire he set?"

"Sounds good to me!" Tash said.

"But you're running out of time! I hear sirens!" Jennifer said.

"I don't! It's only been a couple of minutes! Nice try, though!"

Coltrane felt the heat of the fire through the back of his sport coat. His hair felt warm. Smoke seared his throat. Doubled over, coughing, he knew that he and Jennifer had only a few more seconds before they would have to run toward the stairs. Although the house was made of reinforced concrete, the walls, floors, and ceilings of the interior had conventional wooden frames. Held in by the concrete, the flames would shoot along the wood like a firestorm. We have to get out of—

The vault, he thought, unable to stop coughing. It's fireproof. He almost struggled toward it before he remembered that it had a halon-gas fire-extinguishing system. Not sufficient to put out the flames in the rest of the house but certainly enough to suffocate the two of them if they tried to seek shelter in there.

We have to rush the stairs and hope she doesn't shoot us before we—

As the heat on his back became unbearable and he braced himself to run, he heard a scream from the front-door landing. A shot. But the bullet wasn't aimed toward the lower level. It was aimed toward the figure who toppled down the stairs toward where Tash crouched out of sight at the side of the landing. The figure collided against her and sent her sprawling in full view of Coltrane. The figure was Walt. The blow to his head hadn't killed him. Regaining consciousness, he must have lurched downstairs toward the sound of shouting on the bottom level. His husky body pinned her. His hands groped for her throat as she screamed again and pulled the trigger, blasting a spray of crimson from the back of his already-battered skull. In a panic, she squirmed to get out from under Walt's now-truly dead-weight.

Jennifer took advantage of the distraction and raced toward her. Caught by surprise, Coltrane took a second longer to rush from the fire.

Tash pushed Walt's body off her and down the stairs, then aimed at Jennifer, who lost her balance when she dodged Walt's tumbling body. The bullet meant for her hit Coltrane's shoulder, knocking him backward onto the floor. For an instant, he blacked out. The heat of the spreading fire stung him back to panicked consciousness, the pain in his right shoulder sending his nervous system into spastic overdrive. As the flames seethed closer, he struggled to stand and saw Jennifer grappling with Tash on the landing. Tash pulled the trigger on her pistol, but nothing happened, the slide staying back, the magazine out of ammunition.

She threw the handgun, grazing Jennifer's head. As Jennifer

moaned and stumbled back, Tash turned, slipped, and scurried on all fours up the stairs. Jennifer grabbed for her, snagging the ankle-long hem of her dress. When Tash kicked backward, Jennifer held firm, but Tash's frantic movements tore the dress, exposed her right leg to the knee, and left Jennifer holding a scrap of cloth.

Again, Tash tried to scurry up the stairs. Again, Jennifer grabbed at the dress, ripping more of it away, unable to restrain her. The two of them raced higher.

Jennifer doesn't know I've been hit, Coltrane thought in dismay. His right shoulder throbbed as he wavered up the stairs. She thinks I'm coming to help her.

Amid the roar of the flames behind him, he heard noises outside the house: shouts, approaching sirens. Thank God, he thought, as he managed somehow to unlock the front door. But the crash of something being thrown above him and a wail of pain warned him that Jennifer needed him.

He struggled to climb higher, his mind swirling when for a second time that night he came to the wreckage of the furniture in the living room. And again he heard a commotion from even higher. Dripping blood, he wavered up the stairs.

To the bedroom.

It all came back to the bedroom, he thought.

The place was in darkness. When he groped to flick the switch on the wall and achieved no result, he realized that the crash he had heard was the room's floor lamp being smashed.

The room's silence unnerved him.

"Where is she?" Jennifer asked from the corner on Coltrane's right.

"I don't know. My eyes haven't adjusted to the darkness. I—"

A heavy object struck him in the chest, knocking the wind out of him, aggravating the agony in his shoulder. Dizzied by pain, he fell against a bureau, grabbed it for support, and touched a camera he had set there.

"Are you okay?" Jennifer whispered from the darkness to his right.

"No, I've been—"

Another object walloped against the wall near where Jennifer had spoken. "Where the hell is she throwing from?"

"I don't know," Coltrane said. "She's wearing white. Even in the darkness, we ought to be able to see her."

"She *was* wearing white."

Coltrane didn't understand the remark. Crouching, he grasped the camera.

Outside, the sirens grew closer, louder.

Across the room, he saw what looked like a single pulse from a firefly. The spark came and went so suddenly, he wondered if his eyes were playing tricks on him, baffled until he remembered Tash's problem with static electricity. Readying the camera, he aimed it toward where he had seen the spark, activated the flash, and pushed the shutter button.

The stab of light caught her in midmotion, crawling toward the open door to the balcony. Because the flash was directed away from him, it didn't hurt his eyes and presumably Jennifer's as much as it did Tash's. She winced, her hand raised to protect her vision. At once it was dark again, and Tash scurried toward the balcony as Jennifer leapt from her hiding place. Jennifer's cryptic remark that Tash wasn't wearing white any longer now made sense—because her white dress had been torn from her. She was naked, her sleek tan body hard to see in the darkness. Jennifer's own clothes had been torn, a sleeve of her navy blazer ripped off, the buttons of her silk blouse yanked open.

She caught up to Tash on the balcony, and Tash's supple body fought back in a way reminiscent of a feral cat. She was clawing, twisting, lunging, spitting, streaks of blood suddenly appearing on Jennifer's cheeks.

"Bitch!" Jennifer screamed, the ferocity of her attack increasing.

The flames from the bottom level lit up the night. Smoke rose toward the struggling figures, and from behind. The stairway filled with a haze that drifted into the bedroom.

As Jennifer lunged in a fury, Tash sidestepped, shouldered Jennifer against the railing, grabbed her feet, and upended her, throwing her over the side.

33

COLTRANE'S HEART STOPPED.

With a shock, it restarted, urging him toward the railing. Jennifer had gripped the railing as Tash flipped her over, and now Jennifer dangled, straining to hang on as Tash pounded at her fingers and tried to peel them off. Below, flames roared from both levels, and the swimming pool didn't extend to this side—beneath the flames, there was only a tiled patio.

"No!" Thrusting Tash aside, Coltrane reached his good arm toward Jennifer to pull her up.

The punch to his wounded shoulder drove him nearly insane with anguish. Seeing Tash try to hit him a second time, he managed to block the blow, but not without further pain to his wound.

"I can't hold on!" Jennifer shouted.

But Coltrane couldn't pull her up. He had to let go and defend himself against Tash, who lifted a heavy flowerpot to throw at him as she had at Walt. The effort to raise the pot above her head tilted her off balance, and when Coltrane pushed her as hard as he could, she hit the railing, so top-weighted that when he slammed her shoulders, she, too, went over the side.

Jennifer jerked. "She grabbed me! I can't hang on!"

In a rush, Coltrane leaned over the side and slung his good arm under Jennifer's chest, straining to support her weight. Below her, he saw Tash dangling from Jennifer's ankles, the flames from both levels roaring up at her. Losing his hold, desperate, he tested his wounded arm, using it to try to pull Jennifer up. Blood pulsed. His injured muscle failed.

"No!" He strained harder with his good arm, feeling Jennifer slip. All the while, he stared down at Tash, who clawed her way up Jennifer's legs, almost to her knees.

Coltrane wept with the effort to keep Jennifer from falling.

Tash groped higher.

431

Jennifer jerked her right leg free and kicked.

Tash reached up.

Jennifer kicked again.

"Why . . . don't . . . you"—Jennifer kicked harder, and Coltrane couldn't help thinking about Walt's last words to Tash and where Tash's mother had said she wanted her—"go . . . to . . . hell."

As Coltrane felt Jennifer slipping away from him, Jennifer gave one last kick, and Tash lost her grip, screaming, plummeting into the flames below. The roar of the fire was so intense that Coltrane couldn't hear the impact of her body hitting the patio two levels down.

Jennifer felt weightless. "Hang on to me! Don't let go!"

"I'm trying as hard as I can!"

Jennifer pulled herself toward him. "My shoes are on fire!"

She struggled upward, Coltrane lifting, and abruptly they were sprawled on the balcony, Coltrane ignoring the sharp misery of his wound, burning his hands as he yanked off Jennifer's smoking shoes and threw them away.

But flames filled the stairway to the bedroom. So weak that they could hardly walk, they wavered toward the section of the balcony farthest from the flames. From there, they had a view of the flashing lights of emergency vehicles in front of the house, of the crowd that had gathered and firefighters spraying water at the blaze.

A woman in the crowd shouted, "My God, someone's up there!"

Two firemen stared toward the upper balcony, turned off the hose they had trained on the house, and ran toward the ladder truck, raising it to save the two figures they had seen.

EPILOGUE

FIRE PURIFIES, but how, Coltrane wondered, can you incinerate your mind? The increasing traumas of the previous two months had so numbed him that only after surviving the final horror did he begin to understand the full extent of his psychic damage. The rational part of him had grieved over the murders of his two closest friends and of his grandparents, but the *ir*rational part, he came to realize, had never acknowledged that those murders had occurred, that those loved ones were lost to him forever. Those conflicting parts seemed to be reacting to separate universes, and in one of those universes, the murders couldn't possibly have occurred, just as Coltrane couldn't possibly have been hunted by Dragan Ilkovic. So, if those events couldn't have occurred, they *hadn't* occurred. Otherwise, he would surely have gone insane.

Dragan Ilkovic had seemed the epitome of evil, but then Coltrane had encountered Tash Adler, her malignance existing on such an unimaginably primal level that it had shocked away the numbness created by what Ilkovic had done to him. He wept without warning. He couldn't sleep for fear of nightmares. He needed all his concentration to explain repeatedly to the police and the fire investigators what had happened in his house that night and the events that had led up to it.

When you reach absolute bottom, Coltrane told himself, when you can't possibly fall any further and deeper, you have to start climbing. In that way, Tash had done him a favor. By setting fire to the house that had once belonged to Rebecca Chance and Randolph Packard, she had destroyed part of a festering past that had taken possession of him.

Similarly, the money with which Coltrane had purchased the house was his only legacy from his hated father, and although Coltrane's insurance company would reimburse him for the devastation of the property, he had the sense that the money had been cleansed, that the legacy, too, had been destroyed in the fire. He planned to give some of it to Greg's widow and the rest to various charities. He refused to rebuild the house. He put the lot up for sale.

But there was one other element of the past that he had to deal with, and on a balmy day a month later, he drove to the trailer court in Glendale, where he steered down the lane past the dilapidated playground where his mother had once pushed him in a swing. He knocked on the door of the battered trailer where he and his mother had once lived and where his father had shot his mother and then committed suicide. He knocked several times, but the elderly black woman didn't answer.

"Mister, she don't live here no more," a kid on a beat-up bicycle said.

"Do you know where she moved?"

"She don't live anywhere. She dead."

"Ah." His spirit sank. "And who lives here now?"

"Nobody."

He bought the trailer, had it towed away, and, without ever stepping into it again, watched as a huge metal press crumpled it, destroying it. He bought the best new trailer he could find, had it towed onto the trailer court, found the poorest family in the area, and arranged for them to live rent-free in the trailer. Then he paid for the old playground to be leveled and a shiny new one to take its place. It gave him tremendous satisfaction. He was cleaning house, he told himself, throwing out the past.

One aspect of the past that he was happy to retain, although he felt oddly distant from it, was the special edition of *Southern California Magazine* in which Randolph Packard's classic series of photographs of L.A. houses in the twenties and thirties was mirrored by Coltrane's updates of them, along with the photographs of people and places he had come in contact with during the odyssey of his assignment.

"They're brilliant," Jennifer said. "They're going to give you a whole new direction for your career."

"I feel as if someone else took them," Coltrane said. "I'm a different person now."

"Good. I wouldn't want you to become too complacent." Her tone was teasing.

"I know one thing. I'll never take another photograph that doesn't make me appreciate being alive and part of the world."

"Like *this* photograph?"

"Especially."

The photograph they were looking at showed a wistful, frightened, but determined young woman with wan cheeks, sunken eyes, and a scarf over her head that concealed the baldness that her chemotherapy treatments had caused. The setting sun toward which she peered was a metaphor for the declining days of her life, but the last moments of that setting sun made her face radiant. Her name was Diane Laramy, and Coltrane had taken that photograph on the day he and Jennifer had set out to find the first of the houses that Packard had photographed, Rudolph Valentino's (who, although he hadn't known it, had at the time himself been in the sunset of his life).

Coltrane and Jennifer had suspected that Diane was undergoing treatments for cancer, but they hadn't been certain until Coltrane happened to see his photograph of her in the *Los Angeles Times*. Apparently no one had considered that the photograph might be copyrighted and not available for reproduction without Coltrane's permission. Under the circumstances, it didn't matter—because the photograph was on the obituary page. Diane was survived by her parents and her husband, whom she had married two months earlier. Donations could be made to the American Cancer Society. Coltrane did so.

"I remember something we said the day we met her," Coltrane told Jennifer. They were in the living room of his town house, where he had decided to continue staying.

"What do you mean?"

"We said we admired the way, in the face of death, Diane planned to get married—to grasp at life."

"Yes." Jennifer sounded wistful. "To grasp at life."

"I want to tell you something that I've never said to another woman. It's something I should have told you long ago."

"I'm not sure I can take being hurt again."

"I've learned a lot in the last couple of weeks. About the difference between fool's gold and the real thing."

"I think you should be careful about what you say."

"I love you."

"Now listen to yourself."

"How would you feel about . . ."

"What? A week in Hawaii?"

"No. Getting married."

". . . You keep surprising me."

"Well, *you* wouldn't surprise me if you said no. I can't tell you how sorry I am for having been so stupid, for having hurt you. I'd like the chance to try again."

"Getting married is more than a try," Jennifer said. "I've been there, remember. My ex-husband had his own problems about commitment. Maybe we should just go on as we are for a while and see how things work out."

"But a commitment is what I want to prove to you I'm making."

"How do I know I won't get hurt again?"

"I'd die before I'd ever hurt you again," Coltrane said.

"If you died, that would be the worst hurt of all."

"I made a terrible mistake." Coltrane touched her cheek. "I'm afraid of losing you. I know I can't change the past. But does that mean we should let it drag us backward? All my life I've let the past drag me backward. Can't we learn from it and move forward?"

They gazed at each other.

"Then we're the real thing?" Jennifer asked.

In answer, Coltrane put his arms around her.

And their kiss was indeed the real thing.